ABENI AND THE KINGDOM OF GOLD

ABENI AND THE KINGDOM OF GOLD

P. DJÈLÍ CLARK

STARSCAPE

TOR PUBLISHING GROUP
NEW YORK

ABENI AND THE KINGDOM OF GOLD

Copyright © 2025 by P. Djèlí Clark

A Starscape Book
Published by Tom Doherty Associates / Tor Publishing Group
120 Broadway
New York, NY 10271

www.torpublishinggroup.com

The Library of Congress Cataloging-in-Publication Data is available upon request.

ISBN 978-1-250-82585-8 (hardcover)
ISBN 978-1-250-82586-5 (ebook)

Our books may be purchased in bulk for promotional, educational, or business use. Please contact your local bookseller or the Macmillan Corporate and Premium Sales Department at 1-800-221-7945, extension 5442, or by email at MacmillanSpecialMarkets@macmillan.com.

First Edition: 2025

Printed in the United States of America

0 9 8 7 6 5 4 3 2 1

For Nia and Nya—still

BOOK I

CHAPTER ONE

FORTRESS OF THE LIVING FLAME

The people say the land here was once lush and green. That grasslands extended as far as the eye could see. And that a great river snaked its way throughout, where birds and beasts came to water and drink. But nothing was as grand as the trees. Baobab trees—taller and larger by far than any ever seen, with thick twisting trunks and branches so high they sought to brush the sky. It was said each of the giants housed hundreds, where people lived within and without—stringing long bridges between them that connected an entire kingdom.

But that was long ago.

No one remembers what brought their end. Some say fire rained down from the sky. Others, that a war of men left untold destruction. A few claimed it to be the work of a mischievous spirit. Whatever the truth, the land now is dry and barren, scoured by dust storms and whirlwinds of fire. The river lies cracked and emptied, though it trembles and groans—as if something sleeps beneath. No kingdom stands here any longer. What few plants and creatures now call this place home have grown twisted and hard. The giant baobabs are nearly all gone—felled and burned to ash. Their remains swirl about the sky, casting a shadowy gloom. Not night, not day, but an unending twilight.

One structure, however, dominates the bleak landscape.

The people say that if the great trees could have named a ruler, this would have been the one. It was the oldest and largest of the giant baobabs, with a faded and gray trunk as wide as a small mountain and branches so long and thick they blot out what is left of the sun. It sits alone, the king of a forgotten land. Sharp and pointed massive lengths of black stone have been fitted into the tree, piercing it like immense thorns and curving up to embrace its trunk on all sides like a ring of teeth. From the center of the giant baobab a black spiral tower rises farther than the tallest branches, ending in a point to pierce the sky. At its very top a bright orange flame hovers, burning to rival the sun.

Making its way towards the structure is a long snaking line of people, and others that are not people at all. Each one carries a torch in the gloom and ash, their many voices and different tongues chanting to match their marching feet. Tall doors carved into the giant baobab open to grant them entrance—they who have come in answer to the summons of the eternal living flame.

◯ ◯ ◯

Fulan stood gazing out one of the tall rectangular windows cut into the Fortress of the Living Flame. She had not climbed to the highest part of the tower. But even from here, she could see the entire land spread out—covered as always in a haze of falling ash. In the distance a fire devil began forming from the dark clouds streaked with white lightning, but no thunder—and never rain. The twisting ribbon of flame spiraled down from the sky until it touched the ground, swirling a scorched streak across the charred earth. Most did not realize fire devils were living things—which delighted in burning all in their path. One of her father's creations. Ordinarily, they would cut through the marchers, creating more ash to blanket the skies. But her father had forbidden their usual play. And today, they were not to harm those that carried his standard. They settled for searching out other things to burn—hoping to catch stragglers foolish enough to wander from the marchers. The fire devil would have to snatch them up before any of the other dangerous creatures who called this barren land home.

From her vantage the marchers were barely visible to Fulan's eyes—so that it seemed that a long line of burning flames snaked towards her. Holding to a side of the window, she leaned out to peer below. The height and the danger sent a dizzying thrill through her. From here, she could see the great doors to the fortress swung open, through which the marchers entered to receive the mark of her father. A finger moved to touch the upside-down teardrop etched onto her own forehead—stopping as she recalled she now wore a conical helmet of dark steel topped by a sharpened point, with chain mail that hung to rest along her back and shoulders. She let her hand fall back to her side, eyes still on the marchers.

So many. They came night and day now, only to leave again—off to the west, where her father's armies were gathering in strength. The scholar city of Jenna with its magic-wielding scribes. The famed cavalry of the forest kingdoms of Oyoun and Abomi. Even the great walls of mighty Wagadou. None could stand against the mighty host her father now assembled. He had come to free them from the hold of corrupt rulers, meddling spirits, and indifferent gods. His armies would blaze across the land like fire in dry grass, and one by one, the squabbling kingdoms and city-states of the west would fall beneath his sway. The world would be remade, and a new age of freedom ushered in. Her heart raced at the thought, and she leaned farther out the window—heedless of the recklessness of her action. She wanted to be there, with her father's armies, wielding sword and spear, loosing arrows from her great bow, and shouting a war cry to make their enemies tremble!

Daughter.

The voice in her head was as sweet as a kiss upon her forehead, and as strong as an iron grip upon her heart. She looked down to see one booted foot step out into the open air, as the dizzying rush that had filled her ebbed away. What had she been about to do? Pulling her leg inside, she stepped back from the window. The voice came again.

To me, Daughter. To me.

Fulan turned, starting her descent from the tower. She could never resist her father's voice. There were few who could. She walked a spiral staircase that led out into the vast inner world of the giant baobab. Here, stone archways opened to different parts of the fortress, connected by bridges that crisscrossed the great expanse. Much of this had been created by the people who had built a kingdom here long ago and made this tree their palace. When her father took it for himself he added to it—building the tower to hold his flame and turning the palace into a fortress. Fulan had counted sixteen years now. And for eight of those, this had been her home—when her father had brought her here, rescued her from the tragedy of her past life. The thought shook loose a memory: a flicker of another place, of people clapping, of a woman with twinkling brown eyes, dark brown skin, and a wide bright smile, just like her own. She was singing a lullaby, playfully tapping at Fulan's face as she went.

Daughter.

Her father's call scattered her thoughts, like birds startled by a serpent in the bush. It was stronger now, more insistent. He didn't like to be kept waiting. Glancing to one of the archways, she calculated how many stairs she would have to take to reach him. Too long. As she peered down, a slight smile crept to her lips. But who needed stairs? Breaking into a run, Fulan leapt into the open air, feeling weightless for a moment before plunging. Air whipped at her face as she fell, landing on one of the bridges below—her booted feet touching down on the stone with force. No ordinary girl, no ordinary person for that matter, could have made that leap and lived. But her father had given her many gifts in the time she had spent with him. And this was her home. With a joyous whoop, she ran and jumped again, landing on one bridge before leaping to another, making her way down until she arrived at the main floor of the fortress.

She landed among a group of mounted warriors, recently arrived to answer her father's summons. They sat upon war beasts, great white things larger than a water buffalo with strong stubby legs and bulky bodies with thick folded skin. The hides of the creatures were painted with red symbols that carried down their long faces to a single curved horn that jutted from their snouts. The beasts snorted in surprise at her arrival, ears twitching, stamping hooved feet. Their riders pulled on reins from their leather saddles and gave sharp commands to get the creatures under control. They shot angry glares at Fulan. But then, looking up at the height she had descended from, their eyebrows rose, and their gazes became wary.

Fulan wondered from what land these men had come, and how they had tamed such fierce beasts. She might have stopped to ask, but there was no time. Breaking into a run, she made her way through the throngs of people. Well, not all were people. She pushed through a pack of hyena men, who growled and snapped their dog-like muzzles as she passed. Then had to navigate through a horde of Eloko, whose small greenish bodies reminded her of children—except for the weapons they carried and the way they gnashed their sharp teeth. She was brought up short at a sudden bellowing and pulled back in time to not be trampled by a lumbering giant of a creature that walked on two legs, and whose massive body was covered in bristling black fur. A collar ringed its neck, attached to long chains pulled by several men. Others used whips to lash its back, driving it forward. A zimwi, Fulan recognized—pulled from the lightless caves their kind preferred and brought up from the southlands. Zimwi usually harassed villages and towns, making off with cattle or people to sate their hunger. This one, however, would be fitted with armor and given weapons to march in her father's armies.

At a particularly harsh lash, the zimwi turned about angrily, moving faster than its size would have suggested. A large four-fingered hand snatched its human tormenter, yanking him off his feet and tossing him like a doll into the distance. Its other handlers redoubled their efforts, using whips and pulling on its chains until the gargantuan creature was firmly back under their control.

Fulan skirted around the mayhem, and in her haste ran hard into someone. She looked up to find a tall figure standing in her way, his broad and muscular body looking almost like a man's—except for ridged nostrils and the two small tusks jutting from his jaw. He narrowed yellow eyes at her and sneered.

"Watch where you walk, human!" He spat, and some of it splashed onto her boots.

Fulan looked the creature up and down. A Bikolo. Many of them had certainly answered her father's call. This one had skin like burnt rock and his shaved scalp held a single long topknot studded with small white shells. He was covered in overlapping plates of armor that extended the length of his body. Her eye went to the sword at his waist, with its jagged blade. Then to his several smirking companions. She didn't have time for this. She should just walk away. But he had spit, on her boots. *Her* boots. She drew herself up.

"Or what?" she asked.

The Bikolo looked surprised.

"Or what?" he repeated. He reached a clawed hand to lift a necklace that hung to his chest. It was studded with more of the small shells like those in his topknot. She looked closer. Not shells. Teeth. Human teeth. "Or," he snarled, "I add your pretty teeth to my collection!" His companions laughed, which only made him puff up more. He stepped forward to stand right before her, bending until they were at eye level. "Maybe I take them now anyway, for your insult!"

Fulan had heard enough. Angling her head back, she brought it forward suddenly with tremendous force. Bikolo had notoriously thick skulls. But she had on a steel helmet forged by her father's blacksmiths and magicked for strength. When it struck the Bikolo he staggered back, dazed. Before he could recover, Fulan swept his feet from under him and he went down onto his back hard. She was atop him in an instant, her own knife drawn at his throat. She uttered a single word, and the curved dark blade burst into flames. The heat of it seared the Bikolo's neck, but he did not dare move. His yellow eyes rounded as he took her in anew.

"You are one of his Storm Women?" he asked. "But I had heard—"

"I am no Storm Woman," Fulan cut in, pressing the blade so

that it burned the Bikolo's thick skin. He writhed beneath her. "But my *father* has given me many gifts."

This time the Bikolo's eyes bulged.

"It is you!" he croaked.

"Me," she replied. Pulling the knife from his neck, she sent the burning blade slicing through his topknot. He howled at the loss. Topknots held status among Bikolo. He would lose much standing among his companions.

Rising, she lifted the shorn knot of hair as he scrambled away. "For *my* collection," she said. A small crowd had gathered, and she made certain they all heard. Tying the topknot at her waist, she snuffed out her knife and slid the blade into its decorated bronze scabbard. When she turned to walk away, the crowd parted for her—human and otherwise. She didn't bother to look back.

Descending into the lower floors of the fortress always felt like climbing down into the belly of some monster. As she traveled deeper, the air grew warmer. On one level the clanging of hammers sounded, as blacksmiths worked day and night before blazing fires, creating weapons of war. She went lower still, where rivers of molten rock ran in rivulets along smooth black stone walls, from the ceiling to floor. She tried to ignore the beads of perspiration that formed on her skin, running even beneath her helmet. She was his daughter, she reminded herself. She may not have been born of fire, but she claimed it in her blood. And she would not burn. She stopped before two tall doors of dark iron, where the eternal living flame was emblazoned on the front. Two zimwi stood guard, these fitted in steel armor. They brandished spears tipped by serrated blades big enough to split an ox, and stone maces that looked able to pulverize boulders. Unblinking eyes peered out from behind spiked helmets that only revealed their lower jaws. She met their gazes and lifted off her own helmet—letting long black locs cascade to her shoulders and sweeping a hand over the other side of her scalp that was shaved low. On her forehead, her father's mark blazed to life, the heat and fires of this place making it visible.

Upon seeing it, the two zimwi grabbed hold of the steel doors, pulling them open to the sound of screams.

Fulan gritted her teeth. The screams were loud and piercing. It sounded not like one person screaming, but many—all in terrible pain. She stopped herself from flinching and stepped forward, entering the throne room of her father. Here, sheets of molten rock ran from the high ceiling far above, cascading down like water. The heat of it was almost unbearable, but she clenched her jaws tighter.

"I am my father's daughter," she whispered. "I am fire. I do not burn."

Her eyes found the source of the screaming. A shadowy thing, without true shape or form, hovered near the front of the room. It writhed in agony, as its body stretched and rippled. Between the screams were cries that sounded like the buzzing of many bees. *It burns! It burns! Oh, it burns!* She swung her gaze to another figure, a big man, bowed and kneeling on one leg. Her brow furrowed. That one she did not know. Pulling her eyes away, she fixated on the one who had drawn her here—solitary and seated on an iron throne, his face hidden beneath a great spiked iron mask, behind which blazed a blinding and roaring fire. She stopped before a raised dais and went to a knee, clutching her helmet under one arm and bowing her head low.

"Father," she said.

The Witch Priest rose from his throne, towering, taller even than a zimwi. He was draped in black armor, as dark as his skin—like black rock on which liquid fire ran like veins. Stepping to the edge of the dais, he extended a hand to stroke Fulan's cheek. Fingers gently cupped her chin, lifting her head higher. She looked up into that mask, where blazing eyes stared back. Behind it was a head formed completely of flames, as if a living fire had taken on the form of a man. She thought she might burn away under that gaze, reduced to nothing but ash.

"Daughter." His voice was a muted flame. "I feared you had forgotten your way."

Fulan wet her throat. "I was . . . delayed."

The Witch Priest glanced to the topknot tied at her waist, and there was a low laughter.

"Truly, you are my daughter, not a day goes by that I regret saving you and bringing you into my fold. To think that I would adopt a mortal child as my own. But you have grown strong, dutiful. And I find myself proud." His voice seemed curious, as if he was discovering some unexpected emotion.

"I owe you my life," Fulan said, pride trembling her voice. "I am yours, always, Father."

The Witch Priest nodded. "Such loyalty can be hard to come by." He turned abruptly, gesturing to where the Shadow Thing still screamed. "Look upon these. My minions I gifted with so much power, only to have them disappoint me."

The buzzing sound like bees came again, many voices crying out at once.

We live only to serve you! We are loyal to you!

There was a roar like a firestorm and the Witch Priest surged forward, grabbing hold of his minions in one clawed hand. When he spoke, his voice was a snarl.

"You were to rid me of one of my greatest enemies! You failed at your task!"

No, great one! We saw her die! By our very hands!

"And yet Asha lives! I can feel her, out there, in the world . . ." The Witch Priest's voice faltered, lowering to dying embers. "It has been so long. She hid from me, so that I had almost forgotten her presence. The feel of it. But now it has returned, beautiful in its own way, so familiar. I did not know I could so miss her. And yet . . . could she be my undoing . . . ?"

Fulan frowned. What was he talking about? Who was this Asha, that could be his undoing? She had never heard her father speak this way. Uncertain. Confused. And perhaps even . . . fearful? Impossible!

As if catching himself, the Witch Priest shook his head—releasing the Shadow Thing. He retook his place upon his throne, once more a living inferno.

"For your failure," he spoke, "you will know pain."

At once the screams from the Shadow Thing increased to shrieks—and its body collapsed into many writhing and wriggling things. Fulan looked away, unable to suppress a shudder.

"For you, my daughter," the Witch Priest went on, "I have a special task. You will hunt my enemy. Seek her out. Find her and bring her to me."

Fulan frowned. She was being sent to hunt someone? Now?

"But Father, your armies gather to march on the kingdoms of the west. I would join them. I hoped even to lead—"

The Witch Priest cut her off with the wave of a hand. "I have Kishi to lead my armies."

"Face-stealers?" Fulan straightened. "Those monsters are untrustworthy!"

Her father chuckled. "Truly. But they crave power. And are feared like no other." He glanced again to the topknot tied at her waist. "They will never need to prove themselves to those who march beneath my banner."

Fulan's face flushed.

"Do not assume I set you on a lesser course, my daughter," the Witch Priest assured her. "This task I set before you is perhaps more important than any other. It may determine the course of our great work—to free this world from the meddling spirits and gods who hold it in their sway. We will bring a new order, a new age. And you will sit at my side."

Fulan felt her pride swell again. Clenching a fist to her heart, she bowed low. "Yes Father, as you wish."

The Witch Priest nodded approvingly. "You will not be sent alone. This one will accompany you." He gestured to the other kneeling figure before his throne. Fulan had almost forgotten about the man. At being acknowledged he lifted his head. He was older than she had thought, with white hair streaking the black of his beard. He was big, too—with a thick neck and wide shoulders fitted into a jerkin made from the fur of different animals. The pelts and small skulls of slain creatures hung from his waist, along with a knife with a long, curved blade. Beaded scars rose up on his forehead, encircling his eyes and traveling down his cheeks. Sweat glistened on the dark skin of his shaved scalp to run down to his chin. But if the heat of her father's throne room bothered him he did not show it, his face set and jaw clenched.

Fulan scowled. "I don't need help."

The Witch Priest nodded. "I believe you are capable, Daughter. Or I would not set you on this task. But you have never faced one such as whom you seek. If I know her well, she may look innocent—no more than a mortal girl now. But make no mistake. She is dangerous. I believe she has already thwarted one of my plans, and even now may be working against me."

"A child?" Fulan asked, dubious. "You think I need help finding a child?"

Her father growled suddenly, gripping his throne and leaning forward. When he spoke, his voice was again the raging firestorm. "Do not presume that you know the ways of this world and all the secrets it holds! You have no concept of what power can lurk behind that which you suspect the least!" He sat back, the rage in his voice cooling. "The smallest mouse, my daughter, can start a stampede that trembles the earth, stirring up a storm that can wear down even a mountain."

Fulan bent her head deep. "Forgive me, Father. Truly, you know best."

The Witch Priest turned to the man. "Show my daughter who you are."

The man looked to Fulan and spoke in a quiet voice. "I am called the Huntsman. If a thing lives, it can be hunted. If it can be hunted, we can track it. If we can track it, it will not escape us."

Fulan eyed him, unimpressed. "We? I only see you."

A slow smile crept across his face. Reaching into a pouch at his waist he withdrew something small—a smooth gray stone that fit into the palm of his hand. Pursing his lips tight together, he made a shrill whistle. At once, three shapes flew from the stone to land on the ground before him. Fulan's free hand gripped her knife, readying for an attack. What monsters had this man unleashed? But now she could see the shapes had taken on a clearer form. Hounds—three in all, each larger in size than a hyena! Their bodies were the same gray of the stone, with powerful legs and large jaws that showed sharp teeth. A shadowy haze clung to them, so that they seemed to fade into the darkness. As she looked closer she made out thick rusted chains crisscrossing their chests and backs, running along their flanks. At another whistle from the Huntsman, they sat obediently on their haunches, ears erect and at the ready.

"You see," the Witch Priest said. "I do not burden you unnecessarily. Together, you will find the one I seek. You will bring her to me. Now tell me, who are you?"

Fulan pulled her eyes from this Huntsman and his monstrous hounds, looking up into the iron mask and the scorching gaze that lay beneath.

"I am my father's daughter," she said proudly. "I am fire. I do not burn!"

At this the Witch Priest laughed, his voice echoing through his throne room to mingle with the unceasing screams.

CHAPTER TWO

ENCOUNTERS

A sha! Keep up!"
Abeni burst from the thick bush to run through the tall grass, one hand holding onto Asha while the other carried her wood staff. The wide-brimmed hat tied at her neck bounced on her back, along with the satchel crossed over her chest. Beside her, Songu kept pace—the boy's long legs easily matching hers. Between them Asha laughed as if this was a game.

"They're getting closer!" Zaneeya warned.

Abeni glanced back at the panther girl's warnings, to see a swarm of flying things surging out of the bush and over the tall grass—their many voices chittering in pursuit. A burst of pink mist and the smell of flowers announced Nyomi's arrival. The porcupine girl ran with arms full of honeycombs, the gooey stuff trickling between her fingers.

"I thought," she huffed, "Aziza were supposed to be friendly!"

Aziza. So that's what they were. Abeni had never seen anything like them—small people, able to fit in her hands! With wings too, shimmering in the sunlight so that they glowed!

"They don't seem very friendly!" Abeni put in, as something small whizzed past her. Songu ducked as something else streaked by. There was a sting at her arm. "Ouch!" Slapping at the spot, Abeni turned her hand over to find what looked like a tiny arrow!

Zaneeya growled. "Now they're shooting at us?"

More arrows flew, and Abeni picked up her speed—dragging Asha along.

"I heard that Aziza help travelers!" Nyomi said, letting out a squeak as an arrow zipped by her ear. "That they protect whoever they come across!"

"Maybe they are all of that," Zaneeya shot back, her orange cat eyes narrowing beneath a messy tangle of black locs, "when we don't go digging in their anthills!"

The porcupine girl shrugged, her large black eyes wide. "How was I supposed to know that anthill was filled with Aziza? It's an anthill. It should have . . . ants!"

"Why did you need to eat ants right at this moment?" Zaneeya asked.

Nyomi lifted up the honeycombs. "What else goes with honey?"

Abeni wanted to tell the two to do less talking and more running. But a sudden yank pulled Asha from her grip. She stopped to find the small girl surrounded by the tiny, winged people. A few had taken hold of her long ivory locs, lifting them to stand up on their ends. Others clutched at her clothing and her arms and legs. Songu turned, grabbing at Asha. But the Aziza were stronger than they looked! They hoisted the small girl into the air, taking Songu with them.

"Oh no you don't!" Abeni shouted. Arrows streaked by and she whirled her staff, batting them away. Reaching Songu, she leapt to catch his legs, hoping her weight was enough to drag everyone back down. It seemed to work, as the Aziza groaned in exertion before letting go entirely. The three fell to the ground, tumbling atop one another. Asha sat up, clapping in delight.

"Again! Again!" she cried.

Abeni and Songu exchanged exasperated looks. Definitely not again.

"I've had enough of running!" Zaneeya snarled. In a blur, she shifted into a midnight-black panther—not large, but not too small either. Planting her paws and opening her jaws wide, she roared loud enough to shake the quiet of the day, sending birds flying with startled squawks and smaller animals burrowing in fright. The Aziza all shrieked in terror, diving behind trees and into the tall grass. All was suddenly quiet.

Zaneeya transformed back into a tall girl, wearing a short top and skirt made of the same panther fur, with long muscular arms that ended in claws. She whooped in triumph, baring sharp feline teeth. "And stay down if you know what's good for you! Bunch of buzzing mosquitoes!"

"Awww!" Asha pouted. "You scared all the little flying people away."

Abeni sighed. "That's a good thing, Asha. I don't think they liked us very much."

"Mmm hmm." They turned to find Nyomi stuffing her mouth with gobs of honey and shaking her head. "Some people just get angry over the slightest thing!"

Everyone eyed her. Abeni didn't think having your home destroyed by a hungry porcupine spirit was a slight thing. But it was hard arguing with the girl, especially when it came to food.

Songu gave a lopsided smile, and his hands formed a sign for thankfulness.

Abeni nodded. "Yes, we should be thankful they decided to stop and—"

She cut off at a sudden droning—like dozens of wings beating, hundreds of wings.

"That doesn't sound good," Nyomi whimpered, stuffing her mouth faster.

Before Abeni could even agree, a fresh horde of flying things came streaming from the bush. More Aziza. Definitely hundreds! And they were riding on—she gasped. Bees! The biggest bees she'd ever seen—the size of small birds!

"You have *got* to be kidding!" Zaneeya groaned.

Nyomi squealed, vanishing in an explosion of pink mist, the abandoned honeycombs dropping to the ground. Just as quickly she returned, scooping up the honeycombs before vanishing again.

Abeni didn't bother to yell "RUN!" She scooped up Asha and

sped off. Zaneeya turned back into a panther, taking the lead. The droning only grew louder as the Aziza chased after them. Abeni's mind raced. Maybe if they found a lake? She'd jump in and hold her breath under water as long as she could—anything to get away! Suddenly, Zaneeya braked, running to the right. Abeni saw the problem—another horde of Aziza, coming from the other direction! She and the others followed the panther girl, only to be bought up short again by more Aziza riding those giant bees.

Zaneeya shifted back to a girl, panting. "They're surrounding us!"

She was right. The Aziza had formed around them, chittering in triumph and circling in an ever-tightening ring. Nyomi appeared close to Abeni. The porcupine girl looked to have finally lost her appetite. Her black eyes were wide and the long dark quills that usually lay flat on her head and back like hair bristled in fright.

"Well come on then!" Zaneeya growled, crouched with claws at the ready.

Abeni clutched protectively at Asha with one hand, brandishing her staff in another. She wasn't certain how they would fight off giant bees, not to mention little winged people who now held strung bows, slingshots, and even tiny metal-tipped spears. This close, she could even make out what they were chittering in high-pitched voices.

"Bad ogres! Bad ogres! Bad ogres!" they chanted angrily.

"Ogres?" Abeni asked, perplexed. "Why are they calling us ogres?"

"Aziza don't like ogres," Asha said. Everyone looked to the small girl, who seemed oddly calm. "They're usually quite nice. Very kind to travelers or those who get lost in the forest. But they really dislike ogres, or any monsters."

Abeni blinked at the explanation. She often had to remind herself that the small girl was really a spirit—whom she had once known as an old woman—and sometimes knew things, startling things.

"But why do they think *we're* monsters?" Zaneeya asked.

Everyone stared at Nyomi, who rolled her eyes. "Are we still talking about that anthill?"

Abeni looked back to the swirling Aziza. "We're not ogres!" she shouted.

That only riled them up more, and they drew their circle tighter—so that everyone had to press up against one another. Abeni tried to avoid Nyomi's quills as her eyes remained locked on the stingers of the giant bees. They were very big!

"They also like music," Asha mentioned.

"What?" Abeni asked.

"The Aziza. They love music."

"I don't know how that is going to help—"

Before Abeni could finish, a sweet note sounded. She turned to find Songu, his flute at his lips. The Aziza heard it too. As one, they turned their attention to the boy. Taking a deep breath, he began to play a bright and delightful tune, that seemed to bounce upon the air. The effect on the Aziza was immediate. Smiles appeared on their small faces. They lowered their weapons and began to clap, keeping time with Songu's playing. Their chittering started up, and Abeni could make out one word repeated again and again.

"Dance! Dance! Dance!"

"I think they want us . . . to dance," Abeni said, startled.

"Oh!" Nyomi exclaimed, already breaking into a jig. "That I can do! Have I told you that porcupine spirits are excellent dancers?"

Abeni didn't bother to reply that the girl had—often. Grabbing Asha by the hand she spun the small girl, and the two of them began to dance. Songu moved about too, spinning as he played. Zaneeya crossed her arms, her face set like stone.

"I am not dancing," she said, "for some annoying flighty little—"

"Make the cat dance!" one Aziza chittered loudly. They all took up a chant. "Dance cat, dance! Dance cat, dance! Dance cat, dance!"

"I think they're waiting to see you shake it," Nyomi said in singsong as she leapt about.

Zaneeya ground her teeth. "I'm going to make you pay for this, you walking thorn bush!"

And then, she danced. To Abeni's surprise, the panther girl was quite good! She moved with a dangerous grace, seeming to glide with the music. The Aziza watched her, entranced, oohing and ahhing. Abeni wasn't certain how long their strange performance lasted. But when Songu's flute finally died away, they stopped, exhausted. Everything grew quiet, except for the droning wings of giant bees. With sudden shouts, the Aziza erupted into thunderous applause.

Abeni let out a relieved breath. Songu smiled. Zaneeya merely sniffed. Asha blew kisses. Nyomi, of course, bowed deep.

The music and their dance had a surprising effect on the Aziza. They abandoned their fierce-looking bees and settled down to talk and converse. After a few sharp glares, Abeni and the others got Nyomi to apologize for wrecking their home. A few more stares got her to offer up her honey to make amends. The little people eagerly accepted. It turned out the giant bees they rode weren't the honey-making kind. They insisted everyone join them for a grand feast. And, not wanting to offend, Abeni and the others graciously accepted.

It was morning when she and her companions ventured back across the grass plain.

"Those Aziza certainly know how to throw a party!" Nyomi remarked.

Abeni nodded, blinking bleary eyes. It had indeed been a feast, with food, drink, singing, music, and, of course, dancing. It lasted almost until dawn!

"Do they ever sleep?" Zaneeya grumbled, stifling a yawn.

"At least they gave us gifts!" Asha said, humming a tune she'd learned the past night.

That they had. Abeni patted her satchel—what she called the big bag. It could hold just about anything and not feel any heavier. She'd filled it with jugs of water from a spring the Aziza had shown them, and fruit plucked from trees. The bag would keep the jugs from spilling and the fruit fresh. There was also food the Aziza had prepared for them: tiny portions wrapped in green leaves. You had to eat about a dozen to get full. But they were delicious!

"I think that was the most fun we've had since your village, Songu!" Nyomi said. There was an awkward silence. Realizing what she'd said, the porcupine girl's quills wilted. "Oh. I'm sorry, Songu. I didn't . . . I mean to say . . . I wasn't thinking . . ."

Songu offered a slight smile and a hand sign telling her it was fine.

Nyomi perked up a bit after that and tried to make up by praising his flute playing—claiming she'd only heard similar from a frog spirit who took up the flute after growing tired of croaking in a chorus. She went on to tell a dizzying tale that Songu just nodded at. Once Nyomi got going, she didn't stop until she was out of breath.

Abeni signed quietly to Songu—asking if he was truly okay. He answered that he was and returned a quick smile. She had discovered by chance that she could speak with her hands, an unexpected gift of a prattle stone she had accidentally swallowed, allowing her to speak and understand endless languages. It turned out hand signing was among them. She taught it to Songu and the others, who picked it up quickly. Most times the boy seemed okay—especially when he played his flute. But other times she caught him staring at nothing, with a haunted look on his face.

It had been weeks now since they left the village of Kono—Songu's home, where he once had a family. All of that changed with the Goat Man. He had stolen away the children of Kono like Songu and turned them into monsters. Made them do terrible things, even to those they loved. As a monster, Songu had done the unthinkable—selling away his own parents. The villagers of Kono had been able to forgive the other children, welcoming them back. But they had not been able to forgive Songu. So, he'd joined Abeni's odd little group, one more lost child. One more life torn apart by the Witch Priest.

A hand went to her bag. Inside was the standard she had taken from her own destroyed village: the upside-down orange tear. The eternal flame. The mark of the Witch Priest. Thinking of it made her stomach go hollow. It was because of the Witch Priest that the people of her village had been stolen away, sent to the mysterious ghost ships. It was because of the Witch Priest that Nyomi and Zaneeya had been separated from their families. He had even gifted a sad little goatherd named Brima the power to become the Goat Man and steal away children like Songu. So much suffering. So many wronged.

She felt a small hand slip into her own.

Asha. The girl smiled up at Abeni, as if reading her thoughts.

Once, she had known this little girl as an old woman—whom the people of her village had called a witch. But so much had happened since then. The day of Harvest Festival in her village, her birthday. The Storm Women attacking. The old woman, whom she would come to call Auntie Asha, secreting her away. The time spent as her apprentice in a magic house. A straw man who taught her how to wield a staff. The night Auntie Asha had died—no, had been killed, by one of the Witch Priest's minions, a thing of shadows. Waking up the next morning to discover her as she was now: a little girl who looked no more than five or six, but who in fact was a spirit, newly reborn and in need of a guardian.

Guardian. That never ceased to astonish her. She hadn't seen more than thirteen harvests herself. Asha may have changed a lot, but in her own reflection Abeni still saw the same girl she'd been on her twelfth Harvest Day. The same brown eyes and dark brown face. The same fleshy nose above lips people claimed made it look like she was pouting. Even the same slight overbite. She didn't feel any bigger or more grown-up. She certainly didn't feel like anyone's guardian.

"You're in your head again," Asha said, staring up with her dark, knowing eyes.

Abeni supposed she was. "Better than you being in it," she replied playfully. The little girl had a habit of entering her dreams, though she never quite explained that trick.

"Are you thinking about Songu?" Asha asked.

Abeni started to shake her head, then stopped. "Yes, and no. I

guess I was thinking about all of us, what we've been through."
She lowered her voice. "Do you think he'll talk again?"

"He talks now," Asha said. "You showed him how."

"Yes, but I mean . . . do you think he'll ever talk like he used to?"

Asha looked at the boy. "I can't say. The Goat Man made him
do bad things. He's trying to learn to be himself all over again."

"Like you have to learn how to be yourself again? The old Asha,
I mean?"

The little girl tilted her head in thought. "Maybe. But, like I
told you, I've been an old woman and a girl, many, many times.
I've lived countless lifetimes. Songu only has the one."

Abeni was still trying to get her head around Asha being not
just a spirit, but a very old one. Spirits aged differently. Though
both Nyomi and Zaneeya looked like girls her age, they were de-
cades old. But Asha claimed to have been around when the world
was still new! She was probably more powerful than most spirits.
Only each time she was reborn, she became a child again, forced
to relearn who she had been, to relearn the power she had once
had. That was even harder now, because of her brother.

"Do you really think he's looking for you?" Abeni asked. "Your
brother. I mean . . . the . . ." *The Witch Priest.* She could hardly
bring herself to say it.

Asha's face went grim, and she stared into the distance. "I can
feel him. He's out there. Hunting me. Searching for me."

Abeni shuddered. "Then we get you to these elder spirits, the
ones you said are fighting back against him, who can protect you."
That had been their plan since leaving Kono. She had accepted
her role as the small spirit's guardian. Well, as much as anyone
could accept such a thing. But if the Witch Priest was after Asha,
they needed to find those who could truly keep her safe. The others had agreed to come along. She had met Nyomi and Zaneeya
shortly after Asha was reborn. They didn't always see eye to eye,
but she counted them now as friends. Besides, maybe these elder
spirits could help them find their families. Songu was with them

because truly he had nowhere else to go. She had her own reasons, of course. She wanted to see Asha safe. But she also still hoped to find and rescue the stolen people of her village, something these elder spirits might know about.

"Do you wish you had stayed?" Asha asked. "With your friends, I mean?"

Her friends. The children of her village had been stolen by the Goat Man too and rescued along with Songu and the children of Kono. Abeni had hoped they would join her, to hunt down the Storm Women and the ghost ships. But they hadn't. Even her best friend Fomi. Instead, they returned to rebuild their destroyed village. She thought she understood. Sort of. Fomi and the others had been turned into monsters. Not for as long as Songu had, but long enough. Returning home must have made them feel normal again. She wondered what it would take for her to feel like that once more—normal.

"I want to go back home too," she answered at last. "But not until I find my family." Thoughts came to her then, of the last time she had seen them. Her mother remarking that her bright gold wrap skirt with little red snakes—the very one Abeni now wore— fit her well as a dress. Her father and uncle trading jokes as they prepared for Harvest Festival. Making faces at her older brother. Her twin aunts Awomi and Awami teaching her how to pound yam—and teasing her on being too skinny, claiming boys would want something more to hold onto. Okay, that last part she did *not* miss. But oh, how she missed *them*. What she wouldn't give to have them back.

Not all of her friends had been rescued. One still missing was Ekwolo, a boy whose bright smile had made her belly begin to flutter in strange ways. She wondered if he was one of those her aunts claimed wanted something more to hold onto. She shook her head, cheeks flushing. Where had *that* come from?

Her eyes went down to Asha, who regarded her with a raised eyebrow and a slight smile. Her cheeks flushed further. Could the girl read minds now?

"You're sure we're going the right way?" she asked, quickly changing the subject. "To find these elder spirits, I mean. The ones your sister said were fighting the Witch Priest?"

Asha's sister had been the one they first expected would help them. She turned out to be not a person, but an entire valley! Abeni only hoped these elder spirits weren't . . . trees . . . or some rocks. That was the thing about spirits, they could look like just about anything.

Asha nodded. "Yes. I mean, it *feels* like we are."

Then that would have to do. Abeni was learning to trust the little girl's feelings.

"I just hope our run-in with the Aziza didn't throw us off course."

"Oh, they weren't so bad in the end. Could have been bush babies."

Abeni grimaced. The less she remembered about that misadventure, the better.

They walked much the rest of the day but stopped early—having not slept the previous night. Finding a spot under a shady tree, they made a place to eat. Abeni took food from her bag for herself, Asha, and Songu. Zaneeya went hunting, returning with a hare that she ate raw and bloody—refusing Abeni's offer to cook it even slightly, mocking that as "burnt meat." Nyomi—being a porcupine spirit who was also part hedgehog spirit—ate whatever she could find growing or dig up. This turned out to be fat purple grubs, with a side of bark and flowers. That night, they slept under a starry sky: she, Asha, and Songu wrapped under blankets, Nyomi—who snored loudly—curled up in a ball of quills, and Zaneeya in her panther form, draped over a branch in the tree. It was some much-needed rest.

The next day, they started out early. As they walked, the stalks of grass grew taller, bright green and full of life. Beside Abeni Nyomi snacked on some bushy blue caterpillars and went on with her mouth full about some singing beetles she had known who had made such beautiful music, she had cried at having to eat them.

Zaneeya trotted along in panther form, practicing pouncing in the tall grass at Asha who squealed in delight at the game. Songu trailed behind, playing his flute. It was an uneventful day, and Abeni was thankful. It might have remained that way if not for the masks.

Zaneeya was the first to spot them, changing to her near-human form and pointing far ahead. Something gleamed bright in the distance. As they came closer, Abeni made them out. Masks. Two of them, and each as big as a boulder! They sat upright in the tall grass, one carved in the face of a man and the other a woman. Unrecognizable symbols ran across their foreheads and cheeks, while their heads were surrounded by giant beads. A morning breeze pushed through their open mouths—making a moaning that filled the air. The two shined beneath the sun, both the color of gold.

"I think it *is* gold," Zaneeya said, running a claw across one.

"I've never seen that much gold," Abeni said in awe. "Why make masks so big?"

"Maybe they belong to giants," Nyomi said fearfully.

"There aren't any giants here, Prickly," Asha reassured her, using her nickname for the porcupine girl. "They're all up in the mountains."

Abeni glanced to the small girl with raised eyebrows.

"I don't like giants," Zaneeya muttered.

A tap at Abeni's shoulder made her turn to find Songu. He gestured past the masks to something nearby. Abeni looked to see what he was aiming at. It turned out to be, of all things, two statues.

"What are those doing out here?" Nyomi asked, puzzled.

Abeni shook her head. This was all very odd. They walked towards the statues, stopping before them. These weren't as big as the masks. They were carvings of people and were properly people-sized.

"Gold as well," Zaneeya noted, rapping her knuckles on one of them.

Abeni stepped closer. They were amazingly lifelike—more real than any carving she'd ever seen. Both stood with arms held to their sides, with closed eyes and blank faces. Necklaces with those same odd symbols hung to their chests while long cloth robes patterned in red strips slung over a shoulder reached to their ankles. Lifting a hand, she traced a finger across a golden arm. Hard as metal—as if a real person had been dipped in gold.

"Who could have made these?" she asked.

Zaneeya shook her head. "I've never seen the like. Perhaps—"

The panther girl stopped, her orange eyes narrowing.

"What is it?" Abeni asked, staring about and gripping her staff. Please, no more Aziza.

"I thought I caught the scent of mortals, close by."

"Maybe you're smelling Songu and me," Abeni suggested.

"No." The panther girl sniffed the air. "I know your scents. This is coming from . . ." She trailed off, turning her head back to the statues.

"These two?" Abeni looked at the golden figures again. "But you said it yourself. They're made of gold. See?" With a flick of her staff, she whacked the statue's head. It responded with a surprising yelp.

Abeni yelped just as loud, jumping back. Zaneeya bared her teeth in a growl.

"What's happening?" Nyomi asked worriedly. "Do mortal statues feel pain?"

Abeni shook her head. They weren't supposed to move either! But this statue was doing just that! He held his head where she had hit him and his eyes shot open, revealing bright golden pupils that stared angrily. He shouted out what sounded like words. Immediately, the second statue awoke, glaring at them.

It took a moment for Abeni to make sense of what she was seeing. These weren't statues at all. They were men, covered in gold! Remembering she had struck one, she winced.

"Sorry!" she said. Both men looked to her in surprise. They didn't expect her to speak their tongue. No time to explain a prattle stone.

"I didn't mean to hit you. We didn't know you weren't statues! My name is—"

Before she could finish one of the men lifted a hand and a small golden orb began to form above his open palm. When it reached about the size of a plum he lifted it high without ever really touching it—and flung it at her!

Abeni quickly lifted her staff to bat it away. The small orb struck the wood, breaking apart into golden liquid that quickly spread. She dropped the staff in alarm and by the time it landed in the tall grass, it had been covered completely in gold. Turning back to the statues she found the two men readying more of the golden orbs.

"Run!" Zaneeya growled. "Run now!"

Snatching up Asha, that's exactly what Abeni did. Looking back, she could see the two men forming what looked to be wide flat plates of gold beneath their feet. The plates lifted into the air, carrying both men, who now crouched low and sped towards them.

Streaks of gold flew past Abeni, barely missing her. More of the orbs! Whatever they touched—grass or rock—was quickly covered in shining gold. Her friends dodged the golden streaks as they could. Several times Nyomi appeared, vanishing and jumping from one place to another while Zaneeya bounded through tall grass in great leaps.

Glancing back, Abeni saw in alarm that the two men were getting closer, riding those fast-moving plates. And one was aiming an orb directly for her. Someone yanked her away as it zipped past. She went tumbling behind a large rock, taking Asha with her. She turned to find it was Songu who had saved her. The two men soared past them, going after the others.

Gold streaks rained down on the two spirits. Nyomi appeared in a squeal with bits of gold on her quills. Abeni realized in horror the porcupine girl had been struck! She was vanishing and reappearing, jumping from place to place. But she couldn't shake the gold fast spreading across her body. By her last jump it covered her completely, stifling a shriek. She fell back, falling upon raised quills—all of her now a golden statue with a face frozen in terror.

Zaneeya roared. She turned abruptly, heading directly for her pursuers. Not expecting this attack, the two men tried desperately to take her down. But she dodged their orbs, weaving through the tall grass. One of them cried out as she leapt to knock him from atop his flying plate. She turned and pounced at his companion. But he was ready and met her head-on with a streak of gold. The liquid caught the panther girl in midair, covering her entirely. With a heavy *thunk,* she fell to the ground, a golden statue with claws still extended and mouth fixed in a snarl.

Abeni watched as the felled man jumped back up onto his flying plate and joined his companion. They looked over the captured spirits before turning back slowly, those golden eyes fixing on her.

CHAPTER THREE

PRISONERS

Abeni trudged through the tall grass. Asha walked at her front, and she knew Songu was behind. All three had been bound by their wrists, in bands of gold. It kept their arms tight at their sides and their hands at their waists. She was the only one with a band of gold fitted over her mouth. This she'd gotten after asking her captors where they were being taken, what they had done to be treated like this, and insisting repeatedly they be let go.

Their captors stood perched atop those hovering plates, which carried them above the savanna. On a third and larger plate were Nyomi and Zaneeya. The two had been reduced to golden statues, still caught in their last moments of movement. Abeni's eyes searched desperately for any sign that either was still alive—but they were silent and unmoving. She felt a moment of panic at the thought that her friends might have been turned to gold.

"Eyes forward!" one of her captors snapped. "Or you'll get blinders to join that gag—mouthy girl."

The other one laughed. "Still smarting that she whacked you good with her stick, Kofi?"

Kofi, scowled, the golden features of his face creasing. "Shut up, Ebo. Your fault I got hit." He put on a mimicking voice. "Go still like a statue. They won't know the difference. We'll catch them easy." He sucked his teeth in disgust.

The one called Ebo only laughed harder.

She wished she did have her staff—she'd whack them both again! Or her bag. Something in there might help. Both items, however, had been taken from her. The staff—still gold—rode on the hovering plate with Nyomi and Zaneeya. Luckily, her captors didn't know how to use the bag or what it was. They'd stuck their hands inside, disappointed to find it empty, unaware that you had to *think* on what you wanted before it revealed its contents. Thankfully they hadn't discarded it, throwing the bag on a heap alongside her hat and Songu's flute.

It was as she looked ahead that she first saw the road. That's what it had to be—a road where the tall grass finally receded. Only it was shining. At first she thought it was the heat—although it wasn't quite that hot. But as they got closer she could make out that the road was not made of dirt, but something that glinted yellow. She gasped. More gold! The road was made from gold!

Once she managed to pull her eyes from that startling sight, she noticed people gathered there. More golden people, like her captors. All wore those robes of interwoven red and gold across their golden skin. Some carried long golden spears, and swords that looked to be carved of gold. They stood guarding large white wood carts that seemed joined together by bits of gold, four in all. Each cart held more people—she counted eight. Only they weren't golden. Their skins were brown and dark like Abeni's. And their hands were also bound before them. More captives then, like her.

The new golden people turned to greet her captors. They glanced briefly at Abeni, Asha, and Songu. But their gold eyes rounded at seeing Zaneeya and Nyomi. There was talk about spirits and bush ghosts. In the end, the statues of her friends were deposited into the carts. One of her captors—Kofi—crafted another gold orb that hovered above his palm. He made a set of gestures with his hands, and the orb thinned and grew long—until it was a spear. He leveled the sharp tip directly at her.

"This one speaks our tongue," he said. "Gagged her, because she wouldn't stop talking."

"But she doesn't look or dress like one of us," another man said. He bent to peer into Abeni's eyes, and she reared back. "She carries no flecks and doesn't appear to have ever weaved. I don't even sense the ability."

"Then who is she?" a woman asked, her head covered in elaborate golden braids.

Kofi's eyes narrowed. "Maybe a spy. She was with those two." He gestured to Nyomi and Zaneeya.

"Whatever it is," the one named Ebo said, "we'll let Captain Ekua sort it out when we get back to Makomasi. But first." He walked up to Abeni, holding what looked like a small oval of gold between his thumb and forefinger. She flinched when he reached for her, and he smirked a golden smirk. His fingers pressed the gold oval to the bare skin just above her chest. It felt cool to the touch. And as she watched helplessly it dissolved into liquid, disappearing into her skin. She looked up at him in alarm. But he had already turned to go. The point of a spear poked her back. She was pushed toward the cart and golden hands lifted her easily before depositing her inside. She managed to sit up, watching as Songu and Asha were placed into separate carts. The small girl gave a reassuring look and mouthed silent words.

Stay brave.

A sudden lurch sent the cart pitching forward. Abeni looked over the side to see the wheels spinning and the road . . . moving! She squinted to make certain she wasn't seeing things. No, the road rippled and flowed, like golden water!

"You've never seen the river of gold before?" someone asked.

Abeni looked up to find a man seated across from her, his hands bound. But at least his mouth was free. He wore his hair short to the scalp and decorated in swirling patterns while three small scars marked his cheeks. A smile split his face, as if to calm her. She glanced back down to the moving road. A river? Looking back to the man she made a puzzled face.

"Forgive my brother," a woman beside him drawled. "He thinks he is funny."

"I have it on good authority that I am actually quite funny," he replied.

The woman snorted. "Funny looking . . ."

Abeni took her in, noticing the same smile and matching scars on either cheek. Not to mention the needling jokes. Definitely brother and sister.

"I don't mean it is a real river," the man said. "But that is what we call these golden paths. It is how the Gold Weavers travel, laying down one of their roads that pulls them and their things along. Of course, I never wanted to see one so . . . up close."

Abeni only grew more confused. Gold Weavers? Moving roads? What were they even talking about?

The woman frowned. "I don't think she knows about Gold Weavers. Look at her dress. The way she wears her hair. Reminds me of some forest people I once met through trade. But their home is far to the east, a very long way. What would a girl like that be doing out here? And with them?" She eyed the statues of Nyomi and Zaneeya, sitting just feet away.

"Well, she can't give us much of an answer now," the man said. He nodded at their captors. "Those are Gold Weavers, soldiers of the Gold Kingdom. They can make gold do wondrous things—shape it as they wish. See there?" He indicated two of the golden figures—both women, who hovered on separate plates. They stood with their feet planted, their arms making sweeping movements like some dance. "They're weaving gold even now, causing the road to move."

Abeni gaped beneath her gag. What kind of magic was this?

"Not all Gold Weavers are soldiers, but all are said to be born with the ability," the man's sister said, as if reading her mind. "That you can see in the flecks of gold in their eyes. They can do all sorts of things with gold. Tell me, did they put any inside you?"

Abeni remembered the small gold oval and looked down to her skin.

"Living gold," the man said grimly. "They give it to all prisoners. Lets them control you."

Living gold? How could gold be alive? And what did he mean, control her?

The man gave her a pitying look. "It's a lot to take in at once, I know. But you'll see stranger and grander things when we arrive in Makomasi."

Abeni had heard that name before—from their captors.

"Makomasi?" the man repeated. "You don't know that either? It's the heart of the Gold Kingdom. Where we unfortunates are headed." He jerked a chin into the distance. "You'll see it soon enough."

Abeni turned to look out from the cart, catching a glimpse of something brilliant in the distance. If she could have lifted her hands she would have shielded her eyes. What could possibly be so bright? Their carts moved faster, and she glanced to the hovering Gold Weavers, whose arms now danced furiously, causing the golden road beneath to churn and ripple. As the cart picked up speed, the brilliance in the distance began to take shape. Her eyes rounded and her mind tried to put a name to what she was seeing. A word Asha had once used to describe such a thing formed in her head. She had called it a city.

But she hadn't done it justice.

The city of Makomasi rose up before her. There were more buildings than she could count, great domes and spires that extended high into the air and spread out across an impossible length. Almost every bit was covered in gold that made the city shimmer like a star!

"Bush girl come to town to gawk at market," the man remarked.

Abeni barely heard him, unable to pull her eyes from this sight. In the weeks since leaving Kono, they had come upon other villages—no bigger than her own. How many of those would fit into this place? A hundred? More? Shouts came from atop the city's immense walls, and she realized in surprise that there were people up there! Their captors called something back, and at once two massive golden doors carved with leopards opened. Their party entered the city, passing tall buildings with crenulated walls where people hung out of windows to peer down at them. There were gleaming statues—towering sculptures of people, standing with arms extended and holding long staffs, or spears, and swords. Some buildings looked to be built atop other buildings, with roofs that were flat or rounded or pointed or capped, all carved with symbols—identical to the ones decorating the beads of their captors. Roads led in every direction, as their carts turned this way and that. Everything was built on a grand scale, so that she felt small in its presence.

And there were people—so many people! Men, and women, and children dressed in that richly woven clothing in colors of red, and blue, purple, green, and more—some with golden flecks powdering their dark skin. Every last one, she realized, was a Gold Weaver! She watched several, whose spinning arms took apart a building, one sheet of gold at a time. Others worked the roads of the city, allowing heavily laden carts to be moved without the need of oxen or anything! Elsewhere, people worked what she took for looms—spooling thin lines of gold into cloth. The carts passed under a golden arch and she gaped at what had to be a sprawling market, with dozens of sellers hawking goods from stands as the scents of cooking food wafted through the air. She even saw someone riding on the back of an oddly big mule, with golden jewelry tied into its flowing black mane and more covering its large hooves. A horse! That was its name. Though this was her first time seeing one. Then there was the noise. It had hit her immediately. Everyone talking at once, the rumbling of wheeled carts, people hammering and beating drums and shouting and laughing and children tied to their mothers' backs crying. She shut her eyes as everything started spinning, threatening to drown her beneath. It was all too big, too many, too much!

"It can be a lot your first time." Abeni opened her eyes to find both the man and his sister eyeing her with concern. "Makomasi is not the only city in the west—not even the largest," the woman continued. "But it is impressive. So much gold . . ." She shook her head in awe. "I had only heard tales of the capital of the Gold Kingdom—as they rarely admit outsiders. It is another matter to view it for myself."

Abeni gaped. Cities *bigger* than this one? Trying to imagine that made her dizzy all over again and she was glad when their cart suddenly stopped in what looked to be a rounded clearing. One by one, the golden skin of their captors fell away to reveal people who looked little different than herself. Only their eyes remained gold, along with those giant beads worn about their necks and smaller jewelry on wrists or entangled in their hair.

Nearby, brother and sister chuckled. "Did you think they were *made* of gold?" the man asked. Abeni's cheeks heated. No. Well, maybe. A little . . .

There were more people like her captors here, all holding weapons. They jostled everyone out of the carts with barked shouts. Abeni soon found herself standing among a group of huddled and bound people, trying to catch sight of Asha and Songu. A man walked up to her. Kofi, whom she had struck.

"I'll be needing this back," he said. Opening his palm, he somehow called the gag from her mouth. It re-formed into a gold orb, which he added to the necklace that hung to his chest. She worked her mouth, thankful to be free of the thing.

"This is the one you spoke of?" someone asked. Abeni turned to find a new figure approaching—a tall woman with strong shoulders who moved with a hunter's grace. Her white hair was cut short, and she dressed in the same red and gold patterned clothing as her captors—what Abeni now took to be a kind of uniform. An intricately carved golden eyepatch covered one eye, matching the necklace of large beads she wore, far more than the other soldiers. She fixed Abeni with a measuring gaze.

"Captain Ekua," Kofi said, dropping his arms in salute. "We captured this one near the eastern border, along with these two."

Asha and Songu were pulled from the crowd to stand beside Abeni. The two were still bound but, thankfully, looked otherwise unharmed. Asha craned her neck to stare up at the tall buildings, while Songu kept his face blank.

"Kofi claims you know our tongue," Captain Ekua said. "Is this true? Speak!"

"Yes!" Abeni answered hurriedly. She didn't think it was a good idea to be on the wrong side of this intimidating woman. "I mean, I can understand you."

The captain arched an eyebrow with interest.

"We think she might be a spy!" Kofi added.

Captain Ekua continued to look Abeni over, shifting to Songu and Asha. "The little girl looks like she only wants to run about and climb things. The boy . . ." She paused, frowning. "He stares like a soldier. But they're still rather small for spies." She returned to Abeni. "How do you know our tongue, girl? Don't lie. It will annoy me."

Abeni hadn't even thought of lying. "I swallowed a stone."

"A prattle stone, then," the captain said. She smirked at Abeni's surprise. "I have read of such things—supposedly taken from the belly of some great fish. Are you a sorceress, then?"

"No," Abeni answered quickly. "It happened . . . by accident." She decided to leave out the part about the talking pots that had tricked her into doing it. No need to go into all that.

Captain Ekua gave her that weighing look again, then nodded. "Yes. That seems likely. Not a spy, then, just an overly curious child."

A frustrated Kofi gritted his teeth. "But Captain, what of her *other* companions?" He gestured to the statues of Nyomi and Zaneeya.

Captain Ekua turned to them with interest. "Now this is a greater puzzle." She gave a set of orders, and several soldiers formed a circle about Nyomi and Zaneeya. Some held spears at the ready. Others had their hands up in what Abeni now recognized as a position to weave gold. At a nod from the captain, they began swirling their arms. At once, the gold encasing the two spirit girls rippled, dripping away in a liquid stream to form separate golden orbs. The effects were immediate.

Nyomi picked up the shriek she had been in the middle of since being captured. At seeing the Gold Weavers, her black eyes bulged and she yelped before vanishing. Or at least, she tried to.

The usual pink mist formed faintly, but she didn't disappear. She looked down at herself in surprise and confusion.

"Flowers," the captain noted, sniffing at the air. "Interesting."

Zaneeya's release was far more dramatic. She roared at once, charging her captors. They cried out, falling back in alarm. All except Captain Ekua. The hard-faced woman looked unimpressed as she lifted a hand to make a jerking gesture with her fingers. Zaneeya abruptly broke her charge, shifting into her near-girl form, bent over, and trembling. She looked up to glare at the captain between tangled locs, orange eyes blazing.

"What have you done to me?" she demanded in a strained voice.

Captain Ekua tapped at her own neck. Both Nyomi and Zaneeya reached for theirs, and for the first time Abeni noticed the band of gold there—like a collar.

"We haven't seen your kind in a while," the captain said. "Fitting you with living gold isn't always enough. But we have the means to deal with you. So, none of your tricks."

Zaneeya growled. "I'll show you tricks!" She leapt, claws bared, moving for the older woman. Captain Ekua didn't flinch, instead once more jerking her fingers. The panther girl dropped to her knees, gasping and clutching her sides. But she wasn't defeated yet. Drawing deep breaths, she rose to her feet and stepped forward. Another jerk of the captain's fingers sent her staggering. She tried again, her teeth bared.

"Go on, little spirit," the woman said idly. "I can do this all day."

Abeni stared helplessly as Zaneeya fell to the ground, writhing.

"You're hurting kitty," someone said. Every eye turned to look down at Asha. The small girl stood staring up at the older woman. Her face was calm, but there was something hard in her voice—and the air about them felt suddenly heavy, like just before a storm. Some of the soldiers shifted uncomfortably. Even Captain Ekua frowned. Abeni decided to step in quickly, before something happened they would all regret.

"Please stop," she told the captain. "She'll listen—I promise!"

Captain Ekua gave Abeni a hard look before dropping her

hand. Zaneeya collapsed, panting. No one stopped Abeni when she ran to her, bending to whisper into the panther girl's ear. "Stop fighting! We can't win this!" She indicated the many soldiers surrounding them. Dropping her voice, she added, "At least right now. We'll get our chance."

Zaneeya eyed her dubiously, and Abeni feared she might continue her fight. The spirit girl was incredibly stubborn that way. But finally, she relaxed—though the glare she fixed on Captain Ekua could have burned through stone. If the older woman was concerned, however, she didn't show it. Turning from them, she stared out at the bound captives.

"You have all been found close to our lands or our borders," she spoke loudly, "in violation of our laws. By decree of the king, your freedom is now forfeit. Whoever you were before, does not matter. Whatever your station was before, does not matter. Your lives now belong to the Gold Kingdom. And we will do with you as we wish."

There were murmurs of despair from the bound prisoners.

"For some of you," Captain Ekua said, "this will mean laboring for the royal family, perhaps even in the palace." Stepping forward, she looked the captives over. At a gesture towards a younger man, soldiers moved to pull him away and set him apart. The captain continued her inspection, stopping a second time to indicate an old woman who was similarly pulled away. She came before Asha—bending to inspect the small girl closely, as if searching for something. "This one too," she said at last, watching as Asha was moved away.

"For the rest of you," the captain continued, "it's the mines."

With that, she turned and strode away—with Asha and the other two she'd selected in tow. The soldiers surged forward, grabbing the remaining captives and pushing them into a line. Abeni shouted out for Asha, but lost sight of the girl in the jostle of people. Someone pushed her back, and when she tried again two crossed spears blocked her way. Panic rose inside her. She had lost Asha once. She couldn't do so again! She was set to push past the spears when a hand gripped her shoulder. Turning, she found Zaneeya.

"Heed your own advice, for once," the panther girl said. Her voice dropped to a growl. "We'll get our chance."

Abeni relented. Yes. She looked at the Gold Weavers, a deep anger forming inside. And they'd be sorry.

CHAPTER FOUR

THE MINES OF MAKOMASI

A voice echoed in the dark tunnel. "Remember, your purpose here is to work!"

Abeni hauled the basket of dirt over to dump into a cart. She rapped it once to indicate it was full, and watched as two men wheeled it away. Wiping sweat from her brow, she accidentally smeared her face with dirt. She didn't bother cleaning it. She'd given up on clean long ago. Looking down at her clothing, she grimaced—a drab gown that might have been white once but was now dingy, stained, and torn. They'd all been given such gowns upon arriving here. People from different lands, who spoke different tongues—every last one now set to toil in the mines of Makomasi.

Abeni had seen a mine before, the one run by the Goat Man near the village of Kono—where the children he'd turned to monsters had forced their own parents to harvest gems. She had thought it large. But the gold mines outside the city of Makomasi were enormous—like giants had taken great spoons and dug up the earth. An entire hill had been cut into irregular steps and terraces and run through with tunnels. Hundreds of people worked and moved along its surface, splattered in dust and mud as they dug, hauled rocks, sifted dirt, and more. Others, like her, worked in the tunnels, searching for gold. She had wondered how Makomasi could afford such wealth in gold—to adorn people in it, to build grand statues and structures, to pave their very roads. Now, she knew. They had others work to mine the gold for them.

"Work well to impress your masters!" the shout continued. "Work well, to be rewarded! Work well, and you may regain your freedom!"

Abeni scooped dirt with a shovel, throwing it into her basket. She eyed the short man who spoke. His face was illuminated by torches lining the walls. He paced as he shouted, one hand held forward where he balanced three floating gold orbs above an open palm. Some of the other workers claimed his name was Yooku. But no one, not even the two guards who trailed his steps, dared call him that. He was boss man, and that was all.

"Do you hear me?" he shouted.

"Yes, boss man!" Abeni answered with everyone else. She'd learned that Yooku liked to hear himself talk. He expected them to like it too.

She glanced over to where Zaneeya stood, swinging a long wooden-handle pickaxe that chipped away dirt and rock. The panther girl's blows landed with more force than even some of the biggest men at her side. Her orange gaze, however, was not on her work. It traced Yooku, her eyes glowing like a hunter following prey. Abeni filled a wooden cup with half-clean water from a clay jar and walked to hand it over. Zaneeya stopped to take it, and Abeni clasped the girl's hand, shaking her head.

"Not yet," she whispered. "We're not ready."

Zaneeya downed the water before thrusting back the cup—spitting out grit. "Then when," she growled low. "Three days. Three days we've been at this. And I want *him* to shut up." Her hands tightened on the pickaxe.

"I know. But we can't do anything rash. Remember what they told us—"

"I remember," Zaneeya said, a clawed hand gripping the collar at her neck. They had been warned of the consequences of disobedience. Just attempting to remove her collar had left the panther girl doubled over in pain.

"I miss hunting," Zaneeya said. She gripped the collar again. "This . . . cursed thing. It stops me from shifting. I feel almost . . .

mortal. What if I become trapped like this?" A look crossed her face then—desperate, even frightened. That unnerved Abeni. The panther girl was many things, but never frightened.

"We're going to get out of here," she assured her. "And we'll get that off you." She touched her chest. *And somehow get this living gold* thing *out of all of us.* The thought of it moving around inside her, tracking her movements, able to immobilize her in a moment, made her feel sick.

Zaneeya searched her face, as if looking for certainty, then nodded.

"Have you heard from Asha? In your dreams?"

"No," she answered, hiding her worry. "But we'll think of something. We always do."

Zaneeya sighed wearily, grabbing the pickaxe to return to her work.

"I didn't know there were so many rocks in the world!" Nyomi had trudged over, carrying a large rock that she dropped into a pile. The porcupine girl looked as haggard as all of them, her quills drooping under her ragged gown. "All this dirt, and not so much as a good worm to eat. This collar won't let me disappear or jump away. And the worst of it is—no one here dances!"

"We're prisoners," Zaneeya said, gesturing about. "There's no dancing! No one here wants to dance!"

Nyomi smiled wide, leaning into Zaneeya. "Don't you want to dance though? Deep down inside? In your warm happy place?"

Zaneeya leaned forward, baring her teeth. "The only thing I want deep down inside right now is some porcupine meat."

Nyomi yelped, pulling back. Abeni felt a tap at her shoulder. Songu. His hands moved rapidly in warning. She looked to find Yooku glaring their way. Picking up her shovel, she quickly began scooping up dirt until she felt his gaze drift.

"You lot make way too much noise," a man said, hefting a pickaxe. Abeni looked to find it was one of the siblings she met earlier. She had gotten to know them better over the past three days. Their names were Manu and Naana. They claimed to come from lands to the south and said they had been captured after their river boat got swept off course. The two had been helpful to just about everyone. They spoke a language similar to the Gold Weavers' and translated for the newcomers. It helped keep people calm, and from getting into trouble.

"Maybe they're putting on a show," Naana joked, swinging her own pickaxe. "Is that who you are? A troupe of entertainers?"

"I saw a troupe once," Manu added, huffing as he worked. "It had these men who tamed wild hyenas to do tricks."

They all stopped at Yooku's shout to yell back, "Yes, boss man!"

"I can see it now," Naana said. "The girl who talks many tongues! The scowling panther spirit, and the dancing porcupine girl!" She frowned at Songu. "What is it you do again?"

"Songu plays the flute!" Nyomi piped in.

"And Songu the flute player!" Naana finished dramatically.

Songu smiled shyly.

The brother and sister were always trying to cheer everyone up. They reminded Abeni of her older brother. But it was hard to hold onto laughter in this place.

Seeing her face, Naana turned sympathetic.

"You worry about the little one, Asha," she said.

Abeni nodded. "I'm supposed to take care of her."

Manu chortled. "I think that one can take care of herself."

Naana bobbed her head in agreement. "Better she sit in the palace taking care of some soft-bottomed noble eating golden grapes than be trapped here with us." She sniffed at herself and made a face. "We stink!"

Manu frowned, lifting an arm to sniff as well. "Eh, speak for yourself. I smell great!"

Abeni did smile then, despite herself.

"I think we need a break," Naana said, stopping to wipe her brow. She whistled loudly. "Boss man! I gotta do the necessary!"

Yooku frowned at the interruption.

"You can go at the proper time," he shot back.

Naana puffed her cheeks and blew out. "I don't know, boss

man. I drank a lot of water. If I can't hold it, I'll be standing here doing the pee-pee dance—and these rocks won't break themselves!" She started wriggling, her feet doing a jig. "Not just me! Her too!"

Abeni was uncertain what was happening but joined in, hopping in place.

"I thought we weren't dancing," Nyomi said, confused.

Yooku rolled his eyes. "Enough!" He motioned to guards who stood against the wall. "Escort these two and get them back here fast." Turning his back, he returned to pacing and shouting his workplace affirmations.

Naana winked at her brother before beckoning to Abeni. The two quickly left with the guards, who walked behind them down another tunnel. They had gone some way when Naana flashed her fingers for only Abeni to see. It was some kind of hand talk—not the same Abeni used with Songu, but the prattle stone did its work and she understood. *Follow my lead*, it said, *as I ditch these two.* Before Abeni could respond, Naana turned to the guards.

"Eh, you two go ahead and give us some privacy," she said.

The two men stopped short. One of them shook his head.

"We go where you go," he stated. "Or you go back."

Naana put fists to her hips. "Tweaa! This is what you signed up for? The great Gold Weavers sent to protect the latrine?"

The second guard scowled. "You need to go or no?"

"Yes. But we can't go with you watching! Where are the women guards?"

"Not their shift," the first guard answered. "You're stuck with us."

Naana chuffed. "Mm? Big men can't give a woman and a girl privacy? You follow your own mothers and sisters into the bath? Hoo! Look at how you're frightening this little girl. You don't have any shame?" She kicked Abeni, who put on her best frightened look.

That left the first man tongue-tied. The other one shook his head. "I don't need this. Let them go alone."

"But—" his companion began.

"Ah! I'm not following them to the latrine," he complained. "It smells! Where can they run to, eh?"

The first guard sighed but shrugged, waving them on.

Naana smiled and held out a hand. "Well, we'll need a torch—can't see in the dark!"

The second guard grumbled but gave her his torch. "Don't make us come after you. Remember, we can easily track the gold inside you."

Naana snorted. "How could we forget."

Gathering Abeni, she walked down the dark tunnel, leaving the two men behind.

"That was easy," the woman said. But she sounded relieved. "I thought we'd have to wait forever until there were two men guards on shift! Wouldn't have worked with women." They stopped at a fork in the tunnel before turning right.

"I don't think this is the way to the latrine," Abeni noted.

"Ei!" Naana exclaimed in mock surprise, then winked. "I told you we needed a break. Let's look around, eh?"

Abeni stared down the tunnel, reaching to the rough earthen wall. Being here in the dark reminded her too much of the mines of the Goat Man. Hopefully, there were no monsters.

"So," Naana said. "You ever going to tell me your story?"

"My story?"

"A girl in the company of two—no, make that *three* spirits." She laughed at seeing Abeni's eyes round. "The Gold Weavers are too arrogant to notice what's in front of them. But if that little one you're worried over is just a little girl, I'll eat rocks for my dinner. So, how did all of you end up together?"

Abeni eyed the woman. "You and your brother know a lot about the Gold Weavers."

"I told you. We speak a similar tongue. They say long ago we were part of a single kingdom. I suppose we're like distant cousins." They turned down another tunnel.

"You both also don't seem as bothered being here. I mean, not like the rest of us. You've been that way ever since I met you in the cart. That Gold Weaver, Kofi, was certain we were spies. I figure that must mean there are real spies about. Maybe some even get caught. On purpose."

Naana stopped. She turned to stare at Abeni, who stared back.

"This is the part where we start being straight with one another?" the woman said.

"So, are you two spies?"

"I prefer . . . information gatherers."

"Why did you bring me here into the tunnels?"

Naana took a moment to answer. "We're looking for something. Hidden in the mines."

Abeni nodded. She had come to expect that grown-ups kept secrets. It was annoying at times that they thought no one else could see. "Looking for what?" she asked.

"A weapon of some kind," Naana said. "Something that could harm my people."

"And you brought me along because . . . ?"

"I think you can help. A girl in the company of spirits? You must be someone special."

Abeni weighed this carefully. "If you and your brother got in here, I'm guessing you have a way out. I'll help. But when you go, I want you to take us with you."

"That's a big ask," Naana said. "So many won't be easy. How about we just take you?"

Abeni stepped back. "All of us. Or I leave, right now."

Naana's face hardened, and there was a long quiet. She sucked her teeth.

"Fine," she said at last. "But we don't leave until my brother and I finish here."

"And who is it that sent you?" Abeni pressed.

Naana leaned closer. "Who's that little girl—really?"

Another round of quiet.

Naana smiled. "I guess we all keep our secrets."

"I guess we do," Abeni agreed. And they started walking again.

"How do you know where we're going?" Abeni asked. These tunnels all looked the same.

"My brother and I are not the first to be sent here," Naana replied, turning down another tunnel. "Some never escaped alive. But we follow what others learned before us."

Abeni grimaced. "How do you even know there's anything here?"

"Have you asked yourself where all the gold we're mining is going?"

Abeni shrugged. "Back to Makomasi?"

"You'd think," Naana said. "But no. Nearly all of it is sent to another set of tunnels on the other side of the mines. We don't know why. But the kingdom's finest Gold Weavers come and go from those tunnels day and night, working until exhausted. No one else is allowed near—not even the other prisoners. I want to see what they're hiding."

They came to another place where the tunnel forked in two directions. And stopped.

"What's wrong?" Abeni asked.

"This is as far as our information can take us," Naana said.

"Then how do we figure out which one to take?"

"One of these is a dead end. The other leads to the place where the Gold Weavers have been working—and to the outside." The woman held up the torch to one tunnel. Nothing happened. She held it up to the second, and the flames bent slightly.

"Air!" Abeni said. "There's air coming from that direction!"

Naana smiled. "I knew you were a quick study. Come. Those guards are going to start looking for us, eventually. Let's see what we can find."

They moved down the tunnel, letting the torch guide their way. They hadn't walked long before they came to what looked like a dead end, until Naana held up the torch to reveal a crevice near the ceiling—where the air flowing out made the flames wobble.

"That's it?" Abeni said. "It's pretty small. You won't be able to fit in there."

"No, I won't." Naana gave her an expectant look and Abeni suddenly understood.

"When you said I'm special, you meant I'm small. You were expecting this."

Naana shrugged. "I suspected." She handed over the torch. "Ready to earn your escape?"

Abeni found herself on the woman's shoulders, climbing up towards the crevice. Straining on the tips of her toes, she pushed her arm with the torch through the slight opening. It was dark on the other side, and she hoped that meant no one was in there. Stretching farther, she peeked inside. It was a chamber. A very big chamber! And it was filled with . . . something. Squinting, she caught sight of a golden face and almost dropped the torch— thinking it was one of the Gold Weavers! But this figure didn't move, at all. As her eyes adjusted to the dark, she realized it was a statue of a man—made of gold. And not alone. There were dozens, no hundreds! Golden statues carved like people, in rows as far as the eye could see. It was as she swept the torch back and forth to get a better look that she saw it: a familiar symbol etched onto the forehead of each statue that made her blood run cold. She quickly pulled her arm back out and let Naana lower her down.

"We have to go!" Abeni said. "We have to go right now!"

She didn't wait, heart pounding as she started running. Suddenly it felt too small in here, as if the walls were closing in. She turned down one tunnel, then another. Behind her she could hear Naana calling. A strong tug at her arm told her the woman had caught up. She spun Abeni around, snatching away the torch.

"What?" she asked, face lit by the flames. "What did you see in there?"

"Statues. All golden statues, of people—as big as people. Lots of them. More than I could count. There was a mark on their foreheads . . ."

"What mark?" Naana demanded.

Abeni swallowed. "An upside-down tear. A single flame."

Naana closed her eyes, releasing a deep breath before opening them again.

"You know what that mark is? Whose mark it is?"

Abeni nodded. It seemed wherever they turned, he was there. "The Witch Priest."

Naana frowned. "This is bad." She began walking, muttering to herself. "Even worse than we thought. If they've gone over to him, we're all in danger. The entire westlands . . ."

"Did you know?" Abeni broke in, running to catch up.

Naana glared at her. "That the Gold Weavers had gone over to the Witch Priest? We've gotten strange reports. Odd actions they've been taking. But this . . ."

"What is that in there? Why are they making statues for him?"

"Golden statues," the woman corrected. "Think about it. A people who can control gold. Make it do whatever they want."

Abeni's eyes went wide. "It's an army. They're building the Witch Priest an army!"

Naana nodded grimly. "An army that doesn't need to rest. Or to eat. An army that can march day and night. That can fight without tiring."

Abeni shuddered. "What are you going to do?"

The woman shook her head. "I don't know. I need to talk to my brother—"

"You there! Stop!"

Abeni jumped, ready to run. But Naana put a hand to stop her. "Let me." She broke into a sudden grin. "Over here! We're over here!"

There was the sound of footsteps and a torch flared in the distance. It came closer, revealing the two guards they'd left behind. Both looked tired and angry.

"Where did you go?" one demanded.

Naana huffed. "Go? We've been lost in these tunnels! One wrong turn from the latrine, and we got completely confused. We've been waiting on you two to find us! What took you so long? You fall asleep or what? Planned to just leave us here, eh?"

The guard looked flummoxed. "But you told us to let you be!"

"Don't argue with her," the other guard said. "She'll just get you all turned around. Besides, she's not the one we want." He turned to Abeni. "You're to come with us. They're looking for you."

Abeni stepped back, but the guards grabbed her and pushed her along in front of them. Naana, for the first time, seemed confused. They moved quickly, all but running through the tunnels until arriving back where they'd left. Everyone was there—including Zaneeya, Nyomi, and Songu, giving her questioning looks. What was going on?

Yooku for once wasn't making proclamations. His back was turned as he bowed and apologized repeatedly to another man— who was surrounded by a troop of soldiers. Hearing their arrival, Yooku turned, and his face shifted from anger to relief.

"Oh!" he exclaimed. "There she is. The one you requested. I am honored I could help—"

The man he had been talking to brushed past him, making a face as his long blue and gold robes brushed the ground. The large golden beads he wore around his neck were carved with those odd symbols, and there was more jewelry at his wrists. His dark skin, from his exposed right shoulder to his broad face, was speckled with gold—and his golden eyes shined in the torchlight. He walked with a long staff and Abeni could see it was capped with a golden leopard as he stopped before her.

"You are Abeni," he said in a voice higher than she expected, "daughter of Yayawi and Akanyo, of the Jembe forest."

Abeni blinked. "Um, yes? I mean, that's me."

The man nodded. "I am the royal attendant Akú. I have been sent to summon you to an audience before Otumfuo Nana Kusi Awia, the King in Gold, at the Golden Court." He looked her up and down, wrinkling his nose. "But you will need to be better dressed than that."

CHAPTER FIVE

THE GOLDEN COURT

Abeni ran to keep up with the royal attendant, gaping at the palace about her. She would have stood gawking at it when they first arrived—with its wide walls and many buildings, almost every bit shining with gold—but she had been hurried up what seemed like an endless set of steps and taken right inside.

"You at least clean up nicely," the royal attendant Akú noted. He sniffed pleasantly. "And you smell better too." She'd been whisked from the mines without a chance to speak to anyone, then taken here and immediately put into a bath. A dozen servants had scrubbed her, cut her nails, even washed her hair. They'd applied sweet-smelling oils to her scalp and skin and wrapped her in a gown of interwoven yellow and green patterns, like the ones worn here.

"Where are we going?" Abeni asked, still frazzled by it all.

Akú sighed, not stopping his wide strides—his slippered feet silent on the stone floor. "You've asked me several times, and the answer remains the same. We go to the Golden Court. That's why we had to have you cleaned and properly dressed. Can't have you desecrating the court with your filthiness." He turned to raise an eyebrow. "I believe the words you are searching for are *thank you*."

Abeni didn't feel like saying thank you. Not when she hadn't asked to be taken prisoner to begin with.

"Why am I being taken to this Golden Court?"

They came to a pair of tall doors. Two guards stood in front; their entire bodies were encased in gold that Abeni had learned was some kind of armor. The doors were a bright yellow-gold and carved from top to bottom in those symbols she saw often here. In the very center was one large symbol: a small circle, within a larger circle, within a third even larger still.

"Do you know what these are?" Akú asked.

Abeni shook her head.

"They are emblems of power and sacred to us," the royal attendant explained. "Our society rests upon the wisdom they transmit." He pointed to a symbol like the outline of an X. "This means strength. It represents the seat of authority and the magnificence of this palace." He pointed to another: crossed swords with curved blades. "This grants authority to a ruler. And this one—" He indicated the circles within circles spread across both doors. "—represents royalty. It is the ruler of all the others. In this way our society functions, as all know their proper place, role, and station."

He straightened, fixing her with stern golden eyes.

"You are at the Golden Court because you have been summoned by the King in Gold, Blood of the Dynasty of the Sun, Highest of the High in all the land. These emblems imbue him with that power and right. And be you noble, commoner, soldier, or slave—you *will* give answer."

"So, which am I then," she asked. "A prisoner or a slave?"

Before he could answer, the doors opened. The guards stepped aside as a tall woman emerged, flanked by soldiers. Abeni found herself staring at the familiar face of Captain Ekua. The woman spared her a glance before moving on to the royal attendant.

"Attendant Akú," she greeted. "You're keeping interesting company."

The attendant bowed. "Captain Ekua. I did not know you had business before the court. Tell me, how are the leopards that attend the King in Gold?"

"Do you mean his pets?" she asked. "Or the old men who keep his court?"

Akú chuckled. "Is there a difference?"

Captain Ekua snorted. "Hungry. But it is the old leopardesses that have the sharpest bite." She looked to Abeni. "Watch you don't get eaten."

Then she was gone, marching down the corridor with her soldiers in tow.

"Ready?" Akú asked. He didn't give Abeni a chance to answer before signaling the guards, who pulled open the tall doors. A thought jumped into her head.

"I never asked you how you knew my name? Or where I'm from?"

But the attendant was already walking, and she again rushed to catch up.

The Golden Court was true to its name—a large chamber with walls covered in gold! They led up to a wide rounded dome, its underside carved in a mural depicting people and fantastic beasts. One stood out: what looked like a horned serpent, with wings. Hovering just under the dome was a great spinning gold orb that shined bright. It bathed the chamber in light like a small sun, reflecting off statues lining the room, of men seated on thrones. Guards stood between, holding long spears with fan-like blades. Closer to the front of the chamber, men were assembled, kneeling or sitting on small stools. Most wore colorful robes like Akú and held staffs capped with animals or other figures. They looked to all be old men, with white hair and wrinkled skin. Abeni's eyes roamed past them to a corner where four old women sat in chairs. They were wrapped in golden fabric, their skin speckled with gold and their heads crowned in circlets bearing gold carvings. Each sat bent over a table, eyes intent on a large oval platter. And with them was the most surprising sight of all.

"Asha!" Abeni stopped at seeing the small girl. She was as richly dressed as the old women and sat kicking her legs while studying the golden platter. Her head shot up and at seeing Abeni she smiled, waving excitedly.

Abeni was set to wave back when there was a gasp from Akú. The royal attendant's face was horror-struck—and she realized she had shouted Asha's name. In the Golden Court. Every head had turned to regard her. The men with golden staffs looked as shocked as Akú.

"Attendant Akú," someone said. "Who is this unruly child you bring before me?"

Abeni followed the voice between the attendants to where a man sat on a large golden chair. He wore a robe of many interwoven colors, threaded with lines of gold. But that was nothing compared to the other gold he wore. Giant gold beads hung to his chest, alongside numerous other necklaces bearing carved animals. More gold circled his wrists in thick bands and braided bracelets. His fingers held so many gold rings, it was hard to see his hands. More gold decorated his ankles and there were gold rings on the toes of his bare feet—even gold painted toenails.

Abeni thought it all looked . . . heavy. The man himself was not very big. All those gold ornaments and jewelry looked like they must weigh him down terribly. Even his crown—a circlet with gold carvings—seemed to make his head droop. He sat atop his throne glaring down at her.

"Do not meet the king's eyes!" Akú chided. "And why are you still standing?"

Abeni looked to the royal attendant, only now noticing he was on his knees. She hurriedly joined him—which was about when she saw the leopards. There were two, large spotted cats with gold piercing their ears and noses. They lounged lazily in front of the throne, paying no one much mind.

"Highest and Mighty One," Akú said, his head bowed. "I present the one you summoned."

From the corner of her eye, Abeni saw the king frown. "I summoned? I did not ask—!"

A long "mmm" cut him off. It came from one of the old women, who never looked up.

The king glanced their way before fidgeting with his robes. "I mean, yes. My summons."

Akú went on. "I present Abeni, daughter of Yayawi and Akanyo, of the Jembe forest, to the Golden Court."

Murmurs rippled through the attendants and they strained their necks to look Abeni over. She shifted under their glares, and for the first time noticed at least one was not an old man. A girl was seated there. Older than Abeni, she was as richly dressed as the others, with gold bands on her arms and wrists. Her hair was parted into neatly sectioned knots, each strung with more gold. She carried no staff like the attendants. But she sat straight with a self-important air, and her golden eyes inspected Abeni with interest.

"So, this is the little mine rat," the king said. Abeni pulled her eyes from the older girl. Had he just called her a rat? "Come from some backwater village in the bush," he continued. "Holds no royal blood or office. Doesn't look like much to me."

There was another loud "mmmm" from one of the old women. The king frowned at Abeni in irritation.

"There have been claims about you," he said. "Is it true you cavort with spirits?"

Abeni hesitated, receiving an expectant look from Akú.

"Yes," she said. What was it Akú had called him? "Highest One. They're my friends."

"Friends with spirits. Are you a witch, then?"

"No, Highest One. I'm just a girl."

Another "mmmm" sounded from the old women's corner, this one louder and longer. The king gritted his teeth. "I was getting to it," he muttered. Abeni looked between the two. What was going on?

"Tell us about what happened to your village," the king demanded. "Quick now!"

Abeni opened her mouth, uncertain what to say. "It was destroyed, Highest One," she said at last. "There were these women . . . warriors who came from a storm, with fire in their eyes. They attacked my village, burned it, and took all the grown-ups."

More murmurs swept through the attendants, many looking concerned.

"Ah yes," the king said. "Not the children. They were taken by this . . . Ram Man?"

"Goat Man, Highest One," Abeni corrected.

"But not you. How is it you managed not to be taken?"

Abeni shared a glance with Asha. "Someone saved me. A spirit, who protected our village. She saved me from the Storm Women and the Goat Man."

There was excited chatter at this. The king glared at his attendants—looking annoyed.

"And who did these Storm Women and this Goat Man serve?" he pressed.

Abeni made a face, recalling the golden statues she had seen in the mines and the flame carved onto their foreheads. She looked up, stopping just short of meeting the king's eyes. "The Witch Priest," she said. "But you know all about him, don't you . . . Highest One?"

The king looked surprised at her words, but quickly regained himself, scowling.

"It is claimed you brought the children of your village back."

"Yes, Highest One," Abeni answered. "But not just me. My friends, Zaneeya and Nyomi—the spirits. We went after the children the Goat Man stole. He had turned them into monsters, made them do terrible things. But we stopped him. We freed the children, so that he'll never do that to anyone again."

Silence followed, and Abeni found the attendants studying her with new interest. Even Akú seemed to be reassessing her. The king's voice broke through the quiet.

"You claim not only to have survived destruction at the hands of the Witch Priest's minions, but to have defeated one as well? To have broken his magic? We are to believe one little girl and a handful of child spirits did this? Stood up to him where whole armies and kingdoms have failed?" He scoffed, waving a dismissive hand.

Abeni frowned. "Highest One, that's what happened. I'm telling the truth. We rescued the children of Kono, and my friends—"

"Lies!" the king shouted. His face was a storm cloud. "You dare come into my court? And tell such lies? Who do you think you are, little bush girl? Akú!" He lifted a golden sword, pointing it threateningly. "Take this mine rat back to her digging. I want her and her friends buried so deep in those tunnels that they forget what sunlight is! Then, bring yourself back here to answer for wasting my time with this nonsense!"

This time it was a weary sigh that cut into the king's tirade. Everyone had gone still and now turned to find the old women still seated but staring out upon the court.

"To rule is like holding an egg," one said sagely. "If not held tightly enough it may slip and smash on the ground. But if pressed too hard it breaks. Then what are you left with?"

The other old women nodded their agreement.

"Perhaps the Golden Court should take time to reflect on this advice," a second said.

When no one moved, a third rose to her feet. "Everyone get out!"

There was a flurry as attendants scrambled to stand. In a mass of fluttering robes and sandaled feet, they shuffled to the doors. Akú joined them. He spared Abeni a look.

"I think you impressed them," he whispered, giving a wink before walking away.

Abeni blinked. She had?

The king turned to the old women. "But Nana," he pleaded, almost whining.

A fourth old woman smiled at him. "You did very well. You should rest after such hard work. Attendants, give the king his slippers. Guards, see he gets something to eat."

The king looked ready to protest but wilted under the four sets of golden eyes that now stared at him. Two attendants ran forward to fit golden slippers on his feet. Rising, he almost fell back down under the weight of all that gold—but was caught by his guards. They helped him from the room, his feet leaving behind golden footprints. The last person in the chamber was the older girl with the hair like twisted knots. She hovered by the doors for a moment, looking Abeni over one final time before slipping out.

"Now I can finally hear myself think," one of the old women said. It was the one who had first spoken. She sat back and beckoned at Abeni with an arm that rattled with gold bracelets. "Come, girl."

Abeni rose to her feet uncertainly, one eye on the sleeping leopards.

"Come, come," the old woman said impatiently. "Those kittens will not harm you."

Kittens? They were each bigger than Zaneeya. Abeni crossed the chamber to where the old women sat about their table.

"Greetings, Nana," she said, remembering what the king had called them. The old women stared. The one with the pleasant smile winced. A second raised an eyebrow. Another shook her head, while the fourth scowled.

"I thought you said this child was bright, Nana Afua?" the scowling one chided.

The one with the pleasant smile answered. "Nana Yaaba. We can give her another chance. I'm sure she has more sense than she might be showing, don't you, child?"

Abeni looked to Asha, who nodded slightly to the ground.

Of course. In her village, Nana was a name for grandmothers. But here Nana likely meant more for these women who ordered even a king about! She went to her knees, bowing until her forehead met the floor. "Greetings, Nana."

The four nodded appreciatively, beckoning her to stand. Looking to the golden platter on the table, Abeni found it was fitted with pits like bowls. There were six in all, each filled with small gold beads. This was a game, she realized.

"You are familiar with oware?" the old woman who had called her over asked. Gold dusted her jowly cheeks, spreading across her shoulders and down her thick arms. Her golden eyes traced Abeni while her lips pursed with interest.

Abeni nodded. "Back home, people played something like this."

"Then you know it is a thing of strategy," the old woman went on, pointing a ringed finger at a pit. "Each house must attack, and defend, to outwit their opponents. It is good training for military commanders and rulers."

Abeni wanted to say it must have been good training for the goatherders of her village as well, who played it while tending their flocks. But she thought better of it.

"Yet this little girl has bested you five times, Nana Akasi," Nana Afua said.

Nana Akasi grunted, glancing at Asha, who just smiled. "Strange little one," she muttered.

Nana Afua winked at Abeni. Her pleasant smile lit up a kindly face, so that the gold dust on her plump cheeks seemed to glow. She leaned in to whisper. "No one has ever beaten her at oware more than once!"

Abeni looked to Asha, who she now realized was also playing the game—and had gathered an impressive amount of gold beads. Is that what the little girl had been doing these past three days? While they worked tiredly in the mines? She was relieved—but also a bit annoyed.

Another of the old women snorted—Nana Yaaba, whose narrow face wore a permanent scowl. "Maybe we should have made that boy who sits the throne now play more oware, eh. So he could rule with some sense!"

Nana Akasi grunted. "They say a crab does not give birth to a bird. But this one is nothing like his father."

"That one had a head of stone," one of the old women complained, her wrinkled face creasing. "He fought our attempts to steer him like a bull with a fresh nose ring."

"True enough, Nana Ajuba," Nana Afua added. "But listen he often did in the end. And he was a stronger king for it."

"This one is both stubborn and weak," Nana Yaaba complained.

Nana Akasi sighed. "He is not the first weak king the kingdom has known."

"Yes," Nana Ajuba agreed. "But these are dangerous times for a weak king. Sometimes I wonder if choosing that one for the Gold Throne was wise."

"What choice did we have?" Nana Akasi asked in irritation. "He alone had a rightful claim. Choosing another would have created chaos. You know how thickheaded men can be. All those old tortoises at court, each a chieftain who thinks he should be king. There's a hundred more like them in the kingdom."

"He wasn't the only choice," Nana Afua put in.

Nana Akasi waved a hand dismissively. "We've discussed that enough. It is impossible."

Nana Afua shrugged. "What is impossible for us?"

"Tradition is tradition!" Nana Yaaba insisted, drawing her golden robes about her.

Nana Afua shrugged again. "Is tradition like a rock too stubborn to break? We Ohemmaa were once only advisors to the king. Now, there are four of us—and we do much more than advise."

Ohemmaa. Abeni repeated the word in her head. It meant Queen Mother. She glanced at the old women, perplexed. The king had four mothers?

"I think we are confusing the girl," Nana Ajuba noted.

They all turned to regard Abeni, as if just remembering she was there.

"Yes, girl," Nana Akasi said, tapping a chin. "You are a surprise the gods have dropped in our midst. This little one here." She gestured at Asha. "She was made to serve in my entourage. But she has a peculiar way. Like a child in many things. Yet she speaks in ways a child should not. She has told us interesting things about you."

Abeni stepped back as four sets of golden eyes bored into her.

"Things that you have spoken to the king," Nana Ajuba said.

"Things that seem impossible for a mere girl," Nana Yaaba added, skeptical.

"Things we would like to hear more of, child." Nana Afua beamed.

"Yes." Nana Akasi nodded. "The little one claims you have a song. We would hear it now. But be warned, tell only truths. We will know if you lie!"

Silence followed and Abeni looked to Asha. The little girl had taught her the song—well, when she was an old woman. It told about her village, from the very beginning. And it recounted everything she had been through. *Everything.* She recalled what she had seen in the mines: the army of golden warriors bearing the Witch Priest's mark. Did these Gold Weavers work for him like the Goat Man? Was this some trick? What if these old women then turned them over to him? Doubts swirled in her head, and she stood there, uncertain what to do.

"Abeni," Asha said. The little girl met her eyes. "Just tell them what they need to know."

What they need to know. What they *need* to know. Yes, she thought she understood. She took a deep breath and began. She sang of her village in the Jembe forest. Of its founding and its people. Of being nicknamed Little Rainbringer, born during the first rainfall after a drought. Of her mother and father, her brother and aunts, and her best friend Fomi—whom she missed terribly. Of the Storm Women who came with fire in their eyes. And of the Goat Man who stole away her friends. She told of being saved by the old woman many called a witch and of spending time in her house of many rooms and strange things. She sang of sparring with a straw man. Of the night the Shadow Thing had killed the old woman. And of finding Asha the next day. There were stories of encountering Nyomi, as a thief who stole their food—and of meeting Zaneeya as a girl in a trap. She sang of their adventures, encountering bush babies and a secret vale. And of the village of Kono, where they confronted and brought down the Goat Man.

When Abeni finished, her throat was dry. The old women stared at her in silence.

"You have seen plenty," Nana Afua said, her kind face sympathetic. "And endured much."

"More than I would have thought of one so young," Nana Ajuba said.

"It is . . . quite a story," Nana Akasi said, her voice weighing. "I do not believe anyone could make up such a thing. This girl speaks true."

"She speaks true," each of the old women said in turn. Only Nana Yaaba hesitated, still scowling. Finally, she relented. "The girl speaks true."

Abeni released a held breath. She had been truthful. But in the way Asha instructed. She'd told these old women what they needed to know—leaving out a great deal about who and what Asha truly was. But she'd answered their questions. Now it was time they answered some of hers.

"I've seen the golden army," she said. "The one you hide in the mines."

The reaction was immediate. Gasps rose up. Even Nana Afua's pleasant face looked shaken. Nana Akasi leaned in, her bottom lip trembling in either shock or anger. "Fool girl! The words you speak could end your life this very day if they reach the wrong ears. Have you spoken this to anyone else? Tell us!"

"I haven't told anyone else," Abeni replied. She left out Naana and Manu. It wasn't for her to reveal such things. "But I saw them. An army of golden statues, with his mark. Do you work for him?"

"No!" Nana Akasi said quickly. Her jaw tightened. "And yes. . . . It is a complicated thing."

"And none of her concern!" Nana Yaaba said, glaring. "This girl knows too much!"

"We were warned that she is clever," Nana Afua said appraisingly.

"Too clever!" Nana Yaaba snapped. "We cannot allow her to—"

"Give it up, Yaaba," Nana Akasi said wearily. She rubbed her hands as if washing them. "The girl knows what she knows, and that's that. Once spilled, the soup will not jump back into the pot just because you want it so. At least we can do away with speaking riddles, eh."

"Then we are moving forward with this plan?" Nana Ajuba asked. "It is full of risk."

"If a bird does not fly, it does not eat," Nana Akasi stated. "If we risk nothing, we will gain nothing. And we have already lost so much."

There was a solemn quiet, and even Nana Yaaba's shoulders slumped. Abeni watched them, her eyes sliding to Asha, who sat on the edge of her seat—expectant.

"He came to us," Nana Akasi began.

Abeni tensed, knowing she meant the Witch Priest.

"He praised our strength. Our power," the old woman went on. "Our ability to work gold. The beauty of our cities. And we devoured his words like a child fed sweets. He offered to make us even stronger—to show us new wondrous ways to weave and build. And all he wanted from us was gold." She shrugged. "We have traded gold before, to the city-states of the west. To the stone kingdoms in the farthest reaches of the east. Even far south, where warriors of the grass plains tip their very spears in our gold. What did it matter if we traded also to him—in return for his promises?"

"Only he wanted so much," Nana Ajuba said, frowning. "More than we could ever mine."

"When we protested we could not meet his demands, he had a solution," Nana Akasi said. "He began selling us people to work our mines. This, of course, cost more gold. But he convinced us that with more workers, we could mine farther and deeper. So, it began. The people we bought from him came in a trickle. Before we knew it, the trickle became a flood. We needed so much, we soon began hunting them ourselves. All to mine more gold."

Abeni listened, thinking of her own emptied village.

"Ghost ships," she whispered. "Is that where the people he brings you come from?"

"No, child," Nana Ajuba said. "We heard you sing of ghost ships.

We know of them—great vessels sailed by wraiths from across the sea, with whom the Witch Priest barters people. But we are far from the sea. And the people he brings us travel over land and by river."

"We kept this up," Nana Akasi said. She grimaced. "Then he began demanding we send *him* people. Our people."

"He wanted Gold Weavers!" Nana Yaaba said angrily. "To work gold for him!"

"Did you do it?" Abeni asked. "Give him your people?"

"No!" Nana Yaaba said. "Never!"

"But you didn't care when it was other people," Abeni said with scorn. "People like me."

"Other people are not our kin," Nana Akasi said flatly.

"Perhaps in that we were shortsighted," Nana Afua murmured. "Let the cat get too fat on mice, and soon he will be eyeing you for dinner."

There were grudging nods at this.

"Why don't you just stop?" Abeni asked. "Stop giving him gold. Or any of it. Just stop."

The old women exchanged awkward looks.

"Because they can't," Asha said. The little girl had been quiet all this time. But now she met those golden eyes, as if she was their equal. "He's imprisoned them, just like the people they imprison in their mines."

Abeni didn't understand. She looked to the four women.

"He has taken our throne," Nana Akasi said finally.

Abeni turned to look at the throne atop the dais. Now she was really confused.

"That is only a seat for whoever presides over the Golden Court," Nana Akasi explained. "The true Golden Throne is far greater." She gestured to the ceiling, at the mural on the underside of the dome. To Abeni's surprise, the golden figures carved there began to move—gold weaving!

"Long ago," Nana Akasi said, as she swept her arms, "we belonged to a greater kingdom. This First Gold Kingdom was said to stretch across many lands, so that you could walk for days on end and not reach its end." On the ceiling, Abeni saw a vast kingdom of towering structures, filled with people. "It was the dragon Bida who gave us the gift of gold weaving." The winged serpent Abeni had seen earlier uncoiled, moving sinuously among the people. "With this gift we built even more magnificent structures. The kingdom grew powerful, rich, and fat." On the mural, the people and structures multiplied in number, filling the space.

"But Bida grew jealous. The dragon feared the people had grown too great, creating towers that threatened to pierce the heavens. In his rage, he laid waste to the kingdom and stripped the gift of weaving from the people." Abeni watched as the winged serpent knocked down the structures onto fleeing people. "We might have all perished, if not for a nameless hero with a magic sword." A figure arose, bearing a slender blade. "He fought Bida and struck down the dragon—cutting off his head, to release a shower of gold." In the moving mural, the winged serpent fell from the sky—his horned head spinning away.

"But the great kingdom lay in ruins. Most of its people had forgotten how to weave gold. Broken, they went their separate ways. Only a few held onto what others had lost. These were our ancestors, who passed to us the secret of weaving gold. They built a new home, a golden city named Makomasi, meaning 'the heart has survived.' This city became the new kingdom's capital and its first ruler called on the spirits and the gods to give their blessings. From the heavens, they sent down the Golden Throne: a relic of the First Gold Kingdom, said to have been crafted by the dragon Bida himself." Abeni watched as a shining gold object—a wide stool with a curved crescent-shaped seat supported by two pillars carved with intricate symbols on a broad base—descended from the sky as the people lifted their arms in welcome.

Nana Akasi lowered her hands and the mural went still. "We do not know where the Golden Throne is. The Witch Priest has taken it from us. And without it, we are lost." Her voice trailed off, as if it pained her to say.

"I don't understand, Nana," Abeni said. "Can't you just weave another throne?"

"Truly, you do not understand," Nana Yaaba said harshly. "The Golden Throne was crafted by Bida's magic. We can no more re-make it than we can create life itself!"

"It is more than that," Nana Afua said, her pleasant face sor-rowful. "The Golden Throne holds the very spirit of our kingdom, the spirit of the people itself—the living, the dead, and those yet to be born."

Abeni was perplexed. What were they saying?

"Do you remember the bloodstones?" Asha asked.

Bloodstones. Those she knew. The Goat Man had used those awful gems to turn children into monsters. She herself had been fitted with one, if only briefly. It contained a bit of the soul of its victims. Understanding struck at once.

"He has your souls," Abeni said in horror. "He has the souls of your whole kingdom!"

Nana Akasi touched her chest. "It is like having a chain about your heart. We feel it, always, at every moment. Even as we sleep. He holds our souls prisoner and forces us to do his bidding."

"The golden army you saw has been his greatest task," Nana Ajuba said. "We toil on it night and day, without rest. We mine more gold. We melt down even the structures of our cities, all to meet his demand."

Nana Yaaba scowled. "We can no more disobey than stop breathing."

"His very will bends us to him," Nana Afua said.

Abeni listened. A part of her felt sorry for these Gold Weavers. But another part reminded her they had brought this upon them-selves. They made bargains with the Witch Priest that hurt other people. Now they were being hurt.

"That is why we now turn to you," Nana Akasi said.

Abeni looked at the old woman, startled. "Me? What can I do?"

"This little one." Nana Akasi gestured to Asha. "She has told us of your great deeds. You have done as much with your own song.

You have stood up to him. Fought him and won! We have never heard of anyone doing such a thing—until now."

Abeni stared at the four old women, who eyed her intently. What were they asking?

"They want you to find their Golden Throne, Abeni," Asha explained. "They want you to retrieve the soul of their people from the Witch Priest and bring it back."

CHAPTER SIX

THE QUEST

You told them we would do *what?*" Zaneeya growled.

Abeni sat on a stool supported by three curved golden legs. The panther girl took up another stool across from her. Nyomi stood, inspecting each of her freshly cleaned quills in a mirror. Songu and Asha sat on the floor amid a bunch of pillows, playing the game people here called oware—at which the little girl appeared to be winning. Again. They had been placed in a room within the palace, with tall ceilings, windows that looked out on the city, and even a small pool. Everyone had had a chance to scrub clean. Nyomi had giggled, ticklish as servants bathed her. Songu was bashful, retreating to a corner of the pool. Zaneeya growled and threatened to eat the next person that touched her. After being delivered food they'd finally been left to themselves, which allowed Abeni to explain matters. It was going about as well as she expected.

"I didn't have much choice," she said. "It was the only way to get you free."

Zaneeya sniffed suspiciously at some goat meat. Abeni had requested it raw, knowing her friend's eating habits. The panther girl held up a thin red strip peppered with pungent spices. Nibbling, she made a surprised face before downing the whole thing. Her orange gaze fixed on Abeni.

"Free?" A clawed hand gripped the gold collar about her neck. "I don't feel free. Is that one of those mortal words that never means what it's supposed to mean?"

"I do wish I could get it off," Nyomi said, touching her own collar.

Abeni grimaced. "I'm sorry. That wasn't part of the bargain." She had almost laughed aloud when the old women told her what they wanted—for her to find and bring back their Golden Throne. It was absurd. She thought it must be a joke. But they weren't laughing. They explained it to her. None of their own people could be sent. So long as the Witch Priest held their throne, he held all their souls. It took someone of great will just to defy him, and that the four old women had in abundance. But if he found out they were moving against him, who knew what he might do? Abeni, they claimed, was different. She wasn't one of them. She had confronted and defeated one of the Witch Priest's minions. And, she could be controlled. A hand went to her chest. She may not have been fitted with a collar, but the Gold Weavers had worked their gold inside her. So long as that remained, they held power over her—much as the Witch Priest held power over them.

"Maybe you're just not very good at bargaining," Nyomi suggested. Abeni flinched. Nyomi probably hadn't meant anything by the remark. But it still hurt. Those old women hadn't intended for the others to take part. She'd worked hard to convince them that she needed her friends. Agreeing to this task hadn't been easy. But what other choices did they have? It was this or the mines. Forever.

"If we find this Golden Throne," she said, "they'll remove the collars and this living gold inside us. We'll be able to leave."

Zaneeya huffed. "And all we have to do is find some magic throne that the one person we are trying to hide from stole." She shook her head. "Of all the stupid escape plans you might have come up with, this has to be the stupidest!"

Abeni clenched her teeth, taking deep breaths and counting in her head until her anger cooled. What she wanted to do was shout that the panther girl could go back to those mines if she wanted. Or that she could see if she could do better arguing with four stubborn old women. But she didn't. Abeni knew there was more than spirit nature to Zaneeya's rudeness. When the girl got scared, she lashed out—often at those close to her.

"That's uncalled for, Zaneeya," Asha said. The small girl looked up from her game. "If you want to blame someone, blame me. I'm the one who told Nana Akasi about all of you. It was the only way I could think to get you out of those mines."

The panther girl only grunted, chewing at more meat. "I say when they let us out on this quest, we just go our own way."

Abeni frowned. "But what about the collars on you? The gold in the rest of us?"

Zaneeya waved dismissively. "We find someone to undo it. There must be a sorcerer out there we could convince. Maybe these elder spirits, once we reach them."

"But you can't even shift into a panther like this," Abeni pointed out.

That made the girl scowl, looking down at herself. "I'll get by," she said. But she didn't sound certain.

"I don't know," Nyomi put in, crunching on some snails the servants had brought. "If we make a promise, shouldn't we keep it instead of running away?"

Zaneeya whirled on her. "They imprisoned us! Put us to work their mines! We don't owe these mortals anything!"

Songu cleared his throat, his hands moving. "What about the golden army?" he asked.

"Not our business," Zaneeya replied.

"Are you sure?" Abeni asked. "The Gold Weavers say they'll melt down that army once they have their throne back. If we can keep that away from the Witch Priest . . ."

"Not our business," Zaneeya said again.

"Neither was saving the children of Kono. But we made it our business."

"That was different. We had a choice. No one forced us."

"But what if we can do it? Naana told me this golden army was going to endanger all the kingdoms and city-states fighting the Witch Priest. Maybe we can take this away from him."

Zaneeya glared. "Listen to yourself. Those old women really filled up your head. Told you how great you were, the hero who saved the village of Kono. Do you forget the Goat Man captured us, turned you into a monster? Now you think we can take on the Witch Priest? We have our own quest—to find these elder spirits so Asha can be safe, so Nyomi and I can return to our families, so you can learn about these ghost ships. Stopping some golden army was not part of the plan!"

Abeni was unable to respond. Was the panther girl right? Had she allowed all this hero talk to carry her away? She looked around the room. Everyone was quiet, their eyes on her.

"You're right," she said.

Zaneeya opened her mouth, ready to argue, then stopped, looking surprised. "I am? I mean, of course I am." Her eyes narrowed. "Why are you agreeing?"

"Because you're making sense," Abeni answered. "We didn't come here to help these Gold Weavers get back their throne, or to stop this golden army. I'm Asha's guardian. My responsibility is keeping her safe. All of you have your own quests. Only I can't see a way to get back to that without doing this first." She leaned in close, her voice dropping. "But if we find a way to break the hold they have on us once they let us go, I agree with Zaneeya. We should take it."

"And the golden army?" Nyomi asked.

Abeni shook her head. "Someone else will have to take care of that." She hoped Naana and Manu made their escape and returned with the news. There was quiet before everyone nodded. Only Asha said nothing, giving Abeni an unreadable look before returning to her game.

Just then, the doors to their room opened and a surprisingly familiar figure strode inside. It was the girl from the Golden Court, who had sat among the king's attendants. She carried herself as self-importantly as before and stopped to survey them under a golden glare.

"Well, happy to see everyone is comfortable," she said. "And much cleaner."

Before they had a chance to respond, she walked over and sat down in the largest chair in the room. For a moment she just stared at them, as if waiting for something.

"I don't think we've met," Abeni said. "I'm—"

"I know who you are, child," the girl said, patting one of her twisted knots of hair. Abeni frowned. Child? This girl couldn't have seen four harvest seasons more than her. "I saw the performance you put on for the Golden Court. It seems you've impressed the Ohemmaa with tales of your exploits. Enough for them to send you on a quest to retrieve the Golden Throne. How exciting."

Abeni exchanged glances with the others. Who was this girl?

"I'm sorry, we don't know your name."

The girl fixed her with large golden eyes set into a plump, pretty face. "You may call me Ama. *Oheneba* Ama, sister to the King in Gold." She stopped, waiting for a reaction. "This is the part where you bow."

Abeni played the new word in her head—*Oheneba*. It meant princess. This girl was a princess! She exchanged another look with the others before bowing. They did the same.

"Tolerable," the princess said. Her gaze swung to Zaneeya, who Abeni realized was still standing. "This child, however, is stubborn."

Zaneeya crossed her arms. "I don't bow to mortals with fancy titles. And child? Girl, I'm old enough to be your grandmother. Run along and find someone else to bother."

The princess's face twitched, but she kept calm. "Do you know, Gold Weavers are not equal in skill? As we say in Makomasi, all fingers are not the same. But my teachers claim I show great ability. And I may be as strong one day as Captain Ekua, whom I understand you've met."

Zaneeya bared her teeth.

The princess smiled, gesturing to thick bands of gold covering her forearms. "Until then, these provide me with nearly enough power. So, when I say bow . . ." Her face darkened and her tone became demanding. "You will bow!"

She twisted a hand, as if grabbing. Zaneeya cried out and staggered to her knees, gasping. Princess Ama smiled.

"That's better. Now, let's talk about our quest."

Abeni frowned. "*Our* quest?"

"Oh, weren't you told?" the princess said. "I'm coming with you. Think of me as a . . . chaperone. I'll be overseeing things, to make certain you keep to the task you've been assigned." Seeing their grim looks, she laughed. "Did you think we were just going to send you out into the world? Let me help you understand. The gold now coursing through you has been altered. We call it blood gold. Given time, it will take over your body. Your flesh, bones, skin—every bit will be transformed into gold."

Abeni's insides went cold. "That wasn't part of the bargain!"

Princess Ama rolled her eyes. "It was always part of the bargain, silly girl. As soon as you agreed to take up the quest. The transmutation can be undone. And you yet have the time. But you *will* complete the task set before you."

Abeni looked to the others, who seemed as shaken. This was a disaster.

"Now," the princess said, settling back. "Tell me how you plan on finding the Golden Throne."

There was silence before Abeni finally spoke. "We haven't thought on that yet." It was the truth. They had no idea where to begin.

The princess sighed, drumming fingernails on her chair. "That's disappointing. I thought you were supposed to be adventurers of some sort. The Ohemmaa would have me believe you were gifted with great wisdom. Maybe you're just children after all."

"Maybe we should ask someone who knows where the throne is," a voice put in. It was Asha. She seemed engrossed in her game and didn't bother to look up.

"If it was that simple," the princess snapped, "we would have done so already. The Golden Throne sits here in a room in the palace. Or at least it did. One day we walked in, and the room was empty. No one saw it taken. It just . . . disappeared."

Abeni had been told as much. The Queen Mothers had even shown her the room.

"You're asking the wrong people," Asha said. "In fact, you're probably better off not asking people."

Princess Ama frowned. "Who should we be asking if not people?"

Asha looked up finally, her mind in thought. "What about the Masks of Akani?"

The princess's eyes went wide. "How do you know . . . ?" She shook her head, catching herself. "It doesn't matter. The Masks of Akani are just a story."

Asha shook her head. "No, they're real. Just lost."

Princess Ama looked stunned, her mouth working to form words. Abeni took the moment to ask the obvious. "What are the Masks of Akani?"

The girl blinked, coming back to herself. "You've been told that long ago the Gold Kingdom was part of a much larger kingdom. The Masks of Akani were said to be objects of great power, imbued with wisdom passed down by scholars and oracles through the ages. It was said there was no question they could not answer. It's possible that they would know where the Golden Throne has gone. But . . . no one knows where the Masks of Akani are."

"I do," Asha said matter-of-factly. "Bring me some maps, and I'll show you."

The princess's jaw dropped. She looked the little girl up and down. "Who are you?"

"She's Asha," Abeni answered. "She . . . knows things."

As the princess summoned servants to find the royal mapmakers, Abeni sat eyeing the little girl—the little spirit—with interest. It seemed they were going to be having a quest after all.

CHAPTER SEVEN

ON THE TRAIL

Fulan walked around the small structure that sat in a grassy clearing. It had been a house once. Not very big, with a crumbling round mudbrick wall and what must have been a pointed straw roof. All that was left now was a burnt ruin, where sunlight poured through cracks and holes. There had been a fire. She put a hand to the scorch marks—and stepped back as the mudbrick fell away.

"The fire was set from the outside," a deep voice said.

The Huntsman. The big man came into view where a section of wall had sunken in completely. "It went up all at once." He gave a strong sniff. "Not a natural fire. Sorcery." His eyes lifted to her. "Like your father's."

Fulan leaned in. Despite not having the man's odd ability to smell magic, she did feel something in this place. Something that reminded her of her father, the Witch Priest. But different. Where he was a raging fire, this was cool and crisp. In her mind images came: a drenching downpour of cold rain, turned up rich and black earth, and leafy things in full bloom. A sudden whispering made her spin around to look out past the clearing—where a grove of tall grass stalks swayed in the warm midday breeze.

"What is it?" the Huntsman asked. His sharp eyes were alert, and a hand rested on the knife at his waist. Fulan hesitated as the whispering died away.

"Nothing," she said, eyes still on the grass stalks. *Plants don't talk,* she reminded herself. Her focus returned to the Huntsman. "How long ago do you think this happened?"

The big man released his knife, his broad shoulders untensing. He did that often—relaxed one moment, then coiled and ready to strike the next.

"This clearing was probably always surrounded close by the forest." He gestured to the thick trees surrounding them. "More part of the bush than outside it. See the ground here? Looks to have been a garden once. Now it's becoming overgrown with wild grass." He stopped, calculating in his head. "A short season at most, if that."

A short season, Fulan thought. No more than a quarter of a year, then, since her father's enemy had left this place. It had taken weeks to trek to this forest, which those who lived here called the Jembe. This was where the Shadow Thing claimed to have last seen their quarry—this Asha. Burning the house had likely been its doing. The thing—or the things that made it up—delighted in destruction. It claimed to have killed her father's enemy. But there was no sign of a body or a grave.

A deep growl made the hairs on the back of Fulan's neck rise. One of the Huntsman's hounds stood feet away, tall enough so that its back reached her waist. Even in daylight, the hazy shadow that clung to the creature shrouded it in darkness. Rusted chains criss-crossing its muscled body stretched with each inhale from a deep chest, and it stared at her with black pupilless eyes. This, she had learned, was one of the hounds' oddities. Gaze into those eyes too long and time slowed, leaving you in a trance. On their journey, she'd watched them take down a whole water buffalo, mesmerizing it before tearing it apart. But she was no dumb beast. She met that black gaze, allowing flames to dance in her own eyes. The monstrous hound shrank back, its sharp ears lying flat.

The Huntsman chuckled. He seemed to find these challenging games his monsters played humorous.

"If your dog keeps that up," she said, "I'm going to skin it and make you a new shirt."

That made him chuckle even more, creasing the many dotted scars encircling his face. "I would pay to see that," he remarked.

Walking over, he crouched to where his hound was pawing the grass. "What have you found, Shenzi?"

Fulan joined them, watching as the man picked up a shard of pottery buried in the wild grass. She bent down, finding more pieces. "It's a plate." Her eyes landed on another object. "Here's a broken bowl." Standing, she walked slowly through the clearing, now recognizing more bits of broken things half-buried in the grass. Part of what looked to have been a crocodile mask. The smashed head of a drum. She stopped to root around, pulling up a broken spearhead.

"There was a battle here," the Huntsman said.

A battle of what, Fulan mused. Pottery and drums? She had hoped coming here would give them some clue on where their quarry might be. But this ruined place didn't offer up anything. That whispering came again. She turned her head slightly, thinking to catch a glimpse of whatever might be making the sound. But all she found were the swaying tall stalks of grass. Could they truly be . . . talking? She thought she could even make out words.

Asha's gone, gone, long gone, gone, gone . . .

Her thoughts were interrupted as two more monstrous hounds trotted out of the forest. They moved with eerie silence, their pawed feet leaving no sign of their passing. Unnatural creatures. They went to their master, who bent low as they growled and barked. After a moment, he nodded, then stood and turned.

"Banzai and Nunda say they have found something. A village."

Fulan threw down the broken spearhead. "Show me."

By the time they reached the outskirts of the village, the sun sat low in the sky. It was a small settlement that sat across from a river. Hiding behind a thicket of bushes, Fulan and the Huntsman watched the people within.

"No defenses," the Huntsman noted. "No walls or palisades. A small band could take this village easily."

Fulan had noticed the same. Growing up in a fortress, it was odd to see a place so . . . open. *But you didn't live all your life there,* an inner voice reminded. The flicker of memories came again: a place much like this one, people building things and pounding grain, a woman with a face like hers dancing to hands clapping.

"That's odd," the Huntsman murmured. His voice dispersed her memories like a startled flock of birds.

"What's odd?" she asked.

"The people of this village. They are children."

Fulan looked closer, at the figures walking the village's streets. At the others leading and herding goats. A few in a field tending crops. Two atop a house, mending a roof. Some were younger than her, others her own age or near. But none were full grown. There were no grown-ups in this place!

"I've seen much in my travels," the Huntsman said. "But a village of children is new."

Fulan tried to make sense of it. Maybe all the grown-ups had gone off to hunt or the like. But no, she'd seen children returning from the forest carrying freshly caught game between them. Where were their parents? Or the old people who looked after infants? She crouched lower as several new figures came close. More children, carrying sacks across their backs and bundles atop their heads. By their tired faces and ragged clothing, they looked to have come off a long journey. Someone in the village pointed them out. Almost immediately a group ran up with open arms, helping them the rest of the way.

Fulan prepared to rise.

"What are you doing?" the Huntsman asked.

"I want to find out what's going on with this village. Maybe they know something about the house out in the forest, and who lived there."

"Is that wise?"

"I think they're taking people in—other children. I'll pass myself off as a new arrival."

The Huntsman eyed her skeptically. "You think you can pass for just any other child?"

Fulan looked down at herself—just remembering her weapons. With a grunt, she undid the straps holding her sword to her back.

She pulled free the great bow and the quiver of arrows. Then her helmet. Knives and a few daggers went next.

"How do I look?" she asked, letting the weapons litter the ground about her.

"Like a jackal who has put away his teeth," the Huntsman replied.

Fulan scooped up some dirt, rubbing it over her clothes and face. She slumped her shoulders, putting on a tired look. "Better?" she asked, in a weary and timid voice.

The Huntsman only smiled. That might have been the first time he'd looked impressed.

She made her walk to the village a slow one, trying to look the part of a tired traveler. Her steps made her wobble, as if she might fall over at any moment. Sure enough, a cry went up from the village and people pointed her way. As before, a group ran out. She willed her body not to tense as they approached. This wasn't a fight.

"Hello," one of them greeted, flashing a warm smile. "And welcome." A boy, younger than her by a few years—but not many. He was thin, with long legs he would need time to grow into. "Is it just you?"

Fulan nodded, feigning exhaustion.

"Oh!" the boy exclaimed. "It must be hard traveling alone. Do you come from the Jembe?"

"Farther," she said, on instinct.

He nodded. "That would explain your dress. I've never seen clothes like that."

Fulan noticed he wore only a short colorful kilt to his knees, with his chest bare—a marked difference from her pants, boots, and hooded jerkin.

"I'm from the east," she said, hoping that explained things. "Outside the forest."

He appeared to accept this and dismissed the other boys, escorting her himself.

"We didn't know news of our village had gone so far," he said. "When we put the word out that we would take in children with nowhere else to go, we thought we would get just a few. But it's been one or two almost every few days. You'll make four today alone—that's a record!"

They entered the village, walking narrow streets filled with children. There were small mudbrick houses with thatched roofs everywhere Fulan looked, and a few still under construction.

"We've had to repair more damaged houses to fit all the new arrivals," the boy said. "Good thing my brother and I know how to build them. We haven't really been back all that long, you know, but we started working right way." He blinked. "Oh! I haven't introduced myself or asked your name. Sorry, I get carried away sometimes at all the work. I'm Danwe."

"Fulan," she answered. Easier to remember her own name than making something up.

"Good to meet you, Fulan." They walked until reaching the center of the village, where a great round building stood.

"This is our meeting house," Danwe said. "We don't have a chief anymore. But we do have a council who keeps things in order. Anyone new has to be brought before them." His eyes took her in, and he squinted as if seeing something. Fulan was suddenly self-conscious of the mark on her forehead, though no one should be able to see that. In a blink he was smiling again. "Well, the council's meeting right now. But there's someone you can talk to. This way, please."

They walked down a street to an open area where children worked at various tasks—shaping pots, drawing water from a well, shelling peas, and more. Danwe stopped before a girl, who sat amid a bunch of fish. Short and stout with her hair braided up, she wore a simple brown dress tied up under her arms and across her chest. She wielded a broad knife that she used to chop off the heads of the fish, before using a smaller blade to scale them. Her face was peeled back in a grimace, as if this was the last thing she wanted to be doing. At seeing them, she looked up and fixed Danwe with a grin.

"Hey stork-legs," she said.

Danwe frowned. Fulan glanced to his legs. They did look like a stork's! But just as quick, his face settled—as if he was accustomed to the taunt.

"Fulan, this is Fomi. She's a council member. But today she's missing a meeting to get her favorite work done—cleaning fish."

Fomi made a face. "New people means we need more food. But blech! I hate this!"

"I could help," Fulan offered.

Fomi beamed. "I accept!" She made space on a mat where Fulan sat.

"I'll leave you two before you ask me to start cleaning fish!" Danwe said.

Fomi snorted. "You'd probably try to eat it all up anyway—you big old stork."

Danwe actually laughed this time and wandered off towards the meeting house.

"Don't tell him." Fomi leaned in, whispering. "But he's finally starting to grow into those legs. And he's not bad looking, I think." She winked and Fulan found herself smiling. It was a genuine smile. She couldn't ever remember having a conversation like this with . . . anyone.

"Oh, you'll need a knife." Fomi handed over a blade. As Fulan grasped it the girl frowned slightly and squinted—much as Danwe had done. Fulan resisted the urge to touch the hidden mark on her forehead and smiled awkwardly, her eyes dropping to where Fomi still held the knife.

"Sorry!" Fomi exclaimed, letting go. "I got distracted. Fulan, yes? You just arrived?"

Fulan nodded, picking up a fish and scraping at its red scales. She remembered what Danwe had mentioned. "I heard about your village—a place that takes in children with nowhere else to go."

Fomi nodded solemnly, taking in her clothes. "You traveled a long way?"

"Yes, from the east—outside the forest. News of your village has traveled far."

"So, it seems!" Fomi frowned. "You speak our language very well for someone far-off."

Fulan silently berated herself for making such a stupid mistake. Her father's gifts allowed her to speak and understand nearly any tongue with ease. She hadn't thought to mask that. Careless. "I've been traveling in the forest for some time," she said finally. "Picked up some words along the way."

Fomi seemed to accept this. "You're a quick study! Most people in this part of the Jembe forest speak similar languages. But we've gotten children from all over. The things we've had to do just to communicate! Trader's tongue works well enough. But sometimes, it can take days before we understand each other."

"The children who all come here," Fulan said, "they are fleeing something?"

Fomi looked at her oddly. "Well yes, the war, of course. *His* war."

His war. Her father's war, the girl meant.

"Yes," she managed hurriedly. "The war is moving—spreading. I hear it's going to soon reach the great kingdoms and city-states of the west."

Fomi's eyes lit up. "I've never seen a city, or a great kingdom. I hope they can stop him."

Fulan frowned. Stop him—her father? "So, you are hoping he . . . is defeated?"

Fomi turned to her, quizzical. "Of course. He's awful. Look at all this war he's begun. So many people hurt, their homes destroyed, the people carried off. Someone has to stop him."

Fulan knew she should stay quiet, nod along. But she also felt an urge to defend her father. "I've heard some say that he's only trying to free the land—from corrupt spirits and gods who try to control us. That those who accept his rule are better for it."

Fomi laughed bitterly. "Free? I can tell you about his war to free us. It ended my village. It took my family away. It turned me into a—" She stopped, releasing a breath. "Anyway, there's nothing good about him or his war. He's a monster."

Fulan wanted to keep arguing but held back. That wasn't why she was here.

"Your village seems to have done well for itself," she said instead. "All things considered."

Fomi nodded. "We've been working hard to rebuild. I think Abeni would like it."

"Abeni?" Fulan asked.

A fond smile tugged at the girl's mouth. "My best friend. She's out in the world, having adventures. If not for her, none of this—" She cut off, shaking her head. "Enough about me. I've hardly heard much about you. Was it hard making your way through the forest, alone, I mean?"

Abeni, Fulan thought, marking the name. There was something more there. She would have to find out. But later. "It wasn't so bad," she answered. "I'm just glad I reached—with so many other villages destroyed. In fact, I came across something not too far from here, about a half-day's journey. A small house, alone in the forest. It was burned down. Do you know who might have lived there?"

Fomi paused her cleaning. When she answered, her words sounded careful. "The old woman. She looked after our village."

"An old woman? What happened to her?"

"She died," Fomi said flatly.

Oh yes, definitely more there. Before Fulan could press further, she noticed Fomi's eyes looking past her. Turning, she spotted several people walking towards them—coming from the meeting house. One was Danwe. He was with another boy his age and a tall girl. The three reached to where they sat.

"Finished the meeting already, Sowoke?" Fomi asked.

The tall girl frowned a pretty face, folding her arms. She dressed much like the other girls in the village, wrapped in a long gown— though the green patterned fabric was more elaborate than Fomi's. "We've been in there for hours!" she complained. "Going on about what crops to plant, where to build another granary, plans for digging a new well. Can't believe I once used to want to sit in on those meetings with the grown-ups and the Chief Elder."

Fomi laughed. "Guess you're the Chief Elder now."

The other boy smiled. "You hear that, Danwe? We'll have to get her a staff."

Danwe chuckled. "Maybe we should get her a chief's robes too, Adwe."

They both laughed harder at this. Brothers, Fulan guessed—by their similar looks and easy laughter. One of those memories flickered in her head, of laughing with someone like this. Someone she might have called brother, or sister. From another time, another life.

Sowoke gave both boys a flat look before returning to Fomi. "Don't think I don't know you use scaling fish as a reason to miss meetings."

Fomi exclaimed innocently. "But everyone knows I hate scaling fish. Blech!"

"Mmm hmm," Sowoke replied, but with a slight smile. Fulan supposed the two were good friends. It struck her suddenly—in all her time at the Fortress of the Living Flame, she'd never had a friend.

The tall girl turned a scrutinizing gaze towards her. "A new arrival?"

"Yes," Danwe answered. "The one I was telling you about— Fulan."

"Fulan," Sowoke repeated. "Welcome. Good of you to start helping."

"Hello," Fulan greeted her. "The least I can do. Fomi and I were just talking about your village, what you're building here."

Sowoke nodded, looking around with pride. "It hasn't been easy. And still so much to do. But we try."

"Fulan was asking about the house—the one the old woman lived in," Fomi said.

Fulan thought she saw a look pass between the two girls before Sowoke turned to her with a raised eyebrow.

"Oh? You've seen it?"

Fulan nodded. "On the way here. I was wondering if you know more about the person who lived there."

"Not really," Sowoke replied.

"What do you mean not really?" Danwe cut in. "That's Asha's old house, right?" He turned to Fulan. "We thought she was a witch. But it turns out, she was a spirit and—" He yelped as Adwe stepped on his foot. "Hey! What's that for?"

Sowoke went on, as if Danwe hadn't spoken. "As Fomi likely told you, she died."

"Well, not really died," Danwe started again. "Though smaller now. She's with Abeni, isn't she? After they rescued us from Kono—" This time he shouted, hopping up and down on the foot his brother firmly mashed a second time.

Sowoke sighed lengthily. Fomi shook her head. "I suppose to eat all that fish, storks have very big mouths," the shorter girl muttered.

Fulan took it all in. Asha. The old woman was Asha. But not dead. Instead, truly a spirit! And she was small now? What had she rescued them from? And who was this Abeni? She was set to ask another question when Sowoke spoke.

"Enough," the tall girl said. Her voice had gone flat, and she stared at Fulan. "Who are you—really? What do you want?"

Fulan blinked, pretending to be startled—and in truth, she was. "I don't understand. If I said something to offend—"

"You reek of him, you know," Fomi said. The shorter girl had stopped scaling fish, and now inspected Fulan with hard eyes. "I could almost feel it, the moment you walked into the village. And I noticed it immediately when you sat down. His touch is all over you."

Fulan froze.

"Even Danwe felt it," Fomi went on. "He doesn't know when to be quiet. But he was smart enough to bring you to me."

"And then he came to me," Sowoke added.

Fulan looked to the boy, who winced, still nursing his foot. Then back to the two girls. She'd been played. He'd put her here for Fomi to keep an eye on her, while he went to get their leader. She marveled that these mere children had pulled it off.

"I think I should go," she said, readying to rise.

Sowoke shook her head. "No, I don't think so. If you're thinking of running, you should know we've already prepared for that."

Fulan looked about—and saw that the road out of the village was now blocked. Two older boys stood talking, leaning against a conveniently placed cart. At her look, they turned to stare back. She swung her head in another direction, to find two girls who stood conversing while carrying bundles on their heads. Both ended their conversation and fixed gazes on her. Everywhere she turned, there were more. Children clearing fields, others mending houses, who now all brandished hoes and carpenter's tools menacingly—their cold stares on her. She felt her heart begin to race, then willed it to slow down, and let herself relax. Turning back to Sowoke, she smiled.

"Seems I underestimated all of you," she said. "But I'm not staying. And you can't keep me. Now clear a path and let me pass." A roar of flames danced in her eyes for emphasis. Let these children understand who they were dealing with.

But to her surprise they didn't so much as flinch.

"Is that supposed to frighten us?" Fomi asked. The short girl's voice had taken on a knife's edge. "You dare come here and threaten us? After what he did? You sit there, stinking of him, claiming his war is to free us. Do you know what he did to us?"

"Fomi," Sowoke warned. But the smaller girl went on.

"One of his servants—someone like you—stole us away. A weak little person who called himself the Goat Man. He took us, made us into monsters, forced us to do terrible things! And you think your little fire in the eyes trick is supposed to make us tremble? You have no idea!"

"Fomi!" Sowoke said again, urgent.

"No!" Fomi glared now. "Because she's coming here, asking about Abeni. Asking about Asha. Abeni saved us. She stopped the Goat Man. If not for her, we'd still be his mindless servants! Some of us never came back, like Ekwolo." The shorter girl deftly brandished her scaling knife, and in a flash was on Fulan. Her face was a mask of rage as the sharp edge of the blade pressed at Fulan's throat. "Why do you want to know about Abeni? Who sent you? Do you know where the others like Ekwolo are? Tell me, or I'll—"

"Fomi," Sowoke spoke again, this time gently. "This isn't the way."

Fulan looked down. The girl's hand shook, as if she was fighting for control. At her friend's words, something in her face slackened. That was all Fulan needed. In a burst of strength, she pushed the girl's arm away, thrusting with the scaling knife in her own hand. She intended to make this quick. But once more she was surprised. The girl recovered, her arm darting to block and then aiming to strike. Fulan pulled back, scrambling away and just managing to get to her feet.

She found herself surrounded. Fomi stood now, holding the scaling knife in one hand and the broad chopping blade in another. Sowoke had a knife too, as did Danwe and Adze. Everything about the way they held the weapons, their bodies balanced and eyes hard, said they knew how to use them. Well, so did she. With a yell, she struck, wielding the small knife and spinning in a deadly arc—aiming to cut down as many as she could. Her movement was fast, faster than any person had a right to be. This, along with her strength, was another of her father's gifts. But somehow, she struck no one. The two boys evaded her strikes, while Fomi and Sowoke came at her, their own knives flashing. Fulan should have been able to take down several grown men twice their size! Yet it was all she could do to keep these four at bay! She retreated to a defensive stance, eyeing them in frustration and astonishment. Once again she wondered, what kind of children were these?

"I told you," Fomi said. She circled, twirling her blade. "We were touched by him too—the one you serve. It's how we can sense him on you. Abeni broke the spell that made us monsters. But his touch left us changed. We might never be free of it, not completely."

"But we can use it," Sowoke said, gritting her teeth. "To defend this village and the children who now live here. From him, and from those who serve him. Like you."

Fulan eyed her four opponents, then the others in the village, poised to join in. Not everyone looked ready to fight her. Some had fled into homes. Others sought shelter where they could, watching with wide eyes. But there were enough to provide more than a challenge. And if they were as formidable as these four . . .

Assessing the situation, Fulan made the wisest choice possible— she fled.

It was a mad dash, pushing past startled onlookers, dodging children with hard eyes, and blocking their weapons where she could. But she had to keep moving. She couldn't get pinned down between houses or in open fields. She had to stay on the main streets that led out. Behind her, she could hear the tall girl— Sowoke—shouting orders not to kill her, but to capture her. But Fulan had no intention of being captured. She caught sight of the village's outskirts ahead, and put on a burst of speed, barely touching the ground that raced beneath her feet. Something darted past her face. Another came. She risked a glance back to see figures on rooftops with bows drawn. They were shooting arrows at her! The thought barely registered before a burning sensation shot through her leg, quickly blossoming into a fire of pain. She looked down to see an arrow jutting from her thigh, and stumbled, slowing. Someone yelled to take her. With a snarl, she sped up again, ignoring the lancing pain as she shot out of the village and into the safety of the forest. Despite her wound, she didn't stop until she was far, far, away.

○ ○ ○

Fulan sat with one leg extended, watching the crackling fire and listening to the sounds of night birds and insects. Hours had passed since she'd fled the village. And no parties had been sent in pursuit.

"Something for the pain?" a voice came.

Her eyes flicked to the Huntsman. The big man sat reclined, face illuminated by the fire. He took swigs of some dark liquid from a calabash covered in animal teeth. When she didn't answer, he withdrew with a shrug.

"We could go back to the village." His free hand produced

a smooth gray stone. "Shenzi, Banzai, and Nunda would make quick work of these children who managed to . . . best you."

A smile played on his lips that made her jaw clench. She eyed the stone. The three monstrous hounds somehow existed within and emerged at his call. She imagined them let loose upon that village and memories of another time intruded. People fleeing. Fire and smoke. Roars and screams. She pushed them away and shook her head.

"I don't think my father sent us to cut down a village of children."

The Huntsman gave her a look she couldn't read.

"How did a mortal girl become the daughter of the Witch Priest?"

Fulan looked at him in surprise. In their weeks of travel, he'd never inquired about her.

"He saved me," she answered. "My kingdom was destroyed. My family, my people, were all scattered. He took me in. Raised me as his own."

She had been small, but still remembered some things. Her father, towering and staring down at her from behind an iron mask. When he took it off, there hadn't been fire then, just a face. Dark and beautiful. His eyes, though, were the same—burning like the sun.

"He saved you," the Huntsman mused. "When he has destroyed so many others."

Fulan felt her skin heat.

"He only destroys those who refuse his will. Who refuse the freedom he brings."

"As you say." He took another swig.

Fulan gritted her teeth in annoyance. "I know why I follow my father. Why do you?"

The Huntsman chuckled. "He pays me."

"So you're a mercenary."

"I wouldn't be the first in your father's armies."

Fulan snorted. "You're not loyal to anything."

At that, the Huntsman fixed her with a cold glare. "I am loyal to the hunt. Once it begins, I will not be put off, I will not be dissuaded, until I see it done. Some advice. Walk your own path, girl. Not the one others set for you."

She scowled. He thought he had the right to give *her* advice?

Her leg spasmed and she gasped, looking to the arrow jutting from her thigh.

"You want me to do it?" the Huntsman asked.

Her arm thrust out to him in answer, and he handed over the tooth-covered calabash. She put it to her lips and drank the scorching liquid. Biting down on the calabash's bulbous head, she grabbed the arrow and pulled it free. She screamed and almost passed out. But she held on. A heat joined the pain, dulling it. Where a wound had been, the skin was mended—leaving only a trickle of blood and fire.

Handing back the calabash, Fulan sat in silence. They had learned some things today. Their quarry, Asha, was a spirit. An old woman who had died and been reborn, as a little girl it seemed. Then there was this Abeni, who appeared to be in league with the spirit. She had bested this . . . Goat Man. A servant of her father who turned children into monsters. An exaggeration certainly. But this Abeni had defied her father's power. No one defied her father! If this village was anything to go by, she could prove troublesome.

Pulling a curved knife from her waist, Fulan spoke a word and watched the dark blade burst into flames. Scrawling out a scorched name on the ground, she stared at it like a puzzle.

Abeni.

CHAPTER EIGHT

INTO THE FOREST

Abeni stood on a small hill at the edge of a forest, looking back at Makomasi. The capital of the Gold Kingdom was still visible where sunlight reflected from its shining buildings. They had left the city early. The only ones to see them off had been the Queen Mothers and the royal attendant Akú. This was supposed to be a secret mission. Not even the king knew. Their belongings had been returned—Abeni's staff, the big bag, even Songu's flute—and they'd been gifted new clothing. Then they were offered blessings and wished luck on their journey. Attendant Akú had pulled her aside to speak personally.

"Your time with the princess will probably prove . . . interesting. She can be . . . strong willed? Understand that this quest is important to her, perhaps more than she realizes."

Abeni recalled the attendant's words as she turned to regard Ama. The princess was wrapped in patterned fabrics of blue, red, and green that ended like a skirt above her knees. A necklace of large golden orbs hung to her chest, while matching bracelets circled her wrists and ankles. The two thick bands covering her forearms were there, a constant reminder of her power as a Gold Weaver. A type of sandal woven of golden fabric covered her feet completely. Abeni, Asha, and Songu had each been gifted a pair—which was surprisingly cushioned and comfortable. Ama carried more than one set, along with different dresses and even more jewelry. Or, better put, she had them carry these items for her. Abeni and Songu carried gold-stitched satchels of the princess's belongings slung over their shoulders. Zaneeya had been saddled with a large wood chest painted gold that she hauled on her back. Even Nyomi carried the princess's belongings—a set of a golden pots, plates, and pans. The porcupine girl had stacked the utensils high atop her head, balancing them with what had to be spirit magic. How they were to manage a quest with all these goods to keep the princess comfortable, Abeni had no idea.

At the moment, Ama stood gazing back at Makomasi. There was apprehension in her gaze as she glanced to the forest ahead. Her face creased into a frown, causing the gold dust on her cheeks to shimmer. With effort, Abeni made herself speak.

"Have you never been outside the city before?" she asked.

Ama answered absently. "I've visited the larger cities of the kingdom. But I've never crossed our borders. Certainly not into the bush. It feels like I'm leaving everything behind."

"It was the same for me," Abeni said. "You'll get used to things being different."

Ama's golden eyes narrowed. "Are you comparing leaving your speck of a village to my departing Makomasi? The duties of a princess to . . . whatever it is you did in your backwater forest?"

"I only meant . . ." Abeni stammered.

"Don't presume to know anything about me," Ama said curtly. "Speak when spoken to and remember your place. Now don't dawdle. I want to make good time before nightfall."

With that she turned and walked off—leaving Abeni standing there, fuming. Remember her place?

Zaneeya sidled up to her, watching Ama disappear into the bush.

"How's the bonding going?" she asked dryly.

"I wasn't bonding," Abeni countered. "I was just . . . trying to be friendly."

"Trying to be friendly," the panther girl repeated. "Is that some mortal thing? You talk nice. Then afterward you sit around giggling about boys and braiding each other's hair? Is that what you think is going to happen?"

Abeni was certain she was the first mortal girl—or mortal of any kind—that Zaneeya knew. And she didn't giggle. Or braid hair. Anyway, what boys?

"I was trying to be cordial. We have to be on this quest with each other."

Zaneeya huffed. "Stop trying to be *cordial* with your jailer." She adjusted the chest atop her back, walking into the waiting forest.

"I'll braid your hair if you like," Nyomi offered. "Although, I don't think you can do much with my quills."

Abeni gave her thanks, though she had no plans on letting the porcupine girl, whose hands were often buried in worms, bugs, and other crawly things, near her hair. Besides, Songu was the best braider in their group. The things he did with her hair were amazing! She sent quick hand signals saying as much. He sent back thanks, saying she could make an appointment any time.

"Maybe Zaneeya's right. And I'm stupid for even trying to be friendly."

"You're not stupid," Asha said. The small girl walked up, taking her hand. "Ama might be older, but she has a lot of growing up to do. Maybe that'll happen on this trip. Or not. But don't ever apologize for being kind."

Abeni nodded. At times the girl spoke with a surprising wisdom.

"Ooooh look!" Asha exclaimed. "Butterflies."

And other times she was like this. Abeni let herself be pulled along, chasing butterflies.

For the next few days, they traveled through the forest. It wasn't easy. Tall trees with broad branches created a natural canopy, barely allowing any sunlight. It made even the daytime gloomy. Abeni didn't recognize any of the plants here, that grew in great bunches or long hanging vines. She did see all kinds of animals— from red-furred monkeys chattering high above to a small furry hog with sharp tusks snuffling through the leaf-covered ground. Abeni asked Ama if anyone from the Gold Kingdom lived out here. The girl shook her head.

"Not anymore. Back when the First Gold Kingdom stretched far and wide, it was said people made offerings to this forest—

and it allowed them to enter, creating safe paths for travelers. But, when the kingdom fell, the forest closed itself off. Now, anyone who tries to clear land here finds it grown back almost overnight. Or the small home they manage to build gets completely swallowed up by the bush."

"So this is a magic forest?" Abeni asked.

Ama shrugged, making her way up a hilly slope. The girl was often overdressed, but she seemed capable of handling the terrain. "Or haunted. Keeps people from settling here. Along with the talk of monsters."

"Monsters?" Nyomi asked, eyebrows drooping. "Oh, I don't like monsters!"

"Superstition," Ama dismissed. "Claims of giant bats, ridden by small men."

Abeni stopped, her insides going cold. "Bat riders? There are bat riders here?"

Ama regarded her curiously. "You've heard the stories, then?"

Abeni nodded. She'd heard them. And they weren't superstition. Her eyes searched the sky through the canopy, worried at what she might find.

Since the forest was mostly uncharted—because it changed often—the exact location of the Masks of Akani was unknown. Asha had pored over maps in the palace and pointed to some mountains near the forest's center. How the little girl knew where the relics were, she couldn't say. Not uncommon for the reborn spirit, who remembered only pieces of their past lives. Ama, of course, couldn't know any of that. She'd been skeptical. But Abeni assured her that Asha's guesses were better than most people's facts.

The journey offered other challenges. They'd had to find shallow places to cross streams and so far one river. Sometimes, the land went straight up, and they climbed higher by the day. Rain came in heavy downpours that drenched in moments. Fortunately, the forest's canopy provided some shelter. Unfortunately, nothing could be done about Ama—who only made the already difficult journey harder.

Abeni hadn't thought she could meet anyone more self-assured than Zaneeya. But the princess was in a class of her own. Ama walked through the forest as if she expected it to give way and bow. She might have asked them to bow regularly if she wasn't already busy ordering them about. Fetch water. Cook my food. Cut down that bush in my way. She even now had Songu doing up her twisted knots of hair.

When they stopped to eat or sleep, Ama did nothing—not even collect wood for a fire. She sat watching as they set up camp, and then waited to be brought food. Most of the princess's meals came from her own stores, which she guarded for herself. Nyomi found her own food easily enough. Zaneeya had it a bit harder, still unable to shift into panther form. But she always managed to return with something.

Luckily for the rest of them, Abeni had filled the big bag with food and drinking water before leaving Makomasi. Ama was intrigued with the magic bag, insisting that she be showed how it worked. She watched in amazement as Abeni pulled out bowls of hot peanut soup, balls of fufu, and smoked fish. The princess stuck her own hand inside, commanding a heaping plate of kelewele—which translated as fried plantains seasoned with spices. She frowned when nothing appeared, and Abeni explained that the bag didn't work like that. You could only pull out what you put in. A disappointed Ama called the bag "cheap peasant magic." Abeni was so offended, she wondered if she still had some morning mushrooms in the bag—and whether dropping a few of the mewling and wriggling things into the girl's blankets would be childish. Probably. But she thought of it, a lot.

After three nights of history lessons from Ama—of the Gold Kingdom's many deeds, its heroes, and rulers—Abeni was more than happy when Songu picked up his flute and began playing. Everyone settled down where they'd made camp, listening to the lively melody.

"Those simple songs are nice, I suppose," Ama cut in. "But don't you know anything more . . . sophisticated?" Songu stopped, looking at her in confusion. "Makomasi has some of the finest musicians, you know. Gifted flute players are hired by the wealthiest families to entertain at banquets. I hear that at a funeral a group of them played so mournfully that the clouds opened and wept!" She seemed to wait for Songu to applaud her words. When he didn't, she sat back with a sigh. "I forget at times that you're dumb."

Abeni stiffened, and anger flared in her at seeing Songu's injured face. She shot to her feet. "Take that back!"

Ama looked startled, but quickly recovered. "I don't mean anything. But he doesn't talk."

"He talks fine," Abeni said. "Just differently."

Ama rolled her eyes. "You know what I mean. He doesn't use his mouth."

"Given what comes out of yours, I don't see that makes a difference," Abeni retorted.

Ama's eyebrows rose. "Well, the mouse has teeth. The way you walk around trying to make everyone get along—I began to think tales of you taking on this Goat Man were exaggerated." When Abeni remained unmoved she let out a breath. "Fine." She turned to Songu. "I'm sorry if what I said offended you."

That wasn't much of an apology, but Songu accepted it and Abeni sat down.

"Wasting my time trying to explain grand culture to you anyway," the princess muttered. "What do any of you know about attending high parties or dinners? None of you have ever sat among such important persons."

"I once had breakfast with the meerkat king," Nyomi put in cheerfully.

Everyone turned to her.

"Well, he was king of the meerkats . . . in that one area."

There was an overly loud yawn from Zaneeya. She lay on her back, staring up at a starry sky through the forest canopy—as the many things that came out in the night chittered, hooted, and cawed about them.

Ama turned to her. "Did you have something to say?"

Zaneeya propped up on her elbows. "I was just wondering, if your kingdom is so great, how you ended up making a pact with the Witch Priest. Now you're all but enslaved to him and he's made off with this Golden Throne. Sounds pretty dense to me. But what do I know? Haven't been invited to all the high parties, after all." She lay back down, hands behind her head.

Ama's eyes flashed. She looked set to retort but swallowed it back. "You know," she said calmly, "I remember when I was younger being told about the spirits—how they helped the gods create the world, and how they kept the natural balance. We had grand festivals to your kind—spirits of rivers and good fortune, even yam spirits. Then one day you all went away, left us to fend for ourselves. When the Witch Priest came none of you were there to help. That was when we realized you were useless. We got rid of all our festivals to you, lost our awe of you. You're just . . . beasts, really. To be leashed and used like any other."

There was silence as the princess awaited a response. Getting none, she sat back triumphantly—until an odd growling came from Zaneeya. Abeni tensed, thinking the panther girl was ready to pounce. But she realized in surprise that Zaneeya was laughing. Laughing so hard she shook.

"What's so funny?" Ama asked hotly.

The panther girl had to catch her breath. "You claim you turned away from the spirits when the Witch Priest came. But you don't know, do you?" She sat up. "The Witch Priest is a spirit! All that big talk, and you fools allowed a spirit to trick you, enslave you, and steal your souls!"

Ama watched her, stunned. She turned to the rest of them, a questioning look on her face. Abeni hadn't told the Queen Mothers that part. It came too close to Asha's identity.

"It's true," she admitted. "The Witch Priest is a spirit—not a mortal."

Ama stared at Abeni as if slapped. Zaneeya's laughter only grew.

"Be quiet!" the princess ordered. But Zaneeya was wheezing now. Abeni didn't know the panther girl had this much laughter in her. Ama jumped to her feet, brandishing one of the gold bands on her forearms and squeezing a hand tight. "I said, be quiet!"

At once Zaneeya's mouth clamped shut. She tried to pry it open, but without success. In moments she was scratching at her throat, her eyes bulging.

"Stop it!" Abeni cried. "She can't breathe!"

The princess didn't relent, squeezing her fist tighter. Zaneeya flopped onto the ground.

"Stop!" Abeni snatched up her staff. But Ama saw her coming and extended her other arm—palm flat and open. Something seized Abeni from the inside, and it felt like her limbs had turned to stone. She couldn't move them, and they grew heavier, until it hurt.

"Is that all you know how to do, hurt people?" a voice asked. Asha. She sat watching the princess. "Nana Akasi said only weak rulers believed brute force solved every problem."

Ama stared at the little girl, mouth open but unable to respond. Finally, she dropped her hands. Zaneeya sucked in a deep breath. Abeni felt her limbs return to her control. There was a long moment where no one spoke. They couldn't go on like this, Abeni thought. Something worse was going to happen if they kept at each other. She was set to say as much when Zaneeya spoke instead.

"Why is it so quiet?" she asked, her voice hoarse.

Abeni listened. It *was* quiet. She couldn't say when it had happened, but all the sounds of the forest had stopped. Nothing chittered, hooted, or cawed. Like they had been told to hush. Some silent alarm blared inside her. Warning that this was familiar.

"What's going on—?" Ama began. Then, with a startled scream, she was gone.

Abeni jumped. Something had snatched the girl away right from in front of them—into the forest! There was a flapping sound and a strong wind buffeted them, snuffing out the fire and plunging them into darkness. Burning red eyes appeared in the shadows— like bits of wood left to glow in a fire. There were noises, like claws scraping against branches. As her eyes adjusted, Abeni made out a shape surrounding those red eyes: a large body covered in black fur, attached to leathery wings topped with bony hooks. It was a bat! A giant bat that clung to the side of a tree. It pushed a snub nose forward, pierced by a gold hoop, showing a head with large, pointed ears pierced with more gold hoops. When it opened its mouth, a set of long white fangs showed, dripping saliva. Abeni knew this monster. One whose name she had hoped never to say again: a sasabonsam. And that meant . . .

"Bat riders!" she shouted. "They're bat riders!"

As if in answer, the giant bat let out a piercing shriek. She clutched her ears, falling back and searching for its rider. There. Sitting in a seat bound by leather straps wrapped about the bat's belly was a small man. No, not a man. They were called Mmoatia. Dressed in black, he blended with the night—with gold hoops in his nose and two pointed ears, matching his mount. From his forehead to upper jaw, his face was painted a blood red—and his eyes glowed. At seeing her his downturned lips twisted into a smile, revealing sharp yellow teeth. He snarled, drawing a wicked-looking blade. She threw her hands up protectively and suddenly there was light—a brilliant orb that turned night into day. Asha! The girl had done this once before, as an old woman. As then, the brightness caused both bat and rider to scream, shielding their eyes and rearing back. But as quickly as it came, the light vanished. The bat rider blinked rapidly, trying to clear his vision.

Before he could recover there was a shout followed by the sound of something big crashing through the trees. A figure stumbled out of the bush into view. Ama! The girl looked ragged, her dress torn in several places and with scratches on her arms and legs. One of her shoes was missing. She stared around with wild eyes, stopping on Abeni and raising her hands.

"Ama!" Abeni shouted. "It's me!"

But the girl was already weaving, her arms moving in a whirl. There was a cry, and Abeni turned behind her to see the Mmoatia rider leaning forward, his entire body being pulled—by the gold ring in his nose. With a tear, it broke free, flying into the air. There was another tear, and the large gold ring in his bat's nose ripped free as well, sending up a spurt of blood. The wounded creature squealed and flapped its wings in an attempt to flee. The wind it kicked up almost sent Abeni to her knees. But Ama wasn't done. The two gold rings—small and large—became liquid, merging and forming into a long golden spear. With a shout, Ama sent it hurling at the retreating bat rider. At the last moment, he pulled up his mount, and the spear streaked past.

Then everything went quiet again.

Abeni found her footing, peering around in the dark.

"Asha! Asha! Can you hear me?"

"Abeni!" came a shout. "I'm here! With Songu!"

Abeni breathed in relief. "Zaneeya?"

"Here!" the panther girl said, appearing right before her—claws bared.

"Nyomi?"

"Eek! Hiding!" the porcupine girl squeaked.

"What," Ama said between haggard breaths, "were those things?"

"Bat riders," Abeni said, making her way toward Asha's voice.

"But . . . they're just superstition."

"Superstition just snatched you up!" Zaneeya countered.

The princess glared at the panther girl, then up at the skies. "They wear gold. As long as they do, I can use it against—"

She didn't finish, as a short figure dropped suddenly right before her. A Mmoatia. Startled, she lifted her hands to either push him back or weave gold. But he opened a palm and with a deep inhale blew a fine white powder into the princess's face. She coughed and sputtered before going rigid as a board and dropping to the ground.

Oh no, Abeni thought. Asha.

She hadn't taken two steps before another figure dropped into her path. Lifting her staff, she whirled the form *Crocodile Lashes*

His Tail—catching him on the side of his head. Watching him crumple, she never saw the one behind her. He grabbed her shoulder and she spun about ready to deliver another blow—and received a face full of blown powder for the effort. It had the smell of something sickeningly sweet and the taste of a bitter root. Then her mind was slipping, spinning away with the night.

CHAPTER NINE

CITY OF LIGHT

Abeni was dreaming.

She knew this because she was in Asha's old garden. It looked exactly like she remembered. Flowers and plants grew in neat rows, while a field of tall grass stalks swayed beneath a sunless sky. They whispered as always, the gossiping things. Lying on her back, Abeni turned her head to find Obi. The straw man lay on his back too, his featureless straw face staring up. She smiled. Obi taught her all the forms she knew with the staff. He'd been a friend. But when Asha died, the magic that animated him died too—and he ceased to be, except in her dreams. She liked to think he was still real here, in a way.

Turning to her other side, she saw Asha. The little girl liked to walk Abeni's dreams and was often here. Only this time she lay still, eyes closed as if sleeping.

"Asha?" Abeni gently nudged her. She didn't move.

"Asha?" she called again, pushing her. Nothing.

Bolting upright, she went to her knees, grabbing the girl by the shoulders.

"Asha! You need to wake up! Wake up!"

Abeni blinked awake, no longer dreaming.

She was floating. In water? No. Air. She could feel the night wind on her face—cold and stinging. Her whole body was cold, and she couldn't stop shivering. Why was it so cold? She reached to wipe away tears but found her body bound—unable to move a limb. Fighting a dullness in her head she fluttered her eyelids open. And almost wished she hadn't.

All around her was a dark sky filled with stars. Something white and puffy flew by. Clouds. So close, she could reach out and touch them. But if there were clouds . . . Her eyes swept downward, and she had to hold back a scream. The ground was far, far below. She could make out small shapes she soon recognized as trees. It was the forest canopy, stretching out in a dark mass below.

Asha! She looked around in panic. Where was the little girl? Had she been taken too? In her frantic thoughts, she caught sight of a great black shape moving alongside her. She gulped. A bat! The thing soared through the sky, beating its wide leathery wings. As she watched, the bat turned, revealing its underside. Hanging from one clawed foot was a rope. It led to a long pole to which someone was tied.

Ama! The princess's eyes were closed, and she was unmoving. The white powder, Abeni remembered. That's why her head felt so weird. She caught sight of more bats carrying the others, all tied up and unconscious. Zaneeya must have put up a fight, because she was bound in lots of rope. And with them was Asha. The small girl was tied to a pole with Nyomi. Abeni was thinking of calling out to them when the bat carrying her suddenly plunged. Her stomach dropped away as the world turned upside down. When they righted again, she gasped at what she saw.

It was a city! Almost as big as Makomasi! It sat on the side of a mountain—one of three, whose dark peaks rose against the night sky. And this city—it glowed! Every bit of it was covered in bright lights like a thousand fireflies. There were conical white structures she thought must be buildings that looked cut from the mountain itself. They flew lower to pass over the city, and Abeni soon made out people—more Mmoatia, who bustled back and forth in the night.

The bat carrying her stopped suddenly, beating its wings furiously in place. Abeni found herself dangling uncomfortably close to the ground. More Mmoatia appeared. In swift movements, they undid her ropes until she fell from the pole to the ground. The same was done to her companions carried by the other bats. The Mmoatia started talking in that odd tongue she somehow couldn't understand. They checked each of their captives. Lots of fuss was made around Ama, and her gold bands and jewelry were removed. Abeni watched helplessly as her own staff, hat, and satchel were all taken. A pale gray face rose up before her, and she saw in surprise it was a girl Mmoatia. She didn't look much older than Abeni herself. Unlike the bat riders, there was no red paint on her face or gold hoops in her nose or ears. Her head was shaved, except for long white braids done up in an elaborate style at its center. And she wore all gray, not black. At seeing Abeni awake, her red eyes widened. She pointed a small knife that shook in her hand while crying out. Another Mmoatia appeared, this one bigger and with red paint on his face. Reaching into a pouch he took out a handful of white powder.

"No!" Abeni said. "Wait, I just want to—"

But he was already blowing. And as she inhaled the fine white mist, her words melted away with everything else.

She awoke again to find Asha staring down at her.

"Is this a dream?" she mumbled.

"Nope," Asha said. "I went looking for you there, but you wouldn't wake up."

She was going to tell the girl she'd done the same but became aware of someone yelling. Sitting up she saw it was Ama. The girl stood gripping a set of long iron bars while yelling at the top of her lungs.

"I am Princess Ama of Makomasi! My brother is the king! You will release me at once or face the wrath of the Gold Kingdom! Hello? Does anyone hear me? I'm talking to you!"

Abeni took in their surroundings. A small room with no window or opening, except for the iron bars. A pen of some kind? She was near the back. Songu, Nyomi, and Zaneeya sat around her—propped up against a wall. Standing, she walked to touch it. Stone. There was light in the room coming from something on the ceiling.

"Mushrooms!" Nyomi said, moving to stand beside her.

Abeni squinted, making out the flat caps that grew in bunches. "Glowing mushrooms?"

Nyomi nodded. "They look delicious! Only, I wonder if they'll glow in my tummy?"

"How long have we been here?" Abeni asked.

"Can't say," Zaneeya said. "Most of us woke an hour ago. Seen no one since." Her eyes flicked to Ama. "Hasn't stopped *Your Highness* from trying to wake the dead."

Ama turned to glare. "I'm the only one trying to free us!"

"I don't feel freer," Zaneeya muttered.

"I don't feel any freer either," Nyomi said. "But thanks for trying!"

Ama gritted her teeth. "Does anyone even know where we are?"

"In the mountains," Abeni said. "I was awake when they brought us in."

She quickly recounted all that she saw.

"An entire city?" Ama asked in disbelief. "How has no one known about it?"

"Maybe because you called them a superstition," Abeni said, unable to help herself.

Ama's eyes tightened. "What do you know about these . . . bat riders?"

"The bats are called sasabonsam. The riders are Mmoatia."

"Sounds like you've encountered them before. Know anything that might help us?"

Abeni nodded. She had come across the bat riders once while trying to escape from Asha's house—when she was still distrustful of the old woman. She might have been snatched away if not for Asha's intervention.

"They don't like a lot of light."

"I saw that light!" Ama said. "Who was that?"

Abeni glanced to Asha. Revealing what the small girl had done might also reveal who and what she was. "It was me," she said quickly. "Something from my bag."

Ama nodded. "So, light. Anything else?"

"Not that I know."

Ama grunted and started to shout again—banging the bars. After a while, she turned back to them. "One of you come here and start helping me get someone's attention."

No one moved.

"That's a command," she said. "Come here!"

"Make us," Zaneeya said.

Ama narrowed her eyes. "Do you think I can't?"

"I'm sure you still have your abilities," the panther girl replied. "But they took your bands. Wish they'd taken these collars. But guessing those don't come off so easy. Anyway, without those bands, your powers are greatly reduced. Told us as much when you were running your mouth before, remember? You run your mouth a lot."

Ama turned around fully, raising a hand that looked naked without any jewelry. "Bands or no, I am still a weaver. With power enough to keep that collar on you and manipulate it as I wish."

"Maybe," Zaneeya said. "Or maybe you're only strong enough now to put me off a bit. And by the time I reach you, you're so spent, I can take my time slashing you open." She sat forward, baring her teeth in a sharp grin and flexing clawed fingers. "Maybe we find out?"

Abeni wondered if she should put a stop to this. Or if it was time the princess learned a well-deserved lesson.

She was still pondering when a light appeared outside their pen, alongside the sound of footsteps. Everyone turned to look as four figures emerged from the gloom. All were Mmoatia and stood no taller than her. Two in black had red-painted faces and carried long knives strapped to their chests. Neither, however, wore gold in their ears or noses. They'd learned their lesson about Ama, it seemed. A third was older, his gray skin wrinkled but otherwise unadorned. He wore long gray robes tinged in red. The fourth she recognized as the girl from when she first arrived.

The older one stepped forward and smiled. Abeni noticed his yellow teeth were not at all sharp. Opening his mouth, he spoke.

"Kanewuande'stn?"

Abeni frowned at the harsh clash of sound.

Ama turned back to her. "What's he saying? I was told you can speak any tongue."

The older Mmoatia looked between them.

"Kanewuande'stn?" he asked again.

Abeni shook her head. "I don't know." She looked to Nyomi and Zaneeya. "Do you?" Spirits were supposed to understand most languages. But both shook their heads, looking baffled.

The older Mmoatia reached into his robes and drew out something. A mushroom. It was pale and bumpy, and glowed faintly. But most off-putting, it moved—jumping in his hand and wriggling a set of fleshy tentacles.

"Ugh!" Ama exclaimed, backing away. "What is that?"

Abeni didn't know. She didn't want to know. But the old Mmoatia offered it forward. His other hand tapped his mouth, and he pretended to chew. "I think he wants us to eat it," she said.

"I will do no such thing!" Ama insisted.

"I'll have to agree with the princess," Zaneeya said in disgust. "Just this once."

The old Mmoatia sighed. Behind him, one of the red-faced Mmoatia snarled, pointing angrily at Abeni. She took a step back. What was that about?

The older Mmoatia handed the strange mushroom to the girl Mmoatia—and turned back to the snarling Mmoatia, trying to calm him.

"Why isn't the prattle stone working?" Abeni asked Asha.

The small girl thought for a moment. "Prattle stones are formed in the bellies of great fish who swim the world, learning different tongues. Maybe the fish never came here. Or their language is particularly hard. Maybe we just aren't listening right."

Abeni frowned. How would she fix that? Her gaze returned to the strange mushroom, which let out a sharp and sudden "squeak!" Two black dots opened on its surface. Then they blinked—like eyes!

"Nope! Nope! Nope!" Ama shouted. She'd backed into a corner, rubbing her arms like something was crawling on her. The mushroom squeaked again. Abeni rubbed her own arms. This was too much.

"Awww! It's so cute." Nyomi came to the gate and put her face level with the strange mushroom. She sniffed. "And it smells delicious!" The Mmoatia girl offered the thing again. "Have some?" Nyomi asked. "Certainly! Thank you!"

Before Abeni could stop her the porcupine girl reached out to grab one of the mushroom's tentacles. Breaking it off, she crammed it into her mouth, chewing. It still wriggled.

"I'm going to be sick," Ama said queasily.

Nyomi appeared unfazed. Surprise came across her face and she said something—only Abeni couldn't understand. The Mmoatia girl beamed and spoke back. They were talking to each other! The Mmoatia girl called to her older companion, who walked up to Nyomi, asking questions. The porcupine girl nodded, before turning to them.

"Guys, we have to eat the mushroom. Then we can understand."

Abeni looked to the thing and winced as it blinked at her.

"You're sure?"

"Uh-huh."

With a sigh, she thrust her hand through the gate—grabbing one of the mushroom's tentacles. The thing squirmed even as she twisted and broke it off. She brought it to her mouth.

"Go on," Nyomi urged. "It really doesn't taste bad!"

Abeni shoved the squirming tentacle into her mouth, bit down, and chewed. Nyomi was wrong. It tasted very, very bad. And it wouldn't stop moving! She almost gagged but got it down. All at once, a dull ringing sounded in her ears. She looked up to find the old Mmoatia speaking.

"Kanewuande'stn?"

The ringing began to fade. He tried again.

"Canuunderstandme?"

Abeni shook her head as the ringing vanished and the old Mmoatia spoke one more time.

"Can you understand me?"

She looked at him startled. "Yes! Yes, I can."

"What's happening?" Ama asked. "What are you two saying?"

Abeni realized then she was talking like the Mmoatia. She shifted back. "That I can understand him. The mushroom works. We all need to eat some."

Over the next few minutes, they all had a bite of the mushroom—chewing and swallowing and making faces, and Zaneeya scraping her tongue. Everyone except Ama.

"Absolutely not!" she insisted when offered a piece.

"But you won't be able to understand or talk to them," Abeni countered.

"Then you can translate for me."

Giving up, Abeni moved to return the piece. But Nyomi snatched it up and ate it happily.

"Glad we resolved that," the old Mmoatia said. "My name is Vushu. Let's get the rest out of the way. Now, are you guests or food?"

Abeni blinked. "Excuse me?"

"Are you guests or food?" Vushu repeated. His red eyes stared at them awaiting an answer.

Then Abeni remembered. When she'd first encountered the bat riders, Asha had warned she could end up in their cooking pots. These Mmoatia, they ate people!

"We're guests!" Abeni said quickly. "Not food, guests! Definitely guests!"

The old Mmoatia looked disappointed, and his shoulders slumped.

"What are they saying?" Ama asked. "Are they asking about me? Tell them who I am. That they'll be in a lot of trouble if my people have to come and rescue me! Make sure they know that. Tell them I expect to be released, my belongings returned, and to be properly compensated. Several chests of gold should do. Along with an apology. Go ahead, tell them!"

Abeni stared at the girl. How did she explain that was a bad idea? Zaneeya spoke first, tilting her chin at Ama.

"That one is food."

Vushu perked up.

"She's not food," Abeni countered, glaring at Zaneeya. As annoying as the princess could be, she drew a line at people-eating. "None of us are food."

The old Mmoatia looked disappointed again. "You're certain?"

"Very certain."

He frowned, muttering. "Well, this is all irregular. Not sure what we do with guests."

"Haven't you had guests before?" Abeni asked.

"You'd be surprised how many refuse to eat the mushroom. Our laws say that if what we catch can't claim guest rights, they're food. And it's off to the cooking pots."

Abeni stared in horror. Thank goodness for Nyomi's strange appetites!

"If they're guests, shouldn't we release them?" the Mmoatia girl asked.

"That's not the law, Nula!" a red-faced Mmoatia snarled. He still glared at Abeni. "The council must decide what to do with them!"

"Then they go before the council, Shoma," the girl said. "In the meantime, we treat them as guests and give them free run of the city."

Both the Mmoatia with red-painted faces balked, voicing dissent.

"Everyone quiet!" Vushu shouted, raising his hands in annoyance. "Nula is right. We cannot treat guests as food. They should be released." The girl smiled, showing teeth that were also not sharp.

"But," he went on, "Shoma is also correct. They should be taken before the council. We will move them from the pens to better quarters. It is highly advisable that they remain there, given the mood in the city." That didn't seem to please either party. But they nodded in acceptance.

Abeni felt relief as the door to the pen swung open and they were ushered out.

"What's happening now?" Ama asked, impatient. "Did you tell them who I am?"

"Abeni just saved you from being eaten," Asha said. She walked over to take Ama's hand while the older girl stared down, stunned. "Come, Princess. The Queen Mothers had much to say about you. Would you like to hear?" Ama's eyes remained wide as she was led off.

They were escorted down a corridor. More glowing mushrooms lined the walls. Without them, Abeni didn't think she'd be able to see a thing. She fell in beside the Mmoatia girl.

"Thank you for helping us," she said. "I'm Abeni."

The girl gave her a sidelong look. "Nula," she returned, after a moment. "My pleasure if it means showing up a Blood Skull." She nodded at the Mmoatia with red-painted faces. "Think because they ride sasabonsam that they run everything. Well, times are changing."

Abeni didn't know what any of that meant. "Why is he staring at me like that?" She glanced to the Mmoatia who still glared angrily.

"Oh, that's Shoma. Says you hit him with a stick?"

Abeni remembered swatting him with her staff. "I didn't recognize him. You all look alike." She regretted her words immediately.

Nula shrugged. "You humans all look the same to me. Besides, it's the Gold Weaver that has their ears twitching."

Abeni looked back to Ama. "Why?"

Nula hesitated. "It's complicated."

"Can you tell me where we are?"

"You're in Ile-kun. The Glowing City of the Blunt Nose Clan of the Mowakaii Mmoatia."

Once again, Abeni wasn't certain what most of that meant. But she nodded anyway.

"May I ask, why aren't your teeth sharp—like his." She glanced again to Shoma.

Nula gave her a confused look. "I'm no Blood Skull raider. I wouldn't file my teeth any more than I'd paint my face red."

That left Abeni momentarily speechless, so that she didn't even notice when they passed through a door and stepped outside. She gasped, in part from the cool wind that washed over her—sending up goose bumps on her bare skin. But it was what she stared out upon that left her jaw hanging.

"Welcome to Ile-kun," Nula said, with pride. "The Glowing City."

That it was. Abeni had gotten glimpses as they flew. But that was nothing compared to seeing the city up close. There were those conical buildings she'd seen before, made from white stone. They joined other structures, some that looked formed from the mountain. And it all glowed! There was light everywhere: covering buildings, hanging from bridges and walkways, even lining the streets. All of it looked to come from glowing mushrooms—bunched in large clumps, pruned individually, or growing to cover roofs and walls. They came in hues of white, blue, red, and more. Some changed colors or flickered on and off. It made the city seem like a living thing, made up of light.

"How could anyone have built a city so grand way up here?" Ama asked in wonder.

"It's amazing," Abeni agreed.

"You haven't even seen the heated cavern pools," Nula boasted.

"Ooooh, pools!" Nyomi exclaimed. "I like pools!"

They walked out into the city to find it bustling with Mmoatia. Most were dressed in gray robes, with different colors tinging the ends. They went about tasks that seemed familiar enough: sweeping streets, hauling goods, tending crops, caring for infants. Two Mmoatia women stood talking at what Abeni took for a market, smoking long pipes while haggling over goods. Only a few had the red-painted faces and were dressed in all-black—the Blood Skulls whom Abeni now understood to be the actual bat riders. They swaggered with importance, and other Mmoatia stepped aside or bowed to them. From above came high-pitched barks as giant bats flapped and soared through the air—with riders atop their backs. They moved like acrobats, spinning and flipping at great speeds.

Something struck Abeni.

"Why are people out so late?" she asked. "Shouldn't they be asleep by now?"

Nula regarded her oddly. "Daytime is for sleeping. Night is for doing."

Abeni blinked in surprise. Then she understood. Everything about the Mmoatia—their red eyes, their pale gray skin— seemed suited for night. How very different the world must be to them.

A noise caught her attention. She looked to find a Mmoatia—a Blood Skull—standing on a platform in an open area, speaking loudly. More Mmoatia stood about him. Some cheered and raised their fists in agreement. Most just listened. They were too far away for Abeni to make out words. But as she watched, the speaker pulled out something, waving it about: a crimson cloth with an upside-down orange flame. Her heart caught in her throat. The standard of the Witch Priest!

Asha had once told her the Witch Priest called various people and creatures to his armies. The Mmoatia were among them.

Just then, she noticed more commotion. Another group was approaching, chanting as they came. None of these were Blood Skulls, but they also carried the Witch Priest's standard. Suddenly, the second group's standard burst into flames as they shouted in approval. They were burning it! In moments, everything was confusion—as the two groups began arguing and jeering at one another.

"You've arrived during troubled times," Nula muttered.

New shouts sounded. Abeni turned to find Mmoatia looking their way. Some gaped in surprise. Others stared curiously. A few, however, scowled angrily. Their red eyes especially fixed on . . . Ama.

"Come," Nula urged. "Let's get you off these streets."

They took a turn and walked briskly, crossing a bridge and not stopping until entering a building. There, they were herded into a room.

"Here we are," Vushu said. "You can remain here as guests for the time being. I would suggest you . . . not try to leave. Should you need anything, simply inquire." He gestured to two new Blood Skulls standing outside their door.

As he turned to leave, Nula lingered. She seemed to be contemplating something. Just as Vushu called impatiently for her, she leaned into Abeni, whispering. "Ask for me. It's the only way I can be here." And with that she was gone.

"You think those guards are to keep us safe or keep us in?" Zaneeya asked, once they were alone.

"Some of those Mmoatia didn't look at us very friendly," Nyomi said, eating mushrooms Abeni was certain were meant as lighting.

"Not us," Zaneeya said. "Her." She stared straight at Ama. "Why is that?"

The princess sat on a short chair that looked made for Mmoatia. She folded her arms, biting her lip in thought. At Zaneeya's question she started.

"How should I know how these savages think?"

Abeni said nothing. There was something going on here she couldn't quite place. She walked to where Asha sat, poking at glowing mushrooms. "Are you okay?"

The little girl nodded. It took a lot to ruffle her.

"You may not remember," Abeni said. "But you rescued me once from some Mmoatia. I thought they were demons, but you said they weren't. You even claimed some were pleasant—despite the whole people-eating thing." It was hard to look past that part. "You also said the Witch Priest was calling them to him. Tonight, I saw some of them raise his standard. But I also saw others burn it. What does that mean?"

Asha stopped her poking to look at Abeni, her long ivory locs framing a small brown face. "My brother is good at deceiving, playing on weakness and feelings. But in the end, those who follow him choose to do so. Not because they are born bad, or wrong. Not every human chooses to go over to him. Why wouldn't it be the same for Mmoatia?"

It made sense, Abeni thought. She was viewing all Mmoatia as the same. But how could any people all be the same?

"The Mmoatia girl asked me to call on her. I think she might want to help."

"We could use some," Asha said.

No denying that. Abeni told the others as much. Only Ama was reluctant. But even she agreed they didn't have many options. It took another two hours after Abeni put in the request for Nula to make an appearance. By that time some of them had dozed off, and Abeni was slipping away when the Mmoatia girl entered. A young Mmoatia boy was with her. He wore similar clothing and sported a strip of braided white hair from the front of his head to the nape of his neck. His red eyes took them all in.

"This is Tanka," Nula introduced. "He's with us."

Us, Abeni wondered? The two seated themselves, and everyone—awakened by now—sat in a semicircle around them.

"You saw the burning flag tonight?" Tanka asked. He grinned. "That was me!"

"Dangerous," Nula said, frowning. "You know how fanatical some Blood Skulls can be."

Tanka clicked his teeth. "They don't frighten me."

"That's the problem." Her eyes glanced to the door. "You're certain we're good in here?"

Tanka clicked his teeth again. "Gave them a jug of moon wine—a present, I said, for their hard work. They'll be in their cups for a while."

"Sounds like you went through a lot to come here," Zaneeya observed. "Why? What do you want?" The girl was blunt if nothing else.

The two young Mmoatia exchanged uncertain looks.

"I know you have no reason to trust us," Abeni said. "And we don't know who we can trust. But you must have wanted me to call you here for some reason?"

More silence.

Abeni sighed. This wouldn't do. She turned to Ama. "I'm going to tell them why we're in their forest."

The girl's eyes widened. "What? Why?"

"Because someone has to start talking."

Ama eyed the two Mmoatia—who eyed her back. "What if they work for . . . him?"

"I don't think so. But I won't go into detail." She looked to the two Mmoatia. "We're searching for relics we think are here. Maybe even in these mountains. They're called the Masks of Akani."

Nula shook her head. "I've never heard of these . . . Masks of Akani. I'm certain there's nothing like that in Ile-kun. Our Blood Skulls probably picked you up because they thought you were looking for our city."

"We didn't even know there was a city here," Abeni said.

Nula nodded. Hesitantly, she began to speak. "I told you before these were troubled times. Our city is divided. Our people are at each other's throats. Even the council meetings aren't free from rancor." She looked abashed. "This is not how Mmoatia behave. At least it wasn't, until . . . him."

Abeni didn't need to ask who that was. "I thought all Mmoatia followed him."

"Some," Nula admitted. "Whole clans have gone over to him. Too many. But not all. Not Ile-kun."

"He came to us," Tanka said. "Promised us power, new hunting lands, to join him."

"But you haven't?" Abeni asked.

"Not yet," Nula said. "The decision is what's tearing our city apart. Many were receptive to his offer. Among the Blood Skulls especially, there is an older guard, who have been seduced by his words. They speak of a long-ago time when we supposedly ruled much of this forest and beyond. And claim to want to make the Mmoatia strong again. He has promised to grant the Blood Skulls some foul magic that will allow them to do . . . unnatural things." She spoke this last bit with a grimace.

"Not all of us think that way," Tanka put in. "We don't believe there was ever any such time long ago. Even if there was, we don't want it. We want Ile-kun to be free from ties to him! We shouldn't be whipped along by Face-stealers!"

Abeni frowned. Face-stealers?

"Some who agree with us have called for Ile-kun to stand neutral," Nula went on. "To turn away his gifts and stand apart from the strife now engulfing the world. Others of us . . ."

She trailed off and Abeni understood. "You want to be more than neutral."

"We want to fight back!" Tanka said fiercely, his red eyes wide. "Ally with those who stand against him—the humans and spirits we hear are massing in the west! We want Ile-kun to stand with them when the battle comes!"

Nula made a calming gesture to him. "That may be getting ahead of ourselves. We haven't won the battle *here* yet. But Tanka speaks the truth of it. That's why I wanted to talk. Perhaps you can help us."

"How?" Abeni asked in surprise.

"Get word to the outside!" Tanka said. "The Blood Skulls are the face of Ile-kun to the world. But they must know there are more to us. That some of us will join the fight against him!"

"And," Nula added, "we need her to talk to her people."

Everyone followed the Mmoatia girl's eyes to Ama. The princess had sat by quietly, not asking for a translation. But as their gazes shifted to her, she frowned.

"What? Why are you all looking at me?"

Abeni didn't answer, instead turning to Nula.

"When I asked why your people disliked Ama, you said it was complicated. How?"

Nula grimaced. "We and the Gold Weavers have a history. I

don't understand it all, really. Something about an agreement that was broken."

Abeni translated for Ama, who returned a look of bewilderment. "I don't know anything about that. Why would we have an agreement with . . . them?" Abeni repeated this to Nula.

"It was very long ago," the Mmoatia girl admitted. "Perhaps before her Gold Kingdom. All I know is that after the agreement was broken our peoples went their separate ways. But we had an understanding. This forest was our domain, not to be set upon." Nula frowned. "Now they've broken that agreement too, pushing into the forest, encroaching on our hunting lands."

Tanka grunted in frustration. "It's playing right into the hands of thickheaded Blood Skulls. They say we must join with *him* against the human invaders." He gestured to Ama. "We need her to talk to her people. Get them to stop! Or they'll push Ile-kun right into his hands!"

Abeni turned to the princess, translating for Nula and Tanka. "Is that true? Are your people in this forest?"

Ama hesitated, then straightened. "I'm not at liberty to say," she responded stiffly.

Zaneeya growled. "What does that mean?"

"They're looking for gold." It was Nyomi. The princess made a face like someone who had been found out. The porcupine girl shrugged. "It's all they ever do."

Abeni turned back to the two Mmoatia, sharing what they'd learned.

"Gold," Nula said. "That's why they tear up the land, cutting off whole rivers, making it so that animals can no longer live there." She shook her head. "Are all humans so greedy?"

Abeni wanted to tell her no. But she wasn't sure that was true.

"Your people need to stop," she told Ama. "Or they're going to push this city right towards the Witch Priest."

"We need that gold," the princess insisted. "This forest is filled with it!"

"If you do, you're going to start a war," Abeni said.

"We can defend ourselves!" Ama shot back.

"You really want a hundred bat riders making a night raid on your shiny city?" Zaneeya asked.

Ama opened her mouth to rebut but looked shaken. She stared at Nula, then back at them. "Even if I wanted to stop it, what makes you think I could?"

"You're a princess," Abeni said plainly.

That made her go quiet. Abeni turned to Nula and Tanka.

"I don't know if her people will listen," she said. "But they can at least be told. And we were heading to the west . . . eventually. We can let them know about your city. That there are people here who would stand with them."

The two Mmoatia smiled at this news.

"That's all fine and good," Zaneeya said. "But how are we going to do all of this kept here as your . . . guests?"

Nula shook her head. "You can't stay. The Blood Skulls plan to use your presence before the council as evidence for accepting the Witch Priest's offer. The sooner you're gone, the better. That's the other reason we're here."

Tanka grinned, leaning forward. "We're going to break you out!"

CHAPTER TEN

SANCTUARY

B ut this isn't even half of it!"

Abeni listened as Ama fussed over her things—or at least, what Nula and Tanka had managed to bring. The two had left and returned with their belongings. For Abeni, her staff, wide-brimmed wooden hat, and, thankfully, the big bag. Songu's flute too. Mmoatia, it turned out, loved music. Nyomi and Zaneeya didn't carry anything. But Ama had brought an assortment of items—pots and plates, numerous dresses, even a bathing robe and slippers—most of which were not here.

Abeni translated for Nula and Tanka. The pair looked surprised that had all been for one person!

"We took only what we could carry," Tanka explained. "It'll be hard enough escaping here with all of you—much less all those things. That chest alone was very heavy!"

Zaneeya grunted. "Tell me about it."

An outraged Ama insisted they go back—that all her things could fit into Abeni's bag. The girl wasn't wrong. The bag would open wide enough to fit anything. And it wouldn't be any heavier. But having to drag out an entire chest each time Ama wanted to change clothes? No thanks!

"This is all we we're taking," Abeni told her. "I'll store your food. But you should carry your own clothes if you want to get to them easier."

Ama glared. "And if I order you to do it?"

"You mean force me," Abeni said. She was getting tired of the girl's threats. "If that's what you need to do . . ."

Ama lifted an arm, refitted with a gold band. But for some reason she glanced to Asha. The little girl said nothing. Yet Ama lowered her arm and stalked off. Abeni looked to Asha, puzzled. What was that about?

"Is everything okay?" Nula asked with concern. "The way you all behave with her is . . . different . . . from how you behave with each other."

Abeni sighed. "It's complicated."

The Mmoatia girl seemed to accept this and offered up a bundle of gray robes. "For each of you. There are hoods. Keep them up and we might pass you off as Mmoatia." She stopped to look up at Ama. "This one might have to hunch low." Her eyes went even higher for Zaneeya. "You, may prove a problem."

Abeni slid into her robe. The panther girl was the tallest of them—far taller than any Mmoatia.

Zaneeya turned to Ama. "Let me shift."

The princess folded her arms. "Why would I do that?"

"Because I can get out of here easier. Blend into the shadows and never be seen."

"Or run off," Ama replied.

Zaneeya shrugged. "A chance you'll have to take."

Nula and Tanka made impatient noises, darting glances to the door. Ama scowled but swept her arms in an intricate gesture. Zaneeya's eyes popped, and she smiled slightly. In a blur, she shifted. The two Mmoatia gasped as a medium-sized panther the color of night appeared before them.

"That'll work," Nula said, impressed. She turned to the door. "Let's go."

"What about the guards?" Abeni asked.

A smiling Tanka opened their doors. The two guards sat slumped on the floor—cups of wine still in their hands. "A little sleeping powder did the trick nicely," he said.

Abeni recalled the white powder sprayed in their faces. Sleeping powder. She wondered if she could get ahold of some of that.

"Come on!" Nula urged.

They were taken to stairs that led not out, but up. Zaneeya slipped between them, trotting ahead. At the top of the stairs was a door. Nula pushed it open, revealing the outside. They were atop the conical building and on a long narrow path that connected it to another in the distance. A bridge, Abeni realized. They walked its stone surface, and she peered down at the city below in surprise. They were up so high! Reaching the middle of the bridge, they stopped.

"We're to wait here for our contacts," Nula said, peering about. "They'll get us out."

"Are there many of you?" Abeni asked. "Who want to fight the Witch Priest?"

"More than most suspect," the Mmoatia girl answered fiercely. "Most are young like us. We want to see our society improve for the better. Lots of the older generation are too stuck in their ways, wary of change." There was a pause. "Just so you know, we've talked about refining our policies on people-eating."

"Umm," Abeni said. "That's good?"

"We have a saying." Tanka grinned. "Don't trust anyone over sixty-five!"

Abeni frowned. Sixty-five? They looked Ama's age. "How old exactly are you two?"

"I just turned fifty," Nula said. "Tanka is forty-eight."

"Forty-nine," he corrected. "Well, in a few weeks."

Of course, Abeni thought, shaking her head in wonder when Zaneeya growled, her ears perking as she stared out in the distance. Abeni followed her gaze to see several dark shapes soaring towards them.

"Sasabonsam!" she said, pointing in alarm.

Nula smiled wide. "Our ride out of here!"

Abeni watched the giant bats grow larger as they approached.

Three in all. They reached them in moments, those leathery wings buffeting everyone in gusts of wind. With a gentleness that seemed unnatural for their size, they landed easily, black claws gripping the stone railing. On their backs, three Mmoatia peered down from behind red-painted faces. Abeni inhaled sharply. Blood Skulls!

"Don't be fearful," Tanka said, reading her look. "They're with us."

That was a surprise. "I thought you said Blood Skulls wanted to join the Witch Priest."

"Many, yes," Tanka agreed. "But there are dissenters."

A sudden deep ringing like a very big bell sounded around them. The sasabonsam let out short cries, shaking their heads as their ears twitched. Their riders made clicking sounds, trying to soothe them.

"The alarm!" Tanka said, his red eyes wide. "Someone must have found the guards!"

"We must go!" one of the riders said. "Now!"

In the distance, Abeni saw new dark shapes flying towards them.

"Get on! Get on!" Nula urged, climbing up onto the closest bat. Tanka took another.

It was a scramble for the rest of them, Abeni pulling herself and Asha up until they were in a seat behind Nula and their rider. Nyomi and Songu took the bat with Tanka, which left the last for Ama and Zaneeya. The panther girl had shifted back to girl form, and she and the Gold Weaver glared at each other. Abeni glanced at the approaching shapes, closing in fast.

"Both of you get on, now!" she shouted in a commanding voice—thinking of her mother.

The two actually jumped and climbed aboard. Maybe she should use that voice more often. Without warning, the bats sprang from the railing. There was a lurching drop that pulled at Abeni's middle before the creatures righted themselves and soared into the night. They swerved around buildings and dove beneath bridges, only to rise again, before falling. Abeni fought hard not to empty her stomach. Asha whooped in excitement.

Their rider glanced back and said something to Nula.

"We're about to have company!" the Mmoatia girl shouted.

Something streaked past them. Was that an arrow?

"They're shooting at us!" Abeni exclaimed.

"Just a warning!" Nula assured.

Abeni turned to see two bats racing in their direction. In moments both were right beside them. She recognized one of the Blood Skulls—Shoma, whom she'd struck with her staff. He glared at Nula, then shouted at their rider. Behind him, another Blood Skull was swinging a rope. The rider on the other side of them was doing the same. She had a terrible vision of those ropes catching and yanking her into the darkness!

A sudden shriek came from their pursuers. One of the bats. The gold hoop in its nose was being pulled by some unseen force. It jerked its head wildly, spinning out of control. She looked to see a figure on another bat, her arms extended and bearing those unmistakable gold bands. Ama!

"No!" Nula cried, as the sasabonsam spiraled downward. Abeni watched in horror as rider and mount looked set to crash into the city below. Miraculously, the bat suddenly came out of its dive, flapping back up—but no longer pursuing.

The distraction proved to be what they needed. The three fleeing bats pulled ahead of Shoma and the other Blood Skulls. They sped across the city and Abeni noticed that the lights below were becoming fewer. Soon even those were sparse—and they flew out into utter darkness. She realized in surprise that they had left the mountain city and were now above the forest. Looking back, she wondered if their pursuers had given up. But she made them out, keeping a steady pace and gaining again.

"Just a little farther!" Nula shouted against the whipping wind.

It was then that she saw the dark shape looming ahead—a second mountain. New lights appeared. They were far fewer—paling in comparison to Ile-kun. But she could trace the outlines of a small conical structure cut into the mountain's surface. They had gotten very near when a large shape unexpectedly flew into their path. Their mount pulled up short, flapping its wings furiously.

Abeni gaped open-mouthed. It was another bat. Far larger than any she'd seen. Its massive black wings covered them in shadow like a second night, beating with a slow and powerful rhythm. Woosh! Woosh! Woosh! The creature had thick fur that reminded her of yellow-golden straw. But curiously, no gold hoops fit into its nose or ears. Its eyes were most distinctive: two white orbs that stared out with a luminous glow, peering at them with a lazy interest. Dark straps crisscrossed its chest and she soon made out a figure on its back. Another Mmoatia, dressed in all-white robes.

"Greetings, brethren!" he called loudly above his bat's beating wings. His face was hidden by a cowl, but Abeni could feel those eyes take her in. "And guests, it would appear. Not food."

"Greetings, Healer!" Nula said hurriedly. "We request sanctuary! For our guests!"

The white-robed figure cocked his head. "Not you, sister?"

"No, Healer. We know the law. Any Mmoatia who requests sanctuary must remain with you for a year and a day."

"You could find calm and wisdom in that time," the Healer suggested.

Nula shook her head. "We may. But matters await back in Ile-kun."

"The City of Light remains ever busy."

The Healer's eyes drifted up, and Abeni turned to see Shoma and their pursuers swooping down, stopping short of them. The Blood Skull glared, his red eyes narrowing at her before finding Nula. "You will return at once—all of you. And face punishment for the crimes committed this night!"

"We haven't committed any crimes!" Tanka shot back.

"You aided these prisoners in their escape!" Shoma accused.

"Guests," Nula corrected, her tone even. "Old Vushu said so himself."

"He ordered them confined!"

"For their safety," Nula countered. "We merely . . . provided escort."

Shoma ground his sharp teeth. "You think that will protect you?"

"The law is the law," Nula said, sitting straighter. She turned to the white-robed figure. "Healer. I ask again that you grant these guests sanctuary." There was silence as he appeared to contemplate her request.

"Healer," Shoma said warningly. "Stay out of this. What happens in Ile-kun—"

"This is not Ile-kun, Shoma," the Healer cut in. He pulled back his cowl to reveal an older Mmoatia, with a long scar running from one eye to his jaw.

Shoma bowed. "Wing Commander Osha."

"Not my title any longer," the white-robed figure said. "I am Healer Osha now." He turned to Nula. "Your guests are granted sanctuary, for as long as they wish."

Nula released a held breath before flashing Abeni a smile.

"We could just come in there," Shoma said in threat. "And take them."

"You won't," Healer Osha said, unbothered. "You can be thick-skulled at times, Shoma, but you respect the law. Go home. The raid for you is done this night."

The Blood Skull looked on the verge of a retort. But he instead turned his sasabonsam, sparing a last glare for Abeni before flying away.

"This way," the Healer beckoned. He turned his gigantic bat around, heading towards the mountain. They flew to the conical building. It was much like the ones Abeni had seen in Ile-kun. Its surface was covered in glowing mushrooms; more lined a set of stone steps. All four bats landed and they climbed down to stand before the structure.

"The Blood Skulls can't touch you here," Nula said, walking up the steps with Asha, who held her hand. "The Healers will grant you passage to continue your quest."

"Thank you," Abeni said, following. "We'll do our best to fulfill what you asked."

"It was fun visiting your city," Asha said happily. "Very bright!"

Nula smiled. "You should see it again one day. Under friendlier circumstances." She paused, staring at Asha. "You know, there is something about you . . ."

"You were saying we should visit again," Abeni cut in quickly. "Maybe I might."

Nula turned to Abeni. "That would be nice. Ask the Healers about these Masks of Akani you seek. They . . . know things."

With that, she and Tanka said farewell, climbing back atop the bats, who launched themselves into the night.

Abeni and the others moved towards the conical structure. It looked lonely out here, just one building in all this wilderness. There was a single door, which the Healer opened, gesturing them inside.

"I'll go first," Zaneeya said, shifting into a panther.

The Healer appeared unruffled at the sight and stood waiting patiently. Abeni and the others followed, entering through the door behind the panther girl. Abeni found herself in a dark narrow passage lit only by a few sparse mushrooms. They waited for the Healer, who now took the lead.

"Thank you for taking us in," Abeni told him.

He nodded. "We grant sanctuary to most who ask."

"Are you from Ile-kun?"

"Yes. But we receive others from different cities and clans."

Abeni thought on something she'd heard. "Shoma called you a commander. Are you a Blood Skull, then?"

The Healer chuckled. "I was once. In a past life. Though I still have the teeth." He turned to flash her a sharp smile that glinted yellow in the faint mushroom light.

Abeni tried not to jump. "Are all the other Healers here . . . former Blood Skulls?"

"Not all. Some were artisans or farmers. Others musicians or cooks or teachers." He paused. "But a fair number of us were once Blood Skulls. The Sanctuary offers us . . . tranquility."

They continued walking. Once more, Abeni realized that everything she thought she knew about these Mmoatia was wrong. Asha was right. People were complicated, no matter who they were.

"You've arrived at our harvest," Healer Osha went on. "That's why I was the only one to greet you. The others are all busied with work."

"You grow things in here?" Abeni said, looking at the narrow passage, confused.

"Mostly fruit. We are vegetarians—as are the sasabonsam we dwell with."

Fruit? Those humongous creatures ate only fruit? "They're much bigger than the others," Abeni noted. "Where do you keep them?"

"In here with us. And they are not kept. We care for each other."

Her eyebrows rose in surprise. "You live in here? With your bats? But it's so . . . small."

"Once more," the Healer said, "they are not ours. The sasabonsam have their own minds. In fact, this is their home. They have chosen to allow us to stay. And I assure you, there is room here for everyone."

There was suddenly a light ahead that grew brighter as they approached. The passage was coming to an end. As Abeni watched, Zaneeya seemed to disappear, lost in the light. Then Healer Osha seemed to vanish. She followed both, shielding her eyes as she stepped through another doorway. She blinked to see properly again and gaped in disbelief.

It was like a giant had carved out the inside of the mountain, leaving behind a vast open cavern. The ceiling was hard to make out, much of it covered by long thick twisting green vines that fell like long locs of hair. Bright glowing fruit hung between broad green leaves, each large enough for two people to carry. Across the bottom of the cavern there were more conical structures. They were smaller than the ones in Ile-kun, but numerous—many carved from the very rock. There were Mmoatia everywhere, all in white robes and going about on numerous tasks. Some hung by straps from the vines, plucking the large fruit that they lowered into wide carts. And there were bats. Lots of bats! Gigantic bats that soared in the air, moving through the long vines with ease—sometimes stopping to snatch up glowing fruit. Others clung to the foliage, nibbling contently. Abeni stood in awe. She wondered if the fruit was what made the bats' eyes glow? She was staring so intently that she didn't notice when more Mmoatia walked up.

"They will take you to where you can refresh yourselves," Healer Osha said. "I'll let you rest before joining you." He leaned close. "Please indulge them. We don't get many guests and we are Healers, after all." The other Mmoatia eyed them eagerly, practically bouncing on their feet. Zaneeya's ears lay back, hesitant. Abeni felt the same. Indulge them?

○ ○ ○

Sometime later, Abeni found herself reclined in a chair wrapped in long robes as a Healer rubbed her shoulders. Across from her, Nyomi sighed in contentment, leaning forward as two Healers applied oil between each of her quills. Zaneeya was submerged in a warm pool, only her head visible, with her eyes half-closed.

When Healer Osha said to indulge them, she hadn't expected this. They'd been taken to a room in one of the conical buildings and put through a series of tests. Abeni had stuck out her tongue, coughed, run in place, and more. She'd been poked and prodded and made to drink awful-tasting liquids. The Healers finally declared her to be in good health, and then came the best part. She'd been shown to a hot bath, had her hair washed, her feet rubbed, and her face briefly covered in warm mud that left it clean and tingly after. They might have braided her hair, if Songu hadn't insisted that was his job.

"Un . . . be . . . liev . . . a . . . ble!" Ama said, her voice trembling like a bleating goat. The princess lay on her stomach, as a Healer methodically chopped at her back with his hands.

"You okay, Asha?" Abeni called.

The small girl leaned back as a Healer twisted and oiled her freshly washed ivory locs. She turned to show eyes covered by round slices of some green fruit. "Wonderful!" she said.

Abeni sat back again, inhaling the sweet and pungent scents that came from a bowl of heated oil. She could get used to this. The door to the room opened about then to admit Healer Osha. He looked over everyone with an amused smile on his grizzled face.

"I hope your stay with us is restful," he said.

Nyomi gave a thumbs-up. "Best sanctuary ever!"

He chuckled. "My brothers and sisters feared their skills might grow rusty with no one to practice on. Thank you for allowing them to do the work they love. Please join us for dinner at dawn. Before that, I thought we might discuss the coming days. We have other services you might enjoy. There's a steaming chamber, hot cave springs, and Healer Tia has been perfecting a new treatment where he wraps you completely in well-oiled banana leaves—highly recommended!"

Healer Tia, who was washing a mud mask from Songu's face, looked up eagerly.

"Oh, and there's moon dancing," Healer Osha finished.

Nyomi squealed.

Abeni couldn't believe it was almost dawn. Had they really been up all night?

"Thank you, Healer Osha. But we'll have to be going soon."

Nyomi whined in disappointment.

"We're on a quest," Abeni continued.

The Healer's eyes brightened. "A quest? How exciting!"

"We wondered if you might be able to help. Nula said that Healers . . . know things?"

Healer Osha arched an eyebrow. "Among Mmoatia, Healers are also great keepers of wisdom. What better way to strengthen the mind than to keep it fed with knowledge? Tell me, what is it your quest seeks that brought you into the forest?"

Abeni hesitated, glancing to Ama, who was still engrossed in her healing.

The Healer seemed to read her face. "Share only what you're comfortable with."

"We're looking for something called the Masks of Akani," she said.

Both his eyebrows rose this time. "That is a name unspoken in some time."

Abeni sat up. "So you know them? The Masks of Akani? Can you tell us where they are?" Ama was looking up now as well. The princess couldn't understand them—she still wouldn't eat the mushroom. But she had heard the word Akani, and now looked between Abeni and the Healer with curiosity.

Healer Osha regarded them for a moment before nodding. "I know of the Masks of Akani. And I can tell you where to find them. But . . . I think you should all see something first. Come with me."

It took a while to get ready. The other Healers were disappointed at having to end their work. But they finished quickly. It was only when Asha's last loc had been twisted that they set out, still wrapped in white robes. Healer Osha led them through the vast cavern. As they passed, one of the gigantic bats swooped down, landing nimbly just feet away. Healer Osha greeted the creature, running a hand over its straw-colored fur. Abeni recognized it as the same bat he had ridden on earlier.

"How did it get in here?" she asked.

"She," Healer Osha corrected. The bat flew up again in a powerful gust of wind, using hooked fingers on her wings to cling to the hanging vines. He watched her bite into some fruit before leading them on again. "The sasabonsam have dwelled here for a long time—much longer than us. They have many entrances they squeeze themselves in and out of, some of which we likely don't know about."

They walked a set of steps carved into the rock that weaved about the cavern. There were passages cut into the stone that reminded Abeni uncomfortably of the mines in Makomasi. They finally arrived at another door and Healer Osha ushered them inside. It was a room filled with small holes cut into the rock like shelves. Most were filled with items: gourds, boxes, pouches and more. Several Mmoatia worked within the room. Healer Osha spoke to a very old Mmoatia with white hair coming out of his nose and ears. He lifted a frail hand and beckoned some other Healers over.

"What are they saying?" Ama asked, coming closer.

"I can't make it out," Abeni answered truthfully.

"This room," the princess said. "It's a repository."

"A what?"

"A repository," Ama repeated. "We have them in Makomasi. A place we keep important things—passed down artifacts, sacred relics, and the like."

As they watched, one of the Healers came forward with a brown pouch. He handed it to Healer Osha, who beckoned them on. They were led to a room with a table and several chairs. The Healer sat down and invited them all to do the same.

"You asked if I know about the Masks of Akani," he said. Undoing the string on the pouch, he turned it upside down and emptied its contents onto the table. Abeni eyed them quizzically. They were small gold objects, cut into various shapes: a circle with triangular ridges, an intricately carved scorpion, a turtle with a shell of swirling patterns, and a square box engraved with familiar symbols—like the ones from the Gold Kingdom. Ama noticed as well. Her hand went to the necklace of gold orbs she wore, each bearing similar symbols.

"Where did you get these?" she asked sharply. She turned to Abeni. "Ask him where—"

"You can ask me yourself," Healer Osha cut in.

Everyone looked to him in surprise. He had just spoken the language of the Gold Kingdom!

"You know my tongue?" Ama exclaimed.

The healer smirked. He'd been waiting to do that, Abeni thought. "Something far older. But close enough. You recognize these?" He gestured at the small carvings.

Ama nodded. "They're weights, from the First Gold Kingdom. Used to measure gold for trade. We don't use them anymore and only a few have passed down to us. They're highly valued. This set alone is probably worth more than the wealthiest families in Makomasi!" Her eyes narrowed. "How did you come by these?"

Healer Osha snorted. "You think we must have stolen them, Princess? Yes, I know your title. You carry the symbols of royalty." He motioned to her necklace and forearm bands. "You also carry their attitudes." That made Zaneeya snicker. "As for how we came by these, they were payment from a people who no longer had much to give."

Ama frowned. "Payment for what?"

"Why for helping secrete away the Masks of Akani, of course." That left the princess speechless.

"Not payment to me, of course," the healer went on. "I'm not quite *that* old. But the Sanctuary is. The Healers of that day rendered aid to your people—your ancestors, to be precise. I take it, Princess, that you know none of this?"

Ama shook her head. She looked completely lost.

Healer Osha nodded. "Then let me explain. Long ago, your people and the Mmoatia co-existed. We each held our own separate villages and cities and kingdoms. But we also traded. And worked together. Some of your people even chose to live among my people and learn our ways."

"Why would my people want to—" Ama began, but Abeni cut her off with a raised hand.

"Back then," Healer Osha continued, "Mmoatia still considered this forest our domain. But exceptions were made to allow your people passage, so they could easily reach other human settlements. Spirits visited as well. Both our peoples learned from them and gave offerings. It was a very different time than we know now."

Abeni looked to Asha. The small girl had known about the Masks of Akani and where they might be found. Had she perhaps visited this place in one of her other lives?

"What happened to end all of that?" Abeni asked.

Healer Osha twitched an ear. "We don't know exactly. Our histories are passed down from Healer to Healer, in spoken words. Each of us learns them, adds to them, and passes the new histories down in turn." *Like my song,* Abeni thought in wonder. "But the history of that time is incoherent. Whatever took place to end the kingdom of humans troubled us as well."

"Bida brought the end," Ama said bitterly. "The dragon grew jealous of what we could do—and destroyed our people, breaking and scattering us. The Gold Kingdom is all that survives now. This history we know well. It is painted in gold on the very walls of the palace in Makomasi." Abeni remembered seeing it as the Queen Mothers told this tale—a painting that moved.

There was an awkward quiet from Healer Osha. "I know the history your people pass down, Princess. Of Bida's decimation and defeat by the hero with the magic sword. But . . . there is nothing like that in our histories. All we have there, oddly enough, is a story. It tells of a farmer who had a wondrous hen that laid eggs of gold. Each day, the hen laid one golden egg, and over time the man grew rich, becoming a king. But he wanted more wealth. He begged the hen to produce more eggs, but it only laid one a day. His people began to say the hen was making a fool of him. In anger, he cut off the hen's head—believing he would find more eggs within."

"Did he?" Nyomi asked, her black eyes wide. "Find more eggs?"

The Healer snorted. "Of course not."

"Then there were no more eggs," the porcupine girl said, puzzled. "That wasn't wise."

"Which is why among Mmoatia the story is called The Fortunate Farmer Who Was Also a Fool. It is a proverb that warns against making unwise choices."

"What does that have to do with how the First Gold Kingdom ended?" Ama asked.

Healer Osha spread his hands. "I can't say. I only know it is a story told of those times."

"Well, you said it yourself," Ama countered. "Your histories are incomplete. Not ours."

Abeni wasn't certain how this related either. "What about the Masks of Akani?"

"Yes," Healer Osha said. "I've let my mind wander. In our histories, the Masks of Akani were constructed by the humans of this land in their last days. A way to preserve the wisdom their people had gathered, knowing the end was near. Why they came to the Sanctuary to safeguard the masks, our histories do not say. But I know we did not turn them away."

"Then you know where they are," Ama said, both eager and impatient.

"Yes. We know. And we can take you there." His face turned serious, those red eyes seeming to burn. "However, you should be warned, the way is dangerous. The ones who made the masks placed magic around them, to protect their wisdom. But something went wrong. The *magic* went wrong. There is a darkness there now. A darkness that devours."

"Devouring darkness?" Nyomi whimpered. "That doesn't sound good."

"Why we stay clear of that place," the Healer said. "Besides, the masks are useless to us."

"Useless?" Abeni asked. "I'd think you'd want their wisdom—for your Sanctuary."

Healer Osha smiled. "Those who constructed the masks may have sought our aid to house them, but they did not grant us their use. You see, the Masks of Akani will answer any question you ask—one question, to any seeker. But you must be human. It will not work for any Mmoatia. Or spirit, for that matter."

"Only humans?" Zaneeya asked. "How is that fair?"

The Healer shrugged. "Mmoatia live for a few centuries. I have counted two hundred and fifty years and expect to see fifty more. You spirits live so long you may as well be immortal. Some, perhaps, *are* immortal." His glance flickered to Asha, and Abeni's heart leapt. But he looked away just as quick. "Humans, however, have lives as brief as a weak flame, taking their wisdom with them when it snuffs out. Perhaps in constructing the masks, their makers sought an advantage over that unfairness."

Zaneeya grunted. Abeni, however, couldn't help but feel that this was perhaps the first time she felt as if she held something over the others—with their powers and long lives.

"We want to go there!" Ama said. "At once!" She paused, realizing how she must sound. "Please, I mean."

Healer Osha smiled. "You can't find the masks in daylight. We were the ones who granted it sanctuary, after all. The soonest you can see it is when the moon next rises. In the meantime, you should eat and rest." His face turned grave. "You will need both for what lies ahead."

CHAPTER ELEVEN

DARK WATERS

Abeni looked out at a lake nestled between hills that seemed part of the three mountains. The last rays of sunlight touched its surface, making the blue waters shimmer like gold. She had not seen many lakes in her time. Rivers, she knew. There had been one near her own village. But even she could see that something here was off.

"No animals," Zaneeya said, walking up. "No birds, no creatures drinking. Nothing."

Yes, that was it. The river near Abeni's home had been full of life—birds and different animals that came to bathe or water. By now as the sun set you should hear insects chirping and frogs beginning to croak. This lake had none of that. It was quiet, empty, and still. And after what she had heard of this place she did not like that one bit.

The Healers had flown them here just before dusk—the earliest the sasabonsam would venture out. They couldn't have come any earlier anyway. Healer Osha was right about them needing rest. They'd all slept through nearly the whole day, not waking until late afternoon. Abeni felt refreshed, if not eager for what they were about to do.

"I don't see anything," Ama said. She stood near the lake's edge, peering out.

"Healer Osha said we wouldn't see anything until the sun went down completely," Abeni reminded her. She glanced to the twilight sky. "And the moon was full in the night."

The princess turned to her. "You believe everything that Mmoatia says."

"You must believe some of it," Abeni replied. "Or you wouldn't be here."

Ama gave her a hard gaze and she met it back.

"I think after this is done," the girl said, "we're going to have to revisit the proper respect due someone of my standing." She made an intentional show of the gold bands on her forearms.

Abeni said nothing, turning to the lake. If the girl thought everyone was going to return to being bullied by her, she had another think coming. No one was certain what was going to happen once they found these Masks of Akani. But they would have to face their Ama problem before they moved on.

Asha came to stand beside her. Songu too. The little girl stared at the waters, troubled.

"Do you see something?" Abeni asked.

"No," Asha said. "But I feel it. Songu too. There's something bad here."

The boy signed to her. "I don't like it."

Abeni recalled the Healer's words—a darkness that devours.

"Is it . . . him?"

Asha shook her head. "There is bad in the world other than my brother. This is something else."

"Well, we've faced bad things before." Abeni paused. "I was thinking, these masks can answer any question. If we all get one, we humans, I mean, I could ask about . . . my family."

Asha looked up at her. "You mean, about the ghost ships and the Storm Women?"

Abeni nodded. It was still awkward bringing those things up. She knew the little spirit feared that once she knew those things she might leave. "Whatever they tell me, we're still going to get you to these elder spirits where you'll be safe. I made a promise." She looked to Songu. "You could ask the masks a question too."

He looked at her uncertainly. "But I can't talk," he signed.

"Yes, you can," she signed back. "And if the masks are stupid about it, I'll translate."

Songu smiled and surprised her by taking her hand. She looked at it but didn't let go.

They all stood and watched as the sun slowly vanished and the first stars twinkled to life. The moon had already begun to show early, and it hung large, low, full, and surprisingly red in the darkening sky.

"What do you suppose makes it that color?" Abeni wondered aloud.

"North of my country," Ama said, "there is a lake that turns pink—said to be caused by water spirits. Maybe those spirits have gathered on the moon."

Zaneeya snorted. "That's ridiculous."

"You know a better explanation?" Ama snapped.

"I do," the panther girl retorted. "The moon is a great ball being chased by a panther spirit. It turns red when the spirit catches and bites it. A Blood Moon."

Ama rolled her eyes. "That's gross. And doesn't make sense."

"Well, how would a bunch of river spirits get way up there?" Zaneeya countered.

The princess fumbled for an answer. The panther girl grinned.

"Hmm," Nyomi put in. "My father says the moon is just a big stone and borrows light from the sun. That's what makes it shine. Maybe it turns color when sunlight hits it different—like when you see a rainbow."

Both Ama and Zaneeya stared at the porcupine girl before bursting into laughter—then stopped, realizing they were agreeing.

"Something's happening!" Abeni said, shushing them.

Everyone looked out at the lake. Something was taking shape in its center, becoming firmer with each passing moment. It was a small island, Abeni realized in surprise, forming out of . . . nothing! But most amazing was what stood atop it. There were masks—three in all. Each was enormous, as tall as buildings she'd

see in Makomasi! They stood straight up like three sides of a tri-
angle, their carved faces visible by moonlight and looking out on
the waters.

"By the ancestors of my ancestors!" Ama whispered in awe.

"They're so big!" Nyomi exclaimed.

Zaneeya growled. "Were those things made by giants? I don't
like giants."

"I haven't seen any giants," Abeni assured. "What is it with you
and giants anyway?"

"Ask me that *after* you've met some giants."

"There's something wrong with the water," Asha said.

Everyone looked to the lake. Something *was* wrong with the
water. It looked darker and didn't move right.

"Look!" Ama pointed to something at the edge of the lake. A
boat. It sat on the rocky shore, half submerged in the water.

Abeni frowned. "That wasn't there before."

"Whole island just up and appears, and it's the boat that worries you?" Zaneeya asked.

"I think it's waiting for us!" Ama said and took off running.

"Wait!" Abeni called. "Let's talk about this first!"

She had started to give chase when there came a yelp of surprise. Abeni turned to see Zaneeya staggering back. The panther
girl tried moving forward again but bounced off something—like
she'd hit a wall. Growling, she struck the air with an open palm
and there was a loud SMACK! There *was* a wall! Only it couldn't
be seen! Nyomi walked up, poking the space.

"There's something here," she said. "I can't get past it."

"Because you're spirits," Abeni whispered. She hadn't expected
that rule about who could speak to the masks to be so . . . literal.
Walking up, she knelt before Asha, who placed a palm to the unseen wall.

"Be careful, Abeni."

"I will." She took her staff, satchel, and hat, passing them back
through the barrier. "Keep these for me. I'll be back."

"Wait!" It was Ama. "Why can't the little girl come?"

Abeni realized their mistake, trying to think of an answer. But it was too late. Ama's eyes rounded with comprehension.

"She's a spirit!" the princess whispered. "That explains so much!" Her gaze whipped to Abeni. "You kept this from me! Did any of the Ohemmaa know?"

"You'll have to ask them," Abeni answered tightly.

Ama looked between her and Asha. "When we get back, you're going to tell me everything." She tapped her gold bands. "Everything."

Abeni clenched her jaw. One more problem to deal with.

"What's wrong with him?" Ama asked. "Is he a spirit too?"

She was eyeing Songu, who stood with the others. The boy had a pained look on his face. Abeni was confused until he pressed a hand to the unseen wall, unable to go any further. As his haunted gaze met hers she understood. The Witch Priest. His magic had made Songu a monster. She'd been turned into one too. But not for so long. And she hadn't been made to do so much.

He signed to her.

"What's wrong with me? What am I?"

Something in her almost broke at his questions.

"Night's not getting any younger!" Ama called.

Abeni spared one last look at everyone before walking to join the princess. Ama waited, tapping her foot impatiently.

"So, it's just us girls?" the princess teased. "You keep strange company."

"They're my friends. Do you have any of those? Friends, I mean?"

Abeni didn't wait for a reply, turning instead to look over the boat. It was cut from dark wood, with narrow ends and a wide middle. Swirling patterns were engraved onto every inch. She peered inside to find two paddles with broad leaf-like blades.

Without speaking, they both took hold of the boat's sides and pushed it off the shore and into the lake. To Abeni's surprise her feet stayed dry, protected by the odd shoes woven of golden fabric. But when the water touched her shins, she gasped. It felt like dozens of needles prickling her—so cold it burned. She quickly jumped into the boat. Beside her, Ama did the same.

"The water!" the princess exclaimed, teeth chattering.

Abeni peered over the side, rubbing her shins. "That's not water."

The lake had been transformed. What had been water was now a goopy black sludge.

"Ugh!" Ama made a face. "That's disgusting."

"Better not go swimming in it, then," Abeni said. She grabbed a paddle. Ama said nothing, but did the same.

Rowing was harder than expected. The black water wasn't easy to push through. Abeni strained at the effort. Ama appeared to be having the same difficulty.

"That panther girl," she grunted, straining with the paddle. "We could have used her here. She's a strong one."

"More than you know," Abeni replied.

The princess regarded her, those golden eyes intent. "You think I'm harsh."

"You hurt her," Abeni said. "And the worst part is, I think you liked it."

Ama's face heated. "I hurt her so she would do what I want—what I need her to do. That doesn't mean I like it."

"Then why do you do it?"

"Because I must!" She stopped rowing, glaring now. "You think it's easy being in charge? People are fine giving responsibility but if anything goes wrong, I'm the one they'll blame!"

Abeni laughed.

Ama's eyes tightened. "What's so funny?"

"You!" She put on a mocking voice. "Oh, my life is so terrible. I'm only a princess! I eat gold for breakfast and splash around in a gold bathtub!"

"Pool," Ama corrected coldly.

Abeni rolled her eyes. "Well, I had to watch my village get destroyed. Zaneeya and Nyomi were separated from their families. Songu got turned into a monster! We were minding our own business when your people kidnapped us, put us to work in mines, and forced us on this quest! But you're the one complaining? You can't even see that what your people did was wrong!" Abeni found she was truly angry now. She glared back at the princess, whose golden eyes simmered.

"You think I don't know what we look like?" Ama snapped back. "Stealing people and forcing them to work our mines? I visited them once—it made me sick! This bargain with the Witch Priest only made it worse! I want it all to stop! I want things to be better!"

"Then why don't you make it better!" Abeni shouted.

"Because I'm not the ruler!" Ama shouted back. "Even if it should have been me—!" She stopped, as if she'd said more than she should have.

Abeni couldn't remember feeling this angry before. Her skin was hot, and her head pounded. Both had stopped rowing. Abeni opened her mouth to say more, but the girl raised a hand.

"Did you hear that?"

Abeni listened. She did hear something. Like whispering and laughter. Both girls looked out at the empty black lake. They were far from shore. But the island was still a ways off.

"We should keep going," Ama said.

Abeni nodded, looking out at the waters warily. They began paddling again. But the odd voices only grew, a raspy whispering and creaky laughter in their ears.

Little sweet things come to play. Come, come, little sweet things.

Ama grunted, shaking her head, as if that might make the voices go away.

Sweet, sweet, good to eat. Gobble you up little sweet things. Gobble you all up.

Came to us, came to us. Bright lights to devour, devour. Didn't pay the passage. Naughty. Naughty. So, we're going to eat up you little sweet things. Eat. You. All. Up.

Abeni looked around, her heart thumping as she tried to see where the voices were coming from. The water was moving, roiling enough to jostle the boat. Something suddenly seized her paddle, almost yanking it from her grip.

"Let go!" Ama cried, fighting to hold onto her own paddle. Something black and oozing clung to it. The water! It moved as if it was alive!

No sooner had Abeni had the thought than she saw a head emerge from the water. It looked like a person—a woman. Only she was made up completely of the black sludge: from her braided hair to her eyes, which glistened in the moonlight. She rose to her shoulders right in front of Abeni, her lips peeling back to show black shining teeth. Then she began to sing in a raspy, creaky voice.

Little things soft and meek, give us something sweet to eat.

Another head emerged, this one a man who grinned and sang.

Little things soft and meek, give us something sweet to eat.

The sound came from behind her, and Abeni whipped her head around to see more shapes rising from the water. In moments, there were six. Then ten. Now a dozen. All sang the same words. Not all at once, but different voices all fighting to be heard over the other.

Little things soft and meek, give us something sweet to eat.

"What are they?" Ama asked.

Abeni shivered. "Healer Osha said there was a darkness here. Some magic created to protect the masks that went wrong. This looks very wrong!"

"But what do they want?"

Abeni never got to answer. One of the shapes rose from the black waters right before her, singing its song—then it lunged! She only had time to raise her paddle, smacking the thing right in the face, sending it back into the lake. The other dark shapes drifted towards them through the waters. Hands gripped the sides of the boat, as they tried to haul themselves up. Abeni swung her paddle, pushing them off. But no sooner had she knocked one of the things down than another took its place. Some climbed over each other even as they fell, all trying to reach the two girls.

"They're going to swarm the boat!" Abeni yelled. Her eyes found the island with the masks—they were halfway there. "We have to get to the—"

Abeni's words cut off in a gasp as something cold seized her arm, that feeling of prickling needles biting her skin. It numbed her so that she could barely move. She looked to see a hand made up of that black ooze gripping and holding her tight.

Suddenly, dozens of those cold hands were on her, grabbing her arms, her legs, her shoulders. They pulled hard, and she pitched over the side of the boat. Endless prickling needles seemed to be biting at her entire body, as the black waters swallowed her.

Abeni felt like she was falling forever. There was a weight pushing her down. Forever down in the cold dark. All around her, hundreds of voices spoke at once.

Sweet, sweet. Tried to cross without paying passage. Naughty. Naughty. Gobble you up. Bright lights so shiny. Let us in. Let us in. Give us the lights. So, so, sweet. Want. Want. Want. Give me. Give me. Mine to have. Mine to keep. Mine. Mine. Mine. Sweet to eat. Shiny to eat. Eat. Eat. Eat.

Abeni could barely think between their words. All around her were faces with glistening black eyes and grinning mouths. They pressed in from all sides. She fought to push them away. But her arms felt so heavy. And they were so many. *Just give them what they want,* a small voice inside her said. *Stop fighting and give in. Then you can rest. Rest here forever, with them.* She could feel her mind slowly opening, and all the dark things around her eager to rush inside, to eat, to devour.

Something pulled at her suddenly. Like a hand had reached inside her and yanked hard. It came again. Once more. A warmth began filling her, pushing away the cold prickling needles. Her mind turned away from the dark things. And she heard them howl in anger. They clawed at her, fingers trying to dig into her mind. But she was fighting now, flailing at them, pushing them back. Whatever had come over her, she now wanted desperately to live!

Abeni broke the surface of the black lake, sputtering and coughing, sucking in gulps of air. The voices were still there, but no longer in her head. Someone was shouting her name. There! The boat. The black things swarmed it. Ama stood, her arms moving in a flurry. Gold streaked from her hands, striking the black things down. Seeing Abeni, she shouted over.

"There you are! Well don't just sit there! Swim! Swim!"

The girl made a pulling motion with one hand, and Abeni felt that tug again at her insides. It had been Ama! The tug she'd felt when drowning was the girl pulling at the living gold inside her, forcing her to fight. Taking a breath, she began swimming. It wasn't easy. The water was still frightfully cold. Her limbs were trembling by the time she got close. Some of the black things turned to drift in her direction. A golden orb shot past them, diving into the lake and then coming back up as a flat gold disc beneath her. Abeni rose with it, and then hurtled towards the boat. The speeding disc cleared a path through the creatures, depositing her beside Ama. She grabbed up a paddle, smacking away one of the things trying to crawl inside with her.

"You saved me," she panted. "Thank you."

Ama grunted. The girl looked haggard, and her hair was in disarray—some of the twisted knots unraveled. But she was still standing. "I can't paddle this boat myself."

Abeni didn't see how they could even move the boat. The things still surrounded them. And they didn't seem like they were going to stop.

"Why do they keep coming?" Ama asked, sending gold blasts to sweep them away.

"I think they expect us to pay them passage."

"Passage? What are we supposed to pay with?"

"I don't know." Abeni brought her paddle down on one of the things, kicking it back into the waters. "But we can't last like this. We'll be fighting them until dawn!" She wanted to say they wouldn't last till dawn.

"Fine!" Ama said. She shouted out into the night. "We'll pay your stupid passage!"

Everything stopped.

The creatures all went still and silent. The ones that had been reaching for them stood like statues, their arms still extended.

Then, as one, they slunk away from the boat and sank into the waters. An odd quiet descended upon the now tranquil lake.

"That's it?" Ama asked. She still stood, a gold orb hovering over each palm.

Abeni clutched a paddle, ready. But all she heard was their breathing.

"I think they took you up on your offer."

"Yeah, but what did we offer?"

An eruption broke the quiet like a clap of thunder. Both girls were thrown to the bottom of the boat, lying on their backs as they watched something rise out of the waters. Something massive—so big it seemed to blot out the moon, covering them in its shadow. A black mass stood swaying in the night. A nightmare! Dozens of heads, and backs and torsos and arms and legs and feet, all made up of the black oozing sludge. Abeni stared up in horror, clutching to Ama, who clutched back. Then the monstrous thing spoke with dozens of mouths, all at once.

Flesh things. Weak Things. Payment offered. What will weak flesh things give?

Abeni was too terrified to speak.

With an angry shriek, dozens of hands gripped the front of their boat, causing it to dip.

Flesh things offer payment! Now they go quiet. Naughty things. Speak! SPEAK!

That last part was a roar, jolting them into talking.

"You said to pay for passage!" Abeni stammered. "We want to pay!"

Pay you will, flesh thing. What sweet things do flesh things give?

"What do you want?" Ama panted.

What you have, flesh thing. Sweet thing. Soft, weak thing. Give to us! Give! Give!

"We don't understand!" Abeni told it.

The lights flesh things carry! The sweet! The sweet! What is the light you give?

The lights. Abeni remembered them asking for this when she was in the water.

"What are these lights?"

Lights are the sweet! The sweet you hold dear! The joy! We hunger for it!

Abeni puzzled through the words. "I think it wants what makes us happy."

Ama frowned. "Why doesn't it just take it, then?"

The monstrous thing answered.

Light given is always sweeter than taken. The loss is sweeter still.

"Do we do this?" Ama asked.

Abeni didn't see they had a choice. A silent agreement passed between them before Ama shouted.

"We agree!"

Do you freely offer? Both must speak.

They both answered at once. "Yes!"

Dozens of black shiny smiles appeared across that monstrous body.

Then done. Passage has been paid. Passage will be taken.

With a heave, the terrible thing sank into the lake, leaving no sign of its passing. The two girls lay quiet for a while, catching their breath as the boat swayed. When nothing else happened, they let go of one another awkwardly and sat up.

"Do you feel any different?" Ama asked.

"No," Abeni said.

"Me either. Maybe they don't take their payment until after we're done."

"Maybe. What do you think they took?"

Ama shook her head. "Let's get moving." She reached for her paddle only to realize it was gone. "Great. How am I supposed to get passage if I can't paddle?"

Something shot from the water, landing and clattering between them. The paddle. Ama picked it up.

"Umm. Thanks."

CHAPTER TWELVE

THE MASKS OF AKANI

By the time they reached their destination they were exhausted. They hauled the boat up the rocky shore and made their way onto the island. It was not very large—more like a small hill sitting in the lake. And the objects they had come all this way to see were at its very center.

The Masks of Akani were even larger up close: three carvings of faces standing upright on the earthen ground and towering above them. One was made of a metal that looked like brass. It was covered in spiral patterns and depicted an older man with a scraggly beard and a wide smile. A second was carved of dark wood in the likeness of a long-faced man who scowled. The third was all gold and showed a woman with a pleasant face.

"What now?" Abeni asked.

"I thought you might know," Ama said. "The Queen Mothers told me pieces of that song of yours. Something about talking to plates and a door?"

"Pots," Abeni corrected. "And a door."

"What were they like?" Ama asked.

"Mostly rude. Also, they like to play tricks."

"Tricks? Why?"

"Probably nothing better to do," Abeni said. "Maybe you should talk to them."

Ama looked skeptical. But she stood up straight, fixed a haughty gaze on the masks, and shouted with her best royal voice. "Masks of Akani! I am Oheneba Ama Kusiwaa Awia, Royal Sister to the King in Gold, Blood of the Dynasty of the Sun, an Honored Daughter of Makomasi, and I command you to speak to me!" There was only silence. Ama frowned. "Hello?" she shouted. "Helloooo? Do you hear me?"

Abeni stifled a laugh—or tried to. It came out in snorts.

Ama glared at her accusingly. "You did that on *purpose!*"

Abeni laughed openly now, clutching her sides.

The princess continued to glare, then snorted her own laugh. "Very funny. You try, then."

Abeni let her laughter die away. She stepped forward, looking the masks over. Asha's pots had needed to be touched before revealing their magic. Maybe it was the same here. She put a hand to the gold mask. Nothing. Disappointed, she pulled her hand back—then looked closer. Where she had touched there was a symbol. Etched in black, it was long and curved at the top and bottom. That hadn't been there before. She quickly called Ama over.

"It looks like one of our sacred symbols," the princess said.

"Like on your necklace?"

"The same. This looks like a symbol that means 'if you have forgotten something, go back and retrieve it.' It teaches us the importance of knowing the past. Only . . . it's incomplete." She reached out a finger and drew an identical curving line to face the other.

Almost at once, the symbol faded and the mask suddenly burst into brilliance. Both girls backed away in alarm. The brilliance diminished to a dull glow. But on the forehead of the mask, the symbol had returned—much larger and made of light.

"That's something," Abeni breathed.

They moved to the next mask, the one carved of wood like a scowling man. As before, Abeni put a hand to it. When she pulled away, a symbol was there. This one looked like two joined incomplete circles.

"They're ears," Ama said. "There should be four. It means, 'what I hear, I keep.'" She drew two more joining ears to the pair, and like the last one, it faded. The wooden mask creaked, as if growing firmer. On its forehead, the completed symbol reappeared in light.

They walked to the final mask of brass: a bearded man with a wide smile. This time Ama touched it first. The symbol that appeared reminded Abeni of the top half of a flower, with four long rectangular petals. The princess frowned.

"A spider's web," she said. "It's Ananse. The spider god of wisdom, cunning, and . . . tricks. I grew up with his tales." At seeing Abeni's blank look, her eyebrows rose in surprise. "How Ananse stole the gods' stories? Or how he tried to hoard the world's wisdom in a pot? How about how his rear end got big but his head got small?" She smiled at that last one, as if recalling a fond memory. But Abeni simply shook her head.

"I suppose not everyone has heard them," the princess said. She drew the bottom half of the spiderweb, completing the symbol. It faded as a rainbow of colors flitted across the brass spirals of the mask before reappearing on the broad forehead.

Then all was quiet. The two girls waited. And waited.

"Is something supposed to—" Ama cut off, jumping as a beam of light burst from the center of the masks to shoot straight up into the night like a needle piercing the sky. The light illuminated the three masks, pouring through the holes of their eyes. As the two girls watched, the giant masks began to rise, lifting until they hovered just above the ground. Slowly, they began to spin. Then they spoke.

"Akwaaba. We are the three who are One," their voices boomed.

"Wearied travelers. You have journeyed far to seek us, the Masks of Akani. As reward, we shall answer any question you wish. One question asked. One answer given."

There was a pause.

"Are we done with the speech?" a mask asked. It was the one of brass—the old man with the swirling patterns.

"Yes, Ananse," the gold mask of the woman replied serenely. "We've fulfilled that duty."

"Good! Then can we stop the spinning? I am getting dizzy!" The three masks stopped, still hovering. Ananse sighed. "Medaase! Better, better. Aso, my wife, fetch my pipe. Takooma, my son, bring my slippers!"

"I am not your wife, Ananse," the gold mask replied. "Takooma is not your son. Nor are you truly Ananse. These are merely the names our makers gave us. Besides, you don't have lungs to smoke or feet for slippers."

"Ei!" Ananse looked down in shock. "Who has taken my feet?"

Aso's golden lips smiled slightly. Wooden Takooma just groaned. "Do you ever get tired of that joke?"

"Ah! Now my no-good son speaks," Ananse grumbled.

"I'm not your son—"

"Ahem!" Aso broke in. "If you two are finished, must I remind you that we have visitors?"

All three masks moved at that, breaking formation to face the two girls with eyes that poured light. These were the all-knowing Masks of Akani? They bickered and got on like old people Abeni knew back in her village.

"Saa!" Ananse said. "Long since we've seen anyone. You find my boat? Put that there to help you cross the lake. You made it past the Ekom! Good, good!"

Ekom. The word made Abeni think of hunger or being hungry. Those things in the lake had certainly been hungry. It was all they talked about.

"Shame," Ananse went on. "That magic was supposed to guard us. But it gone bad—like cho left out in sun."

"Too much like its creators," Takooma muttered.

"Interesting, yes?" Ananse asked. "Make I tell you more?"

Abeni did want to know more. But the gold mask broke in.

"Careful, girl," Aso said. "Ananse plays the trickster he is named for well. Should you ask him to tell you about the Ekom, you will have asked your one question. Is that your intent?"

"No!" Abeni said. "I just wanted . . ."

Ananse cackled, his broad grin growing wider. "I almost have she! Hee! Hee!"

Abeni scowled. Why were the inanimate so . . . insufferable?

"Oh, fix your sour face," Ananse chided. "You sit here for hundreds of years with no company but these two bores!"

"I carry myself with the dignity of my station," Aso countered.

"I spend my time in silent contemplation," Takooma added, "seeking to understand the meaning and nature of existence through the acquisition of knowledge and—"

"Yawwwwn!" Ananse broke in loudly.

"Really," Takooma huffed. "You can be so immature."

"Oh, be quiet, wood-head," Ananse muttered. "You're boring me back to un-life."

"Ahem!" Aso cut in again. "While you two bicker, I think this one has something to say."

All three masks looked to Ama. As their shining gazes fixed on her, she shrunk a bit. Then, remembering herself, she stood straighter, with that haughtiness she was so good at.

"Masks of Akani!" she called. "I am Oheneba Ama Kusiwaa Awia, Royal Sister to the King in Gold, Blood of the Dynasty of the Sun, an Honored Daughter of Makomasi. I have come to ask a more pertinent question."

"Oh!" Ananse exclaimed. "See this one. So serious and puffed up." He put on a mocking face and imitated her voice. "Masks of Akani. I'm a biggety big, big. Blah blah! Serious question. Blah blah!"

The other masks chuckled, even Aso. Ama's face flushed.

"Masks of Akani," she tried again. "I come to you burdened with great—"

"Tee hee!" Ananse laughed. "Listen to her now." He put on the mocking voice again. "I'm Miss Biggety-Big-Big and I'm burdened—like a donkey. Hee haw! Hee haw!"

Now all the masks laughed. Aso sounded like she might snort water through her nose—if she drank water. Takooma still scowled but snickered. Abeni had to admit, it was funny. Ama didn't appear to find it funny. At all.

"How dare you!" she exclaimed angrily. "My revered ancestors made you to serve—"

"Revered ancestors," Ananse scoffed. "I bet you don't know the first thing about your revered ancestors. They built us because they saw their end coming. An end they helped bring about!"

"Greed," Takooma said. "It will always bring down the foolish."

Ama looked confused. "I don't know what you're talking about."

"Because you've been sold a story!" Ananse said. "I know something of stories. Weave a good one like the clever spider, and it will remain strong. But pull one strand, and the whole thing can fall apart." His face became menacing. "Tell me, Princess, are you ready to pull a strand . . . and see what happens?"

Ama stared as if her mouth had gone dry. Abeni remembered the story Healer Osha had told them. About the end of the First Gold Kingdom of the Gold Weavers. There was something here she didn't think Ama knew. Or wanted to know.

"You're lying," the princess said—though no longer as certain.

"We cannot lie," Aso said. "But we are straying from your purpose here. Ask your question, while there is still time."

Abeni tensed, waiting for the princess to ask how to find this Golden Throne. She had her own question, one she'd been preparing since the past night. If these masks truly knew everything, they could tell her how to find her family. Maybe some good could come from all this.

Ama composed herself. "Masks of Akani . . ." She drew a breath. ". . . how do I show my people that I am worthy of leading them—as their ruler?"

Abeni gaped. What had the girl just asked? That wasn't what they had come here for.

Ananse let out a slow laugh. "Someone thinks they can do better than their brother, eh?"

Ama flinched.

"It is no easy thing," Takooma added, "to wear the crown."

"Yet, it is what she wishes," Aso said. "More than anything. Let us give answer."

The masks began to spin once again, their voices booming in chorus.

"To become a ruler your people will find worthy, you must prove yourself worthy. Prove to them you are deserving of the crown and the title. Prove it to yourself."

The masks stopped spinning, settling back to face them.

"Your question has been answered," Aso stated.

The princess stared up, puzzled. "But what does—"

"The question has been answered," Aso stated again. "No more can be said."

Ama backed away, clearly frustrated. She looked to Abeni. "You have to ask them about the Golden Throne."

"*You* were supposed to ask," Abeni said, unable to hide her anger.

"I didn't," Ama said flatly. "Now you will. That's not a request."

Abeni wanted to shout that the girl had stolen her turn. She had a good mind to ask these masks what she wanted anyway. Let the princess go back empty-handed. But then how would they get free? She might get her answers but doom her friends. No. Just because Ama did as she wanted, no matter who got hurt, didn't mean she had to do the same. She took a calming breath, trying to ignore the deep loss she felt in her chest—then stepped forward.

"Ei!" Ananse exclaimed. "What's this? Another girl with Biggety Big titles for us?"

"No. I'm just Abeni."

"Just Abeni," Ananse repeated. He squinted. "Oh, you are interesting. More than the other one. Abeni, from the Jembe forest. Friend to spirits. Finder of lost children. Defeater of *his* minions. Interesting!"

That caught Abeni by surprise. She supposed these all-knowing masks truly knew everything. Though she didn't consider herself someone worth knowing about.

"I have a question for you, Masks of Akani."

"Yes," Takooma said. "But not your own. That one stole your turn."

Ama first opened then clamped her mouth shut, folding her arms.

"Oh! She's wondering now if she might have two questions for her troubles!" Ananse said.

Abeni looked up, hopeful.

"We are bound to our rules and cannot undo them," Aso said. "However, I can tell you that the question you will ask—yes, we know that too—will be of greater importance to you than you realize."

"Hee hee," Ananse laughed. "Look at her face! Eyes gone big as melons. I bet she's wondering if we know what question she will ask, if we also know her tomorrows?"

Abeni's heart thumped. Did they?

"Stop taunting her," Takooma scolded. "You know she can't ask that. So, I will answer *you* instead. There are many possible tomorrows. Her acts will determine those that are most *probable*."

"Now child," Aso said. "Ask your question. Time grows short."

Abeni inhaled. "Where can we find the Golden Throne, the soul of Ama's people?"

The three masks grew bright again and began to spin.

"You will find the Golden Throne precisely where her people left it," they boomed as one. There was a pause. "But the question has more than one answer. The soul of her people will be found with the one who forever guards it—the dragon Bida."

The masks stopped their rotation, returning to face them.

Abeni stared, going over each word.

"That's it?" Ama asked in disbelief. "But what does that mean? The place where my people left it? And with the dragon Bida? How can it be in two places at once?"

"The question has been answered," Aso stated. "No more will be said."

"But . . . but . . . !" Ama sputtered.

"Your questions have been answered and your time here is done," Takooma said.

"You'd better be going . . . unless you want to swim back," Ananse said.

Abeni glanced down and yelped. The ground under her feet was fading! The entire island was fading—growing more transparent by the moment. "We have to go!" she shouted.

Ama frowned at her then noticed the vanishing ground and jumped. Without another word, the two girls ran for the boat. It felt to Abeni like she was running on mist. When she reached the boat, she tried to jump. But her feet passed right through the ground, splashing into black water. She shrieked at the familiar feel of freezing needles on her skin, tumbling into the boat. Ama landed beside her. They both looked up in time to see the Masks of Akani fading away.

"Farewell, travelers," Aso called.

"Fate be on your side," Takooma said.

Ama stood up in the boat, glaring at them. "But the dragon Bida is dead!" she shouted.

There was a final chuckle from Ananse. "Hee hee. Is he now?"

Then the masks and the island were gone, leaving Ananse's laughter to echo in the night.

There was a moment of silence—and then Ama screamed. It was a scream of anger, and frustration. When the girl was finished she stood panting, staring at nothing. It was a while before she sat and grabbed a paddle. Abeni did the same.

They rowed in silence. Abeni sat at the rear, staring at Ama's back. Her mind was a jumble, and after a while she could not stand being quiet any longer.

"You stole my question." No anger or accusation. Just a statement.

Ama's back stiffened. "Yes, I know."

Abeni gaped. "You knew I wanted to ask something?"

"Of course. Masks that can answer anything? Who wouldn't?"

Anger surged in Abeni. She stopped rowing. "Then why? Why did you do it?"

Ama stopped as well. "Because what I needed was greater."

"You can't know that!" Abeni insisted. "You didn't have a right—"

"I have every right," Ama cut in. She turned, her golden eyes glinting in the dark. "I need to become ruler of my kingdom. That's important for the sake of a whole people."

"I need to find my family, my village," Abeni countered. "That's just as important!"

"One village compared to an entire kingdom? Be reasonable. Even you can see it."

"All I see is someone who wants to be in charge all the time. Who just wants power!"

Ama shook her head. "I told you before, you don't know me. I was being truthful when I said I want to make changes to my kingdom. I want to see those in the mines freed. I want to make alliances with other kingdoms in the west. When it comes to the Witch Priest, I want us to be on the right side."

"Then why don't you just do that now?" Abeni shot back. "You're a princess!"

"Because they gave my brother the crown!" Ama exploded. "Because even though I'm smarter, and have more experience at court, and understand diplomacy, he is a he—and I'm not!"

The princess took a deep breath. When she spoke again it was in a determined voice. "But I won't become one of the Ohemmaa, wielding power behind the throne as an old woman. I want to rule in my own right. You've met Captain Ekua. Do you know how she achieved her position?" Abeni said nothing, but remembered the hard-faced one-eyed woman.

"She fought for it," Ama continued. "Fought against men and tradition. Fought against those who said she didn't belong. Now Captain Ekua is the chief of our armies. She showed me what I can do if I put my mind to it. Those masks said I had to prove myself. It must be through this quest. I need to find the Golden Throne, bring it back. Then my people will see. The Ohemmaa will see. They'll all see I deserve the crown, not my brother."

"So, you have it all figured out, then," Abeni mocked. "Good for you."

Ama sighed heavily. "My fortune will be your fortune. When I bring our Golden Throne back and gain the crown, I will do what I can to help you find your family. You have my word."

Abeni wanted to ask the girl why she thought her word meant anything, but bit her lip. They picked up their paddles again and rowed back without speaking another word. When they pulled onto shore, Abeni quickly hopped off the boat and was thankful to feel firm ground beneath her feet. She found the others where she had left them. Most were asleep except Zaneeya and Songu. But the rest stirred awake as she came close.

"You okay?" Songu signed.

"Just tired," she signed back.

"Abeni!" Asha came running, embracing her in a hug.

"You made it back!" Nyomi yawned. "About time!"

"Songu and I saw the island vanish," Zaneeya said. "We didn't know what to think. The two of you were gone so long."

Abeni frowned. "We weren't away more than two or three hours."

Her friends stared at her. "Abeni," Asha said gently. "It's almost morning."

Morning? Abeni looked up in surprise to see the moon disappearing. Bits of sunlight were turning the night sky a mix of bronze, orange, and yellow. How had they lost an entire night?

"Looks like you got back just in time!" Nyomi said, gesturing to the shore.

There, the boat was fading into mist too, like the island.

"So?" Zaneeya asked. She eyed Ama, who stood a way off, hugging herself and looking oddly lost. "What happened out there?"

Taking a deep breath, Abeni told them of all that had occurred. Of fighting the black water creatures. Of encountering the masks. Of the questions asked and the odd answers.

"You fought monsters?" Nyomi asked, breathless.

"Did you hear any of that?" Abeni asked. "See the giant thing come out of the water?"

Asha shook her head. "You vanished after you set out."

"Of course, she stole your turn," Zaneeya growled, glancing to Ama. "Typical."

"It doesn't matter now," Abeni said wearily. "We got some answers."

"But now the throne might be guarded by a dragon?" Nyomi said. "Dragons are scary!"

Abeni had never met a dragon. But it did sound frightening.

"I thought these Gold Weavers claimed the dragon Bida was dead?" Zaneeya asked.

Abeni remembered Ananse's parting words. *Is he now?*

There was a sudden mournful wail. They turned to see Ama. The girl was on her knees.

"What's wrong with her now?" Zaneeya asked.

Abeni wasn't sure. They walked over to find the princess fidgeting with the gold bands on her forearms. Her fingers trembled, and she was wide-eyed.

"No, no, no," she kept saying. "No, no, no. Please, no!"

Abeni stared at her, puzzled. "What's the matter?"

Ama looked up, tears streaming her face. "It's gone! They took it! Oh gods, it's gone!"

"What's gone?" Abeni asked, confused. "Who took what?"

Ama held out shaking hands. "I can't weave gold," she stammered. "Those things in the lake. We told them they could take something to grant us passage. They took my weaving! Oh no, no, no! Please not that! Please!"

Abeni stared in shock. "Are you certain? Your eyes are still golden."

Ama put a hand to her face. "But I can't weave. I don't think it happened until we got back. They granted passage both ways. Then they . . ." Her voice broke. "They took it from me."

"You're saying you can't weave gold at all?" Zaneeya asked. "Not one bit?"

Ama shook her head. "Nothing. I can't even feel gold anymore. When I reach for it there's an emptiness, like—"

Abeni barely saw Zaneeya streak past in a blur. Ama went silent as a clawed hand gripped about her neck, forcing her up to her feet.

"No more power," the panther girl growled. Her free hand reached up to rip away the gold collar at her neck, flinging it. "No more control over me."

Ama looked stunned. Her mouth was wide open, but only choking sounds came out. Zaneeya's hand tightened.

"You dared put me in that thing. Bound me. Do you know who I am? What I am? I am the wind that stings your face, the fire racing through the brush, the water that sweeps away mothers and babes. I am one with the earth and stars, and you, pitiful, small, weak mortal, bound me. Tormented me. Me!"

That last part came out in a snarl, and Zaneeya lifted Ama higher—until her feet left the ground. The princess's hands beat at the panther girl's arms. But she might as well have been beating at stone.

Everyone was still, watching. It had all happened so fast. Someone tugged Abeni's arm. Asha. She looked worried, her eyes pleading for Abeni to do something. If Zaneeya listened to anyone it was Asha. That the small girl now turned to her spoke to how dangerous this moment was. Abeni could feel that danger in the air: fear that made her throat dry, that seized her by the heart.

Like what she imagined prey felt like before a predator. It rolled off Zaneeya in waves. A reminder that this being who looked like a girl was really a spirit—not human and beyond her understanding. Someone you did not cross or anger. Ama had foolishly done both.

"Zaneeya," Abeni said carefully. "I understand why you're upset."

"Do you?" the panther girl's voice was a drawn blade. "You know what it's like to be enslaved?"

"I was their prisoner too."

"Then what I do here is for all."

Ama's eyes rolled up as her face turned an unnatural color.

"You do this," Abeni warned. "And there's no going back."

"It won't take long. Unless I want it to."

"You can't kill her," Abeni said bluntly.

Zaneeya turned that orange gaze on her. "Do you think to tell me what to do now?"

Abeni swallowed. She and Zaneeya had only just become friends. This was testing that. She tried a different approach.

"You have every right to be angry. I'm angry with her too. But . . . if you do this, her people will come after us. She's a princess. They won't just let us go."

Zaneeya growled. "Let them come."

"We can't fight them all," Abeni pleaded. "Not an entire kingdom. We could end up back in those mines. That's what you'll do if you go through with this—put us all back in those mines again."

A warring look came over the panther girl's face. She gritted her teeth, then with a snarl threw Ama to the ground. The girl coughed and sputtered, clutching her throat. Abeni released a breath she hadn't known she was holding. She heard the others do the same.

"Fine, she lives," Zaneeya said. "But we don't have to stay with her or complete this quest. We get as far away as we can and don't look back. Her people will have no reason to come after us."

They all looked to each other. Abeni had to admit, it made sense. Why continue with this quest if Ama couldn't force them? They could just leave. Then she remembered what the mask had said. That the search for the Golden Throne was important for her own quest. But how?

"You can't," a voice croaked. Ama. The girl looked worn, her hair and clothes disheveled. Far from a princess. She knelt bent over, trying to catch her breath.

"No one asked you," Zaneeya snapped.

"No, listen," Ama wheezed. "You can't go. The living gold. It's inside you."

"And you have no more control over it, or us," Zaneeya said.

Ama shook her head. "It's more than that. These bands . . ." She touched the gold on her forearms. ". . . these don't just allow me to control the living gold, they keep it at bay."

Abeni didn't like the sound of that. "What do you mean?"

Ama looked up at her. "The gold inside you is like a living thing. The bands allowed me to control it, keep it in tune with your bodies. Without my weaving, I can't do that. Now, it's more like a parasite. And it's growing."

"Growing?" Nyomi asked. She hugged her stomach. "Inside us?"

Ama nodded. "If it continues unchecked, uncontrolled, it will take over. It will turn your blood into gold, your bones, your skin, down to your hair. You'll become gold, alive but trapped like a statue. Forever."

There was silence as everyone stared at her, horror-stricken. Zaneeya broke the quiet, growling and ready to rush the girl. Ama threw out her arms to weave, seeming to remember at the last minute she couldn't. She cowered instead, covering her body protectively with shaking hands.

"No!" Abeni yelled to Zaneeya. "Wait!" She spun back to Ama. "Can this be undone?"

The princess peeked between her fingers, wide-eyed. "Yes. You'll have to go back to Makomasi. Even I can't do it alone. You'll need healers and gold workers. But . . ." She trailed off and Abeni closed her eyes.

"But we'll have to complete your quest first." She didn't need to see Ama nod. There was another angry growl from Zaneeya. But from what Abeni could hear, the panther girl had stalked off to attack a nearby bush to vent her anger—not Ama. She opened her eyes again.

"I'm sorry," the princess said. "I didn't mean for this to happen. I never thought—"

"How long," Abeni cut in.

Ama swallowed. "Three weeks, maybe four. The process inside you has already started. But when it happens, it will be all at once."

There was quiet—except for Zaneeya's tirade—as they all contemplated what this meant. It seemed they would be doing this quest after all. And things had grown even worse. Abeni sat down, putting her head in her hands. She was so tired. There was a weariness inside her, in her body, in her bones, in her mind.

Closing her eyes, she did the one thing that always managed to soothe her. She called up her song. Nothing. She squeezed her eyes tighter, concentrating. She'd sung this many times. The words were right there on the tip of her tongue, tickling the back of her mind. Still, nothing. Her eyes flew open, and she really thought now, hard, searching for her song. But it came back empty. There was . . . nothing there.

Horror crept up inside her and she clutched at her chest, suddenly finding it hard to breathe. Her skin felt hot and cold at once. She couldn't think. She needed to . . . needed to . . .

"Abeni?" It was Asha. The small girl was at her side, her small face full of worry. "Why are you crying?" Was she crying? She hadn't even noticed.

"What's the matter?" Zaneeya asked, her anger seemingly spent.

Songu signed the same thing. But Abeni couldn't speak.

"You look like someone who's lost something," Nyomi said softly.

That was it. She'd lost something. Or rather, it had been taken from her. She looked out at the waters. They'd granted her passage and taken their payment.

"It's gone," she said. "My song. They took it away."

BOOK II

CHAPTER THIRTEEN

KONO

Y ou and your daughter look as if you've traveled far."

Fulan scooped up the last bit of goat stew with some fufu. The meat was tender and peppery, and she relished the taste. She'd had similar food at the Fortress of the Living Flame. But there was something about this stew, its flavoring and simpleness, that reminded her of a time before—a time she had lost long ago.

She looked to the Huntsman, who should have responded but sat busily shoving food into his mouth as if it were his last meal.

"Thank you for your hospitality, Uncle," she told the tall older man with the black and white beard. He acted like a chief of this village, but insisted he was not. And she was uncertain what title to give him. "We have been traveling long. It's good to stop and be so warmly welcomed."

The man with the black and white beard stared momentarily at the Huntsman, who was going through a bowl of seasoned rice meant to be shared by everyone. A woman who sat on the wide colorful mat with them outside her house also watched, looking dumbfounded. Fulan suspected neither had ever seen anyone eat so much at once. She scowled. The Huntsman was supposed to be playing the part of her father, not getting on like a starved zimwi.

"Were you and your father heading anywhere in particular?" the man with the black and white beard asked. He now addressed Fulan, seeming to have given up on the Huntsman. "Not many come to our valley. It's a bit off the beaten path. What is it you do?"

"We're trackers," Fulan replied. She'd decided it was best to be truthful—to a point. "We're hunting after some people, missing children."

"Oh?" The man with the black and white beard looked troubled. "Who are these children? Were they taken?"

"Taken or ran away," Fulan answered.

"What do they look like? Maybe we can help you find them."

I bet you can. "Two girls," she answered. "One younger than me, the other small."

"Where are they from?"

"A place called the Jembe forest."

There. He tried to hide it. But she could see the twitch in his eye at the mention, the way his nostrils flared. Thanks to her father's gifts, she could even hear his heart beating faster. Oh, he knew something. That was expected. It was why they had come here, after all.

Since encountering those strange children, she and the Huntsman had worked to track their quarry. His hounds took up the scent of whoever had lived in that old broken house. They followed it. And it turned out their quarry had left behind clues of their passing.

In one village, three men told of capturing a demon who had hunted their goats. Two girls—one younger than Fulan, the other small—had attacked them to free the demon, alongside a second demon. And they claimed to have barely escaped with their lives. From there the trail led to a hidden field of giant flowers that turned out to house bush babies. Fulan knew of the body-stealers. The creatures had tried to flee, thinking she meant to drag them off to her father's armies. The Huntsman captured one—threatening to wear its furry hide. The thing babbled on in its annoying baby voice, claiming to have encountered a terrible sorceress, who had incredibly turned many of them into flowers!

After that, the trail went cold. Like their quarry had disappeared altogether. But in the village of strange children, that girl Fomi had provided a clue in her anger. She had spoken of a village called Kono. It took some searching, but just at the forest's edge the hounds found the trail again. It led to this valley, and Kono. They arrived posing as father and daughter. And that ruse was now producing results. She glanced to the Huntsman with smug satisfaction—only to find him slurping down some thick yellowish soup with greens and dried fish. He seemed satisfied with just stuffing his belly.

"Did your father teach you to track?"

Fulan blinked, looking to a girl who sat across from her. She was so quiet Fulan had almost forgotten she was there. This was the first she had spoken.

"Yes," Fulan answered. "He's taught me many things. I didn't get your name."

"Damju," the girl replied. "You've come all the way from this Jembe forest?"

"Yes, you've heard of it."

"No."

Fulan looked for signs the girl was lying. But her eyes were unreadable. She just sat there staring with an even expression. Fulan studied the girl's face, comparing it with the older woman seated beside her.

"Your daughter?" she asked.

"Yes," the woman answered. "She helped me prepare this food."

"I hope you enjoy it," Damju said.

Fulan smiled, tasting the soup—which was nutty, slightly bitter, and sweet at the same time. "Very good. Are you and your mother cooks?"

"My mother is a healer. She makes poultices and powders. I'm her apprentice. I suppose we're like you and your father."

Fulan nodded. "I guess so. I must admit, we heard curious things about your village on the way here."

"Oh?" the man with the black and white beard asked. "What things?"

Fulan put on a face of reluctance. "That your village had suffered some great misfortune. I don't understand it all fully. But something to do with your children?"

Quiet descended, and for a moment all that could be heard was the Huntsman's noisy eating. Fulan glanced out upon the small village. It was near sunset. Children still played in the dusty streets. A mother rocked her crying baby. Some men patted brown clay onto a new house. Everywhere, full bowls were being laid out on mats as families sat to eat. It looked like a normal village. And Fulan had the flickering memories again, stronger than before. Of being in a place like this. The laughter and chattering. The scent of cooking food on the warm air. But . . . something was off. The woman who sang to her baby looked around cautiously. One of the men working on the house was missing a hand. She had seen others like him in the village, more than seemed normal. The families gathered to eat clung to one another as if fearful to let go. The children were the oddest of all. They laughed and played, but their games were rough. And their eyes held unspoken secrets.

"The children of our village were stolen," the girl answered finally.

Fulan turned to Damju in surprise. So did her mother and the man with the black and white beard. They looked ready to stop her. Fulan spoke before they could.

"Stolen? By whom?"

"The Goat Man."

That name again, Fulan thought. The Huntsman coughed.

"He worked for the Witch Priest," Damju went on. "You've heard of him?"

Fulan nodded. The Huntsman coughed again.

"The Goat Man came to our village and stole the children away with a song that made you see your greatest desire. A wish song. Many were taken. He changed them into monsters."

Fulan looked closely at the girl. "But he didn't take you, with this wish song?"

Damju smiled. She tapped beneath an eye. "I don't see like other people. The song didn't work on me."

Fulan nodded in understanding. The Huntsman was coughing more now, slapping his chest. Served him right if he choked, the greedy fool. There was a tickle in her own throat, and she cleared it, looking around for some water.

"How did the children become free?"

"A girl named Abeni saved them—though I helped."

Abeni. They had come to that name at last. Fulan rubbed her throat where the tickle had become a slight burning. She must have swallowed too much pepper. She looked around. Where was that water?

"Abeni," she repeated in a rasp that ended in a cough. "Tell me more about . . ." Another cough. ". . . about her."

"No," Damju said simply. "I won't."

Fulan slapped at her chest as her coughing grew worse. Beside her, the Huntsman had gone down to hands and knees, coughing so hard it sounded like he was barking. She met Damju's gaze, at first puzzled, and then in realization.

"What . . ." She choked. ". . . did you do?"

"My mother is a healer. She works with roots and plants. And I've learned a few things myself." Damju patted a leather pouch at her side. "Sprinkle the right things in your food and . . ."

Fulan stared down at her bowl, flinging it away.

"We apologize," Damju's mother said. "But our village has become less trusting. We put the powders in the food of all strangers who pass through. It's easy enough to counteract—water alone will do. If we hear the right things, they drink and are none the wiser. If we don't . . ."

Fulan was coughing heavily now. It felt like her throat and belly were on fire.

"You didn't say the right things," Damju stated bluntly. "Trackers looking for two girls. Bringing up the Jembe forest. Asking about the children of our village. All wrong."

"Who sent you?" the man with the black and white beard asked. His voice was hard now. "Are you one of *his* servants? If you came looking for the Goat Man, he's gone. Your master turned one of our own against us. A wretch named Brima. We exiled him."

"Better than he deserved," Damju's mother said harshly.

"What do we do with them?" Damju asked. "We can't let them go after Abeni."

The older man thought on this. "We put them where we kept Brima for now. Can the two of you make them sleep?" He eyed the Huntsman, who writhed on the ground, gasping like a fish for air. "That big one looks dangerous."

Damju reached into her pouch, pulling out a thick black root. "Have them smell this. Once they're tied up, we have a tea that will keep them too weak to even stand."

Fulan was hunched over, but she could see the girl hand the root to the man with the black and white beard. He brought it close to her and she could smell the strong stink of it. She was certain that if she smelled it too long, she would awaken tied up and drugged with some tea. That wasn't going to happen.

"I am my father's daughter," she whispered between the wheezing coughs. "I am fire. I do not burn."

Then she moved. It took much of her strength, but she rose in a powerful leap, knocking away the root and sending the man holding it onto his back. She staggered over to grip the Huntsman by his leather jerkin, forcing him to stand.

"Run!" she croaked, and took off.

The coughing was so bad she could barely breathe. Her eyes watered and stung. She didn't know where she was going. She just wanted to get out of this place and find some water for her burning throat.

She more stumbled than ran, knocking into people and shoving them aside. Somewhere behind her she could hear the Huntsman lumbering to follow—the two of them probably looking like crazed wildebeests. At one point everything went dark, and she realized they had somehow entered a house. Hanging gourds and calabashes got tangled in her locs. Bowls crunched under her feet and she tripped over pots. People shouted now, heading for the house. She had to get out before they sealed her in. The Huntsman let out a sudden *roar*! With a charge, he ran for a wall, breaking through it in a shower of clay and mudbrick. She staggered through the opened passage, only to find the big man rolling on the ground, trying to right himself.

Fulan grabbed him by the seat of his pants, pushing him ahead. "Go!" she slurred.

He roared again, putting his head down and charging. Now they really were a pair of wildebeests, knocking aside anything and anyone in their path. They almost ended up going through another house, but she shoved him in the right direction, aiming for the low stone wall surrounding the village. They reached it, and ungracefully tripped over the thing, landing in a heap before dashing off again, away from the village of Kono.

ᴏ ᴏ ᴏ

Fulan gulped water from a stream, letting it cool her throat.

The Huntsman had stuck his entire head into the water. When he lifted it again, his face was a mask of anger. "I'm going to go back to that village and skin every last one of them," he growled. "Starting with that witch girl and her mother! Then—" He sputtered new coughs and dunked his head back into the stream.

Fulan sat down, catching her breath.

They'd been outwitted. By a bunch of villagers. And almost captured. This was the second time she'd had to flee—her! This entire venture was turning into a mess. But always there was that name. Abeni.

Who was this girl who inspired such loyalty? Who caused children and villagers to risk their lives for her? Truly, they had to be under some spell. Who else but a sorceress could weave such powerful magic? More and more she wondered if her father was mistaken. If his true enemy was not this spirit, but the girl who was her companion—and possibly her controller.

She gritted her teeth. This Abeni was a formidable adversary. They would need help to hunt her down. And when they did, Fulan was determined that the girl would pay for the humiliations she had suffered. She would have her vengeance.

CHAPTER FOURTEEN

NEW PLANS

Abeni sat watching the sun climb the midmorning sky. Light shimmered off the lake, turning the water into sparkling jewels. There was no sign that there had ever been an island there, or giant masks, or nightmarish creatures.

She turned to Asha, who leaned against her. The girl looked up with eyes full of concern.

"How are you feeling?" she asked.

Abeni opened her mouth to answer, then shrugged. She didn't know how she felt.

"Do you think you know any of it? The song? You taught it to me, after all."

Asha shook her head sadly. "Auntie Asha taught it to you. There are bits and pieces that come to me. But . . . it's like remembering someone else's dream."

The little spirit had told her as much about her past life . . . lives. The song had been a way for Auntie Asha to remember the village that had been lost, and all its people. That was probably what pained Abeni the most. She might be able to re-create the parts of the song that talked about what had happened to her. But everything that came before was gone. All that history lost in one moment.

"It's not your fault," Asha said.

Abeni breathed deeply. It was easy to hear that, but harder to believe. She had handed over her song willingly. How could she have been so careless? So stupid?

"I said it's not your fault," Asha repeated, firmer this time. "You made the only choice that would let you come back. The blame is on those who took your song from you. They had no right."

"Sometimes it feels like the ones who hurt others have all the power in this world," Abeni said. "And the rest of us are just here to be hurt by them."

Asha put her small hands to Abeni's cheeks, turning her face to meet her eyes. "There are many in this world who hurt others because they delight in it. Or they don't care. But there's more in this world than them. There are forces for good like us, that seek to make things better. And there are more of us than them. Always remember that."

Abeni smiled faintly. "Now you sound like Auntie Asha. Maybe you remember more of her dreams than you think."

Someone walked up to them. Zaneeya. The panther girl stood, gazing out at the lake. "I say we go back and get your song. Give me a few moments with these Ekom, and I'll show them hungry."

Abeni raised an eyebrow at that. The panther girl believed every problem could be solved by punching it. Odd to think that she even cared. When they'd first met they were hardly friends. That had taken real work. That the haughty spirit now wanted to fight on her behalf made the hole left by the loss of her song feel a little less empty.

"I don't think that would work. But thanks." For one, the Masks of Akani wouldn't appear again until another full moon. She'd learned about the phases of the moon back with Auntie Asha. That would be another thirty days at least. After what they'd found out about the living gold inside them, they didn't have that long.

Zaneeya shifted uncomfortably, the way she did when showing any emotion beyond anger or annoyance. "Well, you're the first mortal I'm even considering liking. Besides, I'm in that song!"

Abeni smiled. "Considering? I think you like me already."

The panther girl shifted about some more. Oh, that made her very uncomfortable.

Nyomi came to sit beside them. She took Abeni's hand in her

own. "I just want you to know, I thought about jumping into the lake—using my powers—to find these monsters to say I was very cross with them for taking your song, and demanding they give it back. But, then I remembered how frightening that would be, and I got too scared to do it. However, I did seriously *think* about it, for at least a few minutes." She stared at Abeni, her large black eyes expectant.

"Thank you?"

The porcupine girl patted her hand. "You're welcome."

Zaneeya snorted.

Songu joined them. Sitting down, he pulled out his small flute and began to play.

"So, what are we going to do about her?"

Abeni didn't need to follow the panther girl's gaze to know who was meant by "her." She turned to where Ama sat alone. The girl had drawn her legs up to her chin and stared out at the lake, her shoulders slumped.

"What she said about the gold inside us," Nyomi asked worriedly, "do you think it's true?"

"I don't know that we have any choice but to believe her," Abeni said.

"That would mean we have to go along with her quest," Zaneeya said with distaste.

"Yes," Abeni said. "Or we say we don't believe her and take the risk."

Nyomi shuddered. "Of becoming living statues, forever."

"I don't like those options," Zaneeya growled.

"Neither do I," Abeni agreed. "But they're what we have."

There was a long moment of quiet as everyone took this in.

Songu signed into the silence. "Then what are we going to do?"

"The only thing we can," Abeni said.

With a heavy sigh, she came to her feet and made the long walk over to Ama. The princess didn't look up at her approach. It didn't even seem like the girl knew she was there. Unsure about what else to do, Abeni sat down beside her.

Ama jumped, a hand going to her throat.

"It's just me," Abeni said.

The princess looked relieved, lowering a hand to show purple bruises on her dark skin.

Abeni winced. "I think I might have something for that." She rifled about in her bag, drawing out a small gourd filled with a whitish cream. It was cool and tingled her fingers, and when she rubbed it on the bruises, Ama breathed in relief.

"Thank you," she said, her voice still hoarse but stronger.

The princess's puffy eyes were red and tears wet her cheeks. She ran the back of her hand across her face to wipe them away.

"So, your powers are all gone, then?" Abeni asked. Best to be blunt.

The girl flinched. "They got us good, didn't they?"

Abeni sighed. "Yeah."

"I heard about you losing your song," Ama said. She hesitated. "I'm sorry."

They looked at each other then, exchanging feelings of loss. It was hard for Abeni to accept that this girl—whom she didn't even like—was the one person who best understood what she was going through.

"It feels like someone died," Ama went on. "My parents both died when I was still very young. All I had was my brother, and he's . . . well, he's a bit useless. And anyway, they were getting ready to give him the crown. I was left to mourn with cousins and my father's other children that I didn't know, alone with my grief. It feels like that now. Like someone died and left me all alone."

Abeni paused as she finished applying the salve. It did feel like someone had died. Like when her village had been taken. In losing the song, her village had been taken all over again. But at least she'd had Auntie Asha back then. And now, she had her friends. Ama didn't have anyone.

"I'm sure you had friends," Abeni said, returning the salve to her bag.

Ama laughed without smiling. "People who call themselves my

friends either want something or think they should tell me what I want to hear. What you have?" She glanced back at the others. "That's not something I know."

Abeni was surprised at this openness. "Is that why you are . . . the way you are?"

Ama whipped her head around, her golden eyes hard. "I'm the only way I know to be."

Abeni was set to react in kind, then stopped. She had seen this before. It was how Zaneeya lashed out, whenever she was scared and vulnerable. Biting back her first response, she settled for calm.

"Maybe you should try being another way, then," she said.

Ama blinked, not expecting that reply. "I don't know how to do that," she stammered.

"Well, you'd better start learning. After what you told us, it looks like we have no choice but to continue this quest." Relief crossed the girl's face and Abeni made certain to hold her gaze. "But things will be different. We're your companions on this quest. Not your servants. We're all equal from now on. Do you understand?"

Ama wiped her eyes and nose, squared her shoulders, lifted her chin, and nodded sharply.

"If that is what it takes to see this quest completed, I can sacrifice."

Abeni raised an eyebrow. The girl considered *that* a sacrifice?

"Another thing. Get rid of your bands."

"What? Why?"

"You used those things to torment us. To control us. We don't like them. You want to show us you're trying to be different? Throw them away!"

"But I don't even have my powers. I can't use them!"

"Then you don't need them."

This time there was a long stretch of quiet. Abeni thought the girl might stomp off and refuse. But she finally nodded.

"Good. One last thing."

Ama glared in exasperation. "What now?"

"You promise that when this is over, you free us completely." Ama looked set to agree, but Abeni held up a hand. "And, if you do become ruler, you free everyone in the mines."

That left the girl with her jaw hanging. For a moment she sputtered, trying to find words. "But I can't just free them."

"You told me already that you planned to do it. This is just making sure you do."

Ama shook her head. "You don't understand. If there's no one in the mines, how can the kingdom have gold? I want to end the forced labor, yes. But it will take time. Maybe years, before I can free everyone."

"Not years, immediately," Abeni said sharply. "If your people want gold, they should mine it themselves. If you want others to do it, they shouldn't be forced. They should only do it if they want to, and they should receive something in return for their work. It's only fair."

Ama stared as if she'd been asked to retrieve the moon. She let out a low laugh, shaking her head. "For a village girl, you negotiate like a court attendant. Fine. I'll do my best to see the mines closed. Just understand, it won't be easy. Even as ruler. There are many others in the kingdom I'll have to convince, including the Queen Mothers. The politics of rulership are very complicated. But I give you my royal oath that I will do my best to see it done."

Abeni wasn't certain what politics were—and she didn't think she wanted to know. "That's all I ask."

Ama nodded, then looked to the bands on her arms. "I suppose getting rid of them won't be so bad. With my abilities gone, they're heavy now anyway. All this gold is heavy. I never knew how much they weighed." She undid a clasp on each band and they swung open. Rising, she walked down towards the rocky shore. She stood for a moment, then with a great heave, flung one of the bands into the lake, followed by the other. They each landed with a heavy splash, sinking beneath the waters.

Abeni was standing when the girl walked back. "Let's go talk to the others."

They returned to find everyone waiting and watching curiously. Abeni explained matters as briefly and easily as she could.

"I do want to work with all of you," Ama added, standing before them awkwardly. "I hope things can be different between us."

Songu was the first to speak. Abeni translated. "He says you're okay with him." The boy signed some more. "But you're not traveling with us with your hair in such a mess."

Ama touched her disheveled knots. "Thank you."

Asha walked over and beckoned the princess to bend down. Ama looked uncertain but did, meeting the little girl face to face. "The Queen Mothers claimed you had great potential. But that you still had much growing to do. I hope we get to see that happen." Then Asha reached up and tweaked her nose, giggling.

Ama straightened, turning to Abeni. "Are you ever going to tell me what the deal is between you and that strange little spirit?"

"No," Abeni replied.

Ama accepted the answer, then walked up to Zaneeya. She swallowed before she spoke. "I'm sorry for what I did to you. I . . . there really isn't any excuse. I just wanted to say I'm sorry."

Zaneeya huffed. "Save it for someone who cares, Princess." She stalked off, bumping Ama's shoulder hard enough to make the girl stumble back.

"You should probably give her space," Abeni suggested.

"Well, I'm fine with you," Nyomi said pleasantly. "So long as you help me find some breakfast. I saw some rocks that probably have nice wriggly worms underneath." She looped an arm into Ama's. "Wanna help?"

The princess nodded queasily. "I thought porcupines ate flowers and tree bark."

"Oh yes," Nyomi said. "But I'm also part hedgehog spirit. And I respect both sides of my heritage." She pulled Ama along, chattering on about the dietary habits of hedgehogs.

"You're certain about this?"

Abeni turned to find Zaneeya at her side, arms folded as she watched the two go.

"Not really," she admitted.

"Her people kidnapped us, forced us into this quest."

"I know. But we're all in this together now, like it or not."

"I don't trust her."

Abeni nodded. "Then trust me."

The panther girl grunted. "Fine. But just so you understand, at the first sign I see she's attempting to betray us, I *will* kill her."

Abeni stared into those unblinking orange eyes and knew without a doubt that Zaneeya meant it. She said nothing as the panther girl turned and walked away.

○ ○ ○

Sometime later, they all sat eating a late breakfast at the lakeside.

Abeni had enough in her bag to make it a decent meal. She, Asha, Songu, and Ama ate a rice porridge with boiled plantain and a boiled egg. Zaneeya settled for some smoked fish, grumbling that she'd prefer fresh meat. Nyomi had a bowl of red flower petals with strips of bark and earthworms slathered in honey—still wriggling. As they ate, they discussed their plans.

"I don't understand," Nyomi said, slurping down an earthworm and smacking her lips. "The masks said this Golden Throne is right where Ama's people left it, but also somewhere else? How can it be in two places at once?"

"I asked the same thing," Ama said. "The place my people left the throne is in the room where it's supposed to be housed. But I told you already, it's empty."

"Why house a throne in a room?" Nyomi asked. "I thought they were for sitting."

Ama stared at her, aghast. "No one sits on the Golden Throne!"

That caught everyone's attention.

"Are you telling me, we're looking for a throne that no one sits on?" Zaneeya asked.

Ama seemed baffled by their questions. She opened her mouth as if trying to select her words carefully before beginning. "The Golden Throne is more like a stool, which are common in our kingdom. But no ruler sits on it. The Golden Throne houses the soul of our people. In many ways, it is our people, the soul of the whole kingdom. We hold processions and festivals, and the Golden Throne is carried by bearers who hoist it up between their shoulders. Some rulers have even built it a chair—its very own throne. But no one person can think to claim it as their own seat. It is more than any one of us, and made up of us all."

Abeni thought she understood—maybe. "Let's talk about the second place the masks claimed the soul of your people was being held, guarded by the dragon Bida."

Ama shook her head. "That's not possible. Bida is dead. He was slain by a hero with a magic sword. He can't guard the Golden Throne because he's gone."

"That Mmoatia healer claimed your people's histories were off," Zaneeya countered. "Maybe you all got Bida being dead wrong."

Ama frowned. "But what about the hero? The magic sword? If Bida is alive it would mean much of what I was taught was a lie. That what my people believe is a lie."

"Just because something happened different from how you thought doesn't make it a lie," Asha said. "It might still be true—just not the same truth you've been taught."

"Let's say then," Abeni said, "that Bida is still alive. Where would we find him?"

There was quiet.

"Can't say I've met any dragons," Zaneeya said finally. "But I've heard stories. Giant monsters like serpents. Some fly, some swim, some are even said to live in the belly of the world. They're generally described as unpleasant."

"Bida was said to have laid waste to the First Gold Kingdom," Ama said.

"That sounds unpleasant," Nyomi chimed in.

"The stories also say they live in remote places," Zaneeya went on. "Deep in the sea or in the ruins of lost cities, that kind of thing. I think they don't want to be found."

That wasn't going to make it easy for them, Abeni thought. She'd never heard of dragons until this Bida. Back in her village they told stories of enough monsters—like the giant crocodile in the stars that fought the hunter with a bright spear. She wondered if the story of Bida and this hero with the magic sword was like that?

"What we need are books," Asha put in. "They might have something about dragons."

"In Makomasi," Ama said, "we have people who recite our histories from memory. We also have books, brought from other lands. But I doubt any talk about Bida."

Abeni remembered lots of books in Asha's house. All gone now. Songu signed something she didn't quite understand. "What about the Great Library," she translated, ". . . in Jenna?"

Ama's eyes lit up. "Jenna. One of the great cities in the west. There's supposed to be a grand library there, where you can find nearly every book written."

Songu signed. "My father . . ." Abeni translated. He faltered before starting again. "He traveled a lot. He visited Jenna once and brought back many books. Maybe what we need can be found there."

Ama nodded eagerly. She turned to Abeni. "Do you have my maps?"

Abeni reached into her satchel, drawing out several maps. She helped the princess spread them on the ground, weighing their edges down with rocks. Everyone crouched around the unfurled brown sheets of parchment. But Ama scrutinized them carefully, shuffling from one to the next. On one map, she traced fingers along its length before stopping.

"There! That's Jenna. Where the Great Library is housed. It would be a good place to seek information about Bida. Only . . ." She trailed off, not meeting their eyes.

"Only we don't have the time," Abeni finished. She'd never

seen one of these great cities. But she knew they lay far to the west. Ama had said they had three weeks, four at most, before the living gold turned them into statues. They wouldn't make it.

"I remember Jenna," Nyomi said absently. "Very noisy. Lots of mortals."

Abeni looked up at the girl. "Nyomi, you've been to this place?"

"Uh-huh." The porcupine girl spooled an earthworm around her finger before sucking it down. "I was with my cousin's uncle's sister's third cousin. He took me there to see these dancing troupes. It was the first time I had to pretend I was mortal, though I couldn't get the ears right. Mortal ears are hard. They're all small and you can't twitch them and—"

"Nyomi," Abeni interrupted. "The collar and bands that restricted you are gone. Does that mean your powers are working?"

Nyomi sat up. "Ohhh! I haven't even tried. Was too hungry to think about it. Let's see." There was a sudden explosion of pink mist and the scent of flowers.

Ama yelped. "Where did she go?"

"Right here," a voice came. More pink mist and Nyomi appeared right beside her.

Ama yelped again, almost falling over. "How did you do that?"

"She can make it so that you can't see her," Abeni explained. "But that's not all. Show her the other thing."

Nyomi promptly took Ama's hand, and in a poof of pink mist both were gone. They reappeared some ways off, and Ama promptly began shrieking. She cut off as another burst of pink took them away, only to have them step out of pink mist where they'd last been—allowing Ama to finish her shriek. She stumbled away from the porcupine girl.

"The first jump can feel a little weird," Nyomi said.

Ama babbled. "What was that? It was all pink! Where did we go?"

"I call it the mist place," Nyomi said.

"But I was here! And then, over there! Now, I'm back here!"

Abeni smiled. "One of Nyomi's surprises. We call it jumping.

She can move from one place to another. But only somewhere she's been before."

Ama's eyes went round. So did everyone else's. They all looked to Nyomi.

"What?" the porcupine girl asked.

"You can jump us to Jenna, you talking cactus!" Zaneeya snapped.

"Oh!" Nyomi exclaimed. "OH! Yes, I could take us to Jenna!" She looked around, frowning. "Only, there are a lot of you. And it's very far. That sounds tiring. I'll probably have to sleep for hours after. And do lots of eating."

"Maybe you can take some of us," Abeni suggested. "Then come back and get the rest?"

Nyomi gasped. "Jump there and back? I'd have to sleep for a week! And—"

"I know," Abeni cut in. "Lots of eating. Do you think you could take us all?"

The porcupine girl looked uncertain. "I've never jumped such a distance. And with so many people. But I could try."

"Try?" Ama asked. "What happens if it doesn't work?"

Nyomi pondered this. "I don't know. Maybe we end up back here. Or somewhere else?"

"Somewhere else doesn't sound too good," the princess said.

Abeni had to admit the girl was right. "It's risky. But I don't know that we have other options."

"Let's do it already," Zaneeya said impatiently. "Just, do you have to be so flowery?" She waved a hand to clear the air.

"Yes," Nyomi replied. "It matches my rosy disposition."

"I think Prickly will get us there," Asha said. "She hasn't let us down."

"I agree," Songu signed.

That left Ama. She looked wary. But after a while, she nodded.

They packed and freshened up as best they could. Songu did something quick with Ama's hair. In a short while they found themselves standing in a circle holding hands. Nyomi stood between Songu and Asha. Abeni held the little girl's hand and Zaneeya's. Ama had been surprised when the panther girl took her hand firmly, grinning all the while. Abeni knew she was doing that to keep her eye on the princess. Hopefully nothing bad would come of it.

"Okay," Nyomi said. "I'm ready. Everybody hold onto each other. This might feel a little weird. Remember, when we're in the mist place, no matter what happens, don't let go!" She closed her eyes and took a deep breath, shaking out her quills. They bristled before settling down. "Jenna," she whispered. "Jenna, Jenna, Jenna." Her eyes popped back open. "Oh, one more thing. Don't mind the people in there. They're harmless, I think."

Abeni started. People? What people? But before she could ask, there was a large explosion—and the world turned pink.

Abeni found herself floating in that familiar place that smelled of flowers. And there was that curious sensation that tickled her middle, an odd feeling of moving while not moving. She heard someone gasp and saw Ama kicking her legs in panic.

"Relax!" she called out. "You're not falling!"

Ama turned to her wide-eyed, breathing heavily. But her kicking stopped.

The few times Abeni had visited this strange place had been brief. No more than moments. She supposed their stay this time was longer because they were traveling so far. She looked around. A pink mist covered everything. There was no ground or sky. No up or down. Just a pink haze that stretched on forever. Where was this place, she wondered? And what was that last bit about people living here?

Nyomi let out a sudden cry. Abeni turned to see the porcupine girl with her eyes shut tight.

"What's the matter?" she asked.

"Something doesn't feel right!" Nyomi said.

"Is it because there are so many of us?"

"No. Not that. Something inside me—working against me."

The living gold, Abeni thought in alarm.

"Maybe we should go back!" Ama said.

"Too late!" Nyomi answered. "Just let me—unnhh!"

The porcupine girl doubled over, crying out.

"Nyomi!" Abeni shouted. A tremor shook everything.

"What was that?" Zaneeya asked.

Abeni had no idea. It felt like the whole world had moved. Nyomi cried out and the tremor came again, stronger. Abeni tried to call to her, but Nyomi cried out even louder. This time the tremor hit them like a tremendous blow. Abeni felt her hand ripped away from Asha's, and she went tumbling. She could hear the others yelling. But she couldn't make out what they were saying. All around her, the world became a pink blur. She spun end over end, unable to stop as she went hurling away into the void.

CHAPTER FIFTEEN

NOWHERE

Abeni tumbled through pink nothingness. She didn't scream. Because if she started, she didn't think she'd be able to stop. Instead, she tried to focus on what was happening. Somehow she'd broken away from the others. She wasn't falling, she reminded herself. There was no falling here. But if she kept tumbling, she might drift too far away for anyone to find her. She needed to find a way to stop. Just to get her bearings. She flailed her arms, hoping that might work. But it only made her tumbling worse. She was going too fast. She needed to slow down. She needed—

Something hit her hard—and held on. This time Abeni did scream, struggling to get free.

There was a growl. "Stop fighting me!"

Zaneeya? She stopped struggling at once as the panther girl wrapped arms about her, forcing her straight. The tumbling stopped. She was still moving but had slowed.

"Your heart is going like a rabbit," Zaneeya said. "Calm down so you can think!"

Abeni had thought she was calm. But now she could feel her heart thumping and her breathing came quick. Shutting her eyes, she took gulps of air. When she opened them again she was staring into Zaneeya's face.

The panther girl let go and began moving like she was treading water.

"It'll help you keep still," she explained.

Abeni followed her lead, finding her voice.

"Nyomi?"

Zaneeya shook her head. "Saw the porcupine vanish before I went flying."

"What about Asha?" Abeni asked in panic. "I let go of her hand! What if she's—"

"She was holding onto Nyomi the last I saw," Zaneeya cut in. "Went wherever the porcupine went. Same with Songu. Probably to Jenna. We got . . . left behind."

"The two of us?"

Zaneeya made a face. "Three. I can smell one more. How I found you."

Abeni stared out. All she could smell was flowers.

"Who—" she began, then cut off. "Ama."

"We could leave her here," the panther girl said. "Okay, okay. Fix your face. I'm joking."

Abeni wasn't sure she was. "How do we get to her?"

Zaneeya's orange eyes twinkled. "Swim, of course." She let go, and extending her arms and legs, made a sweeping motion that sent her flying away.

Abeni watched, astonished.

"Try it!" Zaneeya called back to her. "Just swim over!"

Swim? How could she swim in . . . mist? At Zaneeya's urging she extended her arms and pushed with her legs. To her surprise she went hurtling. She might have passed by Zaneeya if the girl hadn't reached out to grab her.

"See? Whatever this mist is, only takes a bit to move in it."

Abeni nodded. She could never have moved so fast in water. "Where to now?"

Zaneeya jerked her chin and streaked off. Abeni followed. There was nothing to see as they swam. It was just all pink in every direction. In the endless quiet, the first sounds from Ama reached her ears easily. They grew louder the closer they got. When Abeni finally made Ama out, she saw that the girl was tumbling like she had been—maybe worse. With a grunt, Zaneeya picked up speed and tackled Ama. Abeni pushed forward and did the same from the other end. Together, they wrestled the princess still before letting her go, showing her how to tread the mist. She stared at them wide-eyed.

"I thought I was alone," she said, relieved. "What happened?"

"Something went wrong with Nyomi's jump," Abeni said. She remembered the porcupine girl's cries and the way everything had shaken. "I think she was in pain."

"I wonder why," Zaneeya said dryly.

"The living gold," Ama said, wincing. "It must have disrupted her magic."

Abeni had guessed as much. The jump had been too far. "We got separated," she said. "Nyomi, Songu, and Asha went on to Jenna, I hope. The three of us got . . . left behind."

Ama looked alarmed. "Left behind? In this place? How do we get out?"

Abeni shook her head. "We'll probably have to wait for Nyomi to jump back."

Zaneeya frowned. "That could be a problem. She said she'd need to rest after a big jump. How long before she can come get us? Hours? Days?"

"Days?" Ama asked in panic. "We can't stay here days!"

Abeni agreed. She still had her bag, and it held food and water. But she didn't look forward to spending days here. What if they fell asleep? And floated away from each other? What if—? Her thoughts broke as she spied something in the distance. She blinked, to make sure she wasn't seeing things. But no. A part of the mist was . . . moving.

"Do you see that?" she asked.

"I see it," Zaneeya answered, her eyes fixed.

"See what?" Ama asked, perplexed. "I don't—oh! What is that?"

Abeni wasn't sure. It looked like part of the mist had broken away and started moving.

"It's heading straight for us!" Zaneeya said.

"Do we run?" Ama asked, looking ready to bolt.

Zaneeya growled. "Run where?" She bared her claws.

Abeni didn't think running would help either. Whatever it was, it was moving too fast—like a wave. She pulled her staff from her bag. Though she didn't know what good it would do. They floated there, bracing as the wave of mist rolled forward. When it reached them it suddenly parted. She watched as it formed around them, closing them in a ring. The odd bit of mist hovered there, swirling and churning. Then surprisingly, it changed color. No longer pink, but purple!

"Purple mist?" Zaneeya asked, watching it.

"It almost seems like it's alive," Ama whispered.

It almost seems like it's alive, a set of voices echoed around them. Abeni jumped.

"Tell me you heard that too," Zaneeya said.

Tell me you heard that too, the voices echoed again.

"Is it talking?" Ama asked, perplexed. "How can mist talk?"

Is it talking? How can mist talk?

Then Abeni remembered. Something Nyomi had said before jumping away. That there were people in here! People in the mist! She told this to the others, and dozens of voices echoed her words.

"People?" Ama asked.

"She said not to mind them, that they were harmless," Abeni said.

"That she *thought* they were harmless," Zaneeya amended, scowling as her words echoed back to her.

"Maybe they can help!" Ama said hopefully.

"Or, maybe they don't like intruders," Zaneeya warned.

For a moment, Abeni thought of the dark things in the lake who also spoke. But these voices sounded pleasant, almost curious. Well, only one way to find out.

"Hello?" she called. "Is anyone there?"

For the first time, her words weren't picked up. There was silence for a moment, then . . .

We are here.

Abeni inhaled sharply at hearing the many voices.

"Who are you?" she tried.

The ones who live here.

"Are you the mist?"

There was a pause. *We are the ones who live here.*

"Are you . . . people?"

We are the ones who live here, the voices repeated.

"I don't think they understand what people are," Ama whispered.

We have seen you before, the voices spoke suddenly. *With the one who dances.*

"You mean Nyomi!" Abeni said. "She's our friend!"

Friend. That is good. We like the dancing one.

The mist around them shifted and a shape appeared. It looked sort of like Nyomi, made from purple mist. But her body was oddly distorted, and her arms and legs were too long. They waved around and looped like they didn't have any bones as she hopped about, dancing—before vanishing into the mist.

"Is that what we look like to them?" Zaneeya muttered.

"We got separated," Abeni said. "Left behind."

Something bad was brought here. Something that hurt!

The voices wailed and all around them everything shook—like before.

"Yes," Abeni said. "Nyomi's hurt. We want to get back to her. Can you help?"

We can take you where you need to go.

"Thank you!" Abeni said, excited. "Nyomi went to a place called Jenna!"

There was a pause again. *We do not know Jenna. We can take you where you need to go.*

Abeni frowned, looking to the others. But they only shook their heads.

"We need to go to Jenna," she tried again.

We can take you where you need to go, the voices repeated.

"Maybe they've never heard of Jenna," Ama said.

Abeni tried it a different way. "Can you take us to Nyomi?"

We can take you where you need to go.

Zaneeya grunted. "We'll be here all day with this."

Abeni agreed. "Thank you. We'd very much like it if you can take us where we need to go."

At once, the purplish mist that looked like Nyomi appeared again. It extended a wavy arm forward, and Abeni gingerly reached out to touch misty fingers. It tingled. There was a sudden pulling at her middle, like she was being yanked.

Where you need to go, the voices said.

Then in an explosion of mist, she was gone.

Abeni landed on something hard, bouncing and rolling before coming to a stop. Nearby she heard someone else land with a yelp. A third fall ended in a growl, and she watched from the corner of her eye as a slender shape rolled gracefully before rising to stand. Of course the cat landed on her feet. One thing for certain—there was no more mist, pink or purple. She pushed herself up to find Ama already standing. The girl was staring wide-eyed.

"I don't think this is Jenna," she whispered.

Abeni looked around. They were standing on something hard and firm, made of wood. A boat. All the boats she'd ever known were small, made to travel down rivers. This was bigger than she'd ever seen. But it had to be a boat. Because all around her, as far as the eye could see, there were more boats. Boats of all kinds, some even larger than the one they stood on. Some lay on their side, split open. Others were half sunken. Many looked rotted away. A clap of thunder made her jump, as lightning made the jumble of ships visible. There were dozens—no, hundreds! All of them sat in dark waters that stretched on forever.

"Where's the sky?" Ama asked in alarm. "What's happened to the sky?"

Abeni looked up and almost fell back down. Where a sky should have been there was . . . water! Dark water that roiled and splashed but did not fall. There was no sun or moon. And it left everything shrouded in twilight.

"Where *are* we?" Zaneeya asked, sounding shaken. "Where did those things send us?"

Abeni had no answer. The mist people had said it was taking them where they needed to go. How could this be where *anyone* needed to go! She was trying to think of an answer when something cold and wet wrapped about her leg. She barely had time to cry out as she fell and was dragged towards the edge of the ship. Snarls came from Zaneeya followed by sounds of her claws ripping through something. But Abeni was still being pulled. Just before she reached the ship's edge a shadowy shape dropped down beside her, not making a sound. There was a flash of something black, and whatever held her let go. She turned onto her back and looked up to see a pale fleshy tentacle thrashing in the air. It ended in a stump where it had been sliced clean. From somewhere below there was an angry bellowing that made her insides tremble. The tentacle pulled away, sliding off the ship and into the waters with a heavy splash.

Abeni turned to see a smaller piece of cut tentacle writhing beside her. She scrambled away as a booted foot landed on the thing, pinning it. Her eyes roamed up and she was surprised to find a girl. Older than her, probably Ama's age. Tall and slender, she had a heart-shaped face with small round lips and high cheekbones. Sectioned rows of braided hair ran from her head to her shoulders. Her dress was . . . different. She wore an all-white jacket with gold embroidery running down the arms. Underneath was green fabric with red prints that wrapped her like the top of a dress. But from the waist down, her legs were fitted into white pants with that same gold embroidering, tucked into tall brown boots. She stood staring at Abeni through the glow of a burning torch that lit up the gloom. Releasing the squirming tentacle from beneath her boot, she kicked it over the side of the ship.

"I'd move from there if I were you," she said. "Unless you like being food."

Abeni jumped up at once, reaching for her dropped staff—and backing far from the ship's edge. Ama and Zaneeya were behind her, watching the girl warily. She eyed them in turn.

"Well," she said, leaning back casually, "aren't you three a surprise." Her eyes took in Abeni again. "Don't know about you . . ." She lifted the torch to Ama. "But by those golden eyes, you're a Gold Weaver."

"You speak my language?" Ama asked in surprise.

"I pick them up, here and there," the girl replied. "I have an ancestor who would have belonged to what you call the First Gold Kingdom? Decided I could stand to learn some of your talk. But it's sparse. You speak trader's tongue?"

Ama nodded.

"Good, let's switch to that—make it easier for me." The girl's attention turned to Zaneeya. "And a panther spirit. An odd grouping."

"Who are you?" Zaneeya more demanded than asked.

The girl snorted. "I should be asking questions. You three landed on *my* ship, after all."

"Your ship?" Abeni asked.

The girl smiled proudly. "My name is Zuri, but most know me as the Black Fox!" She made an elaborate bow.

Abeni looked to Ama and Zaneeya, who shrugged. "I'm sorry. We've never heard of you."

The girl looked startled. "The Black Fox? Captain of *The Sea Snake*? Who stole back the magic kora for the scribes of Wagadou? Who rescued the son of a Zhusa chieftain from a ravenous zimwi? Who completed the twelve impossible tasks set by the Queen of Azua? The most celebrated smuggler of the eastern seas?"

Ama leaned in close to whisper. "She sounds like a pirate."

Zaneeya scoffed. "That's quite a lot for a mortal of what . . . sixteen seasons?"

"Sixteen *and* a half," the girl retorted. "There's a song about me!" When they shook their heads she sighed. "Fine, just call me Zuri." She moved to a large wooden chair that looked too grand for the small ship. Propping the torch into a slat along its side, she fell heavily into the chair and swung one leg over an armrest. "So, what are you three doing here? And how did you drop out of thin air like that? One of you a sorceress or something?"

"Where is . . . here . . . exactly?" Abeni asked.

The girl frowned. "The Sea of Monsters, of course. Though some call it the Ships' Graveyard. I like to think of it as . . . Nowhere."

Abeni swallowed. None of those sounded good.

"But again," the girl pressed. "What are you doing here? Come seeking treasure? There's lots of treasure here—if you can get past the monsters. But you look a little young for treasure hunters. Though never can tell with you spirits. Hey cat girl, what are you, like a hundred?"

"Eighty," Zaneeya answered.

"Can we go back to the Sea of Monsters part?" Ama asked.

"It's a sea and it has monsters," the girl said. At her words something very big and covered in reddish scales broke the waters nearby, before disappearing again. "But really, what are you doing here? C'mon, it's just us girls."

"We came here by accident," Abeni said. "Can you tell us, are we anywhere near Jenna?"

"Jenna?" Zuri laughed. "That's clear across the other side of the world! If this place is even in the world. No really, who *are* you?" They hesitated. "I gave you my name. It's only polite I get yours. Besides, I'm the only person you're probably going to meet here."

The girl had a point. "I'm Abeni, from the Jembe forest. This is Ama, of the Gold Kingdom. And that's Zaneeya. Some mist people sent us here by accident, I think. Do you know how far we are from Jenna?"

The girl rubbed her chin. "Mist people? Never heard of them. And I told you, you're very far. I set out in my ship on the Green Sea, near the stone cities of the East." She paused, frowning. "But if you came from near the Gold Kingdom, maybe this place isn't any closer or farther to where either of us started."

"You said this place may not be in our world," Ama said. "What do you mean?"

Zuri jerked a thumb to the roiling sea above. "Not your typical sky. Sailors talk of places like this—that exist outside of our world. Or that hover on the fringes. Lost places for lost things. You get there by being shipwrecked in strange storms. Or you sail out too far for too long."

Abeni knew of a place like that—the Vale of Lost Things. She and her friends had quite literally fallen into it. But she hadn't imagined there could be others.

"How did *you* get here?" Zaneeya asked.

Zuri flashed a crooked smile. "Me? I went looking. They say you can find this place if you want to hard enough."

"Why would you *want* to come here?" Ama asked, appalled.

"Told you, these ships are full of treasure!"

"What treasure would be worth *this*?" Zaneeya asked.

Zuri grinned wider, and for the first time Abeni noticed a dark scabbard at her waist. The girl reached for a round gold hilt and drew out a sword with a long curved black blade. Abeni was certain it had been the one to cut through that tentacle. Zuri swiped the blade at the air. Oddly, it didn't make a sound. She took a step—and was suddenly right before them! They all jumped back and she laughed, only once again there was quiet. In fact, now that she stood so close, everything around them seemed to go silent. The thunder. The stormy sea above. Abeni couldn't even hear her own breathing. Seeming satisfied, Zuri slid the sword back into its scabbard—and the sounds of this odd world came rushing back.

"How did you do that?" Zaneeya asked, teeth bared.

"It's a magic sword!" Ama answered in wonder.

"The Silent Sword," Zuri said, caressing the gold hilt. "It can render a wielder so quiet that your footsteps and breathing can't be heard. It dulls the senses, allowing you to sneak up on an enemy— move without being noticed. It can cut through nearly anything without ever needing to be sharpened and it can't be broken. A seer claimed that it belonged to one of my ancestors. They said finding it would help me fulfill my destiny. So, I went looking. Seemed like a good adventure. But . . ."

"You found your sword," Abeni finished. "Only you got trapped here too."

Zuri nodded grimly. "Hard to keep track of time in this place.

But I'd say it's been twelve days now—or more. Can't sail with all these broken ships clogging the water. Food and water is running low. You're the first people I've seen. I was hoping maybe you know a way out?"

Abeni shook her head. "We were hoping you knew a way."

There was a moment of quiet that had nothing to do with any magic swords.

Zuri's eyes brightened. "Say! I do have a lot of gold I . . . liberated . . . from these ships."

"You mean stole," Ama said with disapproval.

"Nobody's coming back for it," Zuri replied curtly.

Zaneeya snickered. "Got you there, Princess."

"Anyway," Zuri went on. "You could use your power on that gold to lift the ship somehow. And we can sail off!" She made a bizarre sweeping gesture with her arms. "Fwwwip!"

"Is that stupid thing you're doing supposed to be gold weaving?" Ama asked flatly.

Zuri dropped her arms. "It's not stupid. Seen you guys do it. The luck of running into a Gold Weaver! Maybe the gods and spirits are smiling down on me after all!"

"Maybe they're laughing," Ama muttered.

"She can't gold weave," Abeni said.

"What?" Zuri turned to Ama. "Are you weak in the power or something?"

"I'm actually very strong," Ama snapped. Her face dropped. "At least I used to be."

"She can't weave anymore," Abeni explained. Given all that had just happened she'd been able to keep those memories out of her mind. Now the empty loss of her song came back.

"Oh," Zuri said. "That's disappointing." She brightened. "So, a princess, huh? Don't try to deny it, kitty here let it out of the bag."

Ama gave the girl a cold stare, lifting her chin.

"Oh yes, definitely royalty." The girl made an awkward bow. "Tell me, Highness. Will there be a reward for getting you out of this? I'm just kidding. No wait, I'm not. Is there a reward? I'd really like to hear that there's a reward."

Ama looked outraged. She opened her mouth to respond but yelped as she was pulled back. Zuri had her sword out and was moving faster than Abeni could follow. She lunged at Ama, grabbing the girl away from whatever had grabbed her. It took a moment for Abeni to figure out what she was staring at. It looked like a fish—with pale green skin, a broad mouth, and big round eyes that didn't blink. A ridge of yellow fins ran from its head and along its back. But it had a body like a person, with long arms and legs. It stood hunched over, dressed in wet rags that clung to its scaly skin while gills on its neck flapped open and shut. Unhinging a jaw, it showed rows of tiny sharp teeth. But whatever sound it made was lost in the silence of Zuri's sword. The girl didn't give it a chance, swinging her blade in one hand and her torch in the other. The fish person backed away, shielding its eyes from the glare with webbed hands. When it reached the edge of the ship it turned and jumped into the waters. Zuri slammed her sword back into its scabbard and sound came rushing back.

"And keep your barnacled hide off my ship!" she shouted.

"Eww!" Ama said in disgust, wiping green slime from her arm. "What was that?"

"Don't know," Zuri said. "But I've seen them before. Think they were people once."

"People?" Abeni asked in shock.

Zuri grimaced. "Haven't you wondered what happened to the crews of all these ships?"

Abeni looked out at the shipwrecked vessels and remembered the ragged clothing on the fish person. Now that she thought on it, there'd been copper bands on its wrists—like jewelry.

"How did mortals become such creatures?" Zaneeya asked.

"How should I know?" Zuri said. "Maybe if you get bitten? Or stay here too long?" She grabbed the torch and moved to the edge of the ship, peering over. "The bigger problem is, where there's one of them, there's always more."

Abeni joined her at the railing and looked down, shuddering. The glow from the torch revealed fish people everywhere. They swam out of the water, climbing up the side of the ship. Dozens of them!

"Hope some of you know how to fight!" Zuri said.

They were her last words before drawing her sword. Then they were in the thick of it.

Abeni kicked at a fish person that tried to grab her staff, knocking it away with the form *Grandmother Sweeps Her Walkway.* More took its place, reaching clammy hands for her. *Pounding the Yam* sent about three back. But they were soon replaced. Zaneeya had changed into a panther, bowling through fish people. Without her gold weaving, Ama had been reduced to using the torch. She swung it wide and her attackers cowered from the flames. Zuri and her magic sword seemed to be everywhere at once. Sound disappeared whenever she got too close, only to return when she whirled away to fight elsewhere.

It was all they could do to keep the fish people at bay. And there seemed to be no end to them! As her arms grew tired, Abeni wondered what would happen if she became one of these things? Would she remember who she used to be? What would happen to Asha? Who would look for her family? As despair threatened to overtake her, out of nowhere came the smell of flowers. There was a burst of pink mist and the most beautiful sight appeared.

"Nyomi!" she cried, clutching at the girl—not even caring about the quills.

"Found you!" the porcupine girl squealed happily.

"How?" Abeni asked.

"The people who live in the mist told me! But I didn't know if I could—"

A fish person reared up before them.

"Ahhh!" Nyomi screamed. "Fish people!"

Abeni held the girl tight, fearful she might jump away without them. An awful bellowing came suddenly from the waters. The fish people went still, cocking their heads to listen. Without warning, a massive tentacle shot up from the water into the air. It came down on the ship, smashing wood to splinters and knocking everyone to their knees. More tentacles appeared, striking the ship and snatching away anything they found. Fish people were scooped up even as they fled. One tentacle took Zuri's chair—then hurled it back, realizing it wasn't food. It landed on the deck, shattering and almost crushing Zaneeya. The panther girl dodged it in time, shifting to her near-human form and rushing over.

"Ahhh!" Nyomi screamed again. "Tentacles!"

"The ship's coming apart!" Ama said, stumbling to them.

"We have to go!" Zaneeya shouted.

"Nyomi!" Abeni urged. "Get us out of here!"

The porcupine girl nodded briskly, just noticing Zuri. "Is she coming too?"

The girl sheathed her sword. "You think I want to stay here?"

"Okay!" Nyomi said. "Everybody hold on!" She closed her eyes. But Abeni's stayed open, as the biggest tentacle yet loomed up before them. She clenched her teeth as it descended, ready to crush them all. There was a burst of pink mist with the strong smell of flowers. And as they disappeared, she thought she could just see the giant tentacle strike the ship—blasting it apart.

But they were already gone.

CHAPTER SIXTEEN

JENNA

Abeni sat on a comfortable red-cushioned chair with her head resting on her hands as she gazed out a wide half-oval window. The city of Jenna lay stretched out beneath her, a sprawling mass of buildings both great and small—many packed together or even heaped one atop the other. The sun sat high at midday, beating down on buildings in their different hues: mostly sandy brown but also bright reds, greens, and yellows. Trees grew up in orderly bunches between the buildings; some even grew bushes on their rooftops or vines that crept along their walls. The city was crisscrossed with streets and roadways—wide, narrow, straight and meandering—reminding her of a spider's web.

It was hard to believe much of this was made of mudbrick, like the houses of her village. But the angles here were so precise! And some of the buildings were so tall she couldn't imagine the many workers it had taken to create such heights. The building she now sat in—a place called the Happy Wanderer—was four stories high! She had seen things in Makomasi that defied imagination. But that was a city crafted by the magic of Gold Weaving. Jenna was made in ways she understood, with hands, and tools, and water to mold. It felt more solid than the Gold Kingdom, more real.

She had gotten to walk Jenna's crowded streets, see its bustling markets, view the carved statues that lined its paths. She'd even watched a procession of pure white bulls with horns wrapped in gold pulling a funeral barge surrounded by mourners and gazed into the blue waters of a pool filled with colorful fish. There'd been so many scents and smells: jugs of sweet oils, sizzling foods, spices that tickled her nose, the stink of dung. It all mixed together in a city that held something new around each corner.

And of course, there were people—so many people! In all kinds of dress, with all sorts of hairstyles, talking in different tongues. Like the biggest village ever! There were so many people that places like the Happy Wanderer were built just to house visitors. Who had ever heard of such a thing? It all made for a very *loud* city. Everyone here was talking or shouting and arguing—all blending into one big mess of noise! Not to mention the braying donkeys, squawking birds, barking dogs, and the like. It quickly became too much. And she'd been happy to return to their room to just watch it from a window. The city slowed down at this time of day, as people stayed indoors to escape the heat. It wouldn't come alive again until the sun went down. Then there'd be night markets, lit up by lanterns that made Jenna glow like the mountain city of the Mmoatia.

Abeni perked up as a column of tall animals sped by below, ridden by figures in helmets who carried long tasseled spears. Horses! She'd glimpsed one in Makomasi. But here there were many more, ridden by the city guard. She watched them trot in a tight formation, the *clop clop clop* of their hooves echoing.

"You look rested," someone said.

Abeni turned to find Asha. The small girl rested her chin on the window's edge.

"I did sleep a whole day," Abeni reminded her. She had arrived back with Nyomi. And after some hugs and relief at seeing everyone had promptly passed out.

"You had some exciting days," Asha said. "Well, sort of."

That part still amazed her. Turned out, time passed differently where she, Ama, and Zaneeya had been. What felt like an hour was really three whole days! She'd guessed right. The living gold in Nyomi had caused their jump to go wrong. The porcupine girl had needed a long rest to recover before she could go looking for them.

"Exciting is one word for it." She looked to where Zaneeya and Ama were telling their story of being left behind. The two had called a short truce to relate what had happened. This was the third time they'd told it. Nyomi sat attentive though, oohing and ahhing where necessary. Beside them, reclining in a cushioned wooden chair, Zuri sat sipping from a silver cup. She said nothing but watched with a faint smile.

"I tried finding you when you were gone," Asha said. "But you never slept."

"Fish people didn't give me time," Abeni said.

"Did they look like this?" Asha began making sucking sounds with her mouth.

Abeni smiled. "Much, much, worse." She turned serious. "I'm glad you weren't left behind with us. But I was worried."

"I was with Prickly," Asha said. "And Songu. So, I was fine. Are you fine?"

Abeni caught her meaning. Her song. *It feels like someone died,* Ama had said.

"It's hard to believe it's gone. I got used to it being there. Being a part of me."

"You're still you," Asha insisted, her small features softening. "Even without the song."

"I know. I just can't help feeling . . . less."

Asha wrapped her in a deep hug. "You're enough for me."

Abeni hugged her back. She wished she could have said that was enough for her. Over her shoulder, she saw Zuri approaching, carrying two cups. When the girl reached them she handed one to Abeni. It was filled with dark liquid with a foamy top. Abeni sipped it and was surprised by the sweet taste of mint.

"A popular drink here," Zuri said. "In the tea houses, you take three rounds—one bitter, the second minty, and the third sweet. I got something between the second and third. I can do without bitter." She leaned against a wall, sipping her own tea. Asha turned to her.

"Thank you for bringing back my Abeni."

Zuri smiled. "They sort of brought me back."

Asha's eyes roamed to the girl's sword.

"It suits you," she said.

"Yeah? Hope so. Went through a lot to get the thing."

"It was probably calling you," Asha said. "Magic objects are sort of alive. Not like you and me, but they want to be wielded. Just by the right person. Treat it well. But know one thing. Having it is going to change you. Magic always does." Her eyebrows jumped. "Oooh! This is my favorite part! All the tentacles!" She skipped off to sit beside Songu, listening as Zaneeya and Ama continued their tale.

A befuddled Zuri watched her go. "Is she always that . . . strange?"

"We're a strange bunch," Abeni said.

A knock came at the door. At once, Zaneeya shifted into her most human form—a pretty girl with big brown eyes with neat braids parted down the middle. Nyomi became, of all things, an older woman with a plump face—though the eyes were a bit too large. She wore an expensive-looking dress with an elaborate gold and red headwrap. Abeni was impressed. She could recall when Nyomi hadn't even been able to remember to give her illusion clothes. The door opened to admit several figures in white robes and tall red hats. They carried round trays that held more cups of tea and an assortment of sweets.

One of them bowed. "Compliments of Madam Fatouma. The mistress of the Happy Wanderer hopes your party is finding their stay satisfactory."

"Oh, very much!" Nyomi beamed. She reached for a stack of round coins, offering one up. "Tell Madam Fatouma we are quite happy!"

The man took the coin, a wide grin splitting his face. "We will! Most certainly!" He left with the others, closing the door behind him. Nyomi hurriedly changed back. Zaneeya did the same. The porcupine girl scooped up some sweets. She was especially fond of small bars made of sesame seeds, honey, and butter. Beside her, the stack of gold coins became a pile of pebbles.

"I hope Madame Fatouma never learns her rich guest is paying in rocks," Zuri said.

Abeni eyed the pile of pebbles. Nyomi claimed this was the only way to get a place for them to stay. It made Abeni uncomfortable. Ama too. It felt like stealing. But it seemed for spirits tricking mortals was all in good fun.

"What are you going to do now? Head back home?"

Zuri sipped her tea. "Home is no one place for me. Spent the last few years sailing on the other side of the continent. But my ship is lost now."

"I'm sorry about that."

The girl shrugged. "Things turned out the way they turned out. Life's too short to spend it fretting about the way you wanted things to be. Better to adapt to the way they are." She turned to look out the window. "Haven't been back in Jenna in three years. It's an old city. You know it got swallowed up by a big empire once? People say the empire stretched so far you could take a whole season to walk through it. Fell apart. Empires do that. But cities like Jenna that had stood here before, remain."

Abeni looked out at the city, trying to imagine it belonging to something bigger.

"Now Jenna's run by a Council of Scholars instead of a king," Zuri went on. "See there?" She pointed to a building on the western side of the city. It sat taller and bigger than the others, with ridged points rising from each part of its square roof. "That's the main school for scholars, teachers, and students. People come from all over to learn every art there: mathematics, healing, the movements of the stars, magic, philosophy—everything."

"You sound like you've been there," Abeni said.

Zuri smiled. "Briefly. My parents' idea. Sent me off when I was your age. Hoped I might become a scholar or teacher. I don't mind knowing things. But all those rules aren't for me. So, I stole a horse, rode off, and never looked back."

"Did you really do all those things you claimed?"

The girl winked. "More . . . or less."

Abeni hesitated.

Zuri eyed her. "You look like someone with a question."

"Yes. In your travels have you ever seen Storm Women? Warriors with fire in their eyes?"

Zuri lowered her cup. "I've known women warriors—even a warrior queen. But with fire in their eyes? You speak of the Isat."

Abeni's heart jumped. Isat! That's what Asha—Auntie Asha—had once called them. "Yes! Servants of . . . him. The Witch Priest."

Now Zuri's face turned serious. "It is said they were once servants of a king here in the west. His warriors and guardians. Until the Witch Priest whispered in their ears. They turned on their king and became *his* servants, gifted with *his* power. He renamed them the Isat, from an old tongue in the east. It means fire—for they would help him consume the world." She turned to stare out the window again. "Worse than Storm Women march in his armies. Hyena men, Bikolo, even Face-stealers! They've swallowed up smaller kingdoms. Set the southlands ablaze. Now he readies to move on the west. On cities like Jenna."

Abeni felt a chill. She'd seen other sights on the city's streets. Refugees. Men, women, and children with haunted faces. They carried their belongings in bundles or pulled along goats. And told stories to all who would listen about escaping the Witch Priest's armies.

"Is Jenna preparing?" she asked.

Zuri scoffed. "What do a bunch of scholars know about war? They're more concerned with keeping out refugees and stopping talk that scares people. They've convinced themselves it won't happen. Not to Jenna. But it will. And when the other kingdoms and cities of the west fall, he'll turn his eyes to the east. It's the whole world he wants."

Abeni wondered how many knew the Witch Priest was a spirit. A spirit who wanted to see everything burn, so that he could return to a time without all the other beings that now shared this world.

"I've heard there are spirits," Abeni said. "Gathering to stand up to him."

Zuri grunted. "You may have friends in spirits. But they abandoned most of us a long time ago. You want my advice? Don't stay in this city long. Get away however you can. Find someplace to hide, a nice cozy hole where no one can find you. That's my plan."

Abeni looked at her, unconvinced. That didn't seem the greatest plan.

"Have you ever seen them? These Isat?"

Zuri shook her head. "And I don't want to. Heard the stories of what they leave behind." Her gaze on Abeni grew intense. "But you have, haven't you? I can see it on your face. Who are you, Abeni of the Jembe forest? Traveling with spirits, a princess, and that strange little girl who at times *forgets* she's a little girl? Who are you, that you've seen Storm Women in the flesh and lived to speak of it?"

"And if I asked you about ghost ships?" Abeni pressed.

Zuri scowled. "Guess I'll be the one doing all the answering. Fine. I only know what I've heard. Ships sailed by wraiths from across the sea, who steal away the living. Never seen one, never want to." She downed her tea. "Now, will you at least tell me what you're doing in Jenna? Guessing it's not just sightseeing."

Abeni turned again to look out the window, this time east—to a building that stood even higher than the school of the Council of Scholars. It was rectangular, with a raised portion at its front that sloped upward and whose four sides narrowed to create a tower. The mudbrick and clay covering the structure had been painted white, so that it shined under the sun's glare. Zuri followed her gaze.

"The Grand Library?"

Abeni nodded. "We need information."

"That's what libraries are for," Zuri replied dryly. "Anything more specific?"

Abeni scanned the girl's face. If half of her story was true, she might be useful. Was that how she judged people now? Their usefulness? "We're on a quest for the Gold Kingdom."

Zuri snorted. "Not willingly, I'd bet. That porcupine spirit let slip about having living gold inside her. I'm betting it's in the rest of you. And that princess is leading your little expedition. Only she doesn't seem to be in charge."

"She's not. Not anymore."

"Curious. Let me guess. You need to complete this quest to get that living gold out of you or something unpleasant will happen?"

"Something like that."

"And this quest is for . . . ?"

"I can't tell you."

"Right. But what do you want in the Great Library?"

"We're looking for information on a dragon, named Bida."

That sent the girl's eyes as round as Nyomi's fake coins.

"Why would you want information on a—" Her eyes grew even wider. "You want to *find* a dragon? Who goes looking for a dragon? People run the other way when dragons are involved. You know that, right? They shout, 'AHHH! DRAGON!'"

"We need to find this dragon to finish our quest and be free of the Gold Weavers."

Zuri stared at her for a long while. Then, walking back over to the others, she picked up a cup of tea, returned, and downed it in one gulp.

"Okay, I can help you with that."

Abeni blinked. "What? Just like that, you want to help?"

"I owe you for getting me out of that mess," Zuri said. "Can't let it be said the Black Fox doesn't pay her debts."

Abeni stared at the girl. That had been far too easy. Then it struck her. "You think there'll be a reward—from the Gold Kingdom."

Zuri smiled slyly. "It crossed my mind."

Abeni tried to imagine her using that smile on the Queen Mothers. She might actually stick around to see that.

"So," the girl said, leaning close. There was an excited look in her eyes. "When are we going to break into this library?"

CHAPTER SEVENTEEN

THE GREAT LIBRARY

The Great Library of Jenna was much larger up close. It appeared to be made of mudbrick fitted over a frame of painted timbers that jutted out at each floor. There were round towers on the building's four ends, each topped with a bulbous cap. Raised lines and shapes were carved into the library's front, which held two tall doors of dark wood crafted with bits of silver. They opened for men and women in blue robes, who made their way down broad steps and out into Jenna. It was dusk and the city was returning to life. Shops had begun reopening and vendors were setting up for the night markets.

Abeni and her companions stood just outside the library, on a path lined by statues. The one closest to them depicted a reclining man, head in his hand as he read from a book.

"This is what we're trying to get into?" Zaneeya asked, straining her neck to look up. A passing boy offered a smile until her scowl made him duck his head.

Zuri chuckled. "You do know you've chosen to look like a very pretty girl, right?"

Zaneeya rolled her eyes, muttering about mortal boys. The panther girl had put on her best face while out in Jenna. So had Nyomi, who now looked like a girl with large dark eyes. Word had spread of a wealthy woman staying at the Happy Wanderer, handing out gold. That kind of attention they didn't need.

"How are we going to get in?" Ama asked, eyeing Zuri. "Isn't that why you're here?"

"So you keep reminding me," the girl replied. "I've been thinking on a few things." She looked to Nyomi. "Maybe you might jump us in there?"

Nyomi looked at the library and shook her head. "I can only jump somewhere I've been."

"But you found us in that nowhere place," Ama said. "You'd never been there before."

"That was because the mist people showed me."

"Well, can't you just ask them to *show* you inside?" Zuri asked.

Nyomi shook her head. "It doesn't work like that. When I jump, it's like going through a door. I can find the door because I've been there before. I can feel other doors too—endless doors! But I can't see or find them."

"Because you haven't been through those doors before?" Abeni asked.

Nyomi nodded. "It's like trying to visit a place I've only imagined. But . . . I don't think I'm jumping all by myself. I think the mist people are part of it. I never said anything about them before because I thought you'd make fun. I could always feel them. Sometimes hear them. But I never talked to them until I went looking for you."

"They seemed to know who you were," Abeni said.

"Yes," Nyomi said. "When we're in there, I think they can read our thoughts, go through our experiences, see things through our eyes, feel what we feel. When I was hurting, they hurt. And it was worse for them because I don't think they've ever felt pain."

Zuri raised an eyebrow. "That's . . . strange."

"Symbiosis," Asha said. She sat with her head in her hands, imitating the reclining statue. Everyone turned to her. "It's when two different living things work together, sometimes towards a mutual benefit." She returned to imitating the statue.

"I'm starting to think that's how I go through the doors," Nyomi went on. "They see where it is I want to go. And together, we . . . jump. They can't send me through doors to somewhere I haven't been, because there's not enough in my head to pull on."

"It would be like them trying to visit a place *they've* only imagined," Abeni reasoned.

"Exactly. But there must be exceptions. You remember my first jump?"

Abeni nodded. They had been fleeing bush babies set on devouring them. She'd slipped off a cliff and Nyomi had appeared out of nowhere, catching her midair before jumping back.

"How could I do that?" the porcupine girl asked. "I'd never been on that cliff before. But what if in that moment I wanted to get to you so badly—*needed* to get to you—that what I imagined was enough for them to take me through that door? I'm thinking now that something like that happened to you three. When you asked them for help, they must have gone through your minds and sent you through a door—to the nowhere place."

"But why would we need to go there?" Abeni asked. "Why not Jenna? Or to you?"

"I don't know," Nyomi admitted. "Maybe trying to read the three of you is harder than just me—and they got turned around. Or maybe they felt that was where you wanted or needed to go, badly. Like when I first jumped off that cliff. It took *hours* to get them to show me the door to the nowhere place, because . . . well, they kind of forgot where they put you."

"They . . . forgot," Zaneeya said flatly.

Nyomi shrugged. "I think they live in the moment. Things happen, and that's that. I had to keep showing them in my mind that I wanted to find you all—*together*—before they got it. Anyway, trying to explain to them jumping me into the library might take all night. And if they misinterpret my need, who knows where I'd end up!"

Abeni shook her head. She had no idea Nyomi's jumping was so . . . complicated.

"Um, excuse me," someone said. They turned to find the boy who had smiled at Zaneeya earlier—his head clean-shaven and his body swallowed up in light blue robes. "I was wondering—?"

"This is a private discussion," Zuri snapped. She turned back to them. "Okay. New plan. We *break* in. Then, we find some scholar in there—they're always up late reading or doing scholar stuff. And we make them find the information we're looking for—or else!"

"Excuse me?" It was the boy again.

This time Zuri rounded on him, hands on her hips. "Can you not take a hint? The girl doesn't want to talk to you. Keep it moving!"

The boy seemed bewildered, then looked to Zaneeya before shuffling his sandaled feet.

"No. I mean I did notice her. But that's not what I'm saying now."

"Well, what are you saying?" Zuri asked impatiently. "Spit it out."

The boy cleared a narrow throat. "I speak trader's tongue. I couldn't help overhearing . . ."

"Well, you're standing right behind us," Zuri said. "Ever heard of personal space?"

The boy stepped back. "Sorry. But you are, um, blocking the entrance?" He pointed to the path they stood on, leading to the library steps.

Zuri blinked. "Oh." They shifted aside as the boy squeezed past. He had gone a short way before he turned back. "I was saying that I couldn't help overhearing your conversation. I don't think I understood most of it. But if you're trying to get into the Great Library, you don't need to break in. You can just go inside."

Zuri frowned. "Since when is the Great Library open to anyone?"

"For a while!" the boy said. "The Council of Scholars made it public to everyone in Jenna. Didn't you know?"

Zuri stared openmouthed. She straightened, turning to the others. "There you are. Problem solved. You're welcome." Ama rolled her eyes.

"Of course, you'll have to get on the list," the boy said.

"List?" Zuri asked.

"Oh yes. The library has many visitors. They can't all get in at once. You put your names on a list, and you're given a date. You should get in perhaps in a month? Or two?"

Abeni's shoulders slumped. Two months?

The boy caught their disappointment. "I take it you need to be in sooner." He hesitated. "I suppose I could take you."

Zuri looked him over, skeptical. "You're a scholar?"

"A librarian. Well, an apprentice. But I have access to much of the library. Even the restricted areas! I could show you around. Next week? I have a free day—"

"How about now?" Zuri cut in.

The boy looked startled. "Now? But it's near closing. I have books to get in order . . ."

Zuri arched her eyebrows at Zaneeya. The panther girl sighed, then turned to the boy. Her brown eyes seemed to get larger, and her voice turned melodious. "You're certain you couldn't take us in today? It's very important."

The boy beamed. "Maybe I can. Be right back!" He turned, hurrying through the doors.

"That was good," Zuri said. "A little spirit glamour in there?"

The panther girl shrugged. "Mortal boys are easy. And superficial."

The boy's head poked out the doors, and he beckoned them inside. They walked through and Abeni stared in amazement. The Grand Library was even grander on the inside. It was well lit, with candles everywhere. Shelves of books and scrolls lined the walls. Other shelves stood in rows across the main floor. Tables were set up between, where people sat reading. Figures in long blue robes walked about, placing books and scrolls back onto the shelves. There was the scent of leather and burning tallow, along with that inescapable smell of old things.

The boy led them to a green door, opening it. "Your bag will need to stay here," he said to Abeni. "Library policy to guard against theft, with all these refugees in the city." He looked embarrassed. "You're not refugees? I didn't mean offense."

"We're not refugees," Zuri said sourly. "Though the way I heard, lots of your books came from the library taking what it wanted. Every caravan entering Jenna had the city guards going through their goods—looking for any writing. The library ended that policy half a century ago, but never returned anything they took."

The boy cringed. "Those were . . . regrettable times."

Abeni reluctantly gave him her bag. After her song, she didn't want to lose anything else.

The boy eyed Zuri's sword.

"Nope," she said flatly, and he backed off.

"You'll need to wear these." He handed over bracelets made of braided copper and iron. Zaneeya reached to take one and jerked her hand back.

"What is that?" she growled.

"A charm," the boy said. "The library has lots of wards. To preserve books, repel insects, even protect against fire—why we're able to have so many candles. It also stops unauthorized entry. One of the other apprentices forgot to wear his. He got such a shock he was in bed for days!"

Zaneeya took the bracelet and slipped it on. "Just feels . . . funny."

Nyomi did the same and her eyebrows jumped.

"It tickles!" Asha giggled, as Songu fit a bracelet on her small wrist.

Abeni felt nothing.

"I'm afraid I can't give you the full tour," the boy said. "We can't stay too long past closing. The wards won't allow it. Can you tell me what you're looking for?"

Everyone looked to Abeni. She supposed this had been her idea.

"We didn't get your name," she told the boy.

"Seydou," he answered, smiling and placing a palm to his chest.

"I'm Abeni." She introduced the others. "Seydou, we're looking for books you might have about a dragon named Bida."

That made his eyes go round. "Dragon?"

Abeni nodded. "Would the library have books like that?"

"An unexpected request. But yes, of course. Come."

He led them through the library proper, where Abeni looked over the books. Some took up half a table, bound in thick leather.

Others could fit in the palm of your hand. One broad scroll was unfurled to reveal writing in a continuous spiral. They passed a room where a dozen apprentices in light blue robes sat using small, pointed sticks they dipped into jars as they wrote away furiously. A blue-robed librarian walked among them, looking over their work.

"The library gets books from all over," Seydou explained. "One of our jobs as apprentices is copying them, so the originals can be returned."

"Better than stealing," Zuri remarked.

Seydou returned a nervous laugh before taking them to a set of stairs. They climbed up three levels to another floor. This one held books like the first, but also large, framed parchments with writing and colorful drawings that took up whole parts of walls. Somehow, Seydou ended up close to Zaneeya, and tried to start a conversation.

"So, you and your . . ." He looked over the others. ". . . family are visiting Jenna?"

"I'm here and they're here," the girl replied. "So that must be the case."

Zuri stifled a laugh.

"Where, um, are you from?"

"Lots of places."

"That must be nice. I was born here in Jenna."

"Sounds confining."

"Oh, there's lots to do! And with so many visitors. It's like the world comes to us."

"I suppose. But all these people. Pressed against each other. How can you stand it?"

Seydou laughed lightly. "When I want to escape, I climb to the top of the library at night. The stargazing instruments are up there. I just like staring up at it all. The city doesn't seem so big, in the face of that."

Zaneeya glanced at him in surprise. "That sounds . . . sensible."

The boy grinned, as if he'd received the best compliment.

"Aren't you all worried about . . . the Witch Priest?" Abeni asked.

Seydou's face fell. He looked around nervously. "I wouldn't say that name out loud."

"Well, aren't you?" she asked again. "All these refugees talk about him."

"The refugees tell lots of stories," Seydou said uncertainly. "The Scholars' Council insists it's exaggeration. That the troubles are likely the work of bandits who dress up to frighten superstitious common folk."

Zuri scoffed "And you believe that?"

Seydou stopped and looked to them pleadingly, as if he had to believe. Because the truth was too terrifying. But it wasn't right, Abeni decided, to lie to him.

"The stories are real," she said. "I've seen for myself. Your city should prepare."

Seydou swallowed and looked ready to say something. But then it vanished. He resumed walking as if she hadn't spoken.

"Here we are," he said, stopping at a new part of the library. Books and scrolls packed the shelves. On the walls were colorful paintings of fantastic creatures: a great blue bird with a pointed crest and lightning for wings; a small, green-skinned man wearing leaf-like armor; a bizarre four-legged beast with a basket-shaped head and a mouth of dagger-like teeth.

"The library has a rich collection on magical creatures," Seydou said. "But this is where we keep books on the more dangerous ones—hyena men, zimwi, panther women." Zaneeya barked a sharp laugh that caught him off guard. "Yes, well, um, as you can imagine, also dragons." He searched through the shelves, muttering as he went. "Ah! Here!"

He struggled to haul a large book over to a table. Zaneeya lifted it from him with one hand, setting it down easily.

"Thank you! You're quite strong!"

"I get that," Zaneeya replied.

He was starting to say something else when Zuri interrupted. "The book?"

"Right. This is a compendium on dragons. The work of several dragon scholars."

"Dragon scholars?" Abeni asked.

"Oh yes!" Seydou said. "Scholars who search for all they can about dragons. They are rare. And many disappear out in the field. We assume they were eaten."

"Not the smartest career choice," Zuri commented.

"It's dangerous work," Seydou admitted. "But we are indebted to their tenacity." He ran a hand across the brown leather covering. "This compendium was put together by the library. We hired an expert tanner who used worked gazelle skin. Master bookbinders stitched it together."

"You are going to actually open it, right?" Zuri asked.

Seydou gave a half-smile but turned serious as he carefully pulled back the cover. He closed his eyes, sniffing deeply and exhaling with a contented sigh. Opening his eyes, he shrugged sheepishly.

"I like the smell of a book that hasn't been opened in a while."

Nyomi and Asha leaned close on either side of him, inhaling deep.

"Oh! That is wonderful!" the porcupine girl said. Asha nodded excitedly, inhaling again.

"This is obviously going to take a while," Zuri muttered. She plopped down into a chair.

"The dragons?" Abeni asked, trying not to sound impatient.

"Of course." Seydou gingerly turned to a colorful sketch of a large green creature. It reminded Abeni of a very large snake, covered in scales from the tip of its sharp tail to its horned head. But unlike a snake, the thing had four legs, and two bat-like wings on its back.

"That's a dragon?" she asked in wonder.

"Yes," Seydou answered. "Well, more a composite. Actual dragons vary greatly. Not all, for instance, can fly. Some live only in water. Others dwell underground and have bodies suited for burrowing." He turned to another page with what looked like a list of names. "The book is categorized by the scholars rather than the dragons. As you can see, next to each scholar are the dragons they studied. Some have personal names, given by locals. Others more general names. Take for instance the dragons studied by the first scholar in the compendium. Aamadu." He turned several more pages, to a painting of another creature. It looked somewhat like the previous one. But its scales were rainbow hued. It had no wings or legs, just a ridge of spines like a fin running along its back. There were no horns on its head, but there was that same long snout—except these jaws opened wide to show rows of needle-like teeth. All around the painting was writing recounting its size, age, places found, and more.

"Water Lord?" Abeni said, reading the page. "That's a kind of dragon?"

Seydou nodded. "Unpleasant creatures. Very volatile. They live in deep rivers, lagoons, or remote lakes. Their bodies are made for water. They spend their early years at sea, before moving inland." He scanned the text. "According to Aamadu, they're solitary. Their growth seems to depend on the size of the places they inhabit. But some of the largest could easily drag down a water buffalo—as they drown their food before devouring it. There have been claims of multi-headed varieties . . ."

"Multiple heads?" Ama asked, incredulous.

"Well, just claims. Aamadu couldn't confirm. He was, ah . . ."

"Let me guess," Zuri called over. "Eaten."

"While trying to talk to a Water Lord," Seydou explained.

"Dragons can talk?" Abeni asked. She hadn't even thought of that.

"Based on reports, many do," Seydou said. "Though some, like Water Lords, are considered mindless and only concerned with eating. Aamadu wanted to prove they were thinking creatures—but just never cared to talk with humans."

"Guess we'll never know," Zuri quipped. Then added, "Poor Aamadu."

Seydou nodded solemnly. "Now, the dragon you're seeking information on is altogether different." He turned to a section in the back titled Accounts of Unstudied Dragons. "This was the work of multiple scholars who wrote on dragons who are no longer living or whose whereabouts are unknown. Much of it was cobbled together from old histories, folklore, and legends. Your dragon is at the top of the list." He turned to another page that read, simply, *Bida*. There were several sketches. One showed a dragon like the first, all white with gold horns and gold wings. A second drawing gave him a marbled body of black and gold. Yet another showed a short and squat golden dragon, with a face that resembled a lion but with the horns of a ram; this one even had hooves. There were more, each different.

Ama shuddered at the images, hugging herself protectively. This was the monster from her people's stories, Abeni knew. That had destroyed their First Gold Kingdom. It must be hard to see it in this book.

"Why are there so many depictions?" Abeni asked.

"As you likely know," Seydou answered, "Bida is in the legends of the Gold Kingdom and shared by surrounding regions. Their stories vary, as do ideas of what Bida looked like."

"What do those stories say about Bida?" Abeni asked.

Seydou turned a page. "Again, the stories vary. What we generally have is that Bida was a dragon of great power. He is said to have gifted the people of the lands where he resided the art of manipulating gold, held now only by the Gold Weavers." He glanced to Ama, whose golden eyes stood out clearly. "Some tales claim he was a protector. Others, a monster that demanded tribute in maidens, whom he devoured. These differences are likely because the First Gold Kingdom stretched over such a vast region. It's believed the Gold Kingdom of today exists in what would have been its hinterlands."

"Nonsense," Ama snapped. "The Gold Kingdom of today sits at the heart of the First Gold Kingdom and is its direct inheritor."

Seydou said nothing, looking between Ama and Abeni uncertainly.

"Could you tell us what you mean?" Abeni urged.

He cleared his throat. "Well, scholars have long determined the heart of the First Gold Kingdom was much farther away than the present Gold Kingdom—to the north and west. They spoke a tongue closer to what we do here in Jenna and some of the great cities of the west. Why, Wagadou itself shares a name with—"

"I'm sure the scholars of Jenna have their stories," Ama cut in. "But we're not here for the fanciful tales of outsiders trying to lay claim to the First Gold Kingdom. We just need to know about Bida."

Abeni frowned at the girl's rudeness. But she was right.

"Could you tell us what happened to Bida?" she asked.

Seydou scanned the book. "Again, the histories vary. There are numerous stories. All of them, however, carry the same theme. Bida grew to be a danger and was defeated by a hero with a magic sword. According to these tales, Bida is dead."

Abeni shared a glance with Ama. Both knew the Masks of Akani had said differently. That the Golden Throne would be found with the one who created and now guarded it—Bida.

"What if Bida was still alive?" Abeni asked.

Seydou's eyes widened. "That's not possible. The histories . . ."

"But what if you knew he was," Abeni pressed. "What if you knew for certain?"

"I'm not a scholar," he said. "Certainly not one of dragons."

"But you know how scholars think. What would one of them do?"

Seydou stared. "I suppose . . . I'd ask a dragon."

"Come again?" Zuri asked, sitting up.

"I'd ask a dragon," he repeated. "There was one scholar, she believed dragons all knew of each other and could sense another's presence. Dragons are reportedly very territorial. It's important to them that they be the only inhabitants of a region. It makes sense they would have the ability to tell where another dragon resided, to avoid conflict. I'd find a dragon and ask about Bida."

Zuri laughed. Abeni tried to wrap her head around that. Another dragon?

"Where do we even find one?" she asked.

"Well, dragon sightings aren't uncommon," Seydou said. "There've been reports of a dragon in a mountainous region to the west. About a week's travel from here."

A week's travel? Abeni wasn't even sure they had enough time.

"How would we get there?" she asked. Having Nyomi jump was out of the question.

"That I can help with," Zuri said, sitting up. "First, we'll need to steal horses—"

"Or," Seydou said, frowning at the girl, "you could hire out to a caravan. Always some heading that way."

Zuri shrugged, settling back.

"Does this dragon have a name?" Ama asked.

"I don't know," Seydou admitted. "But reports claim the dragon is troubling a small kingdom whose ruler is seeking heroes to drive it off. They've posted calls throughout the city. Although there haven't been many takers. Most people tend to run the other way when it comes to dragons."

Zuri chuckled. "That's what I told them. And screaming." She waved her arms. "AHH!"

"She's not wrong," Seydou said. "Dragons are formidable. The most powerful are said to wield great sorcery, bending even the elements to their will. I wouldn't face a dragon in battle!"

Abeni looked to Ama. This was getting too complicated.

"Unless," Seydou pondered, "I had a magic sword. Like the one that defeated Bida."

He turned the page to a painting of the nameless hero wielding a sword that was said to cut off Bida's head. Abeni squinted. Wait. She *knew* that sword.

"Is that . . . ?" Ama asked, coming closer.

"It can't be," Zaneeya said, leaning over the book.

Seydou looked at them in confusion, then to the sword on the page—a slender curved black blade with a golden pommel.

"Does that sword have a name?" Abeni asked.

"Yes," Seydou answered. "The histories call it the Silent Sword."

Zuri practically jumped out of her chair. "What the—!"

CHAPTER EIGHTEEN

MONSTERS

Fulan walked through the remains of the burnt city. Her boots crunched shards of pottery as she eyed the destruction. This had been the center of a small kingdom, which traded fish and pottery to caravans and the great cities farther west. Its people had been given a choice to join her father. They refused. Now their kingdom was no more. She stopped to look at a man in chains who was led stumbling along. He had been a king. He now stared about dazed, as if expecting to awaken from a bad dream.

She watched him, and there was a familiar *flicker*. She was somewhere else. There was another man, being led in chains. And a woman beside him. All around, everything burned. People screamed. She was so frightened and small. She wanted to run out to the man and woman in chains. But someone put a strong hand on her shoulder. *Flicker.*

Fulan shook away the troubling memories. She turned to stare at the hand on her shoulder. The Huntsman wisely removed it.

"I was calling your name," he said. "It was like you didn't hear me. Where did you go?"

"None of your business," she answered. Where *had* she gone?

The Huntsman grunted, looking through the smoke that covered the smoldering city with the smell of soot. In the sky, the sun slowly began its descent.

"You've been drifting, girl," he said. "Ever since we left that valley. You should have let me gut every last person in that wretched village."

"You tried that. Didn't work out, did it?"

The Huntsman's face darkened and he glared at his three hounds. The monstrous dogs drooped their pointed ears, ducking their heads.

They had left Kono fleeing for their lives. Whatever that girl—Damju—had put in their food, it took hours of drinking water to soothe the burning in their bellies. The Huntsman had vowed to skin the villagers and wear their hides. He released his hounds to wreak havoc on Kono. But the beasts took a few steps into the valley and ran off whimpering.

Fulan had seen what frightened them.

In the valley, among the rocks, trees, and fresh grass, she made out a woman. At first she doubted her eyes. But stepping back she saw it clearly. The valley had the shape and form of a woman who lay on her side, curled up around the village of Kono. The sight staggered her. And the hounds would have no part of it. She had decided, neither would they.

"Then why are we here?" the Huntsman asked.

"Because the trail we follow ended at Kono. Your hounds can't even pick up the scent again. And as leader of this expedition, I decided to bring in some help."

The Huntsman joined her in staring out at the burned town.

It wasn't empty. Like their king, its inhabitants had been put in chains, to be marched off. But the armies of the Witch Priest remained to revel in their victory.

There were mercenaries, people of faraway lands, and others who swore allegiance to her father. They ran through broken buildings, looting for spoils. But more than humans walked the village. Fulan spied packs of hyena men, talking in their odd laughing speech. Their short and hunched human-like bodies were covered in beige hair with dark spots. Ragged pelts hung from their waists down to their knees, which bent back like the hindquarters of a dog. But it was their faces that stood out: each bore the head of a hyena, with rounded ears, and a long black muzzle fitted with sharp yellow teeth. Most clutched crude short swords and shields.

A few held long whips, cracking them at the screaming villagers being hauled away in chains.

Fulan had heard many stories of how hyena men had come to be. Some said they were born of women who married sorcerers who could take the shape of hyenas. Others claimed they were once a beautiful people, struck down and cursed for their vanity. Some even said hyena men were creations of her father—willful men reduced to half-beasts by the Witch Priest's power, now forever bound to his service. None of these were true, she knew. Hyena men were just more of the creatures that inhabited this world. They flocked to her father's armies with promises of power and spoils.

"You want to get the help of hyena men?" the Huntsman asked. He scoffed. "My hounds have as good a sense of smell. And are more trustworthy."

Fulan didn't doubt him. Hyena men made great trackers and could run down prey over vast distances. But they strongly disliked humans. As hyena men only worked in packs, it was impossible to just get one in your service. Worse, they'd turn on you if given half the chance. But she hadn't come here seeking hyena men. She sought another sort of help, that would give them an advantage and help cover far more ground. And she saw them. Not wasting time answering the Huntsman, she trekked across the town, towards what she had come here to find.

Sheltering in the broken shell of a tall building with painted walls were a group of Mmoatia. They sat astride their black mounts: the giant bats called sasabonsam. One or two shifted nervously, stretching leathery wings as if preparing for flight, likely troubled by the scent of the hyena men. But their riders kept them under control, pulling tight on reins attached to a large gold hoop in their noses. Fulan walked up to them with the Huntsman trailing behind.

One of the Mmoatia spoke. He wore a necklace of sharp teeth.

"I am Akul. Wing Commander of the Blood Skulls of Two Peaks Where the Smoke Thunders. Who are you that you bear the mark of the living flame?"

"His daughter," she replied plainly.

"Daughter," the Mmoatia repeated. "I have a daughter. She is fierce, like you."

Fulan gave a deep nod. "Perhaps I will meet her one day. I have need of you, Commander Akul. My father has tasked me with hunting his enemies. On your sasabonsam we can cover much more ground."

"And what enemies can the great lord, the Eternal Living Flame, have?" Akul asked.

Fulan thought back to all that she had endured since the beginning of this quest. "Formidable ones. A spirit. And a sorceress of immense power. It will bring danger."

The Mmoatia commander appeared to consider this. His fingers stroked several gold hoops piercing his steed's ears—much like the ones he wore in his own. He reached to his necklace of sharp teeth. "Do you see this? The teeth of a Water Lord. Young but no less a monster. It sought to make a home in a lake near my people. I led an entire wing against it. Three of my flyers were lost, and two sasabonsam, before we felled the beast. I took its teeth in respect for its ferocity." He dropped the necklace back onto his chest. "If there exists an enemy powerful enough to trouble even the great lord, I welcome the chance to face it in battle."

"Then you'll get that chance," Fulan answered.

She was set to head out when a shiver shook her. She could see the commander go still. Swiftly, he cast his gaze downward. Just behind her, the Huntsman hissed a warning. His hounds began to whine. A coldness struck her that extended over her limbs. She turned and glimpsed the source of their dread.

A giant hyena stalked past, larger than an ox. Midnight black, its yellow eyes reflected in the twilight. Fulan did not need to see the unnaturally tall figure wrapped in black robes that rode the creature. She could feel it. A Kishi—one of the Face-stealers. Of the many creatures in her father's armies, these were true monsters. The Kishi placed its giant beast between herself and the Mmoatia. She felt its cold gaze as it spoke in a rasping hiss.

I was not informed . . . there were visitors . . . in my camp.

"My name is Fulan," she stated.

The Kishi shifted its mount closer. *And who are you . . . that would dare commandeer for herself . . . those under my thrall? Speak wisely . . . girl. For I am always in need of servants for my . . . entourage.*

Its entourage. Fulan's eyes drifted to chains trailing behind the giant hyena. The chains were attached to figures that stood still as statues. At first glance, they looked like ordinary people. Only they had no . . . faces. Where eyes, nose, and mouth should have been, there was nothing. Like something had simply wiped their faces away. There were different names for these unfortunates. The faceless. The soulless. But the one that came to her now was zumbi. She shivered. But there was also anger. This monster was threatening her? HER? With such a fate? That, she decided, was the last time she would be called *girl*.

The Huntsman hissed. "Don't be a fool, girl!"

Fulan growled. The *last*. She lifted her head and stared up at the Kishi.

Like all Kishi, it towered over them. Its black robes covered it completely. But it was its face Fulan sought. At first glance it looked like an impossibly handsome man. So beautiful, you couldn't look away. But the longer you stared, the more the face began to change. As Fulan watched, that perfect face shifted into other faces. Most were of people she'd never met, with expressions of horror, shock, or pain. Some were beasts—a snarling jackal, a hissing serpent, a grinning hyena. These were the Kishi's many victims, those who had dared stare into its face—only to have their faces stolen in turn. They were made into zumbi, forever bound to its bidding. Kishi were her father's generals, whipping along his armies who rightly feared them. But she was no hyena man to be cowed. She stared into its face, unblinking. Defiant. Even as in her head she heard the Kishi singing for her to surrender, to sleep, to give herself to it. A part of her wanted to join those shifting faces. And it grew harder to say . . .

No! She pushed back against that awful song. "I am my father's daughter," she whispered, teeth chattering. "I do not burn." The Kishi's faces faded, becoming a void of nothingness. In her head the song thundered. She pushed harder. "I am my father's daughter!" The void swirled, eager to swallow every bit of light that was the world. "I am my father's daughter! I do not burn! I DO NOT BURN!"

The Huntsman gripped her arm. "You proved your point!"

Fulan at last looked away, wiping at the tears streaking her cheeks.

The Kishi rasped a slow laugh.

Such will . . . you are indeed . . . your father's daughter. Take the Mmoatia. There was a pause. *But he wishes to speak . . . with you.*

Fulan almost looked up. Her father? Of course. He held a connection to these creatures.

"I'll need fire," she said. "And darkness."

A short time later Fulan stood inside a shattered building. It had been someone's home once. Pieces of smashed pottery and broken furniture littered the floor. Her eyes fixed on a small carving. She bent to pick it up. A figurine of a lion. A child's toy. She remembered in Kono, hearing of what this Goat Man had done to children. Before, that girl Fomi spoke of her village's destruction. How many more villages or towns now had such stories? How many families scattered? Was this her father's legacy? The fires that raged inside her, dimmed. Like a candle under a strong wind.

Flicker. The strange images came again, as if she was reliving them. A woman scooping food onto her plate. A man sitting nearby, eating and talking to the woman as both laughed. Another girl, older but still young, showing how to use her fingers to pick up food. Her own voice, giggling as she tried. *Flicker.*

Fulan swooned under the weight of the images, fighting to push them away. No. These people had been given a chance. They had only had to accept her father's rule. He was striving to help them. To save them from uncaring spirits and corrupt rulers. But they were too foolish, too stubborn. The fire inside her roared back to life with her anger. She hurled the figurine into a cooking hearth, as the wood she had gathered there burst into flames. Kneeling before the fire, she stared into it and called.

Father.

The world burned away. She knelt in her father's throne room, where molten rock ran down the walls like water. The heat of it was strong on her skin, though she knew she had not gone anywhere. This was an illusion.

"Daughter," her father spoke. The Witch Priest sat reclined on his throne, a giant who radiated power. "It is good to gaze upon you." His fiery face was hidden behind a spiked iron mask. But as always, Fulan detected the surprise in his voice—at having such feelings, for a mortal.

"Father," she greeted him, bowing her head.

"And how goes your hunt?"

Fulan felt her stomach knot. "The quarry has proved . . . elusive."

"Ahhh. You have encountered difficulties."

"Nothing I can't handle." The fire behind her eyes rose.

A rumbling laugh came from her father. "You are indeed my daughter."

"I do not burn," she whispered.

"What has brought you to this place?" he asked.

"I need Mmoatia. I can track better by air." She paused. "There is a Kishi here. And many hyena men. So large a force to take a city of potters?"

Her father was silent before answering. "The time comes when I must bring my cleansing fire to all who would stand against me. My armies gather to march upon them."

Fulan gasped. "The war with the great cities of the west? It has come at last?"

"It is only a matter of moments."

"Then I should be there!"

"You have your own path."

"But—!"

"This is not to be argued, Daughter."

There was finality to those words, like fire burning brush to ash.

She bowed her head, biting back her frustration. "Why did you summon me, then?"

Her father sat forward on his throne. "I can sense my enemy. She walks out in the world. And my reach has grown greater. Let me be your guide. Let me show you the way."

Fulan clenched her jaw. She wanted to say she didn't need his help. That she could do this on her own. That she could show him who she was. But she already knew this was not a request.

"Of course, Father."

He stood and walked to where she knelt. Reaching down, he pressed a finger to the mark on her forehead. It flared in response and she opened her mouth in a silent and wordless scream.

Fulan staggered out into the night. The Huntsman stood from where he crouched, staring.

"What happened in there?" he asked, matching her stride.

"I know how to find our quarry," she answered.

He frowned. "Your forehead. Have you given yourself over so completely?"

She stopped, reaching to touch the mark that now blazed to life there. It was visible now, the upside-down teardrop, seared into her flesh and soul. "I am my father's daughter," was all she said. And walked on.

The Kishi sat waiting on its giant hyena. She met its gaze and those shifting faces and felt . . . nothing. She had been changed, somehow. This creature could not harm her. Not anymore. The Kishi seemed to sense this as well and bowed its head.

Your Mmoatia . . . await, it said, indicating the three bat riders.

"You're coming yourself, Akul?" she asked.

The Mmoatia commander raised his chin. "I said before that you were as fierce as my daughter. No, you are fierceness itself. This hunt will be an honor." He and his riders bowed to her as well, making their bats do the same.

"Then we go, now," she said.

Before you . . . leave. She turned to the Kishi. *Your father . . . has ordered that I gift you . . . a present.* It gestured behind its mount.

Fulan tensed. Did this creature think she would accept one of its zumbi? But what walked from the shadows to stand before her was not one of the faceless. It was a monster. It looked like a big man—taller and bigger than even the Huntsman. Corded and knotted muscle showed beneath skin the color of grayish rock. Ghostly symbols that glowed in the night were painted on his broad chest, with more on his arms and legs. He was wrapped in tattered red cloth, held together by small clasps of metal. The black hilt of a large sword jutted above his shoulder, while the end peeked from near his waist, showing jagged edges. Curiously, the monster wore one single piece of jewelry: a necklace of iron ringlets that held a small dark stone the color of blood. The gem pulsed like a beating heart.

Fulan looked the monster over. His face was hidden behind a large mask of wood and iron spikes that left only his mouth and chin visible. But his eyes were bright.

"Do you have a name?" she asked.

He answered with a deep growl, drawing back lips to reveal teeth as jagged as his blade.

Right, she thought. One of those.

"Get on one of the sasabonsam," she ordered, then turned, not bothering to see if he complied. She was not fool enough to turn down her father's offer. But if this creature was too stupid to take commands, she would leave him here.

Accepting Akul's aid, Fulan climbed onto the sasabonsam. She sat behind him in a leather seat and tied a harness about her waist. The Huntsman did the same atop another bat. From the corner of her eye, she watched as the monster took the third—though the bat dipped under his weight. The sasabonsam beneath her unfurled long leathery wings and, with a terrific lurch, launched into the air.

"Where do we go, Daughter of the Flame?" Akul asked, his voice carrying on the wind.

Fulan closed her eyes, letting her father's fire course through her. She felt with his senses and reached out across the world. Drawing her knife, she uttered a word to set the blade ablaze and lifted it over his shoulder—pointing.

"There!" she answered.

The giant bat banked, flying as Akul directed. The others quickly joined, so that the three flew in formation. They were like an arrow loosed from a bow and streaking to their target.

"I'm coming for you, Abeni," she whispered. And the fires inside her roared.

CHAPTER NINETEEN

HEROES

A shiver ran through Abeni and she turned to stare out into the approaching night, where the first stars twinkled in the darkening sky.

"What is it?" Ama asked, following her gaze.

Abeni shook her head. "I don't know. I just suddenly felt like . . ."

"Like we were being watched?"

"Yes, but more than that. I can't explain . . ."

Ama looked out across sparse bushes and trees to where dark hills rose in the distance.

"The merchant Antu claims there are predators in this brushland," she said. Her grip tightened on a wood bucket filled with fruit.

"Whatever it is," Abeni said, "I don't think it's nearby. At least not right now."

"Oh." Ama lowered the bucket. Reaching inside, she took out a half melon and placed it into the mouth of the large shaggy creature before her. A set of blocklike teeth crushed the fruit to pulp between broad jaws. "I'll put 'being hunted' on our list of worries. Up there with facing not one but two dragons, finding the Golden Throne, and feeding these beyanaa." The beyanaa responded with a snort from its flaring nostrils and shaking its horned head.

Abeni reached into her own bucket, picking up another half

melon and putting it to the closest beyanaa. It rolled out a thick tongue to taste the fruit before snatching it between those blocky teeth. There were twelve of the beasts in all. Each was about the size of a water buffalo but covered in thick brown fur and with curved deep blue ram-like horns. These beyanaa belonged to Antu—a caravan trader.

Abeni and her companions had left Jenna the day after visiting the Great Library. They'd decided to find this dragon that was harassing a nearby kingdom. But they were less interested in fighting it than they were in learning of the whereabouts of Bida. They had also taken up the librarian apprentice's suggestion of hiring out to a caravan to get there. They had been with the merchant for about a week, and it seemed they had hardly had a chance to rest. Their days were spent getting the beyanaa and the caravan over rocky hills, through streams, or across flatlands. Then there was gathering water, helping to make camp, pitching tents, breaking down those tents, and even more work.

"Ugh!" Ama said as one of the beyanaa spit up chewed green melon rind at her feet. She gingerly scooped it into a bucket. "I hate it when they do that."

"Not used to this kind of work as a princess?" Abeni asked, unable to help herself.

Ama gave her a flat look. "No. Is this something you did in that village of yours?"

"Not really," Abeni admitted. "I only ever got to pound yam once."

"When I was younger I loved watching women pound yam," Ama said. "They moved in rhythm and sang such beautiful songs. But my nursemaids would never let me join in."

The sound of music and clapping broke the awkward moment. They both turned to the small tent that sat off from the beyanaa.

"Well, at least some of us got better chores," Ama muttered.

Abeni couldn't argue there. The caravan merchant's wife had gone ahead to their destination, leaving their daughters with him—six in all, and none who had seen even ten seasons. Nyomi and Songu were charged with watching them. Asha, who the merchant naturally assumed was a small girl, spent her days playing with them. At night everyone gathered in the tent and shared dinner, along with music and dance.

"Do you dream about it too?" Ama asked.

Abeni fumbled her brush at the unexpected question.

"Sometimes I dream I can still weave gold," the girl went on. "In those dreams, I can *feel* myself weaving gold. Then I wake up and . . ."

"Yes," Abeni answered. She'd had dreams like that, where she still had her song.

"I'm sorry," Ama said. "I know you don't want to think about it."

"I think about it all the time," Abeni replied quietly. She'd thought that perhaps with time the loss would get better. But she thought of her song more and more, and the loss just grew worse.

"Me too," Ama said. "I told you I never had friends. That it's hard for a princess to have friends. I'm not used to sharing things like this, about how I feel and—"

"I'm not your friend, Ama," Abeni cut in. The girl flinched. A hurt look crossed her face, breaking through the usual mask that hid her vulnerability. Abeni thought of taking back her words. But hadn't she been hurt too? Wasn't she vulnerable? "Your people kidnapped us, forced us to work. You threatened us, made us your servants, tormented Zaneeya. Now if we don't finish this quest, our lives are in danger. Friends don't do that to each other."

Ama nodded. "I know. I know all that. I just . . ." She swallowed. "When I said I didn't know how to be like someone who has friends, you said I should try being another way."

"We're companions on this quest," Abeni said. "That's all."

Ama flinched again. "I am *trying,* you know."

A flare of anger shot through Abeni. "You can't just expect friendship from people you've hurt."

"I understand," Ama said. Her voice became almost a whisper. "But you're the only one who knows what I'm going through."

There was a pained expression on her face, the mask vanishing to show every bit of her vulnerability. Then it was back up. And she was the princess once more.

"I have a question," Abeni said. "Why do you want the crown of your people?"

Ama looked at her in surprise, then her eyes narrowed. "I want the crown because the kingdom needs an effective ruler. And my brother is not."

"And the Ohemmaa never thought of you?"

Ama's face tightened. "Those old women thought of me. They knew I would be a better pick. But they didn't want to break with custom and grant the crown to a girl. Sometimes I think they chose my brother because they knew he would be easier to control."

Abeni thought she understood now—sort of. "Will your brother just . . . step aside?"

"No," Ama admitted. "He'll try to remain king. But his bungling led us into that awful deal with the Witch Priest. Many in the kingdom see it, even his attendants and chiefs. I've been talking to them. I think they're ready for a change. They won't back me openly, not yet. But, if I can return the Golden Throne, take us from under the Witch Priest's control, I can call out my brother—and demand the crown."

"Wouldn't that cause a war?" Abeni asked. "In all the stories I've ever heard of kings and crowns, wars start over that kind of thing."

Ama looked shocked. "War? Nothing so barbaric! Removing a king doesn't require fighting. He just has to lose the court's confidence. Then they'll take his slippers for certain."

"His slippers?"

Ama smiled. "Our rulers are said to take golden steps. Their feet cannot touch the ground. A king who is left to walk barefoot understands then that he is no king."

"If your brother is such a poor ruler, why doesn't he step down on his own?"

"Because he likes the power."

"And you don't?"

Ama met Abeni's eyes. "To hold the crown is to hold power. Any decent ruler must be comfortable with that. But a good ruler knows that their power resides truly in the people. If the people are not being helped, if they are not protected, if their needs are not met, then the crown means nothing."

Abeni nodded. "Maybe you will make a good ruler."

"Of course I will," Ama replied. Her voice turned somber. "But will my people accept a ruler who cannot weave gold?"

"You two keep at it and you'll brush those shaggy things bald," someone remarked.

Both girls turned to see Zuri emerge from the shadows. She wore deep blue robes over her usual clothing, the kind favored by the merchant and his daughters. One hand rested on the gold hilt of the sword at her side as she smirked at them. She had been hired on as the lone caravan guard. When they camped at night she made numerous patrols, often not even eating with them. She claimed it was to guard against bandits. Abeni suspected other motives.

Zuri's smile vanished into a scowl. "Will you stop looking at me like that?"

"Sorry," Ama said. "It's just . . ." Her eyes darted to the sword. Zuri ground her teeth.

Since finding out the sword the girl held was none other than the magic blade wielded against Bida, Ama had gone through a startling transformation. She now looked at Zuri with a mix of awe and bewilderment. Abeni supposed it must be like seeing a hero from stories come to life.

Zuri looked relieved when someone else arrived.

Zaneeya. The panther girl made her way over, carrying several rabbits strung over her shoulders.

"Did I interrupt something?" she asked, an eyebrow raised.

Several of the beyanaa moaned suddenly. They stamped heavy hooves, glaring at the panther girl as their blue horns changed to a shade of orange.

"Can't fool them with that pretty face you show the merchant," Zuri said. "They know a predator when they sense one."

Zaneeya bared her teeth. "Annoying beasts." Her nose wrinkled. "And smelly." She jerked a chin at Ama. "You finished? I need help skinning these before putting them on a spit."

Ama grimaced. "I don't like skinning your catches."

"I know." The panther girl smiled. "That's why I always have you do it."

Ama sighed. She turned to Zuri. "I hope we get a chance to talk later. There's much I would like to know about you and your past. May our ancestors walk with you."

Zaneeya rolled her eyes. Grabbing Ama's arm, she hauled the girl off towards the tent.

Zuri ran a hand through her rows of braided hair. She had been uncertain how to react when learning about her sword. She insisted it had to be a mistake. But the librarian apprentice had assured her that the drawing was correct. The Silent Sword was the very one wielded by a hero of legend against the dragon Bida—and, according to Zuri, one of her own ancestors.

"I keep asking myself, what are the chances? First I'm sent on a hunt for a sword that takes me to a sea of monsters. Then I run into all of you. Now it turns out your quest and this sword are all tied up together."

"Maybe not just chance," Abeni said. Nyomi was now certain that the mist people had sent her, Zaneeya, and Ama to that nowhere place on purpose. Whatever they picked up from their thoughts, they'd sent them to where Zuri and the sword were. *We can take you where you need to go,* they had said.

"That's even stranger," Zuri muttered. "The seer who set me on this quest claimed it was my destiny. Didn't know having a destiny would make me like a character in a story someone else is telling. You know, I said as much to Asha? She said I was being silly. That we write our own stories and make our own destinies. Then she tweaked my nose. Strange little girl."

Abeni nodded. That sounded like Asha. "Is that why you've been avoiding us?"

"That obvious?" Zuri leaned back against a beyanaa. "This destiny thing comes with a lot of responsibility. And that's something I've avoided. But I don't like the idea of running away either. Besides, you lot finally shared with me what this whole quest is about."

That had been Ama's idea—once they found out who Zuri was. She'd told Zuri all about their hunt for the Golden Throne and what the Masks of Akani had told them.

"Are you thinking of the reward?" Abeni asked.

Zuri grinned. "Never far from mind."

Abeni was no longer certain that was the only thing. She wondered if the girl remembered what Asha had said about the sword. *Having it is going to change you.*

"What I want to know," Zuri said, "is when you're going to tell me *your* story."

Abeni returned to brushing.

"I've only been able to put together pieces," Zuri went on. "That you're from some backwater village. I'm guessing something bad happened there. And that it has something to do with these Storm Women and ghost ships you keep asking about. Don't think I didn't notice your private talk with Seydou."

Abeni stopped her brushing, looking at Zuri, who stared back. She had taken Seydou aside to ask him about the Storm Women— these Isat—as well as ghost ships. There wasn't much about the Isat in the Great Library. Seydou claimed they were too recent to be written upon—admitting that many scholars thought them fanciful tales. Ghost ships, there was more on. Not a lot was known of the frightful vessels. But this was not the first time they had come. The histories spoke of their last arrival almost a thousand years past, to steal away the living. There were sketches of their great ships: giant boats, moved by the wind, that could swallow whole villages into their bellies. No one knew where the wraiths who piloted them came from or where they took people. Thinking of her family packed onto those ships, gone forever, made her stomach roil.

"It's a long story," Abeni said. "I used to be able to sing it . . ."

"Your song," Zuri said.

She nodded. "It's gone."

Zuri looked skeptical. "I don't see how something like that can be taken from you. It's your story, after all. Even if you don't remember the words the exact way, you know what happened. Just tell it again. It'll be different. But it'll be the same story."

"It's not that easy."

"Didn't say it was easy. But have you even tried?"

Abeni opened her mouth to argue but stopped. She hadn't tried.

"Thought as much," Zuri said. She sat up. "Here, try it on me. Just tell your story."

Abeni looked at her for a long moment. And then she did. It was different. She fumbled at some of the words. A few times she had to jump back because she'd forgotten something. And her descriptions didn't have the same feelings as when she sang. None of the magic was there. But she managed to tell a story that was surprisingly close. It was also easier this way to leave out certain things: namely Asha being a spirit, and the Witch Priest her brother.

"Now that's a story!" Zuri said when she'd finished. "I'm sorry about what happened to your village. I can't imagine going through that. And stopping this Goat Man! You're a hero!"

"I'm no hero," Abeni said. "I just want to find my family. Bring my village back."

"I dunno. Betting Songu and lots of others might say otherwise." Zuri stood up, dusting bits of beyanaa fur from her clothes. "Come inside. I'm hungry."

Abeni stared at the girl's offered hand for a moment before

taking it and rising to stand. Together, they walked towards the tent, where the sound of clapping, music, and the promise of stories to come waited.

It was two days later that they arrived at the small kingdom of Foula Jallo.

CHAPTER TWENTY

DRAGON

S o, you've come to face the dragon?"

Abeni eyed the person who spoke. Wrapped in richly decorated robes, he sat on a stool while all about him more people stood. She thought this made him look small. Then again, he was a boy—no older than Songu. So maybe that's what made him look small.

Zuri bowed deep. "Yes, my king. We've heard of your troubles and would lend aid."

A cough came from a man dressed in colorful robes all the way down to his sandaled feet. He had given his title as royal bard and appeared to speak for the king. His eyes ran over them, as if he was trying to make sense of what he was seeing.

"Great king," he spoke, his voice strong in the morning air. "We have had challengers to face the dragon. But these are certainly the strangest. What did you say your name was again?"

Zuri sighed, shifting the blue robes that sat over her clothing. She had accepted them as a gift from the caravan merchant, whom they'd parted with about half a day's journey from Foula Jallo. The kingdom sat in the highlands of several mountains of the same name. Not that they were able to enter. They could see the rounded oval roofs of great houses or buildings in the distance, towering even above the trees. But they were stopped far from it, forced to remain here out on the grasslands where a large white tent stood. The king and the royal bard had met them here, along with others Abeni took to be attendants or officials—all in colorful robes and wearing tall cloth caps. The tent was flanked by horsemen. Both riders and mounts were covered with quilted colorful cloth, embroidered in stars, sunbursts, and other symbols. The horsemen carried spears with wood hilts wrapped in strips of gold cloth and curved blades as long as her arm.

Zuri was set to give their names, again, when the boy king cut her off.

"Does it matter?" he asked. "They're the first to answer our call in weeks."

"My king," the bard said. "We must be certain this is not a trick. They are only . . ."

"Children?" the king said, his cheeks dimpling with a smile. "You're very good as my bard. But I don't think anyone is going to pretend to be ready to challenge a dragon—not unless they don't plan on living long." He turned back to Zuri. "Your . . ." He gestured at the others. ". . . attendants will face the dragon as well?"

"Yes, King," Zuri answered.

The boy shrugged slender shoulders. "More food for the dragon, then, if you don't know what you're doing."

Abeni felt knots in her stomach, thinking of being a dragon's meal.

"How long has the dragon troubled your kingdom?" Zuri asked.

The king sighed wearily. "For several months. We're not certain where he came from, but he settled along the banks of a great river. Then he drank it up."

Zuri blinked. "Excuse me, King, but did you say he drank up an entire river?"

The boy nodded. "Our crops falter. My people grow thirsty. We live on what water we get from our wells and gather through rainfall. But it isn't enough."

Abeni looked at the grassland, which was turning brown from drought.

"Many of our best warriors went out to face the dragon," the boy king continued. "They were led by my older brothers, who each ruled before me. One by one, they met their end. We've had three new kings in the past months. I'm the fourth. And I decided we needed help."

"It is not our first time facing a dragon," the bard said proudly. "One of our greatest kings faced a dragon much like this one a hundred years past, alongside an army carrying eight hundred spears! Under sun and moon they fought for eight long years, until finally the great king pierced the dragon's heart with the last spear!"

The boy king smiled. "Only, my people don't have eight years for me to fight a dragon. If you can defeat this monster, and bring back our river, we can reward you greatly." At a gesture, servants came forward carrying a large rug. They unfurled it to reveal gold and jewels.

"All of this is yours if you succeed," the king said. "I offer any champion, as well, my sister's hand in marriage." He gestured behind him to a tall woman in patterned indigo robes with jewelry embedded into her thick braids. Zuri smiled at her, and she rolled her eyes, pursing dark-stained lips.

"Princess?" Zuri asked. "Would that then make me . . . ?"

"A person married to a princess," the bard replied curtly. "Don't get any ideas."

"You would be part of my family," the king said. "It is a great honor."

Zuri weighed this, looking from the jewels to the princess before returning to the king. She grinned and leaned back in a casual way. "That's quite the offer. So, somebody point me in the direction of this dragon already."

◯◯◯

Abeni looked down at the earth under her feet. It was covered in rocks and sediment. They were walking in a riverbed. But it was emptied and dry now. All the water was gone, and tall banks rose up on either side of them.

"It really drank up the whole river," Ama said in disbelief.

"It must have been very thirsty," Nyomi commented.

"Still, that would be a lot of water," Ama replied. She put her arms out to either side. "We could probably walk side by side like this and there'd still be room in this riverbed to spare. Plus, it's deep enough that when filled we'd have to swim."

Everyone looked at her quizzically.

"That's *really* a lot of water," she said again.

"Maybe it had too many salty snacks," Zuri put in. "Do we know what we're doing? Once we see the dragon, I mean?"

Abeni glanced to the girl's sword. "You aren't planning on fighting it, are you? We're here to ask questions."

"Trust me, not fool enough to fight a dragon." Zuri paused. "Though that was lots of treasure. And a princess!"

"Just questions," Abeni insisted.

"Okay, okay. Better hope the dragon is as civil."

Abeni didn't know what to expect. This was her first dragon, after all.

"Maybe it likes dancing," Nyomi said. "I could dance, and Songu could play his flute!"

"A meal and a show," Zuri commented dryly.

Songu returned Nyomi's smile. But he signed "absolutely not" to Abeni.

Ahead, a small shape came into view, running their way. A panther. It shifted into Zaneeya just feet from them. There was a baffled expression on her face.

"Did you find the dragon?" Abeni asked.

"Yes. Kind of hard to miss."

"And?" Zuri asked.

"You'll have to see for yourself. This way."

The river had mostly gone on straight. But it curved to the right ahead. As they followed Zaneeya, Abeni noticed a black hill directly in their path. She was trying to figure out what a hill was doing here when she saw it. This was not a hill at all. It was a creature. A massive creature. She could now make out the black scales along its body and the ridges that flowed along its back. Its head faced them, flush to the ground and with a long snout like a crocodile's. She made out teeth almost half her size jutting from its closed mouth. Those jaws looked large enough to swallow a water buffalo! The creature's eyes were closed. From the rumbling in its throat, it appeared to be sleeping.

"That's a dragon!" Ama said, breathless.

Abeni was too numb to speak. This monster was ginormous!

"He looks . . . stuffed," Asha said.

Abeni agreed. The dragon did look stuffed. Its pale gray underside was swollen to the point of bursting. Its front legs didn't even touch the ground, instead sitting up in the air. It looked like it was lying atop a big round ball, except that ball was its belly.

"Maybe it *did* drink up the entire river," Ama said.

"Not all of it," Zaneeya commented. "There's water on the other side. The rest of the river, I'd guess. But it's blocking the way."

Abeni could see how. The dragon was wedged into the riverbed, from bank to bank.

Asha tsked. "He drank too much. Greedy thing."

Abeni looked to the girl. "You keep calling it *he*."

"Yes. I think that's right."

"How do you—" Abeni paused. "Asha, do you know this dragon?"

The girl scrunched up her face in thought. "I think I did, once."

"You knew a dragon," Zuri said slowly. "Once."

Asha nodded. "I think I knew a lot of them."

Zuri snorted. "Next thing you're going say you know his name?"

"I can't remember. Fusa? Jesa?"

A sudden tremor shook the ground and Abeni watched the massive dragon shift, the black scales on his body undulating. There was a rumbling from his throat and air burst from his nostrils. He was waking up!

"Everybody behind me!" Zuri yelled.

None of them argued, stepping behind the girl. Abeni held

onto Asha, who was still going through her list of names. She watched in terror as yellow-green eyes opened on either side of that monstrous head.

"Hmm," the dragon moaned. His voice shook the air. "Do you know that dragons can hear in their sleep?" Black vertical pupils in those yellow-green eyes went from wide to narrow as they fixed on Zuri. "Another challenger." He yawned. "Haven't I eaten enough of you?"

Zuri shouted back, drawing and waving her sword. The dragon rolled its eyes.

"Great hearing I may have, but I can't hear you while you're holding that."

Looking a bit embarrassed, Zuri slid her sword back into its scabbard.

"New to using a magic sword?" the dragon asked, sounding amused.

"Maybe," Zuri answered.

"Were you doing the whole *my name is blah blah and I'm here to fight you, blah*?"

"Something like that."

"Right. Okay then. Take it from the top."

Zuri cleared her throat and started again.

"Uh, Dragon! I am the Black Fox! Captain of *The Sea Snake*! Stealer of the magic kora for the scribes of Wagadou! Rescuer of the son of a Zhusa chieftain from a ravenous zimwi! Completer of the twelve impossible tasks set by the Queen of Azua! And I have come to uh, well, ask you some questions, really."

The dragon blinked. "Well, that was fine. Not great. But fine. Questions? That's new. Usually it's, 'I've come to fight you to the death!' What's that silly kingdom downriver offering now?"

"Some gold and jewels. A princess's hand in marriage."

"Is the princess attractive?"

Zuri shrugged. "She's cute."

"Does she want to marry?"

"I don't know, really."

"Feels like someone might ask her . . ."

"Makes sense. Say, are your challenges usually this chatty?"

The dragon pulled back lips on its snout to show more fearsome teeth. Abeni thought this might have been a smile—and it was terrifying. "Most of my challenges don't last this long. They usually start shouting and running at me with sharp things. That's when I—pounce!"

At that last word, he lurched! Zuri jumped back. So did the rest of them—with a lot of "AHHH! DRAGON!" But the massive creature had barely moved. He muttered something and tried again.

"That's when I—pounce!"

Like before, he only moved inches. When he did it a third time, no one jumped or screamed. There was loud straining as he flailed his front legs uselessly before giving up with a groan.

"That's . . ." Zaneeya began. ". . . pathetic."

"Aww, he's too full to move," Nyomi whispered.

"Well, this is awkward," the dragon muttered.

"Bosa? Zisa?" Asha continued, still trying to remember his name.

"I can't help but notice," Zuri called, "that you look a bit . . . stuck?"

The dragon grumbled, wriggling in the riverbed. "It's that annoying kingdom's fault. I just stopped here for a bit to drink and rest. Then they started sending out their warriors to hurl spears at me. Rude! I ate them, naturally. But that made me thirsty. So I drank a bit of the river. They kept sending more warriors, I ate those, and I kept drinking and . . . well." He shifted his belly, and there was sloshing. Abeni often did that with her own belly. But she'd never drunk up half a river.

Zuri grinned. "Guess that makes us lucky. You're probably too full to eat."

"Oh no," the dragon said, his voice menacing. "I plan on eating all of you."

Zuri snorted. "You can't even get to us."

A rumbling came from the dragon's throat that Abeni realized was laughter. "Silly mortal. I'm a dragon. I don't have to chase you. I can just use magic."

At his words, Abeni felt herself suddenly falling—then abruptly stopping. She looked down. She had somehow fallen into the ground of the riverbed, up to her waist! The same had happened to the others. She tried to push up with her hands, but she was held fast.

"Now, we're all stuck," the dragon said, grinning toothily. "And I can take my time."

With a lurch, he moved forward. Not much. And still slow. But he'd reach them in time.

"Knew I shouldn't have put back that sword!" Zuri muttered.

"Don't take this personally," the dragon said, lurching again. "You're probably all perfectly fine people. But you came up here. Wandered into my domain. Now you must get eaten. Those are the rules."

"You don't have to be so tied to protocol!" Zuri shot back.

"I'm a dragon, mortal. We're quite big on rules and formalities."

"Anyone have ideas?" Ama asked, her eyes fixed on the approaching dragon.

"Nyomi! Can you jump out?" Abeni asked.

"No! His magic is holding me here!"

"I can't shift either!" Zaneeya growled.

The dragon started humming. He really was taking his time.

"I remember!" Asha exclaimed. "You're Isa Bere!"

The dragon went still. "Who said that?"

"Me!" Asha waved, peeking from behind Abeni.

The dragon's eyes narrowed on the small girl. "How do you—?"

"Isa Bere!" Asha repeated. She glared up at the dragon, and there was the strength of Auntie Asha in her voice. "A great big preening snake!"

The dragon hissed.

"Maybe don't insult him?" Zuri suggested.

But Asha went on. "You go around gobbling up what you want, drinking up whole rivers. You're greedy and selfish and a big bully!"

Now the dragon opened its jaws wide, roaring. Hot air, and the stink of dragon's breath, whipped Abeni's braids back.

"Rage all you want!" Asha said. "But I know your name!"

The dragon snarled. It thrashed and whipped about. Then, it went still—dropping its head back to the ground and releasing a long sigh.

"Fine. You know my name. So? Names alone don't hold power."

"But dragons have rules," Asha said. "You didn't give me your name. I knew it. That means you have to bargain!"

The dragon rippled in irritation but muttered, "Rules are rules."

The small girl was lifted into the air and brought hovering before him. He stared at her, and Abeni's heart pounded at what might come next.

"Name your bargain," Isa Bere said, lowering Asha to the ground.

"You answer our questions. Then we get you unstuck."

"I can get out of here whenever I want," the dragon said sourly.

"You great big liar." She smacked his swollen belly. "You've been stuck for a month!"

Isa Bere grumbled under his breath. At last, he sighed. "Bargain accepted. However, if you don't get me unstuck, I'm still going to eat you. Rules are rules."

"Of course," Asha said. "Now, my friends?"

Abeni was lifted up to stand again on the riverbed's surface. The same was done to the others. Asha walked over to them, smiling.

"You are the strangest little girl I've ever met," Zuri said, her gaze puzzled.

"That's no little girl," Isa Bere grumbled. "She's a spirit. A wily one at that."

"Oh," Zuri said. Then, her eyes going wide, "Oh!" And finally, nodding, "Ohhhh!"

"For you to know my name," the dragon mused, "it means we've met before."

Asha shrugged. "Probably long ago. I must have looked very different then."

"Hmmm," Isa Bere mused. "I recall your kind usually having a guardian."

"Oh, I do!" Asha beckoned excitedly to Abeni, who walked over, trying not to tremble as the dragon turned its gaze on her.

"A bit small for a guardian," he said.

"Maybe. But she's special. Abeni, this is Isa Bere."

Abeni stared up at the dragon and found her voice. "Hello. It's good to meet you."

"I'm sure it is," the dragon replied. "Are you going to ask your question anytime today?"

Everyone turned to Zuri. She straightened. "We've come to ask about the dragon Bida."

"Bida?" Isa Bere sounded surprised. "You've come to ask about that old blowhard?"

"Is he alive?" Zuri asked.

The dragon snorted. "Quite alive. Though he's gone through much to conceal it. Why do you want to know if—" He stopped, his eyes shifting to Zuri's waist. "Of course! The sword! The one that supposedly slew him. You intend to fight him!" At that, the dragon began to laugh. "Oh, this is wonderful! You should have led with that!"

"Do you know where we can find him?" Zuri asked.

"Of course," Isa Bere said, once his laughter stopped. "I'll gladly tell you where that self-righteous braggart has slithered off to hide. He dwells now in a lost city, one that can only be found by those who know when and where to look. You must call to the city with one clear note, loud and true, for it to appear. The surprise on his face at being discovered will be worth it." His eyes narrowed. "I do ask one thing. If you defeat him with that sword, cut out his golden heart and bring it to me. What I wouldn't give to devour that!"

"Umm," Zuri said. "I'll see what I can do."

The dragon chuckled. "Now your part of the bargain." He wriggled. "Get me unstuck!"

"We're going to work that out," Zuri said. "One moment." She turned, gesturing for them to huddle close. "Any ideas on how to get this dragon unstuck?" Her gaze fixed on Asha. "You seem to be full of surprises. Any special spirit powers?"

Asha shook her head. "None that would help. Or that I remember."

"Could you jump him out?" Zuri asked Nyomi.

The porcupine girl gasped. "Not anything that big! Would be like moving a mountain!"

A memory came to Abeni. "Asha, do you remember when I ate up the magic from your pots? How you helped me get it all out?" She'd been given a bowl of green liquid that made her empty her stomach. It was unpleasant, but it worked. She explained as much.

"Do you think you could make something like that again?" Zuri asked.

"Possibly," Asha answered. She took in the dragon. "But we'd need a lot."

"Are you all quite done?" Isa Bere called. "If you can't do it, I'll just eat half of you. Think that's fair."

"Give us a moment!" Zuri shouted, before turning back to them. "How much is a lot?"

Ama frowned thoughtfully. "Let's see. If Abeni drank a cup brewed for one person, I estimate we'd need a few hundred cups for a dragon. And a few dozen people to work on it—not to mention a way to get it down his throat."

They looked at her.

"Half of ruling is logistics," she said. "I'm good at this stuff."

"But where do we get a few hundred people?" Zaneeya asked.

Zuri smiled. "Well, we know a king who'd give anything to have his river back." She turned to the dragon. "We think we can get you unstuck. But we're going to need some help."

It all went better than Abeni thought. The king was surprised to see them alive—yet confused. When they explained how to solve his dragon problem, however, he was all ears. For the next two days, the resources of Foula Jallo were at their disposal. Healers foraged for the ingredients for Asha's concoction, while blacksmiths and craftspeople worked on a way to deliver it to the dragon. When they went out to see Isa Bere again, the king and his attendants accompanied them. A funnel had been built to fit into the dragon's mouth, and workers used it to pour in jars of the concoction. When it was done, the dragon unfurled a long tongue turned green.

"That is the foulest thing I've ever tasted," he complained. "Blech!"

"It's pretty awful," Abeni agreed, standing nearby on the banks. "What do you plan on doing once you're unstuck?"

The dragon shrugged. "I haven't thought on that. After being trapped so long, not in a mood to travel. If this kingdom keeps sending me more challengers, eating them I suppose."

"Then you might just drink up the river again."

"You have a better idea?"

She had thought on that and shared it with the others. "What if the kingdom brought you food? Then you wouldn't have to eat any challengers. You'd be like a . . . guest."

"A guest?"

She nodded. "When people came to my village, we fed them." Of course, they'd never had to feed a dragon.

Isa Bere thought on this. "I like that. Can I have roasted goat? Or salted pork! I do love salted pork." The dragon went on listing his wants to Abeni then stopped suddenly, as a loud gurgling came from his stomach. He opened his massive jaws wide, and with one terrific heave, threw up everything.

Abeni watched as a torrent of water spilled from the dragon, emptying into the riverbed. Not just water, but fish came flying out, crocodiles, a few canoes, and more! As it all flowed out, Isa Bere's swollen belly shrunk, growing smaller by the moment. When the last of the river returned, the dragon was still immense. But he could stand on his own legs. As he unstuck himself, the rest of the river came roaring back, once again whole. Shouts and cheers went up from those gathered.

"It worked!" the king exclaimed. "And without a spear thrown!"

"The Black Fox does it again," Zuri said. She eyed the others. "With help, of course."

Abeni cleared her throat, then went up to whisper into Zuri's ears.

"Oh yes," the girl said. "We may have told the dragon he would be your guest. You'll need to feed him. He'd like to have his scales brushed, someone to look at his teeth, shave his claws . . ." She listed off the dragon's many requests. "Think of it as a tribute to keep him from drinking up your river. Hopefully, he won't stay too long." Abeni wondered what a dragon who had lived thousands of years considered long.

"He'll eat up half the kingdom's stores!" the royal bard sputtered. "We can't—!"

"I think we can afford to give up some food and see to his wants," the king cut in. "I'll trade that for a river any day. Besides, a dragon nearby will give the kingdom some added protection in these times." He looked back to them. "I must thank you for all you've done."

"About that," Zuri said. "I know the challenge was for someone to *defeat* the dragon."

"Which you didn't do," the bard said.

"But we did get you your river back. Wasn't that the whole point?"

"You've left a dragon at our doorstep!" the bard snapped.

The king held up a hand. "The reward is yours. And well earned." Several servants dropped the rug full of treasure at Zuri's feet. Her eyes glittered as bright as the gold and jewels.

"And my sister's hand in marriage." The princess stepped forward, her face flat.

"Princess," Zuri said, inclining her head. She looked to Isa Bere, who lounged lazily in the river while the king's servants brought him platters of food. Her gaze went back to the princess. "Do you really want to get married to some challenger you've never met?"

The princess seemed surprised. "No. I'm not interested in marriage."

"What is it you want to do?"

Her eyes lit up. "I've long thought maybe I'd like to be a king's bard."

The royal bard made a choking sound.

Zuri chuckled, turning to the king. "Thank you. But I must decline. Marriage sounds like a lot of responsibility."

"I understand," the king said. "Do you have another request? Name it. If it's in my power, I'll grant it."

"There is one thing," Zuri said. "My companions and I have a quest to finish. We need to travel, fast."

"How can I help? Horses? Camels?"

"I was thinking of a canoe for the river."

"We have those. How good are you at rowing?"

"I can manage. Though something with a sail would be better." She sighed. "Times like this, I miss my ship."

The king sat forward. "Yes, you are a captain."

"Was a captain. From the eastern seas. But my ship is . . . lost."

"An eastern ship. The ones with the big triangular sails? We have one of those."

Zuri started. "Wait? What? You have a ship?"

The king nodded. "One of my brothers traveled to study in the stone cities and was amazed by them. He had one brought all the way here, piece by piece, along with the builders. I watched them construct it. They actually *sewed* the planks and boards together! Then put in an inner frame. Fascinating!"

"A waste of an expense," the bard and the princess said at once—then eyed each other.

"Yes," the king said. "Not very useful on our small rivers. Now it just sits in our city as a curious item. I could gift it to you, for the work you've done here."

Zuri's eyes glistened. But when she tried to speak she only let out a small "squee!"

"I think," Abeni said for her, "that was a yes."

CHAPTER TWENTY-ONE

ATTACK

Woooot!"

Zuri shouted with glee into the wind. She stood at the back of her newly gifted ship, holding fast to a long oar as she yelled orders. Above, a great triangular sail curled with wind as the boat, now painted with the bright red letters *The Sea Snake Lives*, pushed across the waters.

Watching, Abeni couldn't help but think the girl had been born to do this.

She pulled a rope at Zuri's command, and the boat tilted with a turn in the river. Finishing, she sat to look at the banks on either side, watching the sun begin to dip low on the horizon. The landscape they had started out on was filled with lush greenery and mountains. In the two days they'd been sailing, that had changed. The land had become flat, first covered by grasslands, and now sandy ground with few bushes or trees.

Songu came to sit beside her and signed. "It's very dry. And hot. But feels cold at night."

"Yes," she signed back. "It's called a desert."

He frowned at the unfamiliar sign, and she tried to explain.

"It's a place made up of sand and little water." A smile touched her lips. Her friend Fomi hadn't believed such a place existed. Now they were traveling to one.

The dragon had been good as his word, giving directions to this lost city. And the king had provided maps. He claimed no one lived in the desert. But it was rumored an ancient kingdom had once stood there.

A loud retching caught their attention. They looked across the boat to where Ama leaned over the side, her back heaving. After more awful sounds, she sat up, her golden eyes dull.

Zaneeya laughed from where she sat near the front of the ship. "Rough going, Princess?"

Ama shook her head, unable to talk.

"Delighting in another's misfortune is beneath you, Zaneeya," Asha chided. She came to sit by Ama, patting her back.

The panther girl sniffed. "Before everyone feels sorry for the princess, need I remind you what's inside us? I know you all can feel it."

There was an uneasy quiet. In the past few days Abeni had begun to feel a stiffness forming—in her arms and legs, her joints. It didn't stop her from walking or running. But she could feel it all the same. It was the living gold, she knew. It was getting worse, creeping its way through their bodies. And time was drawing short.

Songu and Abeni exchanged glances. The boy shrugged, then stood and walked over to offer Ama sips of water. Abeni watched for a moment before joining them. She drew out some green leaves from her bag—fresh as the day they were put in.

"Chew these. It'll help you feel better."

Ama took them with a weak "thanks." Asha smiled at Abeni, who smiled back.

"Okay!" Zuri called. "Who's next?"

Nyomi shot up. "Me!"

She vanished in a pink burst, reappearing near the rear of the ship. Zuri had been offering sailing lessons, giving everyone a chance at the oar. Abeni had already had a turn and the porcupine girl had been begging for a chance. After some quick instructions, Zuri walked over to them, amazingly steady on the rolling deck.

"We're making good time." She took a lid from a wooden cask— one of many on the ship. This one held water, and she scooped a cup. "Better if we pick up a strong wind." Her gaze shifted to Asha.

Since finding out the small girl was a spirit, she had taken to staring at her—as if trying to figure out a puzzle.

"I've been putting some things together. That story you told, of the old woman who saved you from your village. The one who died just before you met this little girl. Going to guess they're the same person?" When Abeni didn't answer, she nodded. "Thought so. You two plan on filling me in on more?"

"It isn't my story to tell," Abeni said. "And you might be better off not knowing."

Zuri frowned. "I don't think I like the sound of that."

Abeni was uncertain what to say and was relieved when Songu interrupted. The boy looked troubled—even agitated. "What's wrong?"

"I don't know," he signed. "I feel something familiar . . . something that shouldn't be."

"What's the matter?" Zuri asked, looking between them.

Abeni didn't have an answer.

"Am I sicker than I thought?" Ama asked weakly. "Or does everyone see those birds?"

They turned to follow her gaze across the late day sky. Bright blue had given way to shades of red, orange, and pink. At first Abeni saw nothing, but then she made them out. Three shapes in the distance.

"Big for birds," Zuri said, squinting. "And fast too."

Abeni could see what she meant. The shapes were growing by the moment.

"Those aren't birds," Zaneeya said. The panther girl was standing on the extended bow, amazingly balanced as her cat eyes peered out. "They're bats. Giant bats."

Abeni inhaled sharply. "Sasabonsam! What are they doing out here?"

Zuri's face was grim. "Whoever they are, they're heading right for us." She bounded across the deck. "Porcupine girl! Hold that oar steady and keep us pointed straight! The rest of you, we need to trim this sail to get more speed! Move!"

Everyone jumped, even Ama. They worked the roping until the sail had a tightly curved pull, bending in the wind. There was a sharp tug as the vessel moved faster.

"More speed!" Zuri bellowed. "We need to lighten the ship!" She moved to the casks.

"We're going into a desert!" Ama said. "I thought you said we needed that water!"

"It's either these things go," Zuri said, "or some of us start jumping overboard."

They all promptly moved to help, dumping several casks into the river. A few more things went overboard, and Abeni could feel them pick up more speed.

"Not enough," Zuri muttered. She was standing on a railing, hanging by a rope to peer at the approaching bat riders. "They're catching up. Gonna be on us." Her eyes went suddenly wide. "Look out!"

Zuri jumped, tackling Abeni to the deck as something zipped past, landing with a dull THUNK! An arrow! More followed. THUNK! THUNK! THUNK!

"Asha!" Abeni cried, scrambling to get from under Zuri.

"I'm here!"

Abeni turned to see the little girl huddled with Songu. A hail of arrows lay broken at their feet, as if they'd struck an invisible barrier. The small spirit's powers had protected her! Thank goodness for that! Songu pulled Asha away, taking shelter under a covered section near the back of the ship. Above came a strong whoosh of wind. Abeni looked up as a dark shape with leathery wings swooped by. There was an ear-piercing shriek as the giant bat soared into the distance. Two more streaked past, joining the first, before banking and turning back to them.

"They're coming back around!" Zuri warned.

Abeni crouched behind a wooden cask as she watched their terrifying approach—those red eyes glowing in the coming dark. They flew lower now, and she could make out the red-painted face of a Blood Skull holding the reins of his mount. To her surprise,

behind him sat not another Mmoatia—but a girl! She wore a conical helmet of dark steel topped by a sharp point, with chainmail
that fell about her shoulders. Drawing back on a large bow, she
released the string to send an arrow flying.

"Take cover!" Zuri shouted as it struck the mast. More followed, with that heart-stopping THUNK! THUNK! THUNK!
The bat rider and the girl sped over them, buffeting everyone with
wind. As a second rider rushed past, Abeni heard a snarl and
watched as Zaneeya leapt from the ship's prow. Her outstretched
claws caught the underside of the sasabonsam, slashing. There
was a screech of pain from the giant bat, and it flapped its great
wings, rising higher as another sasabonsam veered away from the
panther girl.

"Score one for us," Zuri muttered.

A trembling Nyomi appeared in a pink mist, huddling with
Songu and Asha.

"Who's manning the oar?" Zuri asked in alarm.

"No one?" Nyomi said. "I'm too scared to stay there by myself!"

The ship suddenly swayed dangerously and Zuri jumped up,
taking long strides to reach the oar. Songu watched her go, then
leapt up to follow. Ama took the time to scramble over to Abeni as
the vessel pitched and lurched.

"Who are they?" she asked. "Why are they attacking us?"

Abeni shook her head. Her eyes traced the bat riders, who had
regrouped into formation. Zaneeya joined them, watching as the
three shapes banked and dropped into a dive.

"They're coming back!" she growled.

Abeni snatched up her staff. Maybe she could hit one as it
passed—if she could manage not to be struck by arrows. But no
arrows came. Instead, as the giant bats flew close over the ship,
three figures jumped from their backs to land heavily onto the
deck. Abeni stared stunned at what stood before them.

One was a big man—tall and broad with a shaved scalp and
beaded scars on his face. He wore a shirt of fur, while the pelts
and small skulls of animals hung from his waist. His mouth split

into a grin as he thumbed the edge of a knife in a way that made Abeni's blood curdle.

The second figure she recognized, though it should have been impossible. He stood even taller than the big man, with thick muscles beneath skin like grayish rock and painted in ghostly symbols. It was a monster. The very same created by the Goat Man. She could even see the iron ringlets about his neck holding a dark red stone that pulsed like a living heart. Her eyes drifted up to the large mask of wood and iron covering his face, leaving only his mouth and chin visible. What child, she wondered, was locked in that prison—turned into this monster by the bloodstone about his neck? Was this what Songu had felt?

As shocked as she was to see this reminder of her past, it was the third figure that held her gaze.

The girl. She was older than Abeni, closer in age to Ama or Zuri. Tall, she wore boots, long pants, and a dark hooded jerkin that left her muscular arms bare. The bow was gone. But strapped to her chest was an assortment of knives, while the hilt of a sword peeked over one shoulder. She stared at them for a moment, before removing her helmet to reveal long thick locs. A hand swept the tresses to one side, to show a shaved scalp on the other. Whoever this girl was, the set of her face told Abeni she gave the orders.

"I have hunted you for a long time," the girl spoke. "Now at last, we meet." Her eyes swept across them. They hardened at Zaneeya, who bared her teeth. She passed without interest over Nyomi, who promptly vanished. There was surprise at Ama.

"A Gold Weaver. Now what would one of you be doing here?"

Ama said nothing, face drawing tight. But the girl peeked around her, fixing on Asha, who still huddled in the back. She smiled. "Hello, little spirit. My father wants very much for me to bring you to him." She moved forward and Abeni immediately stepped up to block her way. The girl stopped, staring at her and nodding with understanding. "Abeni! The sorceress!" She tilted her head curiously. "I thought you would be, more."

Abeni had no idea what the girl was going on about. But if she thought she was just going to take Asha to her father, whoever he was, she was sorely mistaken. Wait. She paused, frowning. "How do you know—?"

"Your name?" the girl asked. "Oh, I've learned much of you on my hunt, Abeni of the Jembe forest. Friend to spirits. Defeater of monsters. Vanquisher of the Goat Man. Heroine to so many, they seek to block me from reaching you. My father wants this little spirit, for reasons I don't know. But I believe you are the real threat. Enchantress! Trickster! You have undone my father's will at every turn." Her eyes narrowed. "Who do you work with? Has someone set you on this task? To undo my father's plans? Or are you the spider who pulls the strings?"

"I don't know what you're talking about," Abeni said, gripping her staff tighter.

The girl smiled crookedly. "Is this how you gain such loyalty? By playing the innocent? It won't work on me, sorceress. I am my father's daughter. I am fire. I do not burn." At those words she drew the sword from her back as a symbol blazed to life on her forehead. An upside-down teardrop that burned bright with fire.

Abeni's stomach went hollow. She knew that mark.

"Who's your father?" she asked, dreading the answer.

The girl seemed to hear the horror in her voice and smiled wider.

"You know him, the Eternal Living Flame, who will set the world on fire!"

Abeni gasped. "The Witch Priest!" she whispered. At her side, Zaneeya hissed.

"See? You do know. The time for tricks is over, sorceress. I'm here now."

There was a moment of silence as the three figures stood at the front of the ship—and Abeni and Zaneeya stood facing them. Ama had come to her feet and watched the odd standoff. It was a small voice that broke the quiet.

"He's lying to you," Asha said. The little spirit stared at the girl with dark piercing eyes. "Fulan, is it? And daughter? I suppose that makes me your aunt. But you should know, my brother cares for nothing more than his grand plans. He has filled you with his fire. It will burn you up if you let it. And he will discard you once finished—as he has done to so many others."

That seemed to take the girl aback. She looked suddenly stricken, and she closed her eyes, shaking her head. "What are you doing? Get out!"

"You have memories you're keeping from yourself," Asha said. "Let me show—"

"No!" the girl cried. "Get out! Get out!" Her eyes grew wide, and Abeni inhaled at seeing the flames rising within. "I am my father's daughter! And I won't have any of your tricks!"

She launched forward, sword flashing. Abeni moved without thought, her staff blocking the girl's overhand sword swipe with the form *Elephant Swings His Trunk*. The girl came at her again, thrusting, and Abeni returned with *Lioness Swats the Hornet*. The girl spun suddenly, pulling a knife that burst into flames and slashing for her face. Abeni twirled her staff, the forms coming faster than she could name them. *Mongoose Bites the Adder. Gazelle Leaps in the Tall Grass. Heron Spreads Its Wings.* She met each blow, seeking to strike where she could. The girl finally pulled back, stopping but dancing on her toes.

"You're good, sorceress," she said in surprise. "Who was your teacher?"

"A straw man," Abeni replied through clenched teeth.

The girl frowned at this but shrugged. "No matter. We end this now."

She surged for Abeni again, sword and blade a blur. And this time her companions came with her. The monster roared, his bare feet pounding the deck in a run to meet Zaneeya. The panther girl growled back as he swung a jagged sword at her. She leapt over it to slash at his mask, sending chips of wood flying. The two settled into battle, teeth bared, as sword and claws clashed. Ama did not fare as well. The big man came at her, and the princess's arms moved on instinct to weave gold. The man flinched, throwing up his hands protectively. When nothing happened, he lowered them and chuckled.

"Something gone wrong, golden eyes?" He stepped forward slowly, taking his time as the girl backed away. "Always wondered what would happen if I cut one of your kind open. Tell me, do you bleed gold?"

Something about the threat brought a fierce light to Ama's eyes. Planting herself on the deck, she balled up a fist and jabbed it into the big man's stomach. Unprepared for the attack, he doubled over in surprise. Ama followed with a leaping kick to his chin, snapping his head back. He staggered, glaring at her between bloodied teeth.

"So, this prey has some bite!"

Ama glared back. "A princess of the Gold Kingdom is taught many arts of defense!"

The big man's eyebrows rose. "Princess? Well, I'll enjoy this even more."

He barreled forward like a bull, ducking most of her punches and kicks. Grabbing her up, he ignored her fists pummeling his face and shoulders and slammed her onto the deck. As Ama lay dazed, he raised his knife. Abeni cried out, trying to disentangle from her own fight to help the girl. But suddenly a sword appeared, blocking the knife just as it came down. Zuri stood there as if stepping out of thin air. Staring at the big man, she smiled at the shock on his face. He rushed her, seeming to forget Ama. But Zuri moved like water, sliding from the man's blade with barely any effort. Then she pressed the attack. The Silent Sword made not a sound, and neither did she—her feet noiseless on the deck. She gave the slightest twist of her hand, and the tip nicked the big man's cheek. He stumbled back, clutching the wound, startled. Zuri just smiled, urging him forward.

"A magic sword!" A dangerous light flickered in his eyes. "Well, I have some magic too."

Reaching into his jerkin, he pulled out a small round stone. He

barked a word, and three large shapes impossibly leapt out. Hounds!
Monstrous beasts, cloaked in shadow and wrapped in rusting
chains. They bared teeth, snarling as they crept forward. One fixed
its gaze on Zuri, while the other two set their eyes on Asha. Abeni
glanced to them in alarm. Before she could shout, one of the hounds
crouched, ready to pounce on the small girl. There was an explosion
of pink mist and Nyomi appeared between the two. The hound
leapt and the porcupine girl shrieked, holding her hands out in front
of her. A small cloud of purple mist appeared, and the hound vanished inside. It reappeared again, leaping from another purple cloud
high in the air. Its growl turned into a yelp as it fell, splashing into
the river.

Nyomi blinked in surprise, looking at her hands. "Purple?
That's new!"

"Prickly!" Asha cried. "Do it again!"

The two other hounds leapt, and the porcupine girl shrieked
again—her hand extended. The purple cloud appeared, and both
hounds jumped inside. The cloud reappeared near the ship's railing,
and they continued leaping, right into the water.

The girl—Fulan—watched this all in growing irritation. Pushing away from Abeni, she put a hand into the air and made a sig-
nal. A twang sounded and an arrow landed near Abeni's feet. She
backed away and looked up. The three bat riders circled the ship,
the Mmoatia on their backs with bows drawn.

"Enough!" Fulan shouted.

At the girl's words, both the monster and the big man broke off
their fight, backing up to join her. Zuri came to stand beside Abeni.
Zaneeya lent an arm to Ama, who was bruised but able to stand. She
gave the princess a grudging nod, which from the panther girl was
a rare compliment. The two moved to stand with Abeni and Zuri,
creating a line.

"Songu!" Abeni said, looking about worriedly.

"Manning the oar," Zuri said. She had sheathed the sword but
kept a hand on the hilt.

Across from them, Fulan shouted. "You are outnumbered and outmatched! You cannot win against us!" As she spoke, the monstrous hounds began climbing out of the water, hauling themselves up the ship's sides. She pointed her fiery knife at Abeni. "You will hand over that little spirit, sorceress! Give her to me or you will all burn!" Taking her knife, she bent down to slam it into the deck. A line of fire raced out in either direction, covering the wooden planks in flame. "What will it be, sorceress?"

"Not my ship!" Zuri growled. She turned to Abeni. "We make it out of this, and I'm going to have lots of questions." She glanced back to Asha. "Lots!"

"What now?" Ama asked, eyeing the flames and the circling bat riders.

"I don't know," Abeni said, her mind racing.

"Why does she keep calling you sorceress?" Zuri asked. "Wait, *are* you a sorceress?"

Zaneeya snorted. "If she could do magic, we'd have a way out of this mess!"

Abeni looked to the panther girl, her words triggering a memory. "The cat will know."

Zaneeya looked back, confused, then groaned. "Not that again."

Abeni reached hurriedly into her bag, drawing out two stones— one red, one gold.

"What are those?" Ama asked.

"Magic," Abeni said.

"What do they do?" Zuri asked in wonder.

"Can't say. But I was told the cat would know which to pick." Abeni looked to Zaneeya.

"This is ridiculous!" the panther girl said.

"It worked last time! Choose!"

"It doesn't make sense!"

Across from them, Fulan shouted. "Give the little spirit to me now, sorceress! Or we will come for her!"

"Choose!" Abeni said again, this time joined by Ama and Zuri.

"Fine! Red!"

Abeni dropped the gold stone back into her bag and looked out at Fulan.

"You keep calling me a sorceress!" she shouted. "Well, how about some magic!"

Hefting the red stone, she hurled it across the deck, where it bounced, rolled, then stopped just before the line of fire. There was a held breath as everyone waited.

Nothing happened.

"Maybe the cat chose wrong?" Zuri asked.

The red stone suddenly exploded. The roar of it was so loud, Abeni dropped her staff to cover her ears. And then there was wind! It swirled up and out with tremendous force. Abeni and her companions were thrown to the deck. But the greatest impact was nearer the stone. The line of fire snuffed out and those in the wind's path were lifted clear off their feet. The big man and the monster went flipping up and over the railing of the ship. The monstrous hounds went with them. In the skies, the sasabonsam beat their wings furiously against winds that tossed them about—trying not to crash against each other or into the waters below. Fulan was the only one who remained. She lay on her stomach, one hand gripping the knife plunged into the deck. Her eyes were locked on Abeni with a burning hatred as she gritted her teeth, fighting the wind that pulled at her. She looked like she was trying to crawl forward, trying to reach them. But the knife broke free, and she went with it, spinning away!

Abeni watched as above them the sail filled to bursting—and the ship lurched forward. She held on as they picked up terrific speed, hurtling down the river and away.

When the ship finally slowed, the crew of *The Sea Snake Lives* allowed themselves to breathe out in relief. There were no signs of their attackers following. Abeni sat with Asha, cradling the small girl in her arms. Across from them, Ama and Zaneeya, of all people, were trading stories. Nyomi sat cross-legged, trying to re-create the purple mist. Songu sat with her, but his eyes were on Abeni.

"Did you know who that was?" she signed. "The monster?"

"No," he signed back. "The Goat Man sent some of us away. I had just hoped . . ."

He trailed off, but she understood. Like him, she had hoped that once the Goat Man was brought down, the magic holding all the children would be broken. It appeared that wasn't the case.

Zuri called out, and Songu got up, heading to man the oar. The girl came and took his place, sitting down. Abeni steeled herself. She'd known this was coming.

"So," Zuri said. "We've had quite the day."

Abeni didn't answer.

"That girl, the very angry one. She seemed to know you."

"I've never met her," Abeni said. She remembered the hate in the girl's eyes. How could anyone she had never met hate her so much?

Zuri looked to Asha. "She knew you too. Said she'd been hunting you. What you said to her, about your relationship to her father—"

"That's enough," Abeni said.

Zuri glared. "Enough? We haven't scratched the surface! Who is this little spirit? What have you gotten me into?"

"You didn't have to come along," Abeni said.

"Maybe I wouldn't have, if I'd known—"

"You can ask your questions," Asha broke in. Everyone looked to her.

"Asha," Abeni said worriedly. "Are you certain?"

The little girl sighed. "I want to tell them, Abeni. Do you think it's just chance that we ended up captured by the Gold Kingdom? That we've been set on this quest? That we met Zuri and that sword? I told you before, there are forces at work greater than we know." Her dark eyes took them all in.

"Is *he* truly your brother?" Ama asked, both awestruck and terrified.

"Yes," Asha answered simply. "But let me start at the beginning . . ."

○ ○ ○

Fulan crawled onto shore, coughing up water. Beside her, she made out the Huntsman, doing much the same. His hounds dragged themselves out of the river. Behind them, two of the giant bats touched down, landing awkwardly—one nursing a limp. A third all but crashed into the ground, rolling before righting itself. She had seen the creature fall into the river, only escaping with great effort. Its rider had been rescued and ran now to aid the shaken beast. The monster was the last to emerge, striding from the river.

"Akul!" Fulan called, between wheezing breaths. "We go back up now! Find that ship."

"Back up?" the Wing Commander asked, his voice clipped. "Do you not see the skies?"

Fulan looked up. Even in the dark of night that had descended, she could see the swirling clouds above. The work of that sorceress. She looked out at the river, knowing that somewhere the sorceress and spirit yet lived. Opening her mouth, she screamed. It was a scream of anger and frustration. Of being thwarted at every turn. And of failure. She pounded the sand with her fists until her voice grew hoarse. When she could scream no more, she stood. The others all looked at her.

"I need fire," she told them.

A while later she sat on the shore, staring into the flames as she called to her father. As before, the world burned away and she was again in his throne room. He sat reclining and leaned forward at seeing her.

"Daughter. How goes your hunt?"

She clenched her teeth, bitter failure filling her mouth.

"They eluded me, Father. I saw your quarry. But she is protected by a powerful sorceress!"

"A sorceress," he murmured. "Have you found yourself a guardian, Asha?"

"The little spirit told me things," Fulan interrupted.

"Oh? What things would those be?"

In Fulan's head, the little spirit's words echoed. *He's lying to you . . . he will discard you once finished—as he has done to so many others. Flicker.* The odd images came again. This time with screams. Being held in a woman's arms as she ran. Watching homes on fire. The clanging clash of swords. The woman carrying her stopping. Turning to look up at—*Flicker.* She shook her head, pushing them away. What had that little spirit done to her?

"Daughter?" the Witch Priest asked. "What did she say?"

Fulan focused. "She called you her brother."

There was silence. "Yes. But that was long, long, ago."

He said nothing more, and Fulan knew not to press. She changed to something else.

"There was a Gold Weaver with them."

This caught her father's attention. He sat up, his voice a cold flame. "A Gold Weaver?"

"She claimed to be a princess."

A snarling roar rose from her father, like an inferno loosed in tall grass. The halls about them shook. "Treacherous mortals! They side with my enemy against me! They dare!" Then, just as suddenly, his tone shifted. His words came in a jumble, no longer speaking to her but to himself. For the second time she could remember, he sounded uncertain, and, unbelievably to her ears, fearful. "Is this you, Asha? Where are you taking them—to him? Yes, where else can you be heading in those lands. Are you working to undo my plans, yet again? I won't let you! You may be crafty, sister, but I am more cunning by far!"

She spoke up, cutting into his odd ramble. "I need you to grant me more power, to confront this sorceress."

"No," he said, the conviction back in his voice. "I am setting you on another path. You will go to the Gold Kingdom at once. I will instruct you from there."

Fulan reeled. "Am I being punished?"

"You are not being punished, child," her father said, a rare patience in his voice. "There are plans in motion. Plans that must now begin early before they are undone. You must see to them. No other can. This is the destiny I have planned for you."

"Father, please. I must complete this hunt—"

"This is a command, Daughter." There was a harsh finality to his tone.

"Yes, Father. But the Gold Kingdom is far. The bat riders cannot even travel."

"With my power, much is possible. You have wished for it. Would you deny it now?"

Fulan licked her lips. "No, Father."

"Good," he said. His hands reached for his mask, lifting it off to reveal the inferno beneath, showing her his true and terrible face. She gazed into that living flame, bracing herself as it reached out to her, seizing her in its grip and searing her through flesh, bone, and spirit. "I am my father's daughter," she started under the intense heat. "I, I—" She cut off as his fires consumed her, unable to even scream.

Fulan lay staring at the sky. The Huntsman knelt over her.

"You've come back to us," he said. "But what have you done to yourself, girl? What have you allowed to be done to you?"

Fulan sat up. She could see the others looking at her. Behind her eyes the fires burned hotter than ever. And when she looked up at the stars, they looked like burning orbs as well, singing to her with the harmony of the heavens. The whole world looked new, more vivid, more real. She lifted a hand and stared. Beneath her skin, fire swirled, glowing a bright orange in some places. She put a hand to her face and could feel the heat there as well. Her father's power. Now a part of her. She came to her feet feeling a renewed sense of purpose.

"We go to the Gold Kingdom. On my father's bidding."

The Mmoatia Wing Commander stared, uncertain how to address this new version of her. "I have told you, my sasabonsam cannot yet travel. It would take days . . ."

She walked past him to where the bats sat. Their glowing red eyes took her in warily. But they did not flinch when she placed a hand to their furry sides, granting them a bit of the fire inside her. Their eyes burned brighter. Wounds mended and they sat up straight, as if fully rested.

"They will fly. Faster than ever. Ready yourselves."

The Huntsman grabbed her arm. She looked at his hand, knowing she could burn it off if she wished.

"You've given yourself away to him," he said, disappointed. "I told you to walk your own path, girl. It's not too late. You would make a fine hunter. Turn from this. Cut yourself free!"

She pulled from his grip. "The path has been set. I am my father's daughter. I—"

"So you've said," he broke in. "Go your own way then. I will not."

"My father tasks you."

"He pays me," the big man corrected. "To hunt his quarry. Go and do his bidding as you please. But I will not abandon the hunt. The hunt is all that matters."

The two stared at each other, with an understanding that this was where they would part ways. She turned and walked to her waiting mount, climbing up and into the saddle. The other riders, including the monster, joined her. The three bats lifted into the skies, and she stared down to the Huntsman. He stood alone, his only company his three monstrous hounds, each growing smaller as she flew into the night.

CHAPTER TWENTY-TWO

THE LOST CITY

Abeni and her companions sailed two more days after the attack before landing at a place where sand met water. From there they set out on foot to search for the lost city. It wasn't an easy trek, over hot sand that rose in ridges and hills—what Zuri called dunes. Sunlight made the land shimmer, so that it looked like rippling water. They saw no people, no villages, not even a passing caravan. But here and there were insects or lizards, and once even a big-eared fox skittering across the sands. They wrapped up in the blue robes gotten from the caravan merchant. Abeni was thankful for them, even wrapping her face against the sun.

"Are we close?" Ama asked wearily. "We've been walking for hours."

"Hard to say," Zuri said, squinting into the distance. "We were only told to look for a set of black stones."

"I haven't seen any stones," Nyomi grumbled. "Just sand."

"We're going the right way," Asha said.

Zuri gave Asha an odd look. Ama did much the same. They both did that often now—ever since finding out the Witch Priest was the little spirit's brother.

They stopped as Zuri held up a hand. Ahead, a dark feline shape trotted towards them. The panther shifted into Zaneeya, who panted. Abeni handed her some water, which she drank down before speaking.

"It's ahead. About an hour's walk."

It took longer than that. Asha's small legs couldn't move as fast.

And none of them could match Zaneeya. When they crested a tall dune, however, they looked down on what they sought. Black stones. Well over a dozen, placed in expanding circles.

"What is it?" Nyomi asked.

"Maybe somebody's idea of art?" Zuri guessed.

Abeni studied the way the rocks gave off shadows. "It's for telling time. We had rocks like these in our village to record the days and seasons, by how the sun struck them. Our old timekeeper kept track. Though he also thought he could talk to birds."

"Takes all kinds, I guess," Zuri muttered. "What did that dragon say we do next?"

"Wait until the sun is highest in the sky," Ama said. "And our shadows are shortest." She squinted up. "That's not long from now."

"Then we wait," Abeni said.

They sat down on the ridge of the dune, staring at the rocks below.

"What do you think we'll find down there?" Zuri asked.

"Hopefully, this dragon Bida," Abeni answered, drinking some water and sharing with Asha.

"And then?"

"The Masks of Akani said he was guarding the Golden Throne," Ama said, swallowing down her own water. "We'll have to ask him to give it to us. Or take it." She glanced to Zuri's sword. "If your ancestor defeated Bida with it once, you can do it again."

"If my ancestor had defeated him," Zuri replied, "we wouldn't be here facing him, would we? Maybe those stories aren't all they're made out to be, Princess."

Ama frowned, but didn't argue. Abeni had to agree. Nothing they'd been told about Bida and the past seemed wholly correct.

"If the Witch Priest," Zuri said, "is the one who took your throne, and this Bida now guards it, doesn't that mean this dragon is working for him?"

"No," Asha said. "My brother wouldn't summon dragons to his war. They're stubborn, arrogant, ancient. It'd be like trying to summon cats."

"You seem to know more about dragons each day," Zuri noted.

Asha nodded. "The closer we get to Bida, the more bits and pieces seem to come to me." She stood up. "It's time."

The others stood too. The shadows cast by the rocks had grown smaller.

"Okay," Zuri said, frowning. "But I don't see a city."

"The dragon said to call to it loud and true," Ama said.

They all looked to each other, then shouted in a jumble. Nothing happened.

"Maybe if we all said the same thing?" Abeni suggested.

After debating, they settled on the word "Reveal," shouting it as one.

Still nothing.

"Why isn't it working?" Ama asked, frustrated. "He said to call to it loud and true."

"No," Asha said, her small face scrunched up in thought. "He said to call to it with one clear *note,* loud and true, for it to appear." She turned to Songu. "Can you do that?"

The boy stared for a moment. He had been withdrawn since encountering the monster. Abeni couldn't imagine what memories that had brought back for him. Finally he nodded, pulling out his flute. Putting it to his lips, he closed his eyes and blew. The sound was clear and crisp, flowing through the air before dying away.

Abeni felt a slight tremor at her feet. The sand was moving. It grew stronger, a humming that became a rumble that became a roar. They struggled to keep their footing as the world around them shook. Below, where the stones had been, was now covered in sea of churning sand, as something pushed up from beneath the desert—a great white dome that rose higher and higher into the air, sand falling off its surface like water. When it finally stopped, it looked like something out of a dream, so tall its rounded surface seemed to brush the cloudless sky. It was made entirely of white stone that shined brilliant in the sunlight.

"Gods!" Zuri breathed.

Abeni stared in equal awe, clutching Asha's hand.

"Thank you, Songu," Ama whispered. The boy nodded, pride on his face.

"Well, let's go see about finding this dragon," Zuri said.

They made their way down the dune towards the dome. It seemed bigger the closer they got, and Abeni noticed the shapes carved onto the white stone. They reminded her of the symbols on Ama's necklace—only more intricate and complex. She said as much.

"Yes," Ama said, staring at them. "But I don't know what they mean."

They reached the dome and stopped, taking it in.

"I can't even see the top from here," Nyomi said, straining to look up.

"What I don't see," Zaneeya commented, "is a door."

Abeni looked around. There was no entrance. Just smooth white stone.

"There might be some trick here," Zuri said. She placed a hand to the stone, feeling about. "These places often have some hidden mechanism or maybe a magic word or phrase."

"What if we just knocked?" Nyomi asked.

Zaneeya snickered. "That's ridiculous. To think we only need—"

Nyomi promptly walked up and rapped on the stone. She was answered with a scraping sound, and a section of wall slid away to reveal a dark passage.

The porcupine girl beamed. "My mother always says to knock first. It's just polite."

"Score one for mothers," Zuri said. "I'll go first. Anyone have a light?"

Abeni reached into her bag for a small orb, shaking it until it glowed. Holding it up, she walked behind Zuri as the others followed into the dark. The passage was narrow, forcing them to walk single file. Abeni's imagination ran wild as she tried to picture what they would find on the other side. Then, abruptly, there was light. She blinked, shielding her eyes from the sun. No, not the sun—a giant orb of gold! It hovered high in the air, beneath the ceiling of the dome, which was also gold. Together, the two cast a brilliance that shined down on all beneath.

"Now there's a sight!" Zuri whispered, her eyes wide.

The lost city lay spread out before them. Buildings rose up as far as the eye could see, with streets and paths cutting their way between them. It reminded Abeni of Jenna, but on a grander scale. One structure sat like a mound of gold, shining in the false sun. But unlike Jenna, there were no people. It was eerily quiet and empty. Most startling, the entire city was covered in green. Plants and trees grew everywhere, running through the streets. Leafy palms, bushes, and even creeping vines draped entire structures in foliage. Some of the trees grew even taller than the buildings. It was like a forest had taken root here and thrived.

They made their way through the forest city. Asha picked flowers, stringing them in her ivory locs. Nyomi stopped to eat some along the way. Abeni put out a hand for a yellow-winged butterfly to land on her fingers. She could hear other insects, and the cry of birds joining the call of monkeys. She even spotted a small red-brown mother bush pig with a row of piglets moving between the buildings. These, she supposed, were the city's inhabitants now.

"A forest, in a desert," Ama said, amazed.

"Magic," Zaneeya said, sniffing. "Strong magic. I can smell it."

Abeni couldn't smell it. But she had been around enough magic to know the feel of it. Like a tingle on her skin. Songu caught her attention, gesturing to something nearby that glinted between the greenery. They walked towards it and stopped. It was a golden statue of a man, running. He held a spear, as if ready to throw. Songu rapped a hand on it.

"Solid," he signed.

"That's a very good carving," Ama said. She reached up, moving a bit of vine covering the head and drew back, startled. The golden man's face was terrified.

Abeni looked around, finding another statue. This one was a woman holding a bow. Abeni pulled back vines wrapped about its head to reveal another face locked in fright. All about them, they could now see other statues. Many were figures holding weapons, charging forward. A few ran away. All had faces of horror, fear, and pain.

"I don't think these are statues," Zuri said. She pushed back plants concealing a kneeling man. His arms wrapped about his head protectively, as his mouth gaped in a scream.

Nyomi whimpered. "Do you mean they're people?"

"They *were* people," Zuri said. "In their last moments."

People transformed into gold statues, Abeni realized!

"Who do you think they were?" she asked.

A booming voice came in answer. "Mortals who sought riches and treasure."

They spun about, searching. But the voice seemed to come from everywhere.

"Only they found far more, and far worse," the voice boomed again.

Abeni clutched her staff, pushing Asha behind her. Zuri gripped the hilt of her sword. Zaneeya had her claws ready. Nyomi looked ready to vanish. They all searched around, trying to find the voice's source.

"They found me," it boomed.

A sudden motion caught Abeni's eyes. The mound of gold she had thought was some building ahead was moving! It shifted and rippled, and she now made out parts that were great scales—each one golden. She stepped back and looked at the mound, really looked and saw it. They were coils! Each looped tightly against the other. From the very top a great shape was rising. Long gold twisting things she now knew were horns appeared, partially covered in moss. They were followed by a head and two golden eyes that sparkled and stared out beneath ridged brows. A long snout became visible, like something between a crocodile and a serpent. From amid the coils, a great hand emerged, each of its five fingers ending in a long gold claw. It was joined by another. As the massive form unwrapped itself, those claws reached to grip the ground, and the head rose higher on a long neck. But the eyes never strayed from the small figures standing below, now swallowed by its shadow.

"I am Bida," the dragon spoke, in a voice that rumbled. "And woe to those who come seeking and find me."

Abeni gaped. She had thought Isa Bere was large. But this dragon was a giant—a true monster in every way! Being in his presence made her want to fall to her knees. How could they stand against such a being? For the first time, she truly wondered if their quest was hopeless. She could feel the same from the others. Then, without warning, Asha poked her head out from behind Abeni and waved.

"Hi Bida!" she called.

The dragon squinted his great eyes, lowering his head. Then those eyes widened, and, in movement faster than Abeni thought possible, he surged forward. In a few thunderous steps he was before them. Zuri drew her sword, stepping forward to meet the dragon, who brought a horned head down to peer at them. There was a long and drawn moment and the air buzzed. Then the dragon spoke the most unexpected words Abeni had thought to hear.

"Asha," he greeted her. "It has been a long time since I have seen you, Mother."

CHAPTER TWENTY-THREE

A DRAGON'S TALE

Fulan walked through the capital of the Gold Kingdom.

It was midday in Makomasi, and the streets bustled with people. Men, women, and children went about their lives, their golden eyes glinting in the sunlight. None of them paid her any mind, cloaked as she was in shadow and flame. Her father's power kept her out of their sight, even as she passed between them. A man weaving gold to craft a statue shifted to the left as she walked by. A child spinning golden orbs with playmates swerved in his run, missing her. None of them could know why their steps took them just out of her path.

Fulan had journeyed here alone, leaving the bat riders and the monster outside the city. She stopped to look at her reflection on a golden surface. Even in the yellowish hue, she could see the fire that now moved beneath her skin. She traced a finger across her cheek, leaving behind a fiery afterglow. The Huntsman's words came back to her: *What have you done to yourself, girl?*

Flicker. She was somewhere else, again. Everything about her burned. A city burned. Screams and smoke. The man and woman being led away in chains were there. They called out to her. She knew them. Their names were just on her tongue. She reached for them. But that strong hand fell on her shoulder, turning her around . . . *Flicker.*

Fulan frowned, clutching at her head, and shaking it until the images vanished. Her own face stared back at her. She pushed away idle memories and resumed her walk. There was work yet to do.

○○○

Abeni blinked. Had this dragon just called Asha . . .

"Mother?" Zuri mouthed silently, stunned.

Asha tilted her head to stare up at the dragon. "Yes. I think you called me that once."

Abeni thought she might have to sit down.

"It is fitting," Bida said. "You created me. Though not alone."

Asha nodded. "My brother."

"It was the combining of your powers that led to the most wondrous creations," Bida said. "Your affinity for things that live and grow. His fires of unmaking and undoing. We were some of your first attempts at such balance."

"The world must have been very young," Asha said. "I don't remember it well."

"Unsurprising," Bida said. "It is in your nature to re-create. To end and begin again." His gaze took them all in, stopping on Zuri. "I see the sword has returned to me, as it ever does." He sighed tiredly. "Put it away, warrior. If you walk with my mother, I will not call you enemy. Unless it is your wish to battle me and join these others." He nodded to the many statues.

Zuri hurriedly sheathed her sword. "I prefer *not* to be a statue."

Bida chuckled, a sound that made small birds perched atop his horns take flight.

"Tell me, Mother, how did you find me?"

"Isa Bere," she answered. "Says he wants to eat your heart."

Bida snorted, sending up glittery clouds from his nostrils. "Is that greedy dragon still jealous of me? Impudent child."

"I don't think he knew who I was," Asha said.

"No. He was not among the first of us—something that rubs his scales sore. But tell me, Mother, why are you now about in the world? And what strange company you keep. Who is this mortal girl that tries to conceal you from me?"

Abeni realized the dragon was talking about her! Asha stepped from behind her. "This is Abeni. My guardian."

"Guardian," Bida repeated. "I remember when you called such mortals caretakers. Welcome, guardian."

"H-hello," Abeni stammered.

Bida's eyes narrowed. "Are you not young for a mortal?"

"Yes. But Asha needed me early. It's complicated."

Bida nodded. His gaze swung to Zuri. "Another guardian?"

"No," Asha explained. "That's Zuri. She's a friend."

"A wielder of the sword," Bida noted, eyeing the weapon. "Like her ancestor before her."

"How—" Zuri began in surprise, but the dragon had already moved on.

"Song maker," he said, indicating Songu. The boy took a step back. "It takes one of skill to find the proper note to raise this city."

The dragon swiveled to Nyomi, who squeaked. "A porcupine spirit. It has been long since I have seen your kind. Tell me, do you still dance to the moons and the heavens?"

Nyomi's eyes lit up. "We dance to almost anything!"

Laughter like rumbling thunder sounded in Bida's throat before he turned solemn eyes to Zaneeya. "Panther spirit. We are kin in a way, creatures of balance, hovering between light and dark. I was grieved at the passing of the men of your kind from this world. They deserved a better fate."

Zaneeya stiffened but bowed her head. Looking at Ama, the dragon started.

"A child of my gifts!" he said in surprise. "Why have you brought these strange companions to seek me out, Asha—one bearing the sword I know well, and another with eyes that haunt me."

"I should ask you why you're here," Asha said. "In this forgotten place."

The dragon made an uncomfortable sound. He turned to gaze about. "This was once a great mortal city. Where you now stand was a grove, a garden created just for me. I returned to it, rebuilding, and willing the green things to take root and grow again. Here I have rested and slept away the years, apart from the world."

"But why?" Asha pressed. "Why have you fled away?"

Bida's voice grew low. "To escape my mistakes. To not have to face my shame."

"Like destroying the First Gold Kingdom?" Ama asked. She stared up at the dragon, her tone filled with accusation. "You were beloved among my people. Revered for your gifts bestowed upon us. Until you became jealous, devastating all we created. Is that the guilt you've come here to hide away from?"

There was a quiet, and Abeni wondered if the girl had gone too far. But the dragon did not seem angry. Instead, he only sighed again.

"You know not of what you speak," Bida said wearily. "I did not destroy your people's kingdom, child. You have been told a story, created to mask the truth. I should know. I created the story, after all. Much as I created that sword."

Ama stared at him in a mix of shock and confusion. They all did.

"Bida," Asha said. "You're going to have to explain."

"But is it a tale the child wants to hear?" the dragon asked.

Ama didn't answer. There was a stricken look on her face. Abeni put a hand to her shoulder. "You came seeking answers," she whispered. "You're brave enough to hear them." Ama never looked at her, but she nodded.

"Then let us begin," Bida said. He lifted his head, gazing up to the ceiling of the dome. The gold there began to ripple, moving in waves and forming into a mural. Abeni had seen this before—gold weaving as the Queen Mothers had done to tell a story. "I came to your people long ago and taught them the secrets of gold." On the ceiling a dragon that could only be Bida circled and flew among smaller figures meant to be people. "I showed them how to pull gold from the earth, to heat it, and craft it as they wished." In the mural, the people dug into the ground for gold. They made fires and with hammers pounded the gold, molding and shaping it, marveling at their handiwork.

"I gave to them the gift of gold weaving, so that they could use that power to do wondrous things." The dragon blew his golden breath upon the people and when they lifted their arms, the gold about them shifted and heaved. Now they crafted and shaped with their hands, their bodies swaying in rhythm as the gold danced for them. "The people flourished. They built cities and founded a grand kingdom." On the mural, these first Gold Weavers threw out their arms and buildings grew up around them, spreading across the land.

"For a while it was good. I lived among them, and I watched them grow with joy." Bida's tone turned dark, and the golden mural lost its luster as a shadow fell across it. "Then the curse of greed took hold. The people wanted more gold. To build more things. No longer content with what they could pull from their lands, they sought out other lands. They used my gifts to conquer, to enslave others to bring them gold." The mural showed it all. These first Gold Weavers fashioning armor and weapons, forming a golden army that trampled all before them.

Bida shook his head. "But greed destroys. The people began warring among themselves, fighting each other, weavers stealing gold from the very bodies of other weavers, stripping them of their abilities, even their lives." In the mural, Gold Weavers now fought Gold Weavers. The land trembled, and the grand buildings and cities fell to golden dust. "The kingdom crumbled, and I watched it die," Bida finished. "I vowed I would not let such a thing happen again. So I hid. I sowed a story in the people's minds of a nameless hero who ended me, so that all would think I was dead. This way, I could hide from my mistakes and not have to see the wrong I had caused."

Silence fell as the mural vanished. Abeni thought back to the story told by the Mmoatia Healer, of the foolish farmer who slew the hen who laid him golden eggs. It seemed there was truth in that tale after all. Bida hadn't destroyed the First Gold Kingdom of Ama's people. They had destroyed themselves! A truth that now left the princess shaken.

"That's not possible," she whispered. "Our histories—"

"A story of my own weaving," Bida said.

"That would mean everything I know is a lie. What our people believe, is a lie."

"Would you rather have not known? I can take the truth from you if you wish."

Ama's mouth opened, and for a moment Abeni thought she might say yes. But she shook her head. "No. But why keep it from us? Why have us believe a falsehood?"

"The story is not all false," Bida said. "There is truth to it, in a fashion."

"But it isn't true," Zuri put in. "It's a story you created."

"I had to," Bida said. "I could not risk anyone coming looking for me. I could not risk being persuaded to repeat my mistake."

"So, you just gave up on us?" Ama asked angrily. "Because you made one mistake?"

Bida's face furrowed into a frown, a disturbing thing to see on a dragon.

"One mistake?" he asked. "You misunderstand. I bestowed my gifts upon mortals twice before ever encountering your people. You were my *third* attempt!"

◌ ◌ ◌

Fulan stopped as she came to the heart of Makomasi. A set of buildings stood here, many smaller ones attached to a much larger structure. It was part of a walled-in complex that she knew had to be the palace. A palace crafted of gold! She walked right past a column of guards in golden armor, her fingers brushing their tall spears. Her path took her up a set of wide steps flanked by statues of golden leopards and through a gold door decorated with symbols. She stood looking about the inside of the palace, at the many rooms and upper floors, the pathways of gold and the carvings of seated rulers. A pair of real leopards trotted from around a corner, led on leashes by a servant. The beasts fixed bright eyes on her, somehow able to see through her glamour. But the unseeing servant coaxed them on, and they went on their way.

Fulan closed her eyes, letting herself be drawn to her destination. She walked through corridors, passing servants, guards, and people who wore the garb of officials. She didn't stop until she came to a door. She turned to peer down another corridor. That one led to the throne room, she was certain. The king would be there. She could walk in and end him without anyone realizing until it was too late. Her hand hovered near her knife but stopped. That was not the task she'd been set upon. That lay behind the doors ahead.

She walked towards two guards who stood as sentries—and stopped as someone came down the corridor. A hard-faced older woman with close-cut white hair, dressed in red and gold. She moved in a way that made Fulan tense, readying to fight. The woman stopped before the two guards, giving orders, then paused—frowning. She turned to look out from one eye, the other covered in an ornate gold eyepatch.

Fulan watched as that gaze swept the hallway, lingering where she stood. Her heartbeat quickened. Could this imposing woman see through her father's magic? But the woman's eye roamed past, and she finished her orders with the guards. They saluted, and she marched off. Fulan let the tension drain out of her and walked up to the guards. Going up on her toes, she whispered into their ears. The two men didn't flinch, but when she drew back, they turned as one to pull the doors open. Another of her father's gifts. Stepping inside, she let them close the doors behind her and walked towards her destiny.

◯◯◯

"Third attempt?" Zuri asked, confused.

"Why yes," Bida said. "My first attempt to give the gift of gold to mortals was in this very land. I created for the people who dwelled here a river of gold. It allowed them to flourish, to build up a kingdom. I would visit them and stay in this very grove. It was wonderful to see what they had done. But it did not last. Others heard of their wealth and came seeking it, invading and destroying. I came one visit to find the kingdom laid to waste, its people gone. This city is all that remains. They called their kingdom Ouagadougou."

"Ouagadougou," Zuri repeated, her eyes widening. "Like Wagadou! The great city took its name from here?"

"Seydou said something like that at the library," Abeni remembered. "He thought this was the First Gold Kingdom of Ama's people. But it was another kingdom altogether, long before."

Bida nodded his horned head gravely. "After my first attempt failed, I retreated here. I crafted the very sword you now hold, a blade that allows the wielder to make not even a whisper. I found a champion to wield it, who helped me carry out my ruse. I became a legend, a slain dragon forgotten by mortals. Centuries passed, and then a strange thing happened. A young prince arrived, bearing the sword. He claimed it had come to him and led him here. He persuaded me to return with him. So I brought my gifts to mortals a second time—causing gold to rain from the sky. His people created another kingdom and found happiness. I soon learned, however, that though the world had changed, mortals had not. When the prince passed from this realm, his children began squabbling. They used their wealth to raise great armies and fought each another until the kingdom was in ruin. Once more, I retreated here, vowing to never again share my gift with mortals."

"What made you come to my people?" Ama asked. "What made you try a third time?"

Bida's gaze turned wistful. "A boy of your land came seeking me. He had found my sword, like the prince before him. But unlike those seeking treasure, he only came to see a fabled city. I took a liking to him. And I was again persuaded to return to the world, to journey south with him. To his people, I bestowed the gift of weaving. To correct my past mistakes. With weaving, they could protect themselves. And it would give them a connection to the gold, so they would understand it was not something to squabble over. The boy became a ruler, and a great kingdom was born."

"The First Gold Kingdom," Ama said in understanding.

Bida nodded. "Indeed. He was a fine ruler. But . . . well, I have already told you that tale. When this third attempt failed, I understood then that what I thought a gift to mortals was instead a curse. It was a mistake I would not make again. I spun the story of my demise for the last time and bade the new champion who wielded my sword to cast it out from the world, so that none would find it again." He frowned, looking at Zuri. "And yet, here is the sword returned, as if it is my own curse. Is this why you have come here? To persuade me to venture out once again? Do you wish to build for yourself another kingdom of gold?"

Zuri shook her head. "I'm not looking to build any kingdoms." She turned to Ama. "I think it's time you asked him."

Ama took a breath, looking at the dragon. "You talked about the first ruler of my people, the boy who sought you out. The stories say you crafted for his kingdom a gift—a Golden Throne, to house the soul and heart of my people. It is missing. And we have been sent on a quest to find it. The Masks of Akani told us it was here with you—that you guard the soul of my people. I wish to take it back, great Bida, so that we can be made whole."

The dragon stared down at her.

"I am pained to learn that the throne is missing," he said at last. "But it is not here."

Abeni felt like someone had pulled at her very heart. Ama looked as if someone had ripped it out.

"That can't be," the princess said, frantic. "The Masks of Akani said it was here!"

Bida shook his head. "Your throne is not to be found in this city."

Ama put her head in her hands. She looked lost and broken.

"However," the dragon said, "I could tell you where it is."

Ama looked back up sharply. "You can?"

"Of course," Bida replied. "Gold is my element. And the throne was crafted by my power. Such a thing cannot hide from me. I have only to reach out and sense it . . ." He closed his eyes. "Yes, I can see it . . ." His horned head tilted. "Unexpected."

"Where?" Ama asked, desperate. "Please?"

Bida reopened his eyes. "The Golden Throne, child, is not gone. It is precisely where your people placed it."

○ ○ ○

Fulan stood in a dark chamber. But with the fire behind her eyes, she could see clearly. It was a wide square space, with high ceilings and a smooth stone floor.

It was also empty.

Fulan frowned. There was nothing here. Just a great empty space. Why then were guards posted outside? And why had her father sent her here? Closing her eyes, she called to him. She no longer needed to stare into fire. The flames within her were enough. His reply came at once.

"Daughter," he spoke, his voice filling her head. "You have arrived."

"I did as you asked. I came to the palace, to this room. But there's nothing here."

Her father laughed, the type of laugh he gave when pleased with his own cleverness.

"If you want to hide a thing, Daughter, keep it in plain sight. Reach out your hand."

Fulan did so and touched only empty air.

"I don't understand," she said, dropping her hand.

"Because you still think like a mortal when I have made you more. I have gifted you the power to walk among mortals unseen, to bend their will with a whisper. Their minds are small things. To conceal from them, you need only cloud their thoughts. Then, their very senses will betray them. Look again. Reach out again."

Fulan put out her hand—extending her fingers.

Still nothing.

"Stop thinking as a mere mortal!" her father shouted, his voice a fiery hammer. "See with your new eyes! Reach out with your new senses! Remember who you are!"

Fulan concentrated. This time she reached out with both hands, palms open. Inside her, the flames roared higher, building with a heat upon heat. It grew until her body burned from within, a scorching that scoured at her soul. "I am my father's daughter!" she whispered fiercely. "I am fire! I do not burn!" Her eyes flared to blazing—and she saw!

Something appeared in the dark. A great golden structure. It stood taller than her, and wider still. The top was flat and broad, curving upward and jutting out like wings. A seat, she realized. A rounded column thick as her body led down from the center, joining to a flat base. Two curved columns carved in the likeness of golden dragons surrounded the central column on either side, making four in total. All of it shined with a blinding brilliance. Her palms now pressed against the structure's golden surface, and beneath, that light hummed as if alive. She stepped back, staring up at it in amazement.

"Behold," her father said. "The Golden Throne."

Fulan had heard of this—the great and sacred throne of the Gold Weavers.

"Why did you bring me here, Father?"

"Jenna has fallen," he said.

Fulan gasped, staggered by those words. "One of the great cities . . ."

"Burns," her father finished. "Its famed library smolders. Its scholars in chains. My armies have claimed it. I am no longer the Witch Priest. I am the Witch King now."

"My king," Fulan said, falling to her knees. Her thoughts raced. Her father's armies had taken villages and small kingdoms of the hinterlands. But Jenna would force the other great powers of the west to respond. Wagadou. Timbatta. The forest kingdoms of Oyoun and Abomi. Others like Foula Jalou. What of the southlands? The stone cities of the East?

"Be not worried, Daughter," her father soothed, reading her thoughts. "I have long sowed dissent among my enemies. Even now, they bicker on how best to act, and who should lead any force against me. The southlands burn and its fabled spear-bearers fight each other. The stone cities hide behind their walls. My enemies are divided, selfish, distrustful. As they dawdle and scheme, I will strike each, one by one, smashing and rending them to dust."

"So, the great war has come at last," Fulan whispered. Her voice tingled with excitement and disappointment. "But I am not to be a part of it."

"Daughter, I intend you to be the heart of it. My golden spear. Place your hands to the throne and complete your final task here."

Fulan stood up, her mind confused. Reaching out, she touched the Golden Throne.

"Do you feel it?" her father asked. "The souls of an entire king-dom. I intended to come here when my plans had reached their end. To touch it myself. But now, I will do so through you!"

Fulan inhaled sharply as a torrent of fire blazed through her. She feared it would erupt from her skin, turning her to ash. But she couldn't let go. Her father was reaching through her to touch the throne. Her hands were his hands. And as she watched, a shadow began to creep along the throne's golden surface. It moved swiftly, swallowing up the light until the throne was covered in darkness. A muffled BOOM sounded as a wave of force pushed out from the darkened throne, knocking her back and shaking the palace—possibly the entire city. Then there was quiet. She stood up on trembling legs.

"It is done," her father pronounced.

Fulan stepped back, away from the dark throne. Sounds came from outside. She stumbled to the doors, pulling them open—to chaos. Shouts rang throughout the palace alongside screams. She looked to the guards at the door. One knelt over the body of his companion, shaking him awake. She peered closer at the fallen man who lay still, his eyes wide open. There were no pupils, no golden irises in that empty gaze—just shadow. Looking down the corridor she saw others. A guard lying flat with her spear. A servant curled beside a spilled pitcher. A court official slumped against a wall. Each with eyes like smooth black marbles.

"What is this?" Fulan whispered.

"You have given me their throne," her father said. "And with it, their souls. Go now, Daughter. Your army awakes."

Fulan made her way through the hall, stepping past the fallen as throughout Makomasi cries echoed into the night.

CHAPTER TWENTY-FOUR

CHOICES

Abeni stared up at the dragon, trying to make sense of what she had just heard. Zuri frowned in confusion. Ama was at a loss for words. Behind them, Zaneeya barked a bitter laugh.

"What do you mean?" Asha asked, looking genuinely surprised.

"The Golden Throne resides with her people," Bida repeated. "It never left."

"It's been there this whole time?" Nyomi asked. "We came all this way for nothing?"

"We've been played for fools!" Zaneeya growled.

That's how it felt to Abeni. Like part of some cruel joke.

"How is that possible?" Ama asked. "I've been to the room where it was housed. It's gone!"

Bida frowned. He closed his eyes again before opening them.

"You are right," he said. "And you are not. The throne is there. But it is veiled, behind shadow and flame. I know this magic."

"My brother," Asha whispered.

Bida nodded. "This is his touch."

"What are you all saying?" Ama asked. Asha turned to her.

"My brother never took your throne. He hid it. Away from your eyes, and it seems even mine."

"Do not blame yourself, Mother," Bida said. "The magic weaved about the throne is strong. And you are not . . . yourself."

"But he shouldn't be able to trick me so easily," Asha said, troubled. "I underestimated his cunning. And I fear it will cost us."

Bida looked confused. "I do not understand. Why is your brother a part of this?"

"The world's changed since you hid away," Asha said. "There's much you don't know."

"Then show me," Bida said. "As you would in the old days."

He bent his head low, bringing it right beside Asha. Abeni tightened her grip on the girl.

"Fear not, guardian," Bida said. "This is something we have long done."

Asha stepped forward, closing her eyes and resting her forehead against the dragon's.

Abeni gasped as images flashed through her head. The Witch Priest. The war. His armies. They rushed through her and she swooned.

"Are you alright?" Zuri asked, holding out a hand to steady her.

"So much destruction," Bida whispered in shock. "So much suffering. But why?"

"It is in my brother's nature to unmake," Asha said. "And he has let it consume him."

Bida shook his head. "There is no balance in this." He turned to Ama. "Now he has even mired my children in his schemes."

"The children you abandoned, Bida," Asha said.

The dragon reared back in indignation. "I did not abandon—"

"Yes, you did," Asha said, her small face stern. "You weren't meant to idle the years away while the world burns. You were created to maintain balance. I don't single you out for blame. My brother tricked many spirits into abandoning their roles, leaving mortals to face this threat. I was no better. Choosing to hide in the hopes the fires would pass me by. But it has only allowed his power to grow. There is blame enough for us all to share."

The dragon's face pulled into a scowl. "I have tried to be a teacher to the mortals. All my attempts have led to failure. I am not fit—"

"Oh, that again." It was Zuri.

"Pardon?" Bida asked, in a tone that would make most cower. But Zuri went on.

"You've been telling us these sob stories. About how your gifts to mortals turned out wrong. I'll speak for mortals here. We get stuff wrong. A lot. But we don't go hiding away in our magic lairs to brood about it. I guess that's what happens when you live thousands of lifetimes. We just have the one. So, when we mess up we take some time to cry about it, then we pick ourselves up and start over."

"She's right," Zaneeya said. "I'll give mortals this. When they fail, they have an ability to try again, repeatedly, stupidly. It's annoyingly admirable."

"You should hear Abeni's story," Nyomi piped up. Abeni shook her head, but the porcupine girl continued. "She's been through all sorts of terrible things. But she keeps on going. Whenever I hear her story, it makes me a little . . . brave." Her voice dropped. "Don't tell any porcupine spirits I said that."

Bida looked to Abeni with interest. "Guardian. I would hear this story, if you please."

Nyomi clapped. "Ohhh! She can tell it through this wonderful song and—"

"No I can't!" Abeni said. Well, she might have shouted it. Because everyone went quiet. "What I mean is, the song is gone. I lost it."

Bida looked confused. "How do you lose a song?"

"The same way I lost my gold weaving," Ama said quietly.

The dragon looked to them, squinting. "There is a darkness inside both of you, that is not of you. How did this come to be?"

Abeni and Ama shared glances. Then together told of their encounter with the Ekom.

"The Ekom," Bida said with distaste. "That was not always their name. Nor were they always so cruel. The greed that brought down your First Gold Kingdom corrupted them." He paused. "But you give the Ekom too much power. They are not truly real."

"They seemed plenty real," Ama said.

"I do not mean to say they are not dangerous. They feed on fear. It gives them substance. Allows them to shape themselves into that which terrorizes you. This is what they truly hunger for."

"What does my song have to do with fear?" Abeni asked.

"Or my weaving?" Ama added.

"Your song is very dear to you," Bida said. "It gives you strength, connection. The same with your weaving—the source of your pride, how you define who you are. To lose those is a fear buried so deep, you likely never thought on it. The Ekom found that fear and fed on it."

"But my weaving is gone," Ama insisted. "I can't even feel gold."

"Because you *believe* it to be gone. The Ekom cannot take such a thing from you. They can only make you believe they have. To continue in your fear sustains them."

Abeni remembered then the words the things in the lake had spoken.

"Because light given is always sweeter than taken," she murmured. "The loss is sweeter still." She turned to Ama. "I think I understand. The more we believe they took these things from us, the stronger our fear is to them."

Ama nodded slowly. "They even made us believe we gave it to them."

"All that guilt and fear," Bida said. "How they must delight in it."

Abeni looked to the dragon, an anger building up inside. "How do I get my song back?"

"And my weaving?" Ama asked, her tone just as strong.

"Simple," Bida replied. "Choose to believe that it was never taken from you."

There was quiet, as both girls stared at one another.

"I don't know how to do that," Abeni admitted.

"Me either," Ama said.

"It's harder for mortals, Bida," Asha said. "They'll need help."

The dragon nodded. "Share your thoughts, guardian. I will seek your song."

"It's like when I walk in your dreams," Asha explained. "She hasn't learned that yet."

Bida frowned. "I thought all guardians could do such things."

"I think I have," Abeni said. "Just now, when you put your heads together, I saw . . . images."

Bida nodded. "Perhaps your guardian is further along than you know."

"Perhaps," Asha said, looking to Abeni curiously.

"Come, guardian," the dragon said, lowering his massive head. "Show me your song."

Abeni walked up, gingerly placing her forehead against the dragon's—feeling his scales on her skin. They tingled, and—

There was a bright white light like a flash. Abeni blinked and looked around in surprise. She was no longer in the lost city. She was in a place she recognized yet didn't. Her village!

"An interesting choice," someone said.

She jumped, whirling about to find an old man standing beside her, tall and slender with smooth skin dark as night. Tightly coiled golden hair covered his scalp and he wore a robe that looked made from gold scales as he gazed out with gold-upon-gold eyes.

"Bida?" she asked.

He nodded, looking down at himself. "This is how I often appeared to mortals. If I showed my true form to them upon our first meeting, they had a habit of running away screaming AHH! DRAGON!"

"I've heard. Are we really in my village?"

"More like a reflection of your village."

She took in the sight of rebuilt homes and new buildings.

"But it's changed."

"This place reflects the world as it is now, not only how you remember it."

"Fomi, Sowoke . . . all the others," Abeni said in realization. "They must have done this. They made it back! Can I see them?"

Bida shook his head. "In this place we can see structures, plants, trees—things that stay in place. People and animals shift about too much to offer much of a reflection."

"Oh," Abeni said, disappointed. "But why are we here?"

"Only you know that. I asked to hear your song. Does this place hold some significance?"

She nodded. "It's where the song begins."

"Good!" Bida sat cross-legged on the ground. "Sing it for me."

"I can't."

"Try." He motioned for her to sit.

Seeing his expectant look, she sat. Concentrating, she reached for her song—and found nothing. "It's not there."

"Try again. Think on why this place is special in your song."

Taking a breath, Abeni did so. Her village. She imagined the last time she'd seen it, filled with people. The *chok-a-chok-a-chok-a-chok* of her mother and aunts pounding yam. Girls with fresh-painted faces being brought out for first rites. *Inside her, there was a spark.* She thought harder, on Harvest Festival. The masquerade parading through the streets. The sound of music. *The spark grew into a light.* And screams. The Storm Women and the black ropes. People stolen away. The smell of fire and smoke. The Goat Man. And . . . Asha, as the old woman. Their flight from the village. *The light grew brighter and began to hum.* She thought of her time in the witch's house. Of running away. Of talking pots and many rooms. Of a straw man and a shadow that moved at night. Of the old woman dying only to be reborn. Of meeting Nyomi and then Zaneeya. *The humming became a melody.* Abeni's lips moved to familiar words. Words she thought she had forgotten. It was her—

She cut off in shock as Bida thrust his hand into her stomach. It should have been impossible, but his arm went right inside her! She stared at it, wondering if she should scream, if it should hurt. Then his hand came back out, holding something black and wriggling. It looked like a worm, long as her arm. A wide mouth opened on an eyeless head, showing white blockish teeth. She knew what the thing was immediately—an Ekom! It shrieked, whipping about.

Bida squeezed his hand, and the worm burst in a spray of black liquid that turned to motes of gray ash drifting away on the wind. At once Abeni's song rushed back into her! She sang it loudly, savoring every remembered word, every returned memory, as if hearing them for the first time. The last thing she saw was Bida's fascinated face, then the white light took her.

Abeni was back in the lost city. Bida was again a dragon, and he pulled his head away from hers. A smiling Asha came up to wipe tears from her cheeks, and she realized she had fallen to her knees. "It's back!" she sobbed. "It's back!"

"Thank you for sharing your song," Bida said. "You are a remarkable guardian."

"Please." It was Ama. She was staring at the dragon with a desperate hope. "Please help me find my weaving again. Show me the way you showed her."

"You, child, are one of mine," Bida said. "Simply weave."

"I can't—"

"You can and will. Weave!"

Ama lifted her hands uncertainly and began her forms, before dropping them.

"Weave!" Bida insisted, a terrible force in his voice.

Ama tried again, this time finishing the form.

"Again," Bida demanded. "Again. Again."

As he spoke, Ama's arms spun. Sweat slicked her face as she performed each of her weavings like a dance, becoming more confident as she went, the exertion leaving her panting with each repetition. Just as the girl seemed near her limit, Bida opened a clawed hand and pulled at the air in front of her. A black liquid formed in that space, becoming like the worm he had drawn from Abeni. Ama clutched her stomach in revulsion. The Ekom's shriek was cut off as Bida closed his fist, and it burst, turning to ash. Ama was laughing, her face radiant with joy, as a golden orb hovered above her palm.

She stared up at the dragon. "Thank you." Turning back to the others she paused, then lifted her arms and began weaving. Abeni felt something tug inside her. From the others' looks, they did too.

"Please," Ama said, straining in her work. "Trust me."

"I see," Bida nodded. "Allow me to assist."

There was a sudden wrenching and Abeni gasped as something was torn out of her. She looked to see a writhing bit of gold hovering just before her face. It collapsed into a ball, falling to the ground. Several more joined it from the others. Ama dropped her arms, breathing hard.

"What did you do?" Zaneeya began, claws bared and moving forward.

Abeni put an arm out to stop her. "She took it out. The living gold. It's gone."

The panther girl stopped, a hand going to her chest. No doubt she could feel it too. The stiffness that had been growing wasn't there any longer. Abeni looked to the orbs on the ground.

"When I become ruler, things like that will no longer be used," Ama said.

Abeni met her gaze and nodded. "Then you should see about becoming ruler."

Ama smiled. "That's something I still have to figure out—"

The girl cut off as if struck. Abeni had to hold her up as she swayed.

"What is it? What's wrong?"

Ama's breathing came ragged. She looked at them with wide eyes. "I don't know. It felt like I was becoming undone. Like someone was clutching at my soul!"

Bida made a troubled sound. "Something has happened. I can feel it. The Golden Throne. It is no longer veiled. But it is . . . changed. Swallowed by shadow. The souls of an entire kingdom, thousands upon thousands, trapped in darkness."

"Brother," Asha whispered sadly. "What have you done?"

"No!" Ama wailed. "I'm too late!"

"I do not understand," Bida said. "What could your brother want with all those souls?"

"He's used souls before," Zaneeya said. "Turning children into monsters."

"I hope he's not planning to make more monsters!" Nyomi said worriedly.

"In the stone cities of the east," Zuri said grimly, "there is banned sorcery that seals trapped souls into the bodies of small dolls, that are forced to toil for their masters."

"That's awful!" Nyomi exclaimed. "I want you to know that if you become a doll, Ama, I won't treat you any differently. I like dolls."

"Not dolls," Abeni said. Her mind had been racing, going back to something she had seen. Now it was making an awful sense. "I think I know what he plans on doing with all those souls. And we're in trouble."

ꙮ ꙮ ꙮ

Fulan walked the tunnels of the mines just outside Makomasi. Cries and shouts echoed in the distance. The usual sounds of digging and breaking rocks had stopped. Many of the prisoners milled about, having watched many of their guards and foremen fall to the ground—unmoving and with empty eyes turned midnight black. The few Gold Weavers unaffected had fled, leaving the prisoners uncertain of what to do. Now they debated whether to flee or to head to the city to see what had happened. She passed between them unnoticed, moving farther into the mines.

She stopped to stare down at two guards who lay on their backs, empty eyes staring up at her. She had seen many like this on her walk here. People, old and young. *Flicker.* A burning city. Screams and smoke. A man and woman led away in chains, crying out to her. She wanted to reach them. That strong hand falling on her shoulder. She turned around and looked up . . . *Flicker.*

No! Her destiny awaited. Just ahead. She could feel it. Seizing control of herself, she stepped over the fallen guards and walked down the tunnel. More guards lay in the passage—some slumped over as if sleeping. Whatever was down here it must have been important, to station so many. The passage ended, leading into a thick darkness that challenged even her eyes. She pulled her knife, lifting it high and speaking a word to set the blade aflame. There was a burst of light and Fulan gaped at what stood before her.

Golden statues. Of people. They stood tall and erect, arms held at their sides. Fulan moved close to inspect them, noticing the upside-down flames etched on their foreheads. They looked like carvings of Gold Weavers, down to the necklace of gold orbs about each of their necks. Lifting onto her tiptoes she looked out and gasped. This wasn't some small room. It was a massive chamber. And as far as she could see, there were statues—rows upon rows. Silent and waiting.

"You have arrived, Daughter," her father spoke in her mind. "Do you like your gift?"

"Gift?" she asked.

"You have asked for an army. I have given you one. Imagine. An army that does not need sleep, or food, or water. An army that can march day and night without rest. An army bound with souls to serve and obey."

"The Gold Weavers!" Fulan said, understanding. "You've put their souls into these statues. It's why you wanted their throne!"

"How convenient, that they should place the souls of their people in one place—so easy to collect once I made it mine." Her father laughed at his own wit. Fulan was staggered at the revelation. An entire nation now under her father's control. Without striking so much as a blow, he had made them his—mind, body, and spirit.

"These Gold Weavers constructed this army," her father said. "Little did they suspect it was their very souls I would use to power their creations."

"A prison for each of them," Fulan murmured.

"Not all," her father said, irritation in his voice. "There are more chambers adjoining this one, each filled with golden warriors. But even working night and day, enough could not be constructed. My sister has forced me to move sooner than I had anticipated."

"You think this is more important?" Fulan asked. "You're willing to let her get away?"

"Daughter, when you finish here, rest assured . . . she and her guardian will come to us."

Fulan felt a thrill. She would see that cursed sorceress again. And this time, she would be ready. "What do I do?" she asked.

"Your army awaits your command," her father said.

Fulan felt something—a tingling in the back of her mind. She reached out to it. At once, the mark on each of the statues' foreheads flared to life. She absently traced her own mark before she spoke her first order.

"Awaken."

Thousands of eyes opened: gold pinpricks staring out from the darkness, waiting.

◠ ◯ ◡

"An army of gold warriors?" Zuri asked in disbelief.

Abeni had explained what she had seen in that secret chamber, while still a prisoner in the mines. Everyone turned to Ama. The girl shrank.

"He told us we had to build it. To get our throne back. We didn't know . . ."

"That the army you built him would be used to trap your own people?" Zaneeya sneered.

Ama's shoulders slumped. "We did it to ourselves. Now we're paying the price."

"My uncle used to say, *Everyone at the water hole knows the crocodile will eat someone,*" Nyomi put in. "*They just don't expect it to be themselves.*"

Abeni watched the pain on Ama's face. She thought on what it had felt like to lose her own village. She wouldn't wish that on anyone.

"What your people did was wrong," she agreed. "But that doesn't make what the Witch Priest is doing right." She looked to the dragon, who had sat listening. "What are you going to do about it?"

Bida looked startled. "Me?"

"The Masks of Akani sent us to find you," Abeni said. "But we didn't understand them—not exactly." She looked to Ama. "The masks said the Golden Throne was where your people left it. That turned out to be true. They also said the soul of your people would be found with the one who forever guards it." She turned back to Bida. "That's you. You made the Gold Weavers who they are. You gave them this power. You're their guardian—like I'm Asha's. You can't escape that by hiding away."

Ama's face brightened. "We thought the masks meant you guarded the Golden Throne itself. But they meant you guard *us*— the people you helped make!"

"So again," Abeni asked, "what are you going to do about it?"

Bida looked uncertain. "But my mistakes . . ."

"Can't be undone," Asha said. "This is about what you do now."

"I am frightened," the dragon admitted. "Frightened of what I might unleash."

"That's okay," Abeni said. She put a hand to him. "We're all frightened we might get stuff wrong. We still try."

Bida stood quiet and time seemed to stretch. "You are most persuasive, guardian," he said at last. Without warning he lifted, uncoiling his great long body and moving through the garden. They hurriedly followed.

"Where are you going?" Ama asked, running to keep up.

"To your city," Bida said. "To meet this usurper who corrupts what I have created."

The princess smiled, then her face fell. "But Makomasi is days away."

"Do not fear," the dragon said, coming to a stop. "This garden holds a few surprises." They pushed through thick foliage, reaching him. There, a structure stood made of gold, near half the dragon's height. It was carved with the images of animals and fantastic beasts. In its center sat a half-moon face of a woman, her one eye closed and her bold lips pursed in a slight smile.

"It's a door!" Abeni exclaimed. "You have a door! Well, half a door."

"I've seen this," Ama said. "There's one in Makomasi. It sits in a building where we house relics of the First Gold Kingdom."

Bida chuckled. "Doors like these can take you places. Some cover great distances. Others connect to realms beyond our world. This one allowed me to travel to its twin."

Abeni had known a door like this. Though it had been made of wood, not gold.

"How did you . . ." Zuri gestured at the door. ". . . fit?"

In a blur, Bida was the tall man with black skin in robes of golden scales—as he had appeared to Abeni in her vision. The others jumped. Only Asha seemed unsurprised. Ama turned to them.

"You don't have to come," she said. "You're free from any obligation to my kingdom. After what we did, I wouldn't blame you. But . . ." Her golden eyes lowered. "I would very much like not to do this alone."

Abeni looked to Ama, her words striking home. What the girl said was true. Their part in this quest was over. They could go their own way.

"You could have left the living gold in us," Zaneeya said, eyeing her. "Made it so that we had to go back with you to get it removed."

Ama shook her head. "I won't try to force you, not anymore."

Abeni weighed the humility on the girl's face. What a difference from the arrogant princess who once demanded they jump at her call. Had she truly changed so much? *Are you the same girl from a small village in the Jembe forest?* an inner voice asked. *Haven't your experiences changed you as well?* She was still lost in her thoughts when someone unexpectedly stepped to stand by Ama's side.

"Songu?" she asked in disbelief.

The boy had been quiet much of this time—as he had been since the attack on the boat.

"I have to go," he signed. "This talk of captured souls, made to serve others. I know what that's like. I won't just let that happen again."

"But they kidnapped us," she signed back. "Forced us—"

"Yes," Songu cut in. He looked to Ama. "But I've done my share of wrong and lived to regret it. I know what that's like too."

"You couldn't help yourself," she pressed.

"That didn't matter to the ones I hurt. I see their faces." He traced a finger along his own, past the pain in his eyes, ending at his chin. "All the time. I'm not a guardian or a spirit with magic powers. But I've learned I don't have to have those things to stand up for what's right. You taught me that."

"It's hard to forgive," Abeni signed forcefully.

Songu smiled. "Yet when no one would forgive me, you did. Maybe it's not so hard, then."

Ama put a hand to Songu's shoulder. "Thank you."

"Did you know," Zaneeya asked, "that I promised to kill you if you betrayed us?"

Ama swallowed, fingers touching her throat—likely remembering the panther girl's claws about her neck. "I understand why. If it were me, I would probably have done the same."

Zaneeya nodded, then walked to join Songu. Everyone gasped—Ama loudest of all.

"But . . ." the girl sputtered. "You don't even like me!"

Zaneeya shrugged. "I don't like most mortals. And I don't like what you did. But I also get it. Abeni . . . she's always trying to do what's good." The panther girl put on a high-pitched mocking voice. "'Oh Zaneeya! Don't you see? We must do this goody thing—because it's what's right!'"

Abeni's eyes narrowed. "I don't sound like that."

Zaneeya waved her off, turning to Ama. "But you and I understand that sometimes we do what we *must*. Good or not. What you did to us was wrong. But you did it to help your people. Like I would do whatever I thought necessary to help mine. That I understand. That I respect."

The two girls shared a look. There was a frightening hardness to their eyes that Abeni didn't know she could ever understand.

"I want a boat," Zuri said abruptly. She walked to stand next to Zaneeya. "Bigger than the one I'm going to leave behind here."

Ama nodded, grateful.

Nyomi bounced on her toes, looking worriedly between Abeni and the others. "You know I can't choose between you!" she whined.

"You won't have to," Asha said, smiling. "Abeni made her choice before any of you."

Abeni stared at the small girl before smiling back. "How did you know?"

"I told you already. There are forces at work here greater than us. It wasn't chance that brought us all together to face my brother again. You've always known." She walked up to take Abeni's hand. "Besides, Zaneeya's right. When faced with the chance to do good or do nothing, you'll always choose the first."

The panther girl snickered.

"It's not a weakness," Asha added. "It's what makes you the strongest person I know."

Abeni squeezed the girl's hand, and together they joined the others. "You forgot one thing." She met Ama's gaze. "I always choose to help my friends."

Ama looked startled, then mouthed a silent thank-you.

"That was quite dramatic!" Bida said, leaning over to Zuri. "Are they always like this?"

"You have no idea," the girl answered.

"Then let us go, before there is more . . . drama." He turned, calling up at the door. "Atta, we require passage!"

The carvings on the door stirred to life, the lone eye on the half-moon face slowly opening as the mouth yawned. "Bida. Wétin dey happen? Why you wake me so?"

"It has been a long time," the dragon said.

"All ah sudden you want to travel?"

"I was reminded I cannot hide forever. I wish to see your other half."

"That one wey lazy then useless!" The door sucked its teeth, then smiled. "Tell am say his big sisto dey greet am!"

Much of the door vanished, leaving only a rectangular frame.

Within that space, a curtain of shimmering gold rippled. Bida smiled back at them, walking through and vanishing. Ama followed, and one by one so did the rest.

For a time, the lost city was quiet with their passing, except for the birds and chirping insects. No one was there to see the big man who stepped out from behind the trees where he had remained hidden, or the three monstrous shapes that skulked steadily behind him.

CHAPTER TWENTY-FIVE

THE GOLDEN ARMY

Fulan strode at the head of her army.

Night had descended on Makomasi as the Golden Army marched through its streets—their heavy footsteps like ominous drums. A line of guards placed themselves in the army's path, their arms moving and weaving golden orbs that flew like arrows. None touched Fulan, as the forward ranks of her army lifted arms to weave in turn, deflecting the orbs or sending them hurtling back. That the golden warriors could weave like the trapped souls that powered them had been a delightful surprise. What was to come was even greater. As a guard fell, several of the golden warriors surrounded the woman. Before she could raise a hand, they weaved, encasing her in golden armor. One reached down to etch the upside-down flame on her forehead and she ceased struggling. Rising, she fell into formation, joining the army in its march.

Fulan smiled. There had not been enough statues to house the soul of each Gold Weaver. But with her control of the Golden Throne, every soul in the kingdom was hers to command. Once a Gold Weaver was encased in gold and her father's mark placed upon them, they became hers to control. Every Gold Weaver who fell was one who could no longer fight back—and a new recruit. She watched as a family was pulled from their home. The man and woman were quickly encased in gold, going stiff as her father's mark was placed on their foreheads. Their children, too young to be of use, cried after them, left behind.

Fulan stopped, letting her army flow around her. Something would have to be done with these children once the city was taken. She made her way to them, placing a hand on a small shoulder. *Flicker.* Screams and cries. She was frightened, so frightened. A strong hand on her shoulder, turning her around. Her eyes falling on dark armor and looking up to see . . . *Flicker.* Fulan yanked her hand back from the child, who now stared up in horror at her fiery eyes. She backed away, almost stumbling at the fright on the child's face—as if he stared at a demon. Regaining control, Fulan stalked off to rejoin her army. There was a city to conquer and a palace to take.

∘ ∘ ∘

Abeni felt grass beneath her feet shift to solid ground as she stepped through the golden veil. A light flickered to life, and she made out Bida with a bright gold orb hovering above his hand. The light reflected Zaneeya's orange eyes as strongly as Ama's golden ones. Behind them stood a door like the one they'd entered, with one-half of a man's face.

"Is this Makomasi?" Abeni asked. "Did we make it?"

"Whereever I dey, you dey there," a voice said, stifling a yawn. "But who you be, eh?"

Abeni realized it was the door that spoke.

"Hello, Atá," Bida greeted. "Your sister sends greetings."

"Bida!" the door exclaimed. "Long time since I see you o! Wétin carry you come here?"

"Great need," Bida said, looking to Ama. "And a promise."

The princess nodded at him before turning to Abeni. "We're in Makomasi," she said. "Near the city's center. We keep relics of the First Gold Kingdom here—though like this door, we don't know their purpose."

"You never told them what you could do, Atá?" Bida asked.

"Them never asked me. So, I just sleep, eh."

"We could have used you to go directly to Bida!" Ama said angrily.

"Heh heh," the door laughed. "But see the friends you make along the way!"

Abeni looked around. They were in a large room filled with all manner of objects. Some big ones, like the door, sat on the ground. Others were on shelves or atop gold pedestals. Bida walked among them, touching items here and there.

"I haven't seen many of these in quite some time," he said.

Ama caught up with him.

"Is there anything that might help us?"

Bida stopped at a shelf. He took down two items—a pair of gold bracelets and a necklace of thin red ropes attached to a flat gold disc bearing a woman's face.

"This one deflects sorcery." Ama bent as he placed the necklace over her head.

"And these will allow you to weave more gold than you ever have before." He handed her the bracelets. She fitted one on each wrist and jumped in surprise as they expanded, covering half her forearms. Her eyes went to Abeni's. The bands looked much like the ones the others had made her toss before.

"Just don't use them against *us*," Zaneeya said.

Abeni nodded. "Where to now?"

"The palace," Ama said. "Maybe I can reverse whatever was done to the Golden Throne."

"We'll probably have to get past them first," Nyomi said.

Everyone turned to find the porcupine girl looking out a window. Abeni joined her. In the darkened street tall shapes moved with the sounds of heavy footsteps. They were golden people, at least a dozen, marching in formation. A familiar symbol burned on their foreheads—the single flame of the Witch Priest.

"Those your people?" Zuri asked.

Ama shook her head. "Those aren't people."

Abeni watched the golden warriors and shivered. New figures suddenly leapt into the street, all in golden armor and wearing red patterned cloth. Gold Weavers! Their arms moved quickly, sending streaks of gold to strike the marching statues. One—a tall woman—raised both hands, lifting two golden warriors off their feet and hurtling them into a wall.

"Our guards!" Ama exclaimed. "They're fighting back!"

But so were the statues. Several lifted their arms, and gold orbs appeared.

Nyomi gasped. "They can weave too!"

The statues hurled their orbs. Many were deflected, but two found their mark. The guards who were hit fell writhing, as their bodies were fast encased in gold. They went still—then stood up, the flame now etched on their foreheads.

"No!" Ama cried. Before anyone could stop her, she bounded outside. They followed her out the door into the street—and found themselves in the thick of a fight.

Abeni ducked a reaching hand, swinging her staff to sweep a statue off its feet. Or was this one of the guards who'd been turned? She jabbed another in the chest hard enough to stop someone in their tracks. But the statue brushed her aside, sending her sprawling. Weaving a golden spear, it lifted the weapon, preparing to strike. Before it could, its body rippled. And as she watched . . . melted! Abeni looked up to see Ama's hand extending her way. The girl turned and melted three more statues. One turned out to be a guard—who fell to the ground, unmoving. Then there was quiet.

Abeni stood to find no more statues to fight. At least five were smashed together into a golden ball. Bida twirled a finger, causing the ball to spin. He let it drop, and the statues fought to untangle themselves, without success. One of the guards—the tall woman—walked up and Abeni's eyes widened with recognition.

"Captain Ekua!" Ama called.

The tall woman turned, her one eye showing surprise. "Princess Ama! Where have you been? Where did you come—" She cut off at seeing the others. "The prisoners from the mines? The Ohemmaa claimed you were touring the kingdom, Princess. I take it that wasn't exactly true."

"Where are the Queen Mothers?" Ama asked urgently. "The king?"

Captain Ekua grimaced. "The Ohemmaa were struck down by the same affliction that felled many in Makomasi—right before this cursed army marched on the city. Your brother fled."

"Fled?" Ama asked in disbelief. "He abandoned the city?"

"And with quite a bit of gold," the captain said.

Ama turned angry. "That sniveling coward!"

"Careful, Princess," Captain Ekua said. "He's still the king. Just coward will do."

"Who's mounting the resistance, then?" Ama asked.

The captain extended her arms to the few guards behind her. "There's pockets of us here and there. I hear Akú has a group of his own. But we're scattered. And we barely know what's happening. But I'm guessing this golden army is the same one from the mines. The one I warned the court not to build."

"At least one of you had some sense," Zaneeya muttered.

Captain Ekua eyed her. "You don't have a collar."

"No," the panther girl said, eyes narrowing. "And I owe you something."

The captain raised her arms as Zaneeya bared claws. Abeni lifted her staff and Zuri put a hand to her sword—as the guards prepared to weave.

"No!" Ama shouted. "Stand down, Captain, now!"

"You don't hold the crown, Princess," the woman said, eyes fixed on Zaneeya.

Ama seemed to draw on every bit of her royal haughtiness. "Captain Ekua, you serve the crown. I'm the last member of the royal family left in Makomasi. That means you serve me. Now, stand down!"

The force in her voice seemed to work. The captain slowly dropped her arms and bowed. Her guards followed, many looking relieved.

"Good," Ama said. "Now, tell me what's happened."

The captain did so—telling of an odd blast that shook the city, and the affliction that followed. Then the arrival of the golden army.

"They were in the streets before we even had a chance to recover," Captain Ekua said. "Our remaining sentries were quickly overwhelmed. The palace fell next. I barely made it out with about two dozen of my guards. This is what's left."

The captain walked over to the guards who had been encased in gold. They'd been freed, but they remained unmoving—their open eyes dark with shadow. "This is the affliction. Most in the city are like this: trapped in a sleep we cannot wake them from. What's going on, Princess?"

"The Golden Throne," Ama said. "It's been in the palace all this time, concealed by foul magic. Now *he* has taken control of it, capturing the souls of our people. He uses them to power this army."

For the first time that Abeni could recall, Captain Ekua looked shaken. But she quickly recovered. "People say there's a girl leading this golden army."

"Fulan," Asha said, coming to join Abeni.

"The girl who attacked my ship?" Zuri asked, frowning. "With the bat riders?"

"She calls herself the Witch Priest's daughter," Abeni said.

Captain Ekua looked between them. "Attack on a ship? Bat riders? The Witch Priest's daughter? I feel like I'm missing a few things." She took in Zuri and Bida. "And who are these two?"

Zuri sighed. "Captain of *The Sea Snake*, who stole back a magic kora for the scribes of Wagadou, the—"

"You're the Black Fox!" Captain Ekua said in surprise.

Zuri threw up her arms. "Finally!"

The captain looked her up and down. "I always thought you were . . . older."

"I'll take that as a compliment," Zuri said.

Captain Ekua motioned to Bida. "And this one?"

"He's harder to explain," Ama said. "I'll try to fill you in on the way."

"Where are we going?"

"The palace." Ama gritted her teeth. "I'm going to get our throne back."

Abeni held close to Asha as they traveled through the city. They stayed off the main roads, instead taking tunnels left by old gold mines. At their head, Captain Ekua and Ama shared information. Abeni was only partly paying attention, but something caught her ear.

"Wait!" she called out. "What did you say?"

The captain turned. "I said that Jenna has fallen."

Everyone gasped.

"You're certain?" Zuri asked.

Captain Ekua nodded. "Received news—just before all this mayhem. Jenna's been attacked by a massive force bearing the banner of the eternal flame. Its walls were breached, and the Great Library set afire. That was days ago. I expect it's fallen by now. Ama tells me you were all there. Got out just in time."

"The Witch Priest," Zuri whispered. "He's finally done it. The war is starting."

"He calls himself the Witch King, now," the captain said grimly.

"Poor Seydou," Nyomi said. "I hope he's safe. His books too."

Abeni thought back to the librarian apprentice. All those writings he loved, now gone.

"I knew those scholars weren't ready," Zuri muttered angrily. "Needed bigger walls . . ."

The captain grimaced. "None of us are ready. He's taking us down, one by one."

"His strength is your disunity," Asha said. "Your distrust of one another."

Captain Ekua looked at her, frowning.

"We're close. I can feel the throne," Bida said. He had remained quiet all this way, but now his gold-on-gold eyes seemed to brighten. "Also, they are here."

"They—?" Captain Ekua's question was cut off as she rounded a corner of the tunnel and ran straight into a wall of people. Everyone pulled out weapons, lifted hands, and bared claws. The people in front of them looked equally surprised, and hands were lifted to weave and weapons drawn. There were shouts and warnings from both sides. Then it struck Abeni. These weren't golden warriors. And one of those voices . . .

"Manu? It's me! Abeni!"

"The bush girl? Naana! Look who it is!" Two figures stepped forward. Manu and Naana—the brother and sister she'd met when captured.

"You know them?" Captain Akua asked, hands still ready to weave.

"We were in the mines together," Abeni said.

The captain's face hardened. "I heard the prisoners had escaped! Were you all behind this? Are you working with our enemies?"

"I can assure you, Captain, that they are not." A figure pushed to the front, joining Manu and Naana. Ama and the captain gawked.

"Attendant Akú?" both asked at once.

Abeni recognized the royal attendant. His clothes were torn and his face smeared with dirt. Yet he still carried himself a certain way.

"Happy chance, meeting you down here, Captain," he said, before bowing. "Princess." His gaze shifted. "And you, Abeni, daughter of Yayawi and Akanyo, of the Jembe forest."

"What's going on here, Akú?" the captain asked. "What are you doing with these . . ."

"Spies," Manu finished for her.

Naana grinned. "Yep. We're totally spies."

Captain Ekua gaped. "Akú! You're a traitor?"

The royal attendant rolled his eyes "Don't be dramatic, Ekua. If everyone would please put down their assorted weapons, hands and . . . claws, we could talk?"

"Do it, Captain," Ama said, dropping her hands. "I'm sure he has a good . . . reason."

Captain Ekua did as ordered and everyone backed down.

"I'll make this short," Akú said. "The princess has likely informed you of her quest? Well, I wanted to learn more about Abeni and her strange companions through informants I have in the mines. How surprised I was to turn up two spies. I decided, instead of having them executed, to invite them to talk directly. They agreed."

"It was the whole executed part," Manu explained.

"We had some fruitful discussions," Akú said. "I decided it was better to pursue diplomacy, in case things went quite wrong with the princess's quest and we found ourselves in need of assistance."

"You don't have that authority," Captain Ekua snapped. "The Ohemmaa will be furious."

Akú chuckled. "Ekua, who do you think backed my diplomatic overtures?"

The captain's eyes widened. "Those crafty old women . . ."

"Most of the miners fled when this all started," Manu said. "But some of us decided to come into Makomasi. We only intended to get a look and report back. But then, we started finding them." He stepped aside, and Abeni for the first time noticed others in the tunnels. Children. Dozens of them.

"The golden warriors take their parents," Naana explained, "They're just left behind to wander the streets. We started collecting one or two and . . . well. Didn't know what to do with them, until we ran into Akú."

"You saved our people," Captain Ekua asked in surprise. "After all we've done to you?"

Naana looked offended, "They're children."

"We're not monsters," her brother added.

"Thank you," Ama said. "We owe you, all of you, greatly."

"Strange allies in these times," Akú noted, nodding to the assortment of guards and freed miners behind him. "I take it, Princess, from all that's transpired, that things went quite wrong?"

"The Golden Throne is in the palace," she said. "But it's been corrupted. The Witch Pr—, Witch King, is using the souls of our people to power this army."

"Quite wrong, then," Akú murmured.

"We plan to stop him," the princess said. "We need to take back our throne."

Akú looked her over, then smiled. "After your brother fled I feared . . . well, it is good to have you leading us, Princess." He bowed deep. The guards behind followed. Manu began to bow, until Naana cuffed his ear.

"We're not your subjects," she said. "But we'll help stop this army."

"We'll need the help," Ama said. "How far is the palace?"

"Just a few streets away," Captain Ekua said. "We can go up soon."

"One moment." It was Bida. "If it is battle we face, at least be prepared." He walked through them, touching people here and there. The Gold Weavers' armor seemed to gleam brighter. The miners' weapons were fast covered in a thin layer of gold. Even Zaneeya's claws turned gold. Abeni watched as her own staff became a golden rod.

"Who *are* you?" Captain Ekua asked, baffled. Bida only smiled.

"Complicated," Ama said hurriedly. "Let's go!"

They made their way, the two groups now one—about thirty in all. The children were left with two older miners who promised to get them out of the city if this went badly. As they climbed out of the tunnels, Abeni braced for whatever might await them on the streets of Makomasi. And was surprised to find . . . nothing.

"It's empty," Zaneeya said in surprise, as they came to stand in the street.

"Where's the army?" Zuri asked.

"Good question," Captain Ekua said, her one eye scanning everything.

"Maybe they're in another part of the city?" Nyomi asked.

"Or they all had to use the bathroom at the same time," Manu suggested.

Everyone looked to him. Naana cuffed his ear again.

"Wherever they are, the palace is ahead," Ama said. Abeni could see the large structure in the distance, remembering those many steps at its front and the two statues of golden leopards.

Akú frowned. "It would be too easy to just walk through the front doors."

"I agree, Princess," the captain added. "This smells like a trap."

Ama's jaw tightened. "If it's a trap, they know we're coming. So, let's end this and—"

She didn't finish as the palace doors began to open. There was the sound of heavy footfalls from inside, and as they watched, golden warriors emerged from within. They marched in a column, four persons wide, their feet stamping the ground. Their blank eyes stared unblinking, with the fiery mark burning bright on their foreheads. On their shoulders, they carried a throne. It was massive, with a flat base that supported a thick column in the center and two more on each side carved like dragons. The entire throne was shrouded in darkness, so that it looked made up of shadows. At the top was a flat space curving up on either side. And seated there was a familiar figure.

The girl who named herself the Witch King's daughter was on the throne. She wore a long golden patterned robe over her clothing. But it was open, displaying the weapons she still held. She sat casually, one leg folded over the other. Her eyes, however, were as fiery as the mark etched above her brow. It seemed to those who watched that fire lived beneath the girl's skin, as if she was burning up inside. She raised a hand and the procession stopped at the top of the wide stairs. Her lips curled into a smile and when she spoke, her voice thundered.

"Sorceress! My father said you would come! And have you brought me a small present?"

Abeni gripped Asha close. Fulan smiled wider.

"Usurper!" Ama shouted, stepping forward. "You steal the souls of my people, corrupt what is sacred, and now you sit upon our throne? Are we so low in your eyes that you desecrate all we find holy?" Her voice trembled and Abeni saw the same shock and anger on the faces of other Gold Weavers. Of course, she remembered. No one was supposed to sit on the Golden Throne. This was an ultimate act of disrespect, and the girl knew that.

Fulan shrugged. "My father offered your kingdom a place beneath his hand. You betrayed that. So, we have taken your people from you. Now they serve, as you will serve."

"I'll give you one more chance," Ama said coldly. "Give back my people's throne, now."

"You think to command me?" Fulan sneered. "You are ruler of nothing! We are the fire that will sweep over this world!" There was the sound of heavy footfalls, coming from seemingly every direction. "The servants of the Eternal Flame!" The footfalls grew louder, and the ground shook under the weight. "All will bow before us!" Golden warriors poured suddenly from the buildings—in their dozens. "All will serve!" More marched down once empty streets. When they finally stopped, Abeni and the small force that had come to take back the throne were surrounded by a sea of gold that stretched as far as they could see.

Atop her stolen throne, Fulan spoke a final command behind bared teeth. "Now, bow!"

A hush fell, like the quiet before a storm.

Ama stepped forward. "No. We won't bow. Not to you, or *him*. Ever."

Abeni joined her. Then the others all stepped up. Well, Nyomi needed a glare from Zaneeya, but she came. Fulan stared at them all in disbelief—then laughed.

"You stand against me? You and your pathetic friends? Where is your kingdom now?"

"We have each other!" Abeni shouted. "We don't even all get along. We may not get along tomorrow. But today, we stand against you—and the one you serve!"

"I have an army!" Fulan screamed back.

"That you've enslaved!" Zuri retorted. "What? Daddy wouldn't let you lead a real army?"

"You can still walk away!" Asha called. "It's never too late!"

Fulan glared. "None of you matter! None of you are fit to stand against me!" She sat back, a coldness creeping into her voice. "Destroy them all."

Abeni watched as around them the army moved, weaving weapons of gold. Spears appeared out of thin air, joined by axes and swords. As one, they lowered them at the small group at their center.

"This has been interesting," someone spoke. It was Bida. He stepped apart from the others, walking forward. The golden warriors in his path were pushed aside without him even touching them, their weapons curving and bending away. He walked right into their midst, hands behind his back as he stared up at Fulan with those gold-upon-gold eyes. "You," he said in a scolding tone, "are a most unpleasant child."

Fulan laughed. "You send an old man to fight me now?"

"I came on my own," Bida replied. "Though it did take some convincing. Now, I am glad I did. What you are doing here I cannot allow. I must ask you to surrender the throne."

The fires in Fulan's eyes blazed. "Keep talking like that, old man, and I'll have my warriors cut out your golden tongue!"

Bida shook his head. "A most unpleasant child. Very well. Have it your way. Could you at least say, AHH! DRAGON? For old times' sake."

Fulan frowned. "Ahh, dragon?"

Bida smiled. "I do miss that."

Then he transformed.

Abeni gasped loudly. It was quite a thing to see a dragon simply appear. Bida stretched out before them, towering high above the buildings of Makomasi. His golden coils filled the open square before the palace and stretched down a main street, knocking aside golden warriors with his sheer enormity. Even Fulan shrank back, mouth gaping as she stared up, and up, at the dragon. Bida took in a deep breath of night air before swinging his horned head down to fix the girl with a terrible golden gaze.

"I am the dragon Bida!" he thundered. "And you will return my throne!"

Fulan managed to find her voice, screaming out one word. "Attack!"

The golden army surged forward. They scrambled over the dragon, using their weapons to hack, cut, or stab at his serpentine body—trying to breach his shimmering scales. Bida bellowed with laughter. "Warriors of gold sent against me?" He whipped his coils and the golden figures atop him went flying. With a terrific leap, he soared into the air before plunging back down, plowing through them, seizing some between his jaws and flinging them away.

Abeni watched the battle in awe. Most of the golden army seemed focused on Bida. But there were still enough to surround her and the others. She ducked as a golden warrior sailed overhead, crashing into a building. Another stabbed a spear at her. She brought up her staff to block it, now coated in the gold covering Bida had provided. When spear and staff clashed, there was a vibrating clang and the warrior staggered back. Abeni stared in surprise. That was new! The golden warrior came at her again, but something unseen lifted it into the air, hurling it away. She looked to see Captain Ekua's arms weaving in her direction. There was a curt nod before the woman turned and weaved elsewhere, knocking down more golden figures.

Zuri was a blur, somehow everywhere at once. She and her sword moved soundlessly. The blade didn't appear to cut. But it passed right through the golden warriors, and they dropped—lying dazed for long moments.

"Has anyone given thought that some of these are people and not statues?" Manu cried out, striking aside several golden warriors with a pickaxe.

"Don't know that it matters!" his sister said, swinging her own weapon. "None of them stay down long!"

It was true, Abeni could see. No matter how many times the golden figures got knocked away, they eventually came back.

"Too bad we all can't do that!" Manu said, nodding to Ama.

Abeni looked to the princess, who was a force in the battle! Thanks to the bands gifted by Bida, she weaved stronger than anyone—knocking down whole columns of golden warriors and melting others to golden puddles. Those did not come back!

Zaneeya leapt to strike a golden warrior before spinning to rake gold claws at another. "We could use a few more princesses right now!" she said.

"We can't keep this up forever!" Akú said as he weaved.

"We need to get to the throne!" Ama shouted. "If I can undo the dark magic upon it, we can take back our people's souls—leaving this army lifeless!"

Abeni looked to the throne. It wasn't that far. But throngs of golden warriors stood between them and it. The throne might as well be miles away.

"Where's Nyomi?" Abeni asked. They had formed a circle, with Songu and Asha in the middle—the two with no weapons of their own.

Zaneeya snorted. "Squeaked and poofed off at the first sign of battle!"

That was probably for the best, Abeni thought, as she swatted away a golden axe. Though Nyomi's jumping might have helped a few of them reach the throne. She swept another golden figure off its feet, and a sudden ear-piercing shriek sent a shiver through her. She looked up into the night sky searching, and her heart dropped away.

"Bat riders!" she shouted. "There are bat riders!"

"Great!" Zaneeya growled. "Just what we need!"

Abeni watched the dark shapes streak across the sky. She remembered the attack on the ship. Fulan had had three bat riders. Now there were dozens! How were they supposed to fight an army on the ground and another in the air?

One of the bats dove at them, its red eyes intent. She lifted her staff high overhead, readying the form *The Spear Pierces the Sky*. The sasabonsam's black claws opened wide just before it reached them—and sailed right past! She turned in surprise to see it snatch up a golden warrior! The giant bat strained under the weight of the thing, but it rose higher and with a twist sent the living statue plunging into its companions, scattering them. The Mmoatia

Blood Skull stared down behind her red-painted face and gave what looked like a salute before flying off. Abeni sheepishly waved back.

"What just happened?" Zaneeya asked, just as stunned. "Did she help us?"

"Not the only one!" Captain Ekua said. "Look!"

Abeni gazed out at the battle. The bat riders weren't aiding the golden army. They were attacking it! Sasabonsam snatched up golden figures into the air, dropping or hurling them into their own ranks. Others plucked them off Bida's back as he rampaged through the city, while archers fired arrows—that couldn't pierce golden armor, but which hit with enough force to put the living statues on their backs. Abeni watched it all in disbelief. Belatedly, she heard someone call her name amid the noise of battle. She looked up to see a sasabonsam circling above. It dropped down just feet from her, clearing the space. A Blood Skull handled the bat's reins, but a familiar face peeked around him.

"Nula?" Abeni asked, doubting her eyes.

"Abeni!" the Mmoatia girl greeted. "I knew you'd be here!"

"But what are *you* doing here?" she asked, utterly confused.

"So much has happened in the weeks since you left. Where do I begin! They tried to jail us for helping you escape, and it turned into a huge protest. People came out into the streets. We even got some Blood Skulls on our side—especially when Healer Osha spoke on our behalf! The old council resigned. The new leaders listened to us about making alliances with humans. We had scouts watching the Gold Kingdom, to see if we might open up talks. They reported back what happened tonight and it was decided we'd come out and see if we could save anyone. We didn't expect to find a battle! And is that a *dragon*?"

A roar from Bida shook the air as they caught glimpses of him between the buildings.

"A dragon!" Abeni confirmed. "I can't believe you're here and— look out!"

A golden warrior broke through their line and leapt for the sasabonsam. But the giant bat caught the thing in its jaws, shaking it furiously before flinging it away.

"We'd better go!" Nula said. "Safer in the air! How can we help?"

"We need a path to up there!" Abeni pointed to the palace. "We can end all this if we can undo the magic powering this army!"

Nula nodded. Just then, another bat swooped overhead. A figure on its back whooped excitedly, "REVOLUTION!"

"Tanka!" Nula explained. "He's really gotten into this. I'll talk with the Blood Skulls. Get ready to run when we make that path!" The bat rider took off again, soaring into the air.

"What was that?" Captain Ekua asked. Abeni quickly explained and the woman nodded. "Good plan! I'll take the rear with Akú and his people. You get the princess up there."

"Don't you want to guard her?" Abeni asked.

The captain scoffed. "Think she can take care of herself. Besides, you're the ones who've been off adventuring with her. Must be a good team to have gotten this far. Don't stop now."

Abeni supposed they were a team, of sorts. She hurriedly passed on the plan and looked up in time to see a formation of bat riders heading their way.

"Get ready!" she shouted.

The riders swept down in a line, diving at the throng between them and the palace. Golden figures were hefted off the ground and slung away. Others were dropped back onto their companions. The giant bats kept just out of their reach, nimbly avoiding axes and hurled spears while their archers struck where they wished. It was a confused mess, but as Abeni watched, she could see an opening forming.

"There!" she pointed.

They dashed to the palace. Abeni stayed close to Asha and Songu as golden figures fell from the sky or hurtled across their path. Several times she had to fight their way free. Sometimes Zaneeya appeared, a black panther leaping and knocking down living statues. Zuri came and went, her silent sword flashing. One golden warrior in her way was jerked into the air, a sasabonsam clutching its head. Another melted before it could swing a two-sided axe as Ama took up a place beside her.

"Almost there!" the princess shouted.

Abeni could see the steps of the palace within reach. They just had to get past—

Suddenly the golden warriors ahead were jostled aside as a huge form barreled through them. Abeni braked, stumbling back. It was the monster! The one from the ship! He was running straight for them, knocking away anything in his path. Ama hurled golden orbs, but they barely slowed him. He roared—his eyes burning behind his mask of wood and iron. Abeni pushed Asha behind her and raised her staff—just as someone ran past her.

"Songu! No!"

But the boy never looked back. He ran to meet the monster, crying out—the first sound she had ever heard from his lips. Then he changed. She watched in horror as Songu grew. Corded and knotted muscles broke out along his arms, back, and legs, as his skin turned the color of grayish rock. Tattered crimson cloth appeared to wrap him, leaving only his chest bare, as a mask of wood and iron closed over the top half of his face. He had become a monster again! At the sight of him, the first monster seemed to grow enraged. He roared and ran for Songu, who roared back and picked up his speed. When the two clashed, they shook the very ground as they grappled and punched and hit.

"Abeni! Abeni!"

She blinked tears from her eyes and realized that Asha was pulling her arm.

"We have to go, Abeni! The others need us!"

She looked to find everyone else had gone ahead. Slowly she got her feet moving and ran to catch up. There were only a few golden warriors left on the palace stairs and the throne was there! Fulan still sat atop it, staring out at the battle. The girl seemed stunned at this turn of events, but she quickly recovered. With a fierce cry she drew her sword and leapt from the throne, landing right before them. She met Zaneeya first, swinging at the panther girl. Gold claws met metal, sending up sparks. Zuri came in silently. But Fulan somehow sensed her, spinning to meet the silent blade. She dropped to a crouch, extending a leg to sweep Zuri. Jumping back up, she swung again at Zaneeya, forcing her back.

"To me!" she yelled, as the mark on her forehead blared bright.

Golden warriors turned and ran to aid her. More poured from the palace. Abeni and her friends were quickly engulfed, separated and fighting to not be overwhelmed.

"No!" Ama screamed as the golden figures surrounded them. Clenching her teeth in exertion, she moved her arms in a complex weave like a dance and released it with a yell. There was a creaking sound and Abeni watched in awe as the two giant gold carvings of leopards that sat in front of the palace came to life! They twitched their ears and tails, jumping down from their platforms to land before the princess.

"Defend the city!" she commanded.

The leopards turned and pounced at the golden warriors, tumbling many. The fight in front of the palace became even more confused. It was all Abeni could do to keep herself and Asha safe. As she swung her staff, she glimpsed Fulan moving towards her, that familiar rage on her face. The girl pulled a knife that burst into flames and somehow hurled it between the many combatants, aiming for them. Abeni watched the tumbling blade streak towards them, trying to bring her staff to block it. She wouldn't be fast enough! Then suddenly the knife was gone. No, she and Asha were gone! They were floating in a familiar pink place of nothingness before abruptly stumbling onto the steps of the palace, just feet from the throne. Standing there was . . .

"Nyomi!" Abeni said, breathless.

"Hi!" the porcupine girl said. "Got you just in time!"

Abeni looked down the steps to see Fulan searching in confusion. She turned to Nyomi.

"We thought you left!"

"I did. Went to get help. See?"

Abeni followed Nyomi's gesture and jumped. Standing just behind them were . . . things. There were about a dozen or so. Each was a shade of purple so dark they almost blended with the night. They looked like people. Sort of. But with thin wavy arms that were too long or legs too short. Their shapes grew and shrunk by the moment, as their bodies curved and bent as if made of smoke.

"The mist people!" Abeni exclaimed.

Nyomi nodded eagerly. "I thought we could use the help! Some agreed to come back with me. They even tried to look like people." She lowered her voice. "They're really proud of that, so don't say anything." She turned back to them. "This is Abeni! Remember her?"

Abeni raised her hand awkwardly. "Hello."

The mist people didn't speak but waved long fingers that looped and curled.

"Thanks for coming, everyone!" Nyomi said. "It's all the gold people we need help with!"

The mist people turned their wavy shifting bodies, moving to the gold warriors outside the palace. They didn't walk so much as glide above the ground. The first golden warriors they touched disappeared in a purple poof—then reappeared high in the air to rain down on their companions. Others fell into purple holes in the ground. Golden warriors that tried to run them through with spears or swords found their arms sticking out though purple clouds far away. One just kept vanishing and reappearing all over the place, like he was bouncing about. The mist people fanned out to sweep through the golden army, leaving chaos.

Abeni watched it in amazement. "We thought you ran away. I'm so sorry."

Nyomi shrugged. "Don't be. I'm a proud coward. But I play the hero for my friends."

Zuri and Ama hurried up the steps to join them as the golden army was cleared away.

"That's weird," Zuri said, watching the mist people move out into the city.

"The throne!" Ama exclaimed. They all turned to see the Golden Throne—still covered in that shadow, but now unguarded. "I have to find a way to undo this magic!"

"Go ahead," Zuri said. "We'll stand guard." The two giant golden leopards joined her, taking up positions on either side.

"You'll have to do it without Abeni and me," Asha said. "We have other business."

Abeni nodded. This was the only reason she'd agreed to let Asha come along. She looked down to find Fulan. The girl had her back to them, staring dazedly at the mist people wreaking havoc on her army.

"Nyomi. Can you get us to her? We need surprise."

"I can do better."

There was an explosion of pink as the porcupine girl vanished and returned in a blink—depositing Fulan in front of them. She stumbled to her knees, trying to gain her footing. That first jump was always a little disorienting. But Abeni didn't give her a chance. Moving quick, she knelt and grabbed the girl by the back of her head, bringing their foreheads together. Her skin was hot to the touch! Asha joined them. Then reaching up she pressed a finger to Fulan's nose and said, "Boop!"

CHAPTER TWENTY-SIX

HARD CHOICES

Fulan opened her eyes.

She was no longer in Makomasi. Instead of a golden city, she stared at small round houses of mudbrick with brown straw roofs. It was a village. One she recognized. The village in the Jembe forest with those strange children—the friends of Abeni.

"Odd that we ended up here," a voice said.

Fulan spun to find the sorceress standing a short distance away. She reached for her knife, but it was gone. She searched herself. All her weapons were gone!

"None of that!" the sorceress said sharply, gripping her staff.

"What is this?" Fulan asked. "How did you bring me here?"

She remembered watching those odd purple things moving through her army, causing mayhem. Then suddenly she was floating in a place of all pink—arriving right before the sorceress and the little spirit. The sorceress had grabbed her head, then the little spirit said . . .

"Boop," a voice came.

Fulan turned to find someone else. An old woman. She was tall, with colorful shawls wrapped over a long brown dress and bundles of beads hanging from her neck. Her dark skin was the color of freshly tilled earth, and thick ivory locs fell like tree roots to her back. She leaned against a staff of twisted and knotted wood and studied Fulan with piercing eyes.

"Who—?"

"You know who I am, girl," the old woman said gruffly.

Fulan took in the ivory locs again and those eyes. "The little spirit!"

"Auntie Asha?" the sorceress asked, seeming just as surprised. "Is it really you?"

The old woman shrugged. "Perhaps. You can appear here in many ways. Maybe this is how my mind sees myself. Or your mind. Maybe both."

The sorceress frowned. "I thought we were in her head." She pointed a chin at Fulan.

"We're in all our heads, in a way," the old woman replied. "Three heads, together."

Fulan stared. What were they even talking about?

"Did I bring us here?" the sorceress asked.

The old woman shook her head, looking to Fulan. "This is her memory."

The sorceress's eyes widened with alarm. "You've been to my village?" In a blur she was covered in golden armor. She stalked forward, growing larger with each step. "Why were you there? Did you hurt my friends? Answer me!"

Fulan backed away, staring up at the giant.

"Abeni," the old woman said. "Take hold of yourself."

The sorceress glanced at her enormous body. "Oh!" she exclaimed and shrunk back.

"This place doesn't have the same rules as the real world," the old woman warned. "Emotions here can . . . get the better of you." She turned to Fulan. "I'd answer her questions."

Fulan stared between the two. This was crazy! "Hurt your friends? I barely made it out of that wretched village. That Fomi almost took my head off when I asked after you!"

The sorceress grinned. "That's definitely Fomi." She turned to the old woman. "But why did she bring us here?"

"Because she's hiding something. From us. From herself."

Fulan realized the two were talking about her. "I don't know what trick you're playing—"

"We aren't the ones who've played tricks on you, girl," the old woman said. "Look at you. You're burning up inside."

"Asha says you need this," the sorceress added. "That you're his victim too." Her tone hardened. "Personally, I don't see it."

Fulan looked to her arm, where fire swirled beneath the skin. Her face darkened.

"I am my father's daughter! I won't be taken in by you, witch! Or your sorceress!"

"He's lying to you," the old woman said.

"He saved me!" she spat back. "Saved me when no one else could!"

The old woman shook her head. "You are almost consumed by my brother's fires. And his lies. I tried to help you before. You pushed me away. But I will make you see!"

The old woman struck the ground with her staff and the world around them shattered like colorful glass. The pieces fell away to reveal another world beneath. They stood in a city. Nowhere as big as Makomasi, and with mudbrick buildings painted in colorful patterns. Fulan knew this place. It was familiar. And filled her with dread.

The old woman nodded. "Better. But not enough." Her staff struck the ground again.

The city around Fulan burned. It seemed everything was on fire. She could smell the choking smoke, feel the flames. "No." She shook her head. "I don't want to see this!"

"You will," the old woman said. Her staff struck again.

People screamed all about Fulan. Fleeing people with terror on their faces. She watched them move around her, a growing tightness in her chest. "Not this. Please—" The old woman's staff came down without mercy.

Flicker.

Fulan stood staring at the burning building, amid the screams of fleeing people. She had been out on an errand to the fish market. She was only eight, and proud her parents trusted her with this responsibility. Besides, she liked examining the fishermen's catch. She had been staring at a fish nearly half her size when the first shouts came.

She had looked up to see strangers in her city, men on horses wielding spears and torches. They were hurting people, setting things on fire. And following behind them were . . . monsters! Things that looked like people but had heads like hyenas or mouths with sharp tusks. In moments they were everywhere. She had run like everyone else, falling more than once. But each time she got back up, determined to make it home. It would be safe there, she told herself. Her parents were there.

Now she stood staring at her home, on fire. Someone shouted her name. Her parents! She glimpsed them among a mass of people, being led away in chains. She reached an arm out, wanting to run to them. But a strong hand fell suddenly on her shoulder. It turned her around and she found herself staring up at a man.

The sun filtered behind him, so that it looked like he wore a crown of light. He was taller than any man she'd ever seen, with a face as dark and beautiful as the night. But his eyes frightened her. They burned! It was then she noticed he wore armor and carried a large mask of iron under one arm. Behind him a banner hung, showing an upside-down teardrop the color of the sun at dusk. She had seen that banner, carried by the strangers and monsters. He was one of them!

Anger filled her. He had done this to her city. He had taken her parents. She reached for a small knife her father had given her for scaling fish. Pulling it from her waist, she plunged the blade into the man's thigh. He didn't flinch. Not even a wince showed on his face. Instead, he casually reached down to draw out the knife. Fulan gasped as the wound closed and her knife burned away to ash. Was this a man? Or did a god walk among them?

"Such fire in a mortal," he spoke, his voice thundering. "Intriguing. What is your name?"

"Fulan," she stammered.

"Fulan," he repeated. "It is rare that anything yet intrigues me in this world, much less a mortal. I would know more." He extended his hand. Some part of her screamed to run. But his voice was so demanding. Her smaller hand gingerly took his large one as she stared up in awe. Turning, they walked away. The screams and fire and smoke faded from Fulan's mind. So did the cries of her name from somewhere behind her that she knew she would soon forget.

Flicker.

Fulan pulled away from the sorceress and the little spirit, almost falling down the steps of the palace. She was back in Makomasi. Back with her memories, no longer hidden. And she now knew the awful truth that had been kept from her. That she had kept from herself. Her father. All this time, she believed he had saved her. That he had pulled her from the destruction and fires that had taken her family. But he *was* that destruction. He *was* the terrible fire.

"It was him," she whispered. "It was always him. Always, always him. Always . . ."

She folded in on herself, huddled there and trapped with her memories.

○○○

Abeni looked to the girl who sat shaking and muttering under her breath. The mark on her forehead had dulled—as had the fires beneath her skin. Was this the same person they'd been fighting? Who had been filled with so much rage? She looked broken now, her eyes hollow.

"She's just a girl," she murmured. "And she lost everyone, like me." Is this what she might have become, had things been different?

Asha put a hand to her arm, now the little girl again.

"What happens to her now?" Abeni asked.

"That's up to her."

Zaneeya and Nyomi walked up, stopping to glance at where Fulan sat.

"I don't know what you two did," the panther girl said. "But it worked!"

Abeni followed her friend's gaze to the city, only now realizing everything had gone quiet. The fighting had stopped. Or rather, the golden army had stopped. They stood still, some holding weapons in mid-swing—like true statues.

"What happened to them?" she asked.

"I believe I know." They jumped to find Bida beside them. He was a man again.

"How did you get—?" Zaneeya asked. Then, shaking her head, "Dragons."

Bida knelt to examine Fulan. "The one who controls them no longer has control over herself. Until she recovers, they cannot."

"Then let's end this before she does!" Zaneeya said.

They turned to where Ama and Zuri stood staring at the Golden Throne. There was frustration on the princess's face.

"We've tried everything," Zuri explained wearily. "Nothing works."

"I can feel the souls of every Gold Weaver in there," Ama said, pained. "But I can't remove this darkness. It's like they're trapped by it."

Bida moved past the princess and put a hand to the throne—before pulling it back.

His face was grim. "This shadow laid upon your people is like a fire that consumes. It devours them."

"Then we have to remove it!" Ama cried out.

Bida shook his head. "It cannot be removed. The throne has been corrupted utterly. The souls themselves must be freed."

"But how?" Ama asked. Her gaze hardened on Fulan. "Do we have to end her?"

Abeni looked between the princess and the dragon in alarm. Would they truly do that?

"I'll do it," Zaneeya said, her orange eyes flat. "If the rest of you can't."

"That won't work," Asha said bleakly. "The throne must be destroyed." She looked to Bida, her small face on the verge of tears.

"What?" Ama asked, then gasped in understanding. "No!"

"How do we destroy it?" Zuri asked, confused.

"The throne is bound to my power," Bida said. "It can only be unmade if I am unmade."

A quiet dread fell over them at his meaning.

"No," Ama whispered. "That can't be."

"I believe it can and will be, child," Bida said, "if we are to save your people."

"Is there no other way?" Asha asked, her voice quavering. "I just found you again."

Bida knelt to put a hand to her cheek. "Don't cry for me, Mother. You always told us there were forces in this world greater even than you. I do not think it was chance that we met again. That I was fortunate enough to return to the world and make right old mistakes. That I would be allowed to save the people I once abandoned." He gazed to Ama. "Look for my last gift with the dawn." Then those golden eyes turned to Zuri. "Fate has even brought the sword back to me in the end. And a warrior to wield it."

For once, the girl looked completely taken aback. "No. I can't."

Bida stood. "You came to slay a dragon."

"But . . . it's different now. You're different."

Bida smiled. "It is hard to hate an enemy, once you have stared into their eyes." He walked forward, and she backed away. "But I forged that sword for a purpose. It has come to you for that purpose. You will be the hero of legends."

Zuri shook her head. "I don't want that."

"The best of us do not. Here, I will make it easier."

In a blur, Bida was the dragon—towering with shimmering golden scales, his serpentine form beautiful and terrible in the night. He brought a horned head down to glare at them, and the depth in those eyes made Abeni shudder. With a lunge, he brought his open jaws down upon Zuri. She screamed in a mix of regret and defiance, drawing the sword that rendered her silent, and swung. The dark blade passed through Bida, releasing a golden light that streaked like an arrow up into the heavens before bursting with blinding brilliance—like a star being born, momentarily turning night into day before vanishing. Everyone shielded their eyes, opening them again to find the dragon was gone. So was the Golden Throne.

Abeni wiped away a tear. Ama sobbed openly. Zuri's face was drawn, and she sheathed the sword before crouching with her head in her hands. If this was a victory, no one felt like celebrating. Their quiet was broken by a rising murmur. They looked down beyond the palace to find people walking among the still statues. They stared about as if in a daze. The Gold Weavers, Abeni realized—the ones encased in gold! They weren't alone. Guards stumbled from the palace while people emerged from buildings.

"He did it," Ama said in a choked voice. "He freed us."

Jubilant cries went up. People cheered, clapping, shouting, hugging one another. Abeni was soon surrounded by Gold Weavers, eager to celebrate even with strangers. When Captain Ekua and Akú arrived, telling of what they had done, people thanked her. Others surrounded Zuri, calling her a hero. More than a few knelt before Zaneeya and Nyomi, asking if the spirits had returned. Ama was treated as if she already wore the crown. In moments it felt like a festival. Abeni caught glimpses of Asha amid the crowds. The little girl smiled, unable to remain sad in the joyful atmosphere.

Someone made their way towards Abeni and she ran out to hug him. "Songu!"

The boy had returned to normal, but still wore tattered red robes. He looked tired.

"The monster?" she asked.

Songu signed. "Don't know. Ran away, maybe."

"Are you okay? I saw you . . . change."

He nodded grimly. "I can feel it inside me. Like a stain I can't quite scrub clean."

"Oh Songu, I'm so sorry."

He looked at her sadly. "Maybe we can't easily escape our past after all. At least I used it to help. That must be good, right? It means I'm good?"

"Of course," she said, her voice breaking.

The two stood quiet, watching the celebration. Some of the Gold Weavers had started sending up streaks that burst into dazzling golden sparkles in the night sky. Abeni stared at them, glancing back to see if Asha had seen. The little girl was gazing up as well, clapping in delight. A sudden look of surprise came over her face. She seemed confused and opened her mouth to speak, then put a hand to her side. When she lifted it, her small palm was smeared with red. More red appeared on her dress, slowly spreading.

Abeni stared, confused as well. Was that blood? But why would Asha be bleeding? Her eyes went to a figure behind the little girl. A big man with beaded scars on his face and white in his beard. She knew him. From the attack on the ship. He gripped a large knife smeared with red in one hand while the other tucked something long and ivory at his waist. One of Asha's locs. He moved unnoticed in the crowd and met Abeni's gaze with a toothy smile, pressing a finger to his lips—as if they shared some secret. Her eyes left him and went back to Asha, who stood trembling now. Bleeding.

Abeni found she couldn't speak. She couldn't move. It all seemed unreal, like a bad dream. It was Songu who first saw. He raced to Asha, reaching her just as she fell into his arms. Then someone screamed.

Abeni hardly recognized her own voice piercing the night, causing those around her to turn in alarm. Captain Ekua followed her gaze and gave a shout, rushing to where Songu knelt cradling Asha. People backed away from them, while Zaneeya, Nyomi, and Zuri pushed forward. Guards held back Ama, as Akú sent up cries of "Assassin!" But Abeni barely saw them. Her eyes remained on the big man, who rushed to where Fulan still sat. Her guards were so distracted by the commotion that neither saw him coming. Both fell to his knife and the big man grabbed Fulan's arm, urging her up.

Abeni didn't know when her feet began moving. But she could still hear herself screaming. Something was building inside her. It grew stronger by the moment—a rhythm that pulsed to the beat of her own heart. She was pushing past people, running up the stairs, to where the big man still tried to pull Fulan to her feet.

"Get up, girl!" he was saying. "We can get out of here!"

But Fulan just stared at his knife, and the blood that smeared it.

Abeni reached him and he spun, blade at the ready. "More prey. Good. The hunt is all."

Behind her Abeni heard Zuri and Zaneeya shouting. The big man reached into his shirt, pulling out a small gray stone. Three monstrous hounds burst forth. Abeni ducked as they leapt over her to confront the others. The big man returned his attention to her. "Come, sorceress. Show me what makes you so special."

The thing building inside Abeni swelled, filling her up. It was a song. But not her song. This was something different. Hard and unyielding. Strong and severe. A vengeful song. It blared in her ears, and she hummed it on her lips. Then she reached out. And her hands began to glow.

The big man looked surprised when she gripped his arm. He tried to break free, but she held fast, chanting her vengeful song. Her hands shined, as if made from pure light. *My ghost hands,* she thought. Where they touched, the big man's skin turned gray and rough—like the stone he still held. She let go and he stumbled back. But it was too late. First his arm became stone, the gray spreading to his shoulder, hardening. It raced over his chest, swallowing his torso, his legs. When it reached his head he opened his mouth in a scream that never came.

Abeni stepped back, looking at the statue that had been the big man. Growls came from behind her. She turned to find the three monstrous hounds. They crept forward and she gazed right through their shadowy flesh, finding what lay beneath. The song inside her changed, becoming sorrowful. A song of unmaking. When the hounds leapt for her, she casually let her glowing hands brush the rusted chains binding them. The metal fell apart, dropping and turning to dust. The bodies of the hounds did the same, crumbling like fine ash. Dozens of ghostly shapes poured out, barking and yapping. The spirits of dogs tormented and shackled, now freed. They crowded about her, licking and nuzzling to show their gratitude. *Free! Free! Free!* they seemed to say. Then they swarmed the statue, hitting and biting, sending it toppling down the palace steps until it broke and crumbled to pieces. Turning, they ran into the city, knocking over startled people before vanishing, their dying barks echoing in the night.

Abeni walked to where Asha lay in Songu's arms. The boy's eyes roamed to her ghost hands. She placed them gently on the girl, touching the terrible wound. It was angry and raw, and the spirit's hold to this world felt weak. The song changed again—to one of healing. She hummed it like a lullaby, her ghost hands moving to stitch together skin, flesh, and spirit. Beside her, ghostly figures appeared that she knew only she could see. People from ages past, using their hands to guide her own.

"A new guardian is born," they pronounced.

Guardian. That's what they were. Who they had been. Like her.

When Abeni finished, she let Asha lie in Songu's arms. The little spirit would need rest to heal. She stood up, looking around. There were no more threats. Asha was safe. But no. She walked to a figure who sat alone. This one had been with the big man. This one was dangerous. The vengeful song came back to her as she lifted her hands. The girl reared back, her eyes wide.

Someone moved to block Abeni's path. A monster. He stood, shielding the girl. Abeni frowned. She would deal with them both. Her ghost hands reached out and the monster spoke.

"Abeni," came the rumbling voice. "Stop."

She was so surprised, she did. The monster reached for a necklace of ringlets holding a pulsing red stone. He unstrung it and his body shuddered. The corded muscles of his arms and legs grew smaller. Rough gray skin turned smooth and brown. Claws became fingers. He was soon only slightly taller than her. Grabbing his mask, he pulled it off to reveal a human face.

Abeni stared. She knew this face. She tried to remember. But the vengeful song kept intruding, urging her to fight. She pushed it away, reaching for something else—something deeper. *Her* song. The one Asha had taught her, that had been lost and found again. She listened to it, drawing on its memories, its stories, the people it recalled. It drowned out the vengeful song. And finally, she put a name to this face. Her ghost hands turned normal, and the world came rushing back. Whatever had held her, its grip was broken by this face. Her mouth formed a name.

"Ekwolo?"

The boy smiled. A smile that once made her stomach flutter. That still did.

"Hello, Abeni."

She ran to envelop him in a tight hug. He hugged her back as fiercely.

"Ekwolo! They said you were gone!"

"And I thought you were lost, forever," he said in her ear.

She closed her eyes. "I didn't think I would ever find you!"

"You found me." He paused. "But now you have to let us go."

Abeni pushed away from him. "Us?" Her eyes fell on Fulan. "I don't under—"

"I serve her," Ekwolo said. "And the one she serves."

"No, Ekwolo. You don't have to. Throw away that necklace and you'll be free!"

"And what makes you think I want to do that?"

Abeni felt as if someone had squeezed her heart. She stepped back.

"You can't mean that. He destroyed our village! Stole away our people!"

His face grew hard. "Because we were weak. But I'm not weak anymore."

"Ekwolo," she pleaded. "It doesn't matter what you've done—"

"You don't know what I've done!" he snapped back. "You want me to put faith in who? The spirits? Did they protect us? This world is divided between the powerful and the powerless! And I choose power!" There was such anger in his voice. What had they done to him?

"We've both changed, Abeni," he said, reading her thoughts. "We've both come a long way from the Jembe forest. We've just walked . . . different paths."

"Ekwolo," she pleaded. "Don't you see? He's clouded your mind!"

"Clouded?" he asked. "I've never been so certain. Not all who serve do so out of fear. Some of us learn to believe. Some of us learn to accept his blessing."

Before she could stop him, he tied the bloodstone back around his neck—and in moments a monster stood before her once more. A monster once named Ekwolo.

"Why?" was all she managed.

But he didn't answer. Fitting back on his mask, he helped Fulan up. The two turned away, walking down the steps. She watched them go as people rushed out of their way. Behind her Ama shouted, ordering guards to recapture them. But before anyone could reach the pair, two dark shapes dropped to the ground before the palace. Sasabonsam, with Blood Skulls. Fulan climbed onto the back of one while the monster took the other. The bats flapped their wings, rising into the air and soaring away as the first light of morning brightened the sky.

A flurry of gasps sounded, and people cried out. Abeni followed their gazes and gestures. Descending from the sky was a glimmering object. A throne! A replica of the one that had disappeared with Bida. But no shadow marred it, and it shined with a golden brilliance. Abeni remembered the dragon's last words to Ama. *Look for my last gift with the dawn.* He had returned to them their throne, a final gift to his people. It landed gently, and as one the Gold Weavers erupted in jubilation. Despite the celebration, Abeni's eyes sought out the two dark shapes still visible in the sky. They continued to fly away, until they were specks in the distance.

CHAPTER TWENTY-SEVEN

GUARDIAN

Abeni sat on a chair in the large room, staring at her hands. As she had done for days.

They were normal, brown hands. No glowing. But she remembered well what she had done with them. What she had wanted to do. The songs in her head she had never known before.

"You do have nice hands," someone whispered.

Abeni looked up to see Asha, who lay in a bed, her eyes half open.

"You're awake!" It had been two days since the small girl had been healed. And she'd slept all that time. "How do you feel, Asha?"

"Hungry," she answered.

Abeni jumped up, running to the door and calling out. Palace servants soon ran in, bringing food. They placed it on a table along with water. She poured some for Asha and offered goat stew and balls of fufu. The girl ate and drank eagerly.

"You're definitely better!" Abeni laughed. Her tone became serious. "You got hurt. Bad."

"I remember," Asha said. She looked to Abeni's hands. "Tell me all that happened."

Abeni did. She told of the big man. Her ghost hands. She didn't mention Ekwolo. That was still too painful. "Asha, what's happening to me?"

"Something I wasn't certain would," the girl said. "Becoming a guardian makes you my protector and grants you power to keep me safe. For some it never happens. But for those able to call upon it, that power can manifest in unique ways. Yours seems to come through song."

"When I saw you bleeding," Abeni said, "something in me just . . . opened up."

"It's been happening before that," Asha said.

Abeni's eyes rounded. "What? How? When?"

"Do you remember when the bat riders found us in the forest? Someone created a bright light to drive them away. Then when we were attacked on the ship, arrows meant for me were deflected."

Abeni gaped. "I thought that was you!"

Asha shook her head. "I wasn't certain. Not until you were able to see what Bida and I shared in our thoughts—in the lost city. Then I knew."

Abeni shook her head in wonder. She had . . . powers? "Why didn't you say anything?"

"When a guardian's abilities are newly forming, it's like a weak fire. Blow too hard, and it might snuff out. It was important that I didn't interfere. It had to happen on its own."

Abeni stared at her palms. Talk of fire made her think of Fulan. "That power almost made me to do something bad to Fulan. Like I did to the big man." She swallowed. "He's dead, isn't he? I didn't mean to. I just wanted to stop him from hurting you. From hurting anyone else. I didn't mean . . ." She closed her hands into fists, haunted by memories.

Asha gave her a sorrowful look. "The power you now wield, it wants to protect me. It will shape you into a weapon if you let it. Remember who *you* are. Don't let it rule over you."

Abeni opened her hands to look at them. They felt . . . heavy.

Just then the door to the room burst open. Nyomi came running in, followed by Zaneeya. The two dived onto the bed, hugging and making a fuss over Asha, who giggled happily. Zuri hovered in the doorway.

"Good to still have you with us, little spirit," she called.

Asha smiled. Her eyes went to Zuri's side. "I told you that sword fit you."

The girl's face turned grim. "About that. What I did to Bida . . ."

". . . was something he knew had to be done," Asha finished. "You are blameless."

Zuri released a breath, as if she'd been holding it until she could hear those words.

"Where's Songu?" Asha asked. There was an awkward quiet.

"He spends most of his time with Ama," Zaneeya answered. "I think he's ashamed."

"It's not his fault he has a monster inside him," Nyomi said. "We can all get a little cranky. You've seen how I am when I get hungry."

"My brother's touch is hard to wash away," Asha said sadly. "And Fulan?"

Abeni shook her head.

Asha nodded. "She has choices to make. The road ahead for her will be difficult."

"What about our road?" Zaneeya asked. "I'm glad we stopped this golden army—like I was glad to save the children of Kono. But we have our own quest."

Abeni hadn't forgotten. They still needed to reunite Zaneeya and Nyomi with their families. She had a whole village to find. And Asha had to get to these elder spirits. Now more than ever.

"I need a few days' rest," the little spirit said. "Then we can set out again."

"You should rest in the grove," Nyomi said cheerfully. "All that sunlight and green . . ." Her black eyes widened. "Oh! I forgot! Ama said we should come to the grove—quick!"

Asha looked puzzled. "There's a grove?"

Abeni smiled. "Wait until you see it. And there's another surprise!"

She helped Asha dress and they left the room in the palace to walk the city. There were people out, most of them Gold Weavers, working to fix the damage from the battle. There were others too. Manu and Naana were working with the royal attendant Akú to establish normal relations with the kingdom's neighbors. A Mmoatia envoy was coming that night from Ile-kun. It was a new day for the Gold Kingdom, with the possibility of new alliances. Abeni hoped so, considering what was coming.

The Witch King—as he now called himself—might have been thwarted in his attempt to take the Gold Kingdom, but he wasn't going to stop. War was coming. It was coming for them all. But before that looming shadow fell, they could find glimmers of hope. One was the grove.

It had begun to appear the morning after the battle. People spoke of a small grove in the middle of the city, growing inside the building that housed relics of the First Gold Kingdom—where Abeni and her companions had arrived through the doorway. By midday, it had swallowed up the entire building. By night, the streets surrounding it. When they awoke the next morning, a whole section of the city had been overrun by a small forest. Towering trees and plants grew among buildings while creeping vines wrapped everything they touched. At sight of the grove, Asha gasped. She walked through it slowly, brushing leaves and flowers with her fingertips. They seemed to grow taller, brighter, greener, from her touch. Butterflies landed on her shoulders and birds called from the canopy above that filtered sunlight.

Deep inside, they found Ama and Songu waiting. The princess hadn't been formally crowned, but it was all but certain. Her brother had returned, trying to reclaim his title. But his attendants turned their backs. It was Akú himself who refused to let him put on the golden slippers. The king had walked from the palace barefoot, his shame open for all to see.

The Ohemmaa announced Ama as the next ruler—the first true queen the Gold Kingdom would ever have. Though her coronation was weeks away, she had already assumed the role—passing new laws and overseeing Makomasi's rebuilding. She'd kept her word, and all remaining prisoners in the mines had been freed.

Most left for their homes, granted apologies from Ama and as much gold as they could carry. Others had chosen to stay, insisting they deserved to be subjects of the kingdom for helping save it. That was controversial. But Ama promised to see it done. There would be no more raids to capture unwilling workers. The Gold Kingdom would have no more slaves.

At seeing Asha up and about, Ama rushed to crush her in a hug. Songu came slower, more cautious, doing the same.

"I'm so happy you're well!" the princess said. "You'll be able to attend my coronation!"

Abeni and the others exchanged awkward looks.

"I think they're trying to say they'll be gone by then," Zuri said. "Or hope to be."

Ama looked disappointed but nodded. "Of course. If there's anything I can do to help, don't hesitate to ask. Our kingdom owes you a debt. Hopefully the four of you will stay for a feast in your honor."

"I can always eat!" Nyomi said, patting her belly.

"The four of us?" Abeni asked. She looked to Songu.

Ama did too. "You didn't tell them?" she signed. The girl had gotten very good at that.

Songu shook his head, then turned to Abeni. "I'm not going with you," he signed.

Abeni stared in shock. "Why?"

Songu took a moment to respond. When he did, his face was troubled but his hands were calm. "I left with you because I didn't have a place to call home. But Ama has offered me a home here. Her people don't see me as a monster. They think what I did was heroic. Maybe I can use this curse for good, after all."

Abeni was overcome by emotions. Surprise at this choice. Anger at Ama—which wasn't fair. But mostly sadness. She tried to find words for all those feelings, but in the end only replied, "If that's what you want."

Songu breathed a sigh of relief.

"What will you do?" she asked.

"He's going to be a musician in my court," Ama said, beaming.

And unspoken, Abeni thought, a valuable bodyguard. But she nodded. If he was happy, then she would try to be too.

"Though no one asked," Zuri interrupted, "I'll be staying too. At least for a while."

"As my Master of the Ships," Ama said excitedly. "The Gold Kingdom has never had a true navy. But we may soon need one. Who better to train them than the Black Fox?"

"I want that in my title," Zuri insisted. "The Black Fox, *Mistress of Ships*."

A cracking sounded behind them, and Ama jumped. "Oh! It's time!" She ran deeper into the grove, and the rest of them followed.

When they found her again she was inside the building that housed old relics. It was covered completely in greenery, so that the walls and floors were barely visible. Near where the large golden doorway was wrapped by vines was a mound of thick grass. And sitting in its center were two giant eggs of gold.

Asha cried out, running to kneel next to the two. Abeni joined her.

"This is the surprise!" she whispered.

"When Bida died the bands he gave me stopped working," Ama said. "None of the relics do now—not even the door." It was true. With the dragon gone, Abeni's staff had lost its gold. So had Zaneeya's claws. "It was like he put all of his last power into re-creating my people's throne—and this."

Even as she spoke, one of the eggs began to crack again—tiny fractures running along its golden surface. The second egg started to do the same. Small shapes soon poked out of the broken shells. Their chubby bodies were covered in shimmering gold scales, while nubs of horns sat on their heads. One opened its mouth to show tiny sharp teeth and when it started making mewling noises, puffs of gold dust blew from its nostrils.

"Oh, Bida!" Asha exclaimed happily. "You came back! Just like me!"

"Yeah, but he did it twice!" Zaneeya chuckled.

"I think Bida wanted us to raise them," Ama said, gently stroking one of the pudgy little things. "The Gold Kingdom will have dragons again!"

They spent some time with the hatchlings, who seemed intent on investigating their new homes. One hopped into Zaneeya's arms and would not be put back down, licking the panther girl's face, much to her dislike. Or at least she pretended to. They lost themselves in play in the grove, where baby dragons seemed the perfect thing to try and forget about the outside world. Until that world came looking for them.

"There you are," a voice called. They turned to see the royal attendant Akú making his way through the grove, accompanied by two guards. Their eyes all widened at the sight of the dragons, but the attendant caught hold of himself.

"I've been looking for you everywhere," he said. "There's a message!"

"A message?" Ama asked. "Can't it wait a while?"

"I beg your pardon, Princess," Akú said, "but the message is not for you." His gaze went to Asha. "And I don't think they mean to wait."

Abeni and the others exchanged looks, before following the royal attendant. The dragons refused to be left. So Ama carried one, and Zaneeya found herself carrying another. When they stepped out of the grove, Captain Ekua stood waiting with several guards. All of their eyes were fixed upward. The two dragons chirped at the sun, opening small wings that sparkled in the sunlight. But that wasn't what everyone else was looking at.

Abeni stared at what seemed the impossible. There were faces in the sky! Each hovered so large she thought she might reach out and touch them. But she could see that they were not truly here and nearly transparent. One thing was certain: they were not people. Some had manes and faces that looked like lions. Others bore the beaks of birds. Even among such fantastic visions, one drew everyone's eye. She looked like a blending of an antelope and a woman, with long horns rising from thick coils of braided hair and a face that seemed as if it had been carved from black stone. Her eyes twinkled with stars and shined with an ageless wisdom. Abeni knew at once who these beings were.

"The elder spirits!" she breathed.

"You name us true, guardian," the antelope spirit spoke. Her voice was a booming harmony. "Yet, the one in your charge would make us seem as children. Asha."

Asha stepped forward. "Hello. I might know you. But I don't remember things well."

The antelope spirit sighed. "You are at your weakest when we need you more than ever. Two mornings past, a great light appeared with the dawn. We felt the blow you struck against the darkness. Mortals who saw the light took it for a sign of hope. And even now, your brother rages in his fortress. He will soon lash out to show the world his anger. But already, your deed is whispered as stories travel of the defeat of this golden army. Soon all the westlands will know. Like the light, it will serve as a beacon to rally them. We gather to stand against your brother, Asha. We would have you at our side." Those wise eyes turned to Abeni. "You have done well, guardian. But you are not safe. Her brother will seek her out. And he must not be the one to claim her. You must bring her here, at once."

"Of course," Abeni stammered. "But how do we find you?"

A burst of light came in answer, spreading all around them. It was a map, Abeni realized! It hovered in the air, so that it was like they were inside it. She reached to touch a bright spot. But it collapsed, forming into a ball of light that fit into her palm.

"Let this be your guide," the elder spirit said. "Seek us now. The time grows short."

With that, the spirit's voice faded, and the vison vanished.

Zuri whistled, impressed. "That's a message, alright."

Abeni looked to the ball of light in her hand. All this time they had sought the elder spirits, only to have the spirits find them.

"They're right," Asha said. "My brother won't take his loss lightly. He will come for me."

"Let him," Ama said, her voice hard. "We won't give you up."

Abeni knew the girl was sincere. But would she remain so when the Witch King turned his eye once more on the Gold Kingdom? From the uneasy looks shared between Captain Ekua and Akú, she wasn't the only one with such thoughts.

Asha shook her head. "Thank you. But I can't stay. We must go at once."

"I saw that map," Zuri said with concern. "If the Witch King has taken Jenna, there may be an army in your path—one with orders to capture you."

"Maybe I can send some guards as an escort?" Ama suggested.

"No," Abeni said. "That would draw too much attention. The four of us stand the best chance." She gave a questioning look to Zaneeya and Nyomi.

"I'm ready when you are," the panther girl said, resolute.

Nyomi sighed. "I would have liked a feast. And trying to get by a whole army sounds terrifying. I don't like it. But if my friends need help, I'm ready."

Abeni gave both girls thankful smiles before turning to Asha. "And I'm your guardian. I go wherever you go." The little girl took her hand, squeezing tight. She squeezed back.

In her head, Abeni heard her song and she hummed along to it. Finding these elder spirits would mean coming a step closer to finding her family and these ghost ships. As tragic as seeing Ekwolo had been, it oddly gave her hope that they were out there. And she would find a way to save him as well. As she hummed her song, she knew there would be new stories to add. Of all that had happened in the past weeks. Of all that lay ahead. Her song was not yet finished.

ACKNOWLEDGMENTS

When I published *Abeni's Song,* I called it the story I'd been wanting to write my entire life. Now, I get to write book two and introduce readers to even more of this fantastic world! And like before, it wouldn't have been possible without the inspiration, help, and guidance of so many people. I'd like to thank everyone who read the first book and gave it a chance. You were the inspiration that kept me going for book two.

Thanks as always to my agent, Seth Fishman, who encouraged me to pick up this world after I'd set it aside. To my editor, Ali Fisher, at Starscape. Thanks for your invaluable insight in helping craft this sequel. Thanks as well to Dianna Vega, who has worked so hard to get this book over the finish line. To my publicists, Saraciea Fennell and Khadija Lokhandwala, at *Reactor,* thanks for getting me out there to share this book with readers. Angus Johnson, as always, your copy editing is wizardry! And, as before, a great deal of gratitude goes to artist Michael Machira Mwangi for patiently helping me get that glorious cover together!

Thanks to my friends, family, and all the storytellers in my life. Thank you as well to my wonderful partner, Danielle, for the encouragement. And special thanks to Nia and Nya, who help remind me of my own childhood. I hope you get to appreciate these stories one day. Lastly, thanks to everyone who returned to journey with Abeni, Nyomi, Zaneeya, and Asha through this world. I hope it was everything you needed it to be.

ABOUT THE AUTHOR

Le Image Photography | Brooklyn

Born in New York and raised mostly in Houston, P. DJÈLÍ CLARK spent part of his childhood in Trinidad and Tobago, the homeland of his parents. He is the author of the novel *A Master of Djinn* and the novellas *Ring Shout, The Black God's Drums,* and *The Haunting of Tram Car 015.* He has won the Nebula, Locus, and Alex Awards and has been nominated for the Hugo, World Fantasy, and Sturgeon Awards. His stories have appeared in online venues such as *Reactor, Daily Science Fiction, Heroic Fantasy Quarterly, Apex Magazine, Lightspeed,* and *Beneath Ceaseless Skies,* and in print anthologies, including *Griots, Hidden Youth,* and *Clockwork Cairo.* He is also a founding member of *FIYAH Magazine of Black Speculative Fiction* and an infrequent reviewer at *Strange Horizons.*

pdjeliclark.com
Facebook: phenderson.clark
Goodreads: P. Djèlí Clark
Instagram: @pdjeliclark
Bluesky: @pdjeliclark.bsky.social